ASHES
TO
ASHES

_____

CORY TOTH

WARNER HOUSE
PUBLISHING COMPANY

ISBN – 13: **978-1483984988**

WARNER HOUSE

PUBLISHING COMPANY

For Sarah,

Special Thanks to Jessica

1

Calvin Strong wrestled with the steering wheel of his old SUV as he drove as fast as he could up the Northway, fighting to keep the heavy vehicle straight through the snow and slush. His knuckles were numb and white. His eyes strained intensely to peer through the cloud of snow flurries that whirled around his windshield and made it difficult to stay in his lane.

He leaned forward in his seat to wipe some condensation off the inside of the windshield and caught a glimpse of his reflection in the rear-view mirror. He was surprised by how calm he appeared on the outside, although he did have to actively relax his forehead. He could see the tension in his temple. The skin crinkled between his eyes as it did when he was stressed or heavily focused on something. Leah was always on him to relax his forehead and called it his 'unfriendly' face, because she said it made him look like he was mad. It had been the year from hell for him and he was honestly relieved to see he still had his youthful good-looks, although his blue eyes were bloodshot and squinted. From the way he felt, he would expect to see a receding hairline and nothing but gray and wrinkles. Life had taken a toll on him lately.

Calvin picked up his phone from the console and tried her number again. His hand was shaking so badly he could feel the phone vibrating against his ear. It began ringing once again.

He knew she was on vacation, visiting her sister, and might not have her phone near her. It was still early. She would sleep as long as she could when she didn't have to work. He just thanked god that the baby was with her.

The ringing stopped. Her voicemail answered. Calvin swore under his breath.

Exiting from the highway, his senses were quickly overwhelmed by the all-too-familiar character of the town he had grown up in. When passing through this working-class town, one could feel the angst of struggling homeowners treading water to keep from drowning in their everyday expenses, all the while knowing that this was as good as life would ever get for them.

He drove by the same run-down homes he had passed almost every day on the way home from work. There was the tractor supply store, the construction safety equipment store, and the sad bars and restaurants that randomly littered the side of the main road and never stayed in business for very long.

The scenery in the distance was great, though, located in the Adirondacks, with mountain peaks and ski slopes visible in the distance. The air was much more pure than that around Albany, once the exhaust of tractor trailers passing by diffused.

All along this stretch of road, Calvin held gruesome memories of horrendous car crashes—the sort of crashes that changed lives. It's funny how those memories stained that road and became a part of Calvin's daily commute. Someone from out of town passing through would never have a clue what horrible accidents occurred there, but he could never forget.

He passed through the intersection where an elderly couple were killed trying to make a left in their minivan, T-boned by a tractor-trailer traveling at sixty miles-per-hour.

He passed the run-down parking lot of the strip mall where a horrific freak accident occurred. A group of teenagers were whipping through the parking lot in an SUV, swerving around parked cars. While making a sharp right, they struck another car at only ten miles per hour and overturned, throwing a beautiful female passenger through the sunroof as the vehicle rolled. Her head was crushed like a melon underneath. Calvin glanced at the drainage grate in the middle of the lot where her blood had drained. He looked at the Pizza sign behind it. The guys from the pizza shop had come out and rolled the SUV off of the girl. They all later said they wished they hadn't, because what they saw will never leave them.

Those accidents were all cleaned up without a trace. No one would ever know something dreadful and life-altering happened here. People parked in the parking space where the girl's head was crushed. Calvin thought about it and realized he had probably even parked there himself. It was erased, forgotten. Life moved on.

And now he had become one of those circumstances.

Everyone for miles around had to know about it by this point. Calvin knew it was already the talk of the town, as not much happened in the area and big news spread like bad gas. There was nothing he hated more than being the center of attention, and there was an odd feeling for him of having his privacy invaded. Everyone would be asking questions and talking about him. He was in no shape to deal with that right now.

And then, after all the commotion, after all the news reports and rumors, it would just become another forgotten piece of the town's history, just like all the other accidents.

Calvin grabbed his cell phone and tried Leah's number again. After several rings, he was ready to give up when her soft, young voice answered with an indiscernible croak. He had obviously awoken her.

"Leah, it's me," Calvin said desperately, his voice trembling unexpectedly. "I need to talk to you."

"What's wrong?" Leah mumbled in a daze, still half-asleep.

"There was a fire at my house this morning—a bad fire."

He could hear rustling in the background as Leah sat up from under the covers. He could picture her dirty-blonde hair a tangled mess, her eyes barely open, and her forehead scrunched with confusion.

"Oh my god…" Leah muttered, still in shock. "Calvin, are you okay?"

"Yeah. Yeah, I'm fine. I'm fine…" He hesitated for a moment, trying his best to maintain his composure. "It's Hobbes, Leah." Saying his name instantly brought up the image of the little puppy he had rescued from the kennel. He had been abandoned on the side of the road somewhere in Alabama, left for dead in a tied sack. Calvin named him 'Hobbes' because of both the comic strip in the funny pages and the funny hobble in his walk from an injured hind leg.

"What about Hobbes?" Leah asked.

"Hobbes was in the house."

"Oh my god…"

Calvin could feel the news hit her the way it had hit him earlier.

There came a silence before she quietly asked, "Do you think there's any way he made it out?"

"No," Calvin replied. "I want to. But I know he didn't. He was locked in there. And I left him there."

"Is there any way he could've survived?"

"According to what I've heard…no, there isn't."

"You don't know that for sure…"

"Yes, I do," Calvin said loudly, letting his sorrow manifest as anger.

"I'm sorry!" she said defensively.

Calvin realized that he was being abrasive with her and calmed himself down. "It's okay."

"I know how much you loved that dog, Calvin. He was your life. Before me, anyway."

"He was the only real friend I had. At least I felt that way lately."

"I'm sorry," she said again.

"I just can't believe this happened," he said softly, doing everything he could not to cry.

"What happened? I mean, how did it happen?"

"I don't know yet," he said. "I know very little at this point. I just got off the phone with the police a little while ago."

"When did it happen?

"It happened this morning. Early this morning. I think they said like five-thirty."

"You weren't sleeping there, were you?"

"No, no, I wasn't there. I'm heading up now. I was at your house last night."

"Oh, thank god," she said in a sigh of relief.

"It's a good thing I wasn't there, too," Calvin continued. "From what they've told me so far, it was a hell of a fire. They said I wouldn't have gotten out if I had been upstairs in the bedroom. They said it spread so quickly and burned so hot that no one would have gotten out alive if anyone had been sleeping there at the time."

"I'm so sorry about Hobbes, Calvin."

"I'm just glad the baby is safe and sound with you," Calvin said. "I don't want to think about what could've happened if I had her with me and I happened to stay up at my house with her."

"I don't want to think about it either. I'm just so glad I have her here with me. I'm a little freaked out right now. I'm, like, shaking. I just can't believe it. It just doesn't seem real."

"It still doesn't seem real to me either," Calvin said distantly. "I didn't want to drive up. I'm afraid to see what happened."

"You put so much work into that house, too," Leah said sullenly.

"Seven years. Seven years worth of hard work into fixing up that dump. I finally got it in pretty nice shape, too. I just can't believe it's totally gone."

"Totally gone? Can part of it be salvaged, or rebuilt or something?"

"No. Like, totally gone. Obliterated."

"Oh, Calvin... Did the police call you this morning about it?"

"No. They never called," he said bitterly. "I had to call them."

"Then how did you find out about the fire?"

"That's the weird part. I got a call that woke me up this morning. My phone was next to the bed, so I answered it, even though I was totally out of it. A man's voice asked for me. I told him I was Calvin. He told me that my house burned to the ground and then he hung up."

"Was it anyone you know?"

"I didn't recognize the voice at all."

"Your phone should have his number in the call log, right?"

"I checked. It came up as a blocked call," Calvin said. "I didn't take it too seriously at first, but the more I thought about it, the more it disturbed me. I didn't really understand why someone would call me and say that. I mean, what sort of prank would that be? So I laid there thinking about it until it drove me crazy and I went into a panic attack. Then I finally called the police department up there. They had me talk to the cop who was on the scene first about it. He told me they got a call from a neighbor driving by, heading to work at six thirty this morning, saying that there was smoke pouring out from the basement doors by the driveway."

"Were they able to get inside?" she asked.

"No. He said the fire was so hot and so intense that they couldn't even approach the structure. The fire chief wasn't about to send men into a situation *that* dangerous and volatile. They didn't know if there was anything explosive in the house, or if the gas lines were open."

"But what if *you* were in the house?" Leah became enraged. "What if *our child* was in the house, Calvin?"

"The cop I talked to said he *did* go up to the house once. He ran up and kicked in one of the doors. The heat almost blew him backwards down the steps. It practically exploded in his face. He could see that no one seemed to be home. No one was screaming or yelling for help. There were also no cars in the driveway or any other signs that anyone was in there. I don't think they really knew for sure that the house was empty. I think they were just hoping it was because they didn't want to risk lives trying to find out. They probably figured anyone in there was a goner by that time."

"The fire is totally out now, right?"

"Oh, yeah," Calvin said. "They've had it out for a while. They had to call in fire companies from four other towns to put it out, though. The cop said there was six feet of water in my basement by the time they were done. They had to pump all that out afterwards."

"Calvin, all your things…"

"I know. It doesn't sound like there was much left. He told me it was a total loss. Not a whole lot to salvage. I'll see if there is anything I can save, but at this point I've kind of accepted it. I've lost everything. My house and all my furniture, everything I own, is gone."

"What are you going to do now?" Leah asked eagerly. "You need a place to stay."

"I don't know yet…" Calvin was starting to feel frustrated. "I have no idea what to do. I'm still trying to get my head on straight and figure this whole situation out. I'll deal with the living situation later."

"Why don't you stay with me?" Leah asked as casually as she could, making an obvious effort to be respectful and not sound excited.

There was a long pause from Calvin.

"Are you still there? Cal, did I lose…"

"Yeah, I'm still here," Calvin said, sounding more annoyed than he intended. "I don't know about that."

"You've already been staying there half the time anyway. Why don't you just move down for the time being?"

"Full-time, for the time being?"

"Yes, full-time, as you put it, like it's a job," Leah said sweetly.

"Leah...there's a big difference between staying there a few nights a week and permanently living together."

"We work opposite schedules now, though, for the most part," she reasoned. "Right? We can just take shifts with the baby, and I have friends who can help out with the rest."

"I may end up living with my friends again if we try that," Calvin said. "I just don't want to end up homeless, moving in with my friends until I find a place to live. I had to kick my tenants out last time before I could even have my house back. I can't handle more drama. I've got enough problems going in my life right now, financially and now this."

"You'll be paying so much less if you move in with me than you were for your house. It totally makes sense, for the baby and for you."

"I couldn't afford the house anymore, Leah, and I probably won't be able to afford my share with you either. I'm dying here. Ever since the business went under I've been a wreck financially. I just can't get back on my feet."

"You need to be full-time again at work, Calvin. You need to talk to them..."

"I know I need to be full-time again," he cut her off loudly. "Unfortunately, they gave away my full-time position when I left to buy the business. They hired *two* full-time staff to cover my position. I'm stuck where I am, part-time. And I'm lucky to have that in this economy. I'm damn lucky I held onto that part-time position as a safety net, or I'd be totally screwed."

"So, get a job somewhere else, somewhere you can go full-time and get better benefits."

"I've been trying like crazy," Calvin said, getting irritated. "There's nothing out there right now." He realized he was getting loud and lowered his voice. "No one even responds to my resume, no matter what I put on it. I'm going to start making shit up just to see if someone will actually call me."

"Just come home after all this today, Calvin, and we'll talk. For now, just stay at home with me, even if you don't contribute anything to bills for the time being. As long as you do next month, if you're there that long. You need to be with me right now, with all that you're going through. You need to be with your child."

"I know. It's killing me being away from her, my little Pearl. I miss her so much."

"So come home to us," Leah pleaded, knowing she was wearing him down. "We'll try it again. Look, I have no interest in staying in a bad relationship either, baby or no baby, but I think we need to put in a little more effort. For her—and for us. Maybe we should try counseling."

"No, I'm not going to counseling," Calvin snapped.

"We should at least give it a try. What's the harm?"

"There's nothing some shrink is going to tell me that I don't already know. That's just some prick, sitting in a chair, mediating our arguments, who has no clue what we're both actually going through. I already know what the problems are with our relationship, thank you. I live them every day and I don't need someone drawing overly-broad conclusions about our innermost thoughts and feelings. That's stupid. If you're not with us twenty-four hours a day, it's impossible to understand our problems."

"We'll make it work," Leah insisted in a soothing tone.

"Listen, I just can't talk about this right now," Calvin said. "I appreciate the offer and we'll talk about it more later. My head's just not in the right place at the moment. I need to deal with the house. This was all just so sudden and…final. I was just there, too. I just saw everything as it had been all those years I lived there. And I just saw my dog last night when I left him."

"I'm sorry."

"Me too. I need to get off the phone now. I'm almost to the house. I'll talk to you later."

"Okay. I don't know what to say...I am so sorry. Love you."

Calvin paused a moment, ill at ease. Without emotion, he then said, "Love you too."

Calvin's heart pounded as he approached his street. He felt like he might get sick. He knew the sight was going to crush him, from everything he had been told so far, but nothing could have prepared him for the actual sight of his ruined home.

Calvin's truck stopped dead in the middle of Route 7.

The property looked like a war zone. There was red tape around the entire blackened perimeter. Burnt debris was spread across what used to be the lawn. The structure appeared to be a hollowed-out shell of what was the day before a beautiful old colonial. The white pillars still stood on the front porch majestically, now holding up only charred remains of the entryway. The original slate roof was gone, most of it collapsed into the second floor and some of it strewn across the front yard. The whole yard was debris, ash, slate, and mud.

All the windows and doors were now blackened holes, hauntingly empty and dark, like eye sockets of a skull.

It was burnt on all sides, from all openings. The fire had obviously made its rounds and taken its time devouring his home in his absence, savoring every plank of ninety-year-old wood.

Calvin jumped at the horn blast from behind him. A

tractor trailer was on his tail so close that he couldn't even see the entire grill in his rear-view. He realized he had stopped in the middle of a very busy road and quickly pulled onto the side street, next to the remains of his home.

There was a man on the side of the street opposite it with a white helmet on. He was taking pictures of the property and reminded Calvin of a surveyor. He was wearing work gloves and an absolutely hideous sweater with multicolored diamonds.

Calvin pulled past him and parked along the edge of his destroyed property. He stepped out of his aging SUV and let the heavy door clunk shut. He stood at the edge of his property as though it wasn't his, as though he had arrived at the site of a plane crash and he had no right to set foot on the scene.

"You must be Kevin," said a hearty voice from the man with the helmet and the bad sweater as he approached.

"It's Calvin," Calvin corrected him.

"Melvin?"

"No, *Calvin.*"

"Alvin?"

"It's *Calvin.*"

"Oh, *Calvin.* Like the…the underwear designer guy?"

"Yes. Like the underwear guy," Calvin answered, a little aggravated.

"He has a house around here, somewhere, doesn't he?"

"I have no idea," Calvin said, staring at the house.

"I heard he did, anyway. My name's Marshall Hamilton. I'm the insurance adjuster assigned to your case."

"Do you know anything about my dog?" Calvin asked with desperation.

Calvin examined Marshall up-close for the first time. He was a peculiar-looking man. He was not ugly, but just strange enough in appearance to keep Calvin staring longer than he should have as he tried to figure out what was so abnormal about his face. His pale skin was plastic-like in appearance, rubbery, and there were dark patches under his eyes that almost looked like eye shadow. Neatly-trimmed gray hair was visible on the sides under his white hard-hat.

"Yes," Marshall answered cautiously, looking Calvin in the eyes. "I do know something about your dog."

Calvin's heart surged.

Marshall said sullenly, "I have his collar and tags for you."

Calvin had finally heard the words he had been dreading. Any hope he had that somehow Hobbes had managed to survive the fire was lost. His heart ached as he imagined the horror that his dog went through, trapped in the burning house alone and being reduced to ash. Calvin refused to let himself cry.

"I left them inside the house," Marshall continued. "I'll get them for you a little later."

There was something about Marshall's expression that troubled Calvin, though, when he broke the news. He couldn't distinguish if it was disgust, disbelief, or anger that crept over Marshall's face as he looked him in the eyes. It definitely disturbed him.

"How are you holding up?" Marshall asked, changing the subject.

"Okay, I guess." Calvin shrugged. "Still in shock. Trying to understand everything."

"We're still trying to understand everything as well," Marshall said. "We've got a hell of a mess here. We're still trying to put together all the pieces. Maybe you can help us out with that."

"Sure. I can tell you plenty about the house," Calvin offered. "I know almost every square inch of it. I did a lot of work through the years, inside and out. Now it looks like a bomb hit it."

"Well, this was one vicious fire," Marshall said, shaking his head and turning to face the house. "It started low in the house, possibly the basement—you may have already heard this from the police—and it worked its way up the house. Once it got into the walls, forget it. It was over. It shot right up through the walls and into the attic. The attic ignited easily, all those exposed beams dry and aged. And then, well, the roof had nothing supporting it and collapsed into the upstairs. The first floor is actually down in the basement."

"What was that?" Calvin asked in a stupor.

"The first floor living room dropped right into the basement," Marshall repeated. "Most of the first floor is missing now. Calvin, this was an extremely hot and dangerous fire. One of the hottest I've seen in years. Your possessions inside were incinerated, most of them destroyed beyond recognition. It's definitely a total loss."

"Yeah, they told me that," Calvin said, sounding very depressed.

"There's really no part of this structure that could be rebuilt," Marshall said, gazing at the ruined home. "Even though the garage section appears mostly intact, it isn't worth saving. You'd have to build a whole new house around it, anyway. It wouldn't make sense financially and you'd be better off totaling it, anyhow."

"Yeah, I know. I can see there isn't much salvageable from this."

"Practically nothing that we can see. That, over there," Marshall pointed to a twisted heap of metal in the middle of the lawn, "is your front door."

"It's rolled into a ball...coiled." Calvin shook his head. "That was a steel weatherproof door."

"And that was on the outermost point of the house. That gives you an idea of what we're looking at inside."

"Was it the furnace?" Calvin asked.

Marshall cocked his head and looked at Calvin with an odd half-smirk. "What makes you say that?"

"I just had a brand new furnace installed about a month ago, just before it got really cold."

"Ah, yes, I believe there was mention of that. One of the neighbors told us there was a new furnace just put in. They had seen the plumbing and heating van over here. The fire inspector did check it out and didn't see anything wrong with it. We'll take another look at it a little later. I'll even take a look personally. But we're pretty sure it was an electrical fire, plain and simple. I'll show you myself in a little bit. But first I'd like to sit down with you and ask you a few questions...maybe more than a few. Would you mind maybe sitting down at a coffee shop or somewhere warm?"

"No, not at all," Calvin said, shivering. The thought of walking into coffee-scented warmth and getting some caffeine in his system perked him up. "There's one just a couple doors down."

"Oh, yes. I've become quite familiar with it already," Marshall said with a smile. "I'm about due for a refill."

They sat down across from each other at the local coffee shop after ordering coffee and a doughnut. Marshall was nice enough to pay for Calvin's.

"So, where to start?" Marshall said while flipping

open three folders and sifting through them. "This is a huge loss for you."

"Yes, it is. I'm just glad that no one besides my dog was inside."

"It could have been a lot, I mean *a lot* worse. Believe me. I deal with this sort of thing every day and I've seen it all. I'll spare you the details, but a good percentage of my investigations involve charred human remains. You're very lucky."

"That's a funny word to use right now," Calvin said with a bitter smile. "But yes, I suppose we are."

"When you say 'we,' you mean you and your wife?"

"She's not my wife. But yes, my girlfriend, and we have a baby together."

"How old?"

"She's about seven months now…seven and a half." Calvin shook his head. "It's flying by."

"So will the next fifteen years or so," Marshall said with a grin. "So the three of you were not in the house at the time. Where were you staying last night?"

"I was at my girlfriend's house last night. I stayed down there to watch her dog for her."

"Where is she?" Marshall asked with unusual interest.

"Oh, she's out in Buffalo visiting family. Her sister lives out there so she brought the baby to see them for a few days. She's actually heading back today."

"So this was your house, correct? You owned it?"

"Yes, I own it…I owned it."

"There was no one else on the title or the mortgage, no cosigner?"

"Nope. Just me," Calvin said. Despite what had happened, it still made him feel proud to say he had bought the home on his own.

"And how long have you owned the home?"

"It's been about seven years now. Seems a lot longer."

"So, Calvin, this was your house and your girlfriend has her own house, you mentioned. Where is her house located?"

"It's down on Grave Lake."

"Grave Lake…where is that, just approximately?"

"About ten miles Southeast of Albany," Calvin answered.

"Oh, ok. So you stayed there last night while she was out of town?"

"Yes. To take care of her dog."

"Why didn't you take your dog with you to her house?"

"Our dogs get along about as well as she and I do."

"Oh. I see," Marshall said with an understanding smile. "So your house is way up here, way up North, and she owns her own home way down on…ah…"

"Grave Lake."

"Grave Lake. Sorry. That's a pretty morbid name for a lake, huh?"

"Part of the land that was flooded when they made the lake had a graveyard on it."

"When they made the lake?"

"They made it the way it is now by widening the narrow lake that was already there. They built a dam on one end of it for hydroelectric power. The lake is actually three lakes separated by two roadways. If you dive down in the middle lake, you can still see some of the gravestones on the bottom."

"What did they do with the bodies?" Marshall asked, intrigued.

"Well, that's the thing. There are all kinds of stories, about how they didn't bother moving the bodies and some floated up a few weeks after the flooding. There was supposedly a big cover-up about that. I'm not sure I believe all that, but it makes for all kinds of creepy tales surrounding the lake. That it's haunted and people have been pulled underwater and out of boats by the dead people under the lake."

"Wow," Marshall said with a chuckle. "That's enough to stop me from ever kayaking there. So...you and your wife maintain separate residences even though you have a baby together?" Marshall looked puzzled.

"She's not my wife. But yeah," Calvin said with a sigh.

"Geez, that must get expensive."

"It is what it is right now."

"That must be a lot of commuting for you, Calvin, back and forth. That's, what, a good hour drive?"

"A little less than an hour, depending on traffic and how fast you're going. I've gotten used to it. I've worked in Albany for the last six years or so, so it doesn't really faze me anymore. It does take a nice chunk out of my free time, though."

"I would imagine," Marshall said. "So you were staying at the house on a regular basis, right?"

"Yeah, pretty regular. I mean, there was no schedule set in stone or anything. I was up here at least three days a week."

"Oh, ok. All right...So far everyone we've had contact with up here, the police department and fire department, have referred to your property as 'vacant'."

"No, that's a mistake," Calvin said firmly. "It wasn't vacant."

"You were actually living there?"

"Yes. Not all the time, but I was still living there."

"We met some of your neighbors this morning as well," Marshall said. "They came up to us—we didn't approach them. They said they thought you were renting out the home, that you had moved elsewhere, maybe in with your girlfriend and the baby?"

"Well, yes, I did. But it didn't work out."

"With the renters, or living with the girlfriend?"

"Both," Calvin said, getting irritated. He could feel his face turning red as he noticed other patrons of the coffee shop starting to pay attention to their conversation. There wasn't much background noise and it made him very uneasy knowing everyone in the shop could hear everything they said.

"Sorry…relax. This isn't an interrogation," Marshall said with a reassuring smile, sensing that he was making Calvin uncomfortable. "We're just trying to figure out the whole situation, the circumstances. It's my job. The insurance company requires us to do this."

"Ok, no, I understand. It's been a rough morning."

"I only brought that up because your neighbors did, and I have to at least ask you about it. They mentioned something about your car—that you drove a very flashy sports car, the type of car you can't miss, and they hadn't seen it in a while."

"Well, yeah, that would be my Porsche. They haven't seen it because I sold it months ago."

"Because of the baby?"

"Because of the baby, because it was totally impractical, and I had a business go under recently. My Porsche days were officially over," Calvin said with a careless chuckle.

"That must be the car we had a claim on recently. I noticed a claim for that car, a rather pricey one."

"Oh, right," Calvin recalled. "The convertible top was replaced. Totally forgot about that."

"Wow— a $3800 top?" Marshall was marveled.

"Yeah, well, leave it to Porsche. The guy who installed it would only use a Porsche factory top, not a knock off. It was actually all over a little tear in the plastic rear window. I had the top down late at night and pulled into my garage. I left the top down, since it was inside. The temperature dropped overnight and when I raised the top in the morning the plastic just ripped, since the cold made it brittle."

"You can't just replace the plastic rear window?"

"No, you actually have to replace the entire top. It's not a zipper-in window."

"There's a scam if I ever heard one," Marshall said with an awkward laugh. "Funny, this car seems to be what stands out most with your neighbors. They describe the comings and goings of the car, this beautiful Porsche of yours, but it seems like they rarely saw you."

"I wasn't around much, I guess, with the baby and all. When I'm not working, I'm with the baby or driving."

"Now, Calvin, did anyone have access to the house besides you?"

"What do you mean by access? Keys?"

"Well, yes. Keys. A way to get in?"

"No. No, just me," Calvin said, struggling to determine what Marshall was driving at. "You don't think someone set the fire, do you?"

"Oh, no, nothing quite like that. Seems pretty open and shut to me. We have to ask all these questions. I wouldn't be doing my job if I didn't cover all the bases. Like I said earlier, it was an electrical fire, plain and simple. The electric was a mess, by the way. It was an accident waiting to happen."

"I was always worried about that," Calvin said, drooping his head and nodding. "I mean, I thought I was fairly safe, but, you know...you never know for sure."

"Ever notice anything funny with the electric while you were living there? Any burning smells you couldn't explain?"

"Not really." Calvin stared off into the background of the coffee shop, trying to remember any information that might help. "There were a few strange abnormalities through the years...but nothing consistently strange or concerning."

Marshall's interest was piqued. "What do you mean by 'abnormalities'?"

"Well, you know, like once in a while an outlet suddenly wouldn't work," Calvin explained the best he could. "Then it would suddenly start working again the next day without me fixing anything."

"Did you ever have that problem with the outlet on the wall below the stairs, where there was a TV plugged in?"

"Not that one in particular...I don't think," Calvin said. "I don't really remember that."

"I ask because your last tenants stopped by this morning when they saw the fire on the news. They indicated to us that that outlet gave them problems on a number of occasions. The circuit that it was on would trip very easily. We can see in there, now, that this happened because there were way too many outlets run on that circuit. The entire thing was overloaded, and totally not up to   code."

"I had no idea," Calvin said defensively.

"We're not trying to blame you. It's not your fault unless you yourself wired that system and never got the permit and inspection for the work."

"No, I never touched the electric in that house, even though I did a lot of other work. That's the way it was when I bought it."

"Ok. Enough on that for now. When was the last time you were up here at the house?"

"Last night," Calvin said.

"About what time?"

"I left about seven or so to go down to my girlfriend's and spend the night there."

"And everything seemed normal to you when you left?"

"Yeah. As far as I can remember, everything seemed like it always did."

"All doors locked, all the windows closed?"

"Yeah, the doors were dead-bolted."

"Are you sure you dead-bolted them when you left?"

"I'm pretty sure...yeah..." Calvin hesitated. "I mean, I don't specifically remember doing it, but I know I don't leave without dead-bolting the back door—and that's the only door I use."

"So the front could've been not dead-bolted, or even unlocked?" Marshall asked.

"It's—it's possible, I guess I couldn't really say for sure since I didn't specifically check it last night on my way out to make sure the front was locked. Since I don't use that door, I'm sure I assumed it was locked...look, are you trying to say that someone broke into my house?"

"No..."

"Because it sure seems to me like you think someone intentionally lit my house on fire."

"Not at all, Calvin," Marshall soothed him, opening his palms over the table. "Not at all. We just need to have all our facts straight," Marshall said slowly, calmly, in a tone that troubled Calvin. It sounded as though Marshall knew more than he was acknowledging.

"Sure," Calvin replied, unconvinced.

"Do you lock the windows as well?"

"I do," Calvin said. "They were all new windows, only about a year old, and they all had locks on them. I locked them all—except one. I left one closed but unlocked in case I ever locked myself out of the house. It had happened enough times that I started leaving myself a secret way in, in case I did it again."

"Which window was unlocked?

"One of the two on the backside of the house, first floor, by the basement doors."

Marshall wrote something down in his notes. "So you had a mortgage on this property, correct?"

"Yes, that's correct."

"Just the one mortgage?" Marshall asked. "No home equity loans or lines of credit?"

"Nope. Just the one."

"And how is your payment history with your mortgage company?"

"Very good," Calvin said. "Until just recently."

"Until recently? So you're behind on your mortgage then?"

"Well, yes," Calvin said reluctantly. "But only because of this disaster I went through with my business failing—or buying a failed business, I should say. Then I had these tenants in here who were always late on their rent and then just didn't pay it. That's when I kicked them out. So I got a few months behind. I was going to get caught up again."

"A few months…that's probably a good four to five thousand dollars," Marshall said.

"Roughly, yeah. But I just got approved for a

mortgage loan modification, a government program that was going to drop my payment almost five-hundred a month and clear away all the late fees."

"Wow, that's quite a difference," Marshall said, taken back.

"Yeah, it was going to be a great thing for me. Help me get back on my feet," Calvin said.

"This business you had—you mentioned it a couple of times now. What happened with that?"

"I bought a restaurant franchise about six months ago. It was a major ordeal to go through all the training and certifications to be able to buy it, and it cost me a fortune..."

"Wiped you out?" Marshall asked boldly.

"Basically, yes," Calvin replied, keeping a level head. "Within a couple weeks of taking over the restaurant I could tell something wasn't quite right with the numbers. The sales and expenses weren't adding up. The store was losing tons of money. Then I discovered the records of the previous owner on the store computer. He had lied about how well the store was doing, and had given me sales sheets that showed strong numbers, numbers he had made up. He was desperate and shoved his failing business off on me, right when we were having a baby."

"You're working with a lawyer on this matter?"

"Yes, I have been," Calvin said. "And, fortunately, I have some proof. We're hoping to get more proof when we subpoena the franchise headquarters for all the former owner's sales records. Then we'll be able to show that he falsified every document he ever gave to me. Years worth of sales records, the same numbers he reported to the IRS."

"How long did you manage to stay open?" Marshall asked with an odd interest.

"I fought to stay open for two months. I did

everything I could to keep that store open. I went door-to-door advertising, gave out coupons. I was working there myself almost twelve hours per-day in addition to working every weekend at my part-time job. It was a living hell. I had never intended to be slaving away in fast food, not only making less than the teenagers I employed, but actually doing it for the privilege of losing a fortune."

"How much exactly did you lose?"

"Exactly?" Calvin thought for a moment. "I don't know for sure, exactly how much. I haven't really had the heart to sit down and add it all up."

"Well, ball park?"

"Ball park...maybe ninety-thousand," Calvin said.

"Ninety thousand? That's an awful lot of money for someone your age."

"That's an awful lot of money for any age," Calvin said.

"That was just for the actual restaurant?"

"It was buying the actual restaurant—not the space, of course, that was leased—and all the other things involved with buying an official franchise. There was the franchise fee, flying out to Colorado for a week of training and paying for the hotel, buying the existing food off the previous owner, and a ton of other things. Not to mention the money I had to sink into the restaurant to keep it open for the two months."

"So that was probably pretty much all the money you had, right?" Marshall asked.

"Pretty much. It wasn't all of it, though. I had money left over to put a new furnace in the house."

"Yeah, about that furnace," Marshall said. "You kept bringing it up in your conversations with the police. Just curious, now why do you seem so sure the fire had something to do with the furnace?"

"I'm definitely not sure about that. Just a good guess. If I had to pick something in the house, a reason for why this happened, I would instantly assume the furnace because it was the only thing recently replaced."

"It was installed only about a month and a half ago?"

"That's correct," Calvin said. "Roughly a month and a half, two months maybe."

"Did you install that yourself?"

"Oh, god no," Calvin said. "I wouldn't mess with that."

"You hired a professional?"

"Yes, a professional company. I've hired the guy for work on other houses. He's fully insured and seems to do good work. I've always trusted him. He was a straight-shooter from the start, so I stuck with him any time I needed plumbing or heating done."

"Well, from our determination, the fire had nothing to do with the furnace," Marshall stated.

"Yes, they told me that already."

"Does that surprise you?"

"Yes. It does."

"Well this was a very old house…" Marshall looked at his paperwork. "Let's see here…built in 1925. Does that sound about right to you?"

"Yes. I believe that's exactly right."

"These old houses weren't built the way they build them nowadays. They didn't use sheetrock. They used strips of wood covered by plaster. Do you know if the walls were ever updated, replaced with sheetrock?"

"Some of them were. Most of the walls I guess I don't know. I never tore into them or moved any walls or anything like that. So I have no idea."

"Looking at the structure from the inside, it's quite

apparent that they were practically all the old style. Once the fire made its way into the walls there wasn't much stopping it. It had all the fuel it needed to shoot straight through the roof, and then some."

"And the fire crews couldn't do anything?" There was some lingering anger in Calvin's voice. "There's a fire house not even a quarter mile up the road."

"There was a bit of a delay in getting there, from what I've heard," Marshall said. "Then, supposedly, a problem with water pressure. It was a busy night for fires around here. They had six calls before the one on your house last night. My guess would be that the equipment just wasn't ready to handle another fire, especially one this intense. They're certainly not going to say that they couldn't handle the fire, but I'm getting the impression that that was the case. Well," Marshall said, shifting in his seat, "How about we take a look now?"

Calvin crossed what used to be his backyard, stepping over scattered rubble and piles of unidentified charred remains. He had never seen anything like it.

"We'll have to enter through the basement steps," Marshall said. "It's the only way to safely get in, since the first floor is half-gone and the rest of it is totally unsafe. We'll only be able to walk through the basement. Just please watch your step. It's a mess in here," he said as he led Calvin down the concrete steps.

The ash and black of the charred beams and walls made it look like he was entering a dungeon. The ceiling of what remained on the first floor was jet black. The floor crunched under his shoes and was soft and uneven. Looking down, he could see it was pure ash and charred remains of the first floor. It looked deep, possibly six inches.

Calvin entered the area of basement that used to sit underneath the living room and his eyes were drawn to a bright beam of light from above. He could see up, through the first floor, second floor, the attic, and straight through where there used to be a slate roof far above.

Calvin stood in the basement of the devil's cathedral, a giant blackened tomb of his once beautiful home, looking up and all around. He felt as though he was in a giant well or a cave with a funnel of daylight high overhead. The second floor seemed impossibly far above.

"Oh, I almost forgot," Marshall said in a gloomy tone, picking something up from the charred floor. "I was able to find this in the rubble down here." He held his hand out to Calvin.

Calvin's heart sunk. He wanted to drop to his knees. It was Hobbes's collar and tags, blackened but unmistakable.

"Poor guy never had a chance," Marshall said, shaking his head and staring at the ground.

"No. And it's my fault," Calvin said, overcome with grief. He wandered away from Marshall in the basement, uncertain if he wanted to cry or punch something.

A few minutes passed before Marshall approached again. He inhaled deeply through his nose, sounding satisfied, like a man taking in the smell of a new car. "After so many years," he said, "you can tell what was in the fire, what burned. Everything has a slightly different smell when it's burnt. Did you know that, Calvin?"

"No. I didn't," Calvin answered in a daze. "It just smells like charcoal to me. Like a campfire."

"Couches, carpet, plastic, wood, even alcohol or gasoline," Marshall said, shrugging. "It all gets left behind, even if there's nothing you can see. You can smell it.

That's what old dogs like me do, Calvin. We sniff it out. We use every single one of our senses to sniff out the situation."

"Where is everything?"

Marshall turned to face him with a serious expression. "What do you mean?"

"The furniture—my things," Calvin said, troubled. "There were things in here. I don't even see remains of anything."

"It was all incinerated," Marshall stated plainly. "This was an incredibly hot fire. One of the hottest we've seen in a long time. You had six feet of water where you're standing, too, don't forget. This place was a disaster area."

"I just thought I'd still see some remnants or remains of my things. Did they pull anything out of here?"

"Did we pull anything out of here? No, we haven't changed a thing," Marshall said calmly. "We never remove items from a scene unless it is something that could have been directly responsible for the fire."

"Do you think the fire department took things out?"

"No, I don't think so. I don't know why they would do that. If they did, nobody told us. You can always ask them yourself," Marshall said as he crunched across the floor to the base of the stairwell. "Well here's the culprit," he said, holding up an ancient-looking electrical outlet box. The box dangled from bare copper wire that connected all the other outlet boxes on the circuit and suspended them like a long string of party lanterns. "This wiring is doubled back," he said, holding it closer to Calvin. "It's frayed at the top, outside of the box. The wiring has been pieced together, some new and some old. With all the plastic melted off the wiring you can see, plain as day, how many outlets were running on this circuit. This was a very dangerous situation."

There was something about the way Marshall gazed at him while he explained it that made Calvin very uneasy. It was as though Marshall didn't really believe what he was saying.

"God...I had no idea," Calvin said, staring at the box. "To think I was living here that whole time," he added dramatically, feeling as though he was acting out a scene in a play.

"It burnt right through this thick support beam, here, and then grew outwards and upwards," Marshall said with fascination. "Fire is like a living organism. In order to exist, to survive, it needs to breathe. It will snake through the house until it finds even tiny cracks in walls or doors so that it can breathe. It went straight for those covered up windows, there." He pointed to the front wall. "It must've found some air seeping in and burnt straight through them. Meanwhile, it was building heat and worked its way up through the stairwell and the first floor."

They stood together in silence for a moment, gawking at the burnt skeleton of the house. Calvin tightly clutched the dog collar in his right hand.

"Well, if you don't mind, I do need to get back to work here," Marshall finally said. "I've got a long day ahead of me and other stops to make. No rest for the wicked, Calvin."

"No," Calvin said, forcing a slight smile.

"I've seen a lot of fires in my career," Marshall said as Calvin headed for the steps up into the light outside. "People like me, it's what we do for living. It becomes second nature to us," he said with an unnerving frozen smile. "These investigations usually last a while. Someone almost always comes forward with something to say. We'll keep our eyes and ears open." Marshall headed further into the dark basement. Then, in a teasing tone, as if chanting 'I know something you don't know', he said, "And we'll keep a close eye on you, too, Calvin."

Calvin stopped dead in his tracks on his way up the stairs. His heart thumped. He turned around to see Marshall fully disappear into the blackness below, into the dead heart of his house, to become one with the ominous charred remains of the devil's cathedral.

2

I t was late afternoon when the winding back roads took Calvin far into the country landscape towards Leah's house. It was beautiful out there, with snow-covered trees and mountains in the background from any angle.

Driving that long country route often brought up memories of the first time he came out there a year-and-a-half earlier, following Leah home from work to see her house on Grave Lake. He never would have imagined that he would still be with her, let alone moving in with her.

He pulled into the gravel driveway next to her car and shut off the engine. He sighed and slumped in his seat for a moment. It had been a long day, a long drive, and he just needed a minute to get his head straight before entering her home. The icy surface of the lake down below was beautiful, shimmering in the late afternoon sunlight on either side of the house. The trees were bare and frosted with icy snow that glistened in the last bit of sunlight with a purplish hue. Night was slowly settling in.

The house had been a fixer-upper, an old camp that had been converted into a small year-round home. Leah had done most of the work on it herself, rearranged the floor plan and made it her own. It needed tons of work, and plenty more still needed to be done. The back porch was turned into the master bedroom and two tiny bedrooms were turned into one large one with a closet, now the baby's room. It wasn't much, but it was cozy. It was peaceful and the scenery was picturesque. It would be home for a while now.

He saw the front door of the cottage open. Leah came out holding the baby. Calvin took a deep breath and popped open the door. As soon as he stepped out of the truck, the baby's arms started flapping and she had a huge smile on her face. He waved back to her. "Hi, my little Pearl," he said to her, waving happily back.

Leah had her long, dirty-blonde hair pulled back into a ponytail and she was wearing jeans and a hoodie. She still looked surprisingly beautiful every time he saw her, especially when he hadn't seen her in a few days. She had the prettiest blue eyes and the softest fair skin he had ever seen. She was twenty-four, soon to be twenty-five, but she looked about eighteen—a fact which Calvin had been very proud of, since he was thirty-two and feeling about forty-two. He was so proud of her youthful looks that he loved showing her off and making sure everyone knew they were together—until he found out she was pregnant.

"You look so young when you're with her," Calvin said as he passed through the porch gate. She did look young because she *was* so young. Although she was twenty-four, Calvin felt that her age never really matched her behavior. She acted too young sometimes, almost like she was trying to play grown-up, like a little girl playing house.

"I made you a steak for dinner," she said sweetly.

"Really?"

"I hope you're hungry. I figured you didn't eat all day, knowing you," she said, smiling and looking into his eyes.

"I haven't had much of an appetite at all. I'm starving now."

The three of them sat at the kitchen table devouring their food in silence. Baby Pearl sat strapped into her high chair, dropping fistfuls of peas and carrots onto the floor for Leah's large husky, Miko.

"No, Pearl. No feeding the dog. *You're* supposed to eat it." Leah sighed, putting some more food on Pearl's tray. "*You* eat it." She looked at Calvin. "Rough day, huh?" she said, seeming to instantly realize how stupid that sounded. It was her first attempt at conversation since he arrived.

"Rough year," Calvin responded with a mouthful.

"I know. Things will get better soon."

"I sure hope so. Somehow I don't feel like they're going to, though. I guess they can't get much worse, though, right?"

"Don't say that," Leah said dreadfully. "They can always get worse. Just be grateful we have a healthy, beautiful baby with no issues. That's the most important thing." She paused a moment, uncertain of how to bring up the subject that Calvin seemed to be avoiding. "So...that must've been hell for you up at the house today, huh?"

"You have no idea," Calvin said, rolling his eyes.

"It was bizarre."

"Like, how do you mean?"

"I mean the guy, this investigator or whoever he is—I thought he was a claims adjuster at first, but then he turned out to be some sort of special investigator—he asked a lot of questions."

"Questions about the house?"

"Questions about everything—about the house, my cars, us. He touched on pretty much everything going on in my life right now."

"What does anything besides the house have to do with the house fire?" Leah asked.

"*Dat*," Pearl said, pointing at Calvin. "*Ooooooooh*."

"I don't know," Calvin said, a little frustrated. "He said it's procedure, that's what they have to do. They have to ask all those questions or he wouldn't be doing his job."

"Leave it to insurance companies," Leah said. "It sounds like they're trying to get the full picture, make sure they don't miss anything."

"Yeah," Calvin said with uncertainty. "It left me with a really bad taste in my mouth. I didn't like the way that guy talked to me, Leah. And the way he looked at me. It creeped me out."

"What was creepy about it?"

"Everything. He kept telling me they knew what caused the fire and it was open-and-shut. There was no question about it. But then he kept probing, insinuating. I felt like I had done something wrong."

"But you didn't," Leah said. "Right?"

"Of course I didn't. He just made me feel dirty, like I was hiding something. The way he talked about the fire, it was like he knew something more than I did and he was trying to see how I would react, or something. I just got the feeling there was more going on than I realized."

"You've been through a lot, Calvin. I'm sure your head isn't exactly clear. You haven't even eaten all day, and you know how you get when you don't eat..."

"But I'm telling you there was something weird with this guy, Leah," Calvin argued, flailing his arms. "You always do this—you're not listening to what I'm saying..."

"I'm listening, I'm listening. I just think you're still in shock and this guy was just trying to do his job. It can't be easy looking at burnt-out houses all day for a living. Can you imagine?"

"I know," Calvin said with some disbelief. "He was telling me how in a lot of the house fires there are bodies, or remains of bodies."

"I don't think anybody cleans them up. If there's hardly anything left of a body, there's nothing for an ambulance or hearse to take. The remains probably just get left there. And this poor bastard has to walk in and see all that."

"Yeah," Calvin agreed with a snort. "He was wearing this ugly Mr. Rogers sweater...it was probably a ploy to make me feel comfortable around him so I wouldn't feel threatened if I had done something wrong."

"Oh, would you stop," Leah said, growing annoyed with his paranoia.

"*Babababababababa,*" added Pearl from her highchair.

"That's right. Blah blah blah blah," Leah said to little Pearl. "You tell Daddy."

"Listen, I need to talk to you about something," Calvin said, suddenly changing the subject and his tone.

"Sure."

"Let's just keep the house fire to ourselves for now, please."

"Why?" Leah stopped feeding the baby and glared

at him.

"I just can't deal with other people knowing this now…I have enough problems as is. I don't want the attention. I don't want pity or charity."

"Calvin, there's nothing wrong with people feeling bad for you, or…"

"Or looking down on me."

"No, *helping* you," Leah said forcefully. "There's nothing wrong with people caring and trying to help you out when you're down."

"I'm fine. Please just keep this to yourself. Please."

"I've already told some people," Leah said with a shrug. "I mean, this was a pretty major event, Calvin, and it would seem kind of strange if I didn't tell people I know."

"Ok, just don't tell any more. There's no need to, other than for you to have something to talk about, some new exciting news to spread."

"Because it's something people *should* know, Calvin."

"Ok, I understand, you've already told your family."

"And a few friends," Leah added.

"Ok, that's fine. Please, let's just keep it out of work. I don't need people at work knowing about this."

"What's the big deal?"

"Because you know they're going to draw their own conclusions about it based on absolutely nothing. They'll just assume I had something to do with the fire without having any facts at all to support that, and then tell everyone they know like it's a goddamn proven fact. That girl, remember, way back, who had her house burn down…"

"Janice," Leah interjected.

"Yeah, Janice. Everyone assumed she did it. They

don't know. They don't know anything about what happened to her house. It's just fun and convenient to simply say she burnt her house down and talk behind her back like she's a criminal."

"It's not like that even worked out well for her," Leah said.

"No, it didn't. And she had to leave the job because everyone gave her such a hard time about it. Once people make up their minds about something like that, once they get an idea in their head that something scandalous might have occurred, that's it."

"Okay," Leah said, nodding her head. "I agree. There's no need to bring it into work."

"Thank you."

"It won't do any good, anyway, to tell people," Leah said. "And this way you can go to work and not think about it. You won't have a dozen patients a day telling you how sorry they are."

"I need that like another hole in my head right now."

"Another hole?" she said with a smile. "You already have a hole in your head?"

"The gaping void that was left when you took my free will."

Pearl sneezed mid-spoonful and sprayed strained peas all over herself, Calvin, and Leah.

"Oh, baby..." Leah said, reaching for the roll of paper towels.

Pearl grinned widely with her few teeth exposed and laughed a little.

"Yes, sneezes are hilarious," Leah said while wiping up the mess.

Calvin felt Leah's eyes on him while he continued to eat ravenously.

"See? You were hungry," she said.

"I guess I was."

She paused for a moment and continued staring at him. "Calvin, what happened to us?"

He stayed silent and chewed his food.

"This is so nice, the three of us together like this," she said cheerfully. "Isn't it nice, Calvin?"

"Yes. It is," he said drearily.

"Why can't it be like this all the time?"

He finished chewing and swallowed. "I don't know."

"Okay. It's obvious you're avoiding the conversation," Leah said, starting to sound upset.

Calvin shrugged. "I'm not avoiding it. I just don't know what to say. I don't have the answers you want to hear."

"But I was thinking all day," she began. "Maybe this was a sign."

"A sign?" he raised his eyebrows.

"A sign that we are supposed to stay together as a family."

"Right. A sign from God," he said with heavy sarcasm.

"So? Maybe it is. Maybe this is someone's way of telling us that we belong together."

"It's a sign from God that someone did a shitty job of wiring my house."

"See? Why do you have to be like that, Calvin?"

"Like what?"

"Like, totally disinterested in me. You don't care at all about me. I mean, I know we're not entirely together as a couple at this point, but would it kill you to show just a little affection? Or at least act like you care? I am the mother of your child."

"Of course I care about you," Calvin said compassionately, putting his fork down. "There just isn't much excitement…or romance left. I'm sorry. I'm trying. I can try harder, but I don't know if I can force something that just isn't there."

"But it was there before, right? I mean, why did we even start dating, then?"

"We only dated a week before you got pregnant," Calvin said bluntly.

"It doesn't mean we wouldn't have stayed together if I hadn't gotten pregnant."

"Well, it wasn't going so great by the end of the week, or week-and-a-half, whatever it was." Calvin instantly realized how hurtful his words were to her.

"So it was supposed to be what, just a meaningless fling?"

"No…I'm just saying, we weren't even really together. I wasn't even sure if we were dating, or…or…"

"Or what? Or if you were just using me for a good time? Because that's not how I saw it."

"Things are just a lot different now than when we first started dating." Calvin struggled to find a way to make her understand.

"In what way?"

"It was fun, exciting. It wasn't serious and dramatic. It made me feel like a teenager again, like we were running around doing something we weren't supposed to, trying not to get caught."

"We *were* doing something we weren't supposed to," Leah said.

"Exactly. Like when we first started dating, it was a secret. It was fun because no one even knew. No one would ever have guessed."

"Because we had worked together for three years

and couldn't stand each other most of the time?"

"Yes. It was a big secret that we couldn't let anyone find out about. Remember what that was like? Stealing kisses in the back hallway, making out in the storage room? Taking breaks in my car together and you ducking down every time someone walked near the car?"

She smiled a little.

"And then we were seeing each other almost every day outside of work and no one even knew that we were together."

"And then getting called into the office and disciplined for it by the bosses," Leah added. "That was great."

"Yeah, the two of us almost getting fired over it because us being together pissed everyone off so much." Calvin laughed and shook his head. "Why did it piss everyone off so much?"

"I don't know. Jealousy."

"Yeah. People have affairs all the time in that company, married people, and you'd think we'd started a war from the way everyone reacted to the two of us getting together. What were they thinking?"

She was silent for a moment. "I'm sorry, but I just have to ask...All that sneaking around and trying to stay under the radar...is that because it was fun, or because you were embarrassed to be with me?"

"Why would I be embarrassed to be with you?"

"Because I'm so much younger than you, for starters."

"Only, what, eight years?"

"That's a lot."

"Who cares?"

"I know that you always thought I was a little too immature for you. That's why I thought you were trying to keep things 'light'. You never really saw us as anything long term. I was just a fling gone wrong."

"That's not true. And Please stop calling it a fling," Calvin said. "You may not have been exactly the person I pictured myself ending up with, but I definitely pictured a future with you. At least back then." Calvin realized what he had said and instantly felt like a scumbag.

Leah lowered her head a little. She looked ready to cry, but angry at the same time. "It's been tough lately to picture us together at all. I know. I feel the same way, so don't feel bad."

"Look...things are so different now. So real and serious, and not fun. I guess I started to wonder what the point was in this—in us. Everything positive between us has vanished."

"Life can't be a party forever, you know, Calvin."

"I don't want to party forever, or even now for that matter. We used to have fun, though. Now there's no fun. Just work and the baby. And, of course, we both love spending time with the baby."

"She's probably the only thing bringing me joy at this point in my life."

"Well, mine too," Calvin agreed. "But there should be more than that making you happy. I know she comes first, but we can't sacrifice every other bit of happiness for her."

"We don't *have* to stay together, Calvin."

"I don't want her to grow up in a broken home. I feel like I don't have a choice, though. And that's my fault. I did it, we did it, we brought her into this world."

"She'll always be loved, no matter what, Calvin."

"It's not the same, though," he contested.

"That's why we need to try a little harder," she said amiably. "You're here now, and together we can work on being a family."

"Well, we can try. I guess we don't have much of a choice at this point. I just don't want you to get the wrong idea by me moving back in here. This isn't permanent."

"I figured," she said as though he was stating the obvious.

"My heads just a mess right now," Calvin said. "I've had such long string of bad luck."

"You don't have to explain your head to me. It's okay. I understand. I accept you for who you are."

"Thank you for dinner," Calvin said, sliding his chair back a little from the table. "And thank you for being here for me."

"Of course I'm here for you," she said in a motherly tone.

"Well, you could've kicked me out on the street."

"You're the father of my child. No matter what, you'll always be a part of my life and I'll always care about you. Even if we don't make it, it doesn't matter."

She came up behind his chair and slipped her arms around him.

Calvin could see the reflection of the two of them in the front kitchen window. He was taken aback by how pretty she looked. After all this time and all the fights they had endured, he was still extremely turned on by how pretty she was, and in particular how young she looked next to him. Her skin was so vibrant and soft to the touch. Her dirty-blonde hair was so silky soft and shiny. She still had her nice hourglass figure, even after her pregnancy. It was times like this that made him wonder why they couldn't work their problems out. If only they could work through their issues, she would be the perfect wife and they would make the perfect family.

She rested her chin on his head. He put his hands on

her arms and caressed them, exhaling. A feeling of peace and comfort came over him.

A little while later, they held each other naked in bed. Calvin ran his hand up and down the smooth, soft contours of her waist and thigh. Leah finally broke the beautiful moment they had shared without the baby and without concerns by nudging him with her elbow.

"Can you please let Miko in before you come to bed?" She asked him, sounding half-asleep.

"Yeah," Calvin grumbled, struggling his way to his feet and staggering across the bedroom floor. He was surprised that Miko hadn't been clawing at the front door to come inside. The more he thought about it, Miko had been out for quite a long time, and it was freezing out.

Calvin opened the front door and was slammed in the face with bitter-cold air. He flinched and lost his breath for a moment. Outside it was dark and silent. It was a perfectly clear night, and after his eyes adjusted to the dark, Calvin could see stars very clearly. There didn't seem to be a cloud in the night sky. He could smell the woodstoves burning from the nearby neighbors' houses.

"Miko," Calvin called, a little surprised that he hadn't been waiting outside the door to come in from the cold. He waited a moment, listened, and then impatiently called for him again. Then he spotted the outline of the dog in the corner of the fence, just a black blob in the dark.

Calvin closed the door behind him and ventured out onto the icy patio in his slippers. He pulled his coat closed around him, shuddering from the nipping wind.

"Miko," Calvin said as he approached the motionless dog, "What are you doing, boy?"

Miko didn't acknowledge him.

Calvin put his hand on the dog's head. "What's a matter, bud?"

Miko stared intensely into the woods across the street. Calvin strained to see what had caught his attention, but couldn't see anything at all out of the ordinary. Just trees, road, snow, and forest.

Miko let out a low, suspicious growl as he gazed out at a fixed point in the night landscape.

"What do you see out there, bud?" Calvin asked. He knew he saw something that had him spooked.

Miko stood up abruptly, maintaining his focus on whatever he saw out there. The hair on the back of his neck was raised.

A chill ran through Calvin, and it wasn't from the freezing cold. There was something—or someone—out there.

Calvin couldn't stay out any longer. It was late. He was tired and cold. And now his mind was playing tricks on him. He grabbed Miko by the collar and led him towards the door, but not without much resistance. Calvin shrugged it off as a deer that had wandered through the property. He did, however, look back over his shoulder with every couple steps he took towards the door.

3

Calvin stood amidst the rubble that occupied the front lawn of what used to be his home. He stared into those empty window holes with his own mouth hanging open in a catatonic state. The ground was covered with ice and snow, but he didn't feel any coldness at all.

He couldn't take his eyes off the dark empty eye sockets of the misaligned skull face of the house. It looked like some morbid, rotting Jack-O-Lantern a kid carved with the mouth hanging off to the left side.

He did not want to be there. He did not know why he had come.

The opening to the basement beckoned him with its frightening, empty darkness. It sent shivers down his spine, but he couldn't turn away. He could only move towards the house, headed for the dark basement opening that summoned him.

He did not feel his feet as he descended into the

dead house's mouth, down the concrete steps into the basement, into its blackened heart.

He stood in the dark basement as he had the day before, this time alone. He felt sick to his stomach. He should not be there. There was something very wrong with his presence in the lifeless house, but that only pushed him further inside.

The wind howled around the burnt structure, swirling snowdrifts down through the house from the open roof.

Calvin stood silently, waiting. He thought he heard something else—a sound, some noise in the distance, just barely within reach of his ears.

There *was* something else, he was sure of it now—a very faint, high-pitched noise that wasn't coming from the wind. It was a whimpering.

He looked up at the bright light beaming through the hole in the top of the house. *"Hobbes?"* he yelled to himself. His voice seemed to echo forever.

He listened again. The wind moaned deeply. He could definitely hear it now, a high-pitched whining. It was coming from upstairs, somewhere high within the structure.

"Hobbes!" Calvin yelled up at the white light above. *"Hobbes! It's me, bud!"*

He put his foot on the staircase in a desperate attempt to climb it, but it had been reduced to fragments of burnt wood and simply crumbled to pieces under him. He stared up at the second floor high above.

"I'm coming, bud! It's okay!" he shouted. *"I'm coming for you!"*

He pulled his old ladder down from the garage and maneuvered it into the house through the missing basement doors. He swung it around clumsily, teetering as its weight shifted and clunked noisily into the blackened walls.

He opened the ladder and extended it to its full twenty feet. He shifted it around on the uneven grit of the floor until he found a somewhat stable place. He leaned the top of the long ladder against the upper wall of the house, which had been stripped to its bare wood skeleton.

He couldn't feel his feet or hands as he ascended the ladder, one rung at a time, his eyes fixed on the strong white light above. He climbed past the first floor and peered into what remained of it. The refrigerator was melted into a distorted rectangle, a mangled mess of metal. The kitchen was completely gone.

A strong wind suddenly rushed through the house, groaning at Calvin angrily through a tornado of black ash. Calvin was stopped for a moment, flinching and covering his face. Then he pushed forward, unafraid, upwards towards the light. He was going to save his dog.

The wind howled more fiercely than before. The ladder swayed. The house shook. The groaning of the trapped wind began screaming at him, circling his head and crying right in his ears.

He couldn't hear Hobbes anymore.

The ladder swayed far out from the wall. Someone was shaking it. Someone was down there, trying to knock him off. Calvin looked down in shock, but the bottom of the ladder vanished in the blackness below.

"*Hobbes!*" he hollered at the top of his lungs. The ladder shook violently again, nearly throwing him off. There was someone down there, or something, below him. There had to be.

The snowflakes and ash swirled around his head and stung his eyes. He cowered and hid his face between his arms. He couldn't hang on. The ladder was ripped from his hands. Calvin fell through the house, flailing and screaming at the top of his lungs.

"Calvin!" a voice cried at him. "Calvin!" It cried again.

Calvin jolted awake with a holler.

Directly over him was what looked like a demon head in the dark, peering down. He hollered again.

"Calm down!" Leah shouted at him, trying to keep her arms around him. "It's okay, Calvin, it's okay…"

Calvin squirmed in bed for a moment and panted. He was drenched in sweat. The demon head above him moved, and then jumped onto his stomach.

"Damn cat!" he yelled, trying to get a hold of himself and shake off the nightmare, which had followed him into consciousness.

"Holy shit, Calvin…"

"Bad dream…Bad dream."

"Are you okay?"

"Yeah," he said, sitting up in bed breathing heavily. "I'm fine. I'm okay," he said insincerely, hopelessly trying to cover up his fright. His alarm started buzzing. "What a way to start the day," he said as he pounded a fist on the alarm clock to silence it. "No rest for the wicked."

After a few moments of sitting up in bed and getting a firm grip on reality, he grudgingly swung his legs out and left the warm comfort of bed. His feet hit the ice cold wood floor of the bedroom.

"Try to have a good day," Leah mumbled, mostly asleep.

"Sure thing," he groaned. "Living the dream."

"You'll find another job soon," she said reassuringly while yawning.

"I know, I know."

She blew him a kiss.

He never understood why he felt so terrible waking up so early. His body had never gotten used to it, even after six years of doing the same job. He often asked coworkers if they felt this way when they awoke for these early hours. Of course they all hated it, but no one seemed to feel the way he did when he first woke up. There was a terrifying feeling of hopelessness and desperation. He knew it wasn't just the waking up at four, though. It was his life in general.

Leah often told him that if he felt that bad then maybe he needed medication. His answer to that, every time, was, 'The problem isn't in my head. It's everything else around me. I need to fix all the problems in my life to stop feeling this way. Something from a bottle isn't going to help anything. All that will do is mess me up worse.'

He grabbed his work scrubs and tip-toed across the creaky wood floors like a burglar trying not to get caught. He would do anything to avoid waking the baby. The last thing he needed at this hour was the baby waking up and Leah having to get up with him to take care of her, since he wouldn't have time to get the baby back to bed. She'd be mad, they'd start a fight, and another day ruined.

He was soundlessly creeping toward the kitchen when a flash of light caught his eye. He froze and crinkled his forehead. He knew it was something unusual at this hour, although he didn't instantly understand why.

It was car headlights that beamed through the front windows in the kitchen for a moment, an unusual sight at this hour. Then he heard a very quiet car engine head up the street, past the house and up the hill.

He'd been waking up there several days a week at this hour for almost a year, and it was definitely unusual to see any car at that hour heading back up the hill.

He continued into the kitchen and retrieved his coffee, already brewed and awaiting his weary brain. He poured a good amount of creamer into his 'I love Dad" mug with his daughter's grinning pictures on it. He did not use sugar, though. Too much sugar in his diet already, so years ago he decided to stop using it completely. He couldn't drink coffee with it now. It would be way too sweet for him, and there was a certain taste that he loved about the sugarless coffee, in much the way that a fine wine connoisseur would never be satisfied by the sappy sweet nectars of the Riesling variety.

Coffee had become his lifeline. It was the only thing that could pick him up and get him through the day, besides the glowing smile and laughter of his daughter.

He kept the lights off in the kitchen. Not only would light be too much for his red eyes to bear at this early hour, but he didn't want to risk waking the baby with that, either.

The kitchen suddenly lit up again in flashes from the front kitchen window, startling Calvin slightly in mid-sip of his coffee.

He rushed over to the window. A car was turning down the street again, from the main road. He anxiously watched it buzz by, up the street. From what he could see through the trees it was a mid-size car, sedan shaped, light color, maybe white or silver. The headlights seemed to reflect that of a new car model, even although the body didn't appear to be very new.

He bent his neck and watched the car go up the street as far as the view from the front window allowed. The headlights illuminated the trees up the road in progression, but did not stop. It was out of view.

Calvin waited at the window for a good five minutes. All was quiet, as usual. He rarely saw a car on the street at this hour, and if he did it was heading down the street, not up it, to turn onto the main road, someone heading to work. The street was a dead-end street, although it did have a through-road that made it into a block, so a car could loop around on the upper street and turn back onto the main road again.

His coffee went cold on the table.

After another five minutes or so of nothing, his attention was suddenly grabbed again.

The trees on the main road lit up. He watched anxiously to see what type of vehicle it was. The headlights looked similar to the car that had gone up the road. As it passed, he became certain they were the same headlights and the car had the same overall shape. It was on the main road, now, traveling much faster, although still quietly, heading down the hill towards the bridge over the lake.

Calvin was fascinated. He was pretty sure that was the same car, although it was impossible to be certain in the dark with some trees and shrubs in the way.

He waited again. He couldn't pull himself away. He knew the car would come by again. He waited for it excitedly, knowing it would validate this strange obsession he had picked up at this un-godly hour. He couldn't bear the thought of missing this vehicle passing if he left the window to continue his morning routine.

What seemed like five minutes later, his wish was granted. He saw the headlights again coming down the hill on the main road. He couldn't believe it. He was right, he had been right to wait at the window this whole time.

The headlights slowed and the sedan smoothly and quietly whipped around the corner onto their street and quickly made its way up their road again.

"Gotcha," Calvin muttered to himself, delighted by his discovery.

"Calvin," Leah's voice fired from behind him with no attempt to be quiet.

"Jesus," he exclaimed after jumping and flailing his arms.

"What the hell are you doing?" she said angrily.

"Nothing. Getting ready for work."

"It's five thirty—almost quarter to six," she said, pointing to the digital clock on the stove.

"What?" He looked at the digital clock on the stove. "Oh, shit,"

"Ah, yeah," she said obnoxiously. "What the hell were you doing?"

"Nothing...nothing."

"When I came out here you were just staring out the window."

"I know. I didn't realize what time it was. Lost track of time."

"Is there something out there, or what?"

"No...there was," Calvin said. "There was a car I kept seeing. The same car kept coming back and going up our street."

"What? Calvin? Are you serious? You've been standing there for...what? Almost an hour? Are you serious?"

"Yes, I'm serious. I didn't realize it was that long, but there's a car that keeps coming back and driving up our street."

"People drive up and down this road all the time."

Calvin shook his head, growing frustrated.

"People live here who have to go to work."

"But it wasn't someone going to work. They made a left onto this road from the main road, and then never came back out again."

"So someone stayed out late and is just making their way home now."

"Three times?"

"Well it probably wasn't the same car all three times."

"I'm pretty sure it was."

She stared at him across the room in the dark with her arms folded against her chest.

"Listen, I know cars, it was the same car," Calvin said firmly. "And then it went past us on the main road towards the bridge."

"So someone's driving around. Maybe they're lost. Maybe they're trying to pick someone up to go to work and they can't find the house...I don't know, Calvin, it could be anything. Maybe it's the paper delivery guy and he forgot to drop off a paper and came back for it."

"That car definitely did not belong on this street."

"It didn't belong here? Calvin, are you listening to yourself?" she said, glowering at him like he was crazy.

"It wasn't someone's who lives on this street. I know all the cars. I see them passing and wave to most of them. I know all their vehicles and which houses those vehicles belong to, and this one did not belong on this road."

A whiney cry came from the second bedroom.

"Oh goddammit," she said, throwing her arms. "That's great. Now the baby's up."

"Well, I didn't tell you to get out of bed and come check on me. What the hell."

"I kept waking up. I don't know why," Leah said, annoyed. "I checked the clock and realized I never heard you leave. I always wake up when you go out the door."

"I don't need you keeping tabs on me, thank you," Calvin snapped.

"Well it's a good thing I was. You're late for work. You need to leave now—you needed to leave half-an-hour ago. You better get moving."

4

Calvin cranked AC/DC's 'Thunderstruck' until he could feel the music as he dropped his foot and let the engine roar him through the back roads. His bloodshot eyes were glued to the small range of view in front of him, limited by the reach of the headlights through each twist and turn. He had driven these roads a hundred times, maybe more, and he knew every bend, every twist, turn and bump. He even knew when to swerve over the line a little to avoid a set of potholes. Nothing ever changed on those back country roads. In a way it was boring, numbing, but provided some creature comfort in routine, like his morning coffee did. The only thing different was the occasional drunk driver or random deer crossing. There was nothing like playing deer-slalom at five in the morning to get his adrenaline going.

Calvin always blasted music on his way to work. Hard rock, classic rock, the occasional popular dance music that he would never admit listening to, anything to keep his heart pumping at that hour and keep his mind from wandering too much.

He always wondered on these early morning drives if today was the day it would happen. Would he slam into a deer? Maybe he would hit a moose that would kick inside his car after smashing through his windshield and kill him? He remembered the one morning when he almost hit a large horse standing in the middle of the road. That was different.

The commute from Leah's house was much shorter than the one from his house up north. He had to be grateful for that, a twenty-minute drive versus the old hour haul early in the morning—especially when there was a snowstorm. The plows weren't even out yet when he would be heading down the Northway for work. There were so many terrifying drives down the highway through a foot of snow when he couldn't see the road in front of him and there wasn't another vehicle in sight.

He pulled into the blood bank parking lot and parked next to all the other employees cars parked in a row, just like every other morning.

Even though he was already late and pretty stressed about it, Calvin sat in his truck for a minute preparing himself for the day. It was tough to find the motivation to go in there and join the other walking zombies at this hour.

All would be fine if his coworkers hadn't found out about the house. He had thought about it quite a bit. It was unlikely that any of them would know about it because none of them lived even close to as far north as he did. Even if someone did happen to drive past the house or had heard about it on the news, they wouldn't make the connection that it was his house, as long as he didn't mention it.

He had worked there for over six years and knew how his coworkers operated. The only thing they loved better than spreading juicy gossip was embellishing it and falsifying it to the point where no part of it was any longer true.

"You're late, superstar," were the words that greeted Calvin when he walked through the door. Billie stood near the entrance with his arms crossed. He was not a large man, by any means, and very boyish in appearance, but had the temperament and stance of a drill sergeant. Everything about him screamed asshole.

"Yeah, sorry, overslept," Calvin said without remorse, refusing to make eye contact with Billie.

"Not everyone can set an alarm right," Billie said, following him for a moment. "McDonalds is hiring. My nephew can probably get you a job there."

Calvin bit his tongue and stayed quiet.

"Man, oh, man," Billie said. "I don't know what someone like Leah ever saw in you, but I think it's time for her to find a real man."

"Oh?" Calvin stopped and raised his eyebrows at him, his temper escaping. "A real man? Like you?"

"At least I'll still have my job next week."

"*Little prick*," Calvin muttered under his breath as he walked away from him.

"What was that?" Billie snapped at him.

"Nothing," Calvin said, disgusted with Billie and himself. He shook his head and swore to himself as he walked into the break room and found Sam in there working on a crossword puzzle in the newspaper. Sam was middle-aged, gray, mostly bald, and not a single day went by without him complaining about how he should be retired at his age.

"Ignore that asshole," Sam said to Calvin as he walked in.

"That gap between his front teeth is about to get a lot bigger."

"Just ignore that ridiculous crap," Sam calmed him.

"Forget about it."

"It's getting harder and harder."

"Yeah, well, you got bills to pay, right?" Sam shrugged. "You do something to him, chances are you'll lose your job, the way things have been looking."

"I know."

"I know you don't care about yourself, but you need to take care of that beautiful little girl of yours. You have to be the adult now, as her father, and be the provider. If that means you have to deal with some bullshit from some little asshole, well, then you just have to suck it up."

"Yeah. Well, I don't have to like it," Calvin said.

"Hey, look at *me*. I'm fifty two years old. How do you think I like being bullied around by some twenty-four year-old kid who didn't graduate high school? I have a master's degree. I have two grown kids and a wife, and up until a year ago I had a job that paid four times what I make here."

"He didn't graduate high school?"

"You didn't know that?" Sam chuckled. "Yeah. Didn't graduate. And they still not only hired him but ended up actually putting him in charge of other people. Real people, like you and me."

Calvin threw on his white lab coat and headed out onto the lab floor. The fluorescent lights were unpleasant on the eyes, reflecting off the white tiles. The open space was filled with the humming of the Apheresis machines as one fired up after another in a line, warming up for a long day of high-tech vampire work.

It had been his home away from home for the last six years, the little prison in which he spent the majority of his waking hours. Many dreams had come and gone for him while he worked there. No matter what happened with his ventures outside of work, there was always the blood bank to fall back on. It was a constant in his life. He knew the procedures for the blood-collecting machines backwards and forwards. He knew how to fix every problem, every alarm that occurred. He knew which veins worked and which veins didn't on each particular donor. Every day was a painful reminder that his life had gone nowhere and he needed to move on.

But there were occasional irregularities that made the job exciting. There were giant bruises, donors occasionally passing out and/or throwing up, power outages, and line breaks within the machines that produced horror-movie-worthy explosions of blood.

Calvin said good morning to all of his coworkers as they came in. And then there was Sadie. Calvin was always so taken back by her beauty. Calvin was usually the one being pursued by girls, but he found it very humbling to be in her presence. She made him feel like a shy little boy around the coolest girl in school. And everything she did was cool; the way she moved, talked, and responded to anything anyone said. She always knew exactly the right thing to say at the right time without any effort. There was never an awkward moment for her. She completely owned every moment and lived it to its fullest.

There was something very intriguing about her, besides her sleek and sexy exterior. She was very mysterious and seemed to have a bit of a dark side to her. She never talked much about her life outside of work or what she did in her free time. Even when questioned directly about her personal life she would answer only with an amusing comment or sarcastic remark. Or, depending on her mood, she would go on for minutes giving every detail of a story, only to then tell the listener that she was bullshitting him and have a good laugh about it.

Calvin went to work setting up a machine. His day had begun, and no one had mentioned a thing about the house. And suddenly a cloud was lifted from his conscience. The sick feeling in his stomach subsided as he realized that no one knew, he wasn't going to be the center of attention, and everyone wouldn't think he did it. He would lose it if they did find out. He knew he would. He was barely hanging on as things were.

Later that morning, Calvin sat in the break room alone, staring at the wood-grain Formica surface of the table that seemed to sadly remind him of his life. There were all sorts of lavish woods and beautiful tables in the world that had been created my master craftsmen, but they were intended for those living better lives. The old scratched surface of the cheaply produced table, which he propped his elbows on, appeared as shoddy and inferior as he felt.

He had no appetite. He would normally never consider skipping lunch, with his fast metabolism, but at the moment he could only drown his sorrows in yet another cup of coffee. It was thick, burnt, and tasted terrible.

Sadie suddenly barged in, flipping her long dark hair and throwing a pack of cigarettes on the Formica table top.

"I've never seen so many people be so fucking miserable doing such a good thing for other people."

Calvin looked up at her and shrugged. He knew exactly what she was talking about, and he didn't have to answer because she knew what he would say. They had had this conversation many times before.

"I'm just glad I have a job," Calvin grumbled, unavoidably staring at her ass as she threw her keys up on a shelf. "I don't like it any more than you do."

Sadie plopped herself down in the chair across from Calvin. Its legs scraped as she pulled it up under the table, pulling herself closer to him. She leaned her elbows on the table, propping up her chin, imitating his defeated appearance. Her big brown eyes glistened at him through thick eyelashes.

Calvin smiled.

"But you're good with needles, though," she said as though she had just figured it out. "You're way better than me."

"I'm not better than anyone else."

"Sure you are. I fuck up all the time."

"So does everyone."

"You don't fuck up," Sadie said firmly. "I watch you. You don't fuck up. Why is that, Calvin?"

Calvin shrugged.

"It doesn't bother you at all, does it? Sticking needles in people all day?" she asked with sick fascination. She leaned even closer to him on the table, seeming to relish making him nervous.

"I don't really think about it," he said, making a conscious effort to keep a cool demeanor. "I forget I'm working on a person. I think of an arm like it's a piece of meat."

"Freak," she said with a twinkle in her eyes.

"I don't know...there is something very satisfying about slipping that needle under the skin just right, like hitting a perfect bulls-eye in darts. It's not just getting it in the vein; it's getting it in so that there's no way it could possibly have gone in better. It's like artwork to me, I guess. Everything in me goes into that needle stick because I want it to work so badly that it just can't go wrong. For a brief moment, nothing else matters and I feel validated, like I serve some actual purpose, as small and insignificant as it may be."

"Wow," Sadie said quietly, cocking her head a little and squinting as she peered into his eyes intensely. "That's pretty fucked up."

"I know."

Billie opened up the break room door abruptly and interrupted their conversation. "Hey, there you are," he said to Sadie harshly. "Break's over, sweetie." He slammed the door shut.

Sadie sighed in disgust and looked at Calvin. "What a loser," she said. "And my lunch isn't even over. I have another…three minutes left."

"He just doesn't want you in here talking to me," Calvin said with a laugh.

"He doesn't want me talking to anyone, besides him, and I have absolutely no interest in talking to him. "Did I tell you he called me at home one day?"

"He called you?"

"Yeah," Sadie said, clearly disturbed. "And I don't mean about the schedule. He just called me."

"For what? I mean, what did he say?"

"Nothing," she said in disbelief. "I was expecting to hear something about work, that the schedule changed or he needed me in early, or had a question about something I did the day before because there was a problem, or *something*."

"So, what? He just called to chat?"

"Apparently. After a few seconds of talking to him I realized that he really didn't have any reason at all to be calling me, not to mention it was almost nine at night."

"What the hell?"

"Once I realized he didn't need anything I was pretty freaked out and was just like, 'okay, well I need to get to bed now'."

"Bed, where your boyfriend is," Calvin added.

"Right," she said sarcastically. "Billie doesn't care that I have a boyfriend."

"He's like that with Leah, too," Calvin said in disgust. "That's been going on for years now. You'd think the guy would give up at some point."

"So much creepiness and so little time to stalk."

"I could never be a stalker," Calvin said. "I'm way too lazy and I couldn't find the time. I swear..." Calvin began, a little irritated. "Leah and I have been together for like a year-and-a-half and we have a baby together. Where does he think it's happening between him and her?"

"Hope springs eternal."

"You'd think at some point along the way he would just give it up already and move onto someone else."

"He has. Me," she said with a big fake smile.

"Yeah, I see that, but he's still trying with Leah. He's always flirting with her and trying to put his hands on her. He practically jumps out of his way to have any excuse to reach a hand out and touch her," Calvin said, his anger showing. "It's really starting to piss me off."

"Have you talked to her about it?"

"Yeah, but it never goes well," Calvin said. "She thinks he's just being friendly."

Sadie laughed.

"I understand being friendly and some people are more touchy-feely than others, but I don't think she gets what's going on in his head. He's not just being friendly."

"Right. You don't see him going around touching Amy like that, just because she's not very...well, it's Amy."

"So, what? He only hands-on with the girls he finds attractive?"

"Well I sure wish I wasn't his type. No way no how that would ever happen."

"Leah is just so naïve about it," Calvin continued. "She really doesn't believe it means anything, because she tends to be a little too touchy-feeley with people, even when first meeting them. But she feels it's just her way of expressing herself. She doesn't see it as sexual or an advance or some way of saying she's interested."

"That's probably why she always has these strange guys chasing after her hopelessly."

"Yeah. Great," Calvin said with a sigh. "We can't seem to get rid of them, and it's always the strangest ones of the bunch. Leah just acts the way she does, super-friendly, without meaning anything by it, and of course they take it the wrong way since she's probably the nicest looking girl to have ever actually been nice to them. She plants that seed in their head, totally unintentionally."

"And once they have that idea rooted in their heads, they can't get it out," Sadie said. "It's like they spend the rest of their life chasing after something that was never there in the first place."

Sadie shrugged her shoulders like a carefree child. "Well, if Leah can't change and you've talked to her about it, I guess you just have to ignore it."

"Not so easy since we work in the same place."

"At least it's better now that you work opposite schedules here."

"Opposite for the most part," Calvin said. "We still have our days together. In a way it made things worse, since now I wonder what goes on when I'm not around, or you're not around to watch what that prick is doing." He nodded his head towards the door Billie had stormed through earlier. "And then when I'm here with her it really bothers me that everyone knows every detail about our relationship. When we're fighting, when we're having problems, when she got pregnant and we didn't want anyone to find out."

Sadie took on an incredibly guilty look. "I'm so sorry about that."

"It's okay, it's not your fault," Calvin said. "I didn't mean to bring that up to make you feel bad."

"Well, I do. I had no idea that it was a secret. I hadn't worked in a few weeks and found out from one of my friends while I was on vacation. I didn't mean to spill the beans about it when I got back."

"You mean saying how she was going to be the cutest mom ever?"

"Yeah…that. Sorry."

Calvin laughed. "It's not like we could keep it a secret much longer anyway. She was getting huge and her boobs just about doubled in size. It was getting tougher and tougher to keep telling people she had just gained some weight and acting offended when they asked if she was pregnant."

Sadie was quiet for a moment. She stared at Calvin, who was no longer making eye contact with her. She leaned far over the break room table, her chin coming to rest on her folded arms on the table. She peered up at him with those glossy eyes. "So…" she started slyly, "what's going on with you?"

"What? How do you mean?" Calvin was stunned.

"I mean what's bothering you, fruitcake You're not eating."

"No. Nothing's wrong."

"Come on," Sadie insisted, seeming to know that he was defenseless against her. "I won't run and tell anyone."

Calvin stayed silent for a moment, and then hesitantly said, "You can't tell anyone else."

"I swear I won't. You can trust me, Calvin. I'm not like the other people here."

"I really shouldn't tell you this, because I wasn't planning on telling anyone at work," he said nervously, knowing there was no going back. "There was a fire at my house yesterday. My house burnt to the ground."

"Oh my god, Calvin..." Sadie said, shocked, and stared at him in silence.

"My dog was inside," Calvin told to her, fighting off the unexpected tears that were starting to glisten his eyes.

"Calvin..." she said, sounding upset that he hadn't mentioned it sooner and had been holding it in. "The baby, and Leah..."

"They're fine. They're fine."

"Oh thank god...that is just so crazy, I don't even know what to say."

She rose from her chair a little and dove into him with a hug.

Calvin was very surprised by this act of kindness and humanity from her. She had never touched him before, although they had talked quite a bit. She smelled of perfume and her morning cigarette. Her embrace made him feel wonderfully comforted, as though everything was going to be okay. It made him feel very warm inside that she actually cared about him.

The door to the break room swung open again.

"Sadie, *let's go*," Billie said with some hostility in his voice this time. He froze when he saw the two of them embraced.

Calvin and Sadie quickly ended their hug and Sadie moved back to her chair.

"My break just got over, tard," Sadie said back to him. "I don't know what clock you're looking at."

Billed stood in shock, holding the door open. He looked as though he wanted to break down crying. He slowly moved out of the doorway and shut the door behind him, this time without slamming it.

Sadie turned back to Calvin and said, "I'm going to punch that little fucker in the face." She gathered her things from the table, irritated, and hurried out of the break room.

"Mr. Strong," Calvin's attorney, Alfred, answered the phone.

"Alfred, good morning."

"How is everything, Calvin?"

"Could be better."

"I know. This hasn't been the best patch for you lately."

"I'm in my own personal hell right now," Calvin said bitterly.

"Well, listen—do you have a few minutes?"

"Yeah. A few," Calvin said. "I'm on my lunch for just a little bit longer."

"Okay, because I have some news I'd like to share with you about your franchise lawsuit."

"Please let it be good news."

"It is," Alfred said. "It is very good news, as far as the strength of our case is concerned."

"Thank god. What's up?"

"Remember several weeks back when I sent a subpoena to the Franchise Corporate for the previous sales records?"

"Yes. I thought they weren't going to give those up," Calvin said.

"They had to. And they finally came. It took a number of rather assertive phone calls from me, but they finally cooperated and sent me everything they had on this asshole who sold you the business. They sent me the last two years of his sales records, every single document, showing every daily sales figure that he reported to them for the last two years."

"I didn't expect that much."

"Needless to say, I spent the last two days looking over them," Alfred said. "I haven't gotten much sleep, and in fact I was up all night writing these into our argument and analyzing these documents."

"And?"

"And every single sales figure Mr. Caruso had provided you with was falsified."

"Are you serious?" Calvin said incredulously.

"Gloriously, fabulously, wonderfully dead serious, Calvin. We have the original sales figures that he had given to the broker, who in turn sent them to you. Now we have the 'real' records from the actual franchise, the numbers which he reported to the IRS. The two sales figures, which should be identical, are completely different. He went through each day and each week and changed all the numbers before giving you these documents. You purchased the business on pure lies. The restaurant was never profitable. Not by a long-shot. It never made a dime for you because it hadn't made a dime in the last two years, and we have absolute proof of that, thanks to these new documents that absolutely nail him to the ground."

"I can't believe it..." Calvin said, taking it all in.

"And if you look at the numbers on the falsified pages and compare them to the originals, you can see that on a lot of the days he got lazy and didn't even bother changing the cents after the decimal. He actually just added two-thousand dollars to some of the weeks, whole numbers, without altering the fifty-six cents that followed the final number."

"Sloppy arrogance," Calvin said, sickened.

"He thought he was being smart about it," Alfred said. "As the pages went on he got more and more careless, probably figuring that you wouldn't go through all the pages, maybe just look at a few. In any case, what this means is that when, if, this case gets ruled in your favor, we could be looking at a couple hundred-thousand dollars."

"That would be phenomenal. So we have a slam-dunk."

"No. No, there's no such thing as a slam-dunk in law," Alfred said. "Anything can happen."

"How could any judge see all that fraud and not rule in our favor?"

"You'd be surprised," Alfred said. "It all depends on the judge. I'm only telling you that because I don't want you to get your hopes up too much. Things can go wrong. But chances are you will win this case, eventually."

"Eventually?"

"Everything in law takes an eternity. Don't expect anything anytime soon."

"Alfred, how long are we talking here, assuming we win this case?"

"Who knows? It won't be quick."

"I'm just in a real bind here. I'm in real financial trouble right now because of this whole ordeal…I'm working all the hours I can at my job, but it doesn't pay much and I'm only part-time."

"They won't let you go back full-time?"

"They filled my full-time position as soon as I switched to part-time to buy the business. There's no other full-time opening now, and I don't think they would hire me anyway. I'm a great worker here, but they don't like me now, unfortunately, for reasons beyond my control, and there's not much of a chance of getting my old job back with them. I'm paying three times as much for health insurance now, too, being part-time, and God forbid something actually happens to me. The insurance I have is terrible and I'll be in debt for the rest of my life if I have an accident or something."

"Just don't count on the money from this lawsuit to bail you out," Alfred warned. "If we do win, you won't see money anytime soon. And then there's the matter of collecting money in this case. That's another challenge in itself."

"Collecting from the seller?"

"Yes. Unfortunately, we don't have much of a case against Davis Edwards, the broker of the deal. The broker company has insurance, so that would be a goldmine for us. The seller, Jake Caruso, however, is just a normal guy with his bills and debt. Collecting your money from him may prove especially difficult, since he'll probably just try to declare bankruptcy."

"He can do that?" Calvin asked.

"It really depends on how the judge rules. If it is determined beyond a doubt that fraud has been committed, a crime has been committed, then we can pursue his assets, such as his house, his cars, and his savings. Pretty much anything is fair game, even if he declares bankruptcy. If he isn't found guilty of fraud, we may walk away with nothing. Bankruptcy will mess up his credit for a while, but that's a hell of a lot better for him than paying you the six-figures he owes you out of pocket."

"Great," Calvin said, sounding defeated.

"Things will get better soon, Calvin. Keep your head up. And keep those payments coming to my office."

Calvin collapsed into the driver seat of his SUV and clunked his head against the headrest, which had a spot worn through the material where the back of his head always settled. Pulling out of the parking lot, his phone lit up the interior and hurt his eyes in the dark. It was the same number he noticed had called his phone six times already that day. He assumed it was a telemarketer or a bill collector and had ignored it. But it was late. They weren't allowed to call so late. If it was a collections agency, he couldn't wait to take out his aggressions on whoever was unfortunate enough to be on the other end of that phone line.

He answered it.

"Calvin," a hauntingly familiar voice said on the other end. "Calvin, it's Davis Edwards…from the Parks Broker Agency. How are you doing today?"

Calvin was silent for a moment. Davis was the last person he expected to be calling him. His voice was all-too familiar from the many extended conversations he and Calvin had regarding the transaction of the business purchase. "I'm doing awesome today, Davis. How are you?"

"Well, hey, Calvin," Davis chuckled nervously. "Hey, I just wanted to let you know how sorry I was to hear that you had to close the restaurant down…You should've called me first, Calvin."

"The restaurant wasn't making any money, Davis. I lost a fortune."

"That is just…just unbelievable. I can't believe what Jake did to you. I've known Jake Caruso for a long time, and he was always a man of his word. Believe me, no one is more shocked than I am about this. I'll do anything I can to help you. You just let me know what you need. I'll testify against Jake in court if that's what you want."

"I think you've been help enough, Davis."

"Hey, the reason I'm calling you, though, Calvin, is that I need to talk to you about this lawsuit you filed."

"We shouldn't be talking about that, Davis. You know that."

"Why not? Oh, come on, Calvin. Let's get real. We're both men, here, right? Why can't you and I, man to man, have a conversation about this and work out some of these issues?"

"Our lawyers will work out the issues."

"Calvin, Calvin, listen…This was all Jake. It was Jake Caruso, Calvin. He's the bastard who did this to you. He's your man. You don't actually blame *me* for all this…do you?"

"Yes, Davis. Actually, I do."

"What? Oh, no, Calvin. You don't think I would have done this to you on purpose, knowing that you had a *baby* on the way, do you?"

"Hey, Davis?"

"Yes?"

"Go fuck yourself." Calvin hung up.

"Hey, Leah," Calvin said with a sigh when she answered the phone.

"Hey," she greeted him warmly. "Where are you?"

"About half-way home." Calvin was briefly blinded by the headlights of an oncoming car. "Be there in about ten."

"You're later than I expected," she said, sounding

bothered.

"I know. We ran late. It's pitch-black out. I'm exhausted. And starving."

"Good," Leah said. "I made some dinner earlier and saved you some."

"Hey, thanks."

"So is the baby asleep yet?" he asked, hoping to see Pearl.

She sighed. "No...I was just sitting here with her trying to get her to take a bottle when you called. She's been a little cranky today. I'll probably try to get her to bed a little early tonight. So...how did it go today?" she asked with some apprehension.

"So far so good. No one said a word about the house."

"Good. So no one there knows anything?"

"Well...I did tell Sadie about it," Calvin said nervously, now realizing his mistake.

"What? Calvin, why would you do that? Why would you tell Sadie about the house?"

"I'm not sure why. I guess I had to talk to someone about it."

"Then you talk to *me* about it," she snapped at him. "Sadie? Why on earth would you tell Sadie? I thought you were trying to keep this a secret, Calvin."

"I am. Sadie isn't going to tell anyone. Don't worry about it. It was my idea, anyway, not to tell people."

"Yes, it *was* your idea."

Calvin glanced in the mirror. The headlights behind him made him squint a little.

"Damn it, Leah, I've got someone riding my ass."

"So? Who cares?"

"He's been on me for a while and I think it's a cop," Calvin said, growing agitated. "Otherwise I wouldn't care."

"Ok, just calm down," she said like she was talking to a child scared of a monster in the closet.

"Great, I've been speeding the whole way home and I'm talking on my cell phone. He can probably see the phone lit up."

"Calvin, just relax, you don't even know it's a cop."

"I can't afford a ticket right now, let alone two...I can tell by the headlights, the way they're narrow and spaced far apart. I'm pretty sure it's a cop. But it's hard to tell now since the county started changing all their cars to newer different models."

"You and your headlights," Leah remarked.

"I'm going to turn off on some random road."

"Calvin, just come home."

"No. I can't drive with a cop behind me like this. If he's going to give me a ticket, then he can go ahead and pull me over. It's making me nervous having him behind me like this."

"If he hasn't pulled you over, then he probably isn't going to," she said. "If it even *is* a cop, that is."

"Not too many other people take this way home. The combination of roads I've taken...what are the odds that someone else would be traveling exactly the same way as me?"

"I think you're being paranoid."

"It's practically impossible."

"You're impossible."

"I've just had a really long day," Calvin complained. "I don't need this right now. Wait...here's a turnoff coming up." He flicked his signal and braked abruptly.

"Great, get rear-ended by the cop now," Leah said, obviously considering this little game childish.

Calvin turned up the side road, which took him at a

steep angle up-hill and around a tight bend. "He's still behind me!" he hollered at her.

"Calm down. So you get a ticket. It's not the end of the world."

"I don't like being followed," Calvin said intensely. "I don't like someone else having that power over me, to make me nervous like this. He should just pull me over already. There's no way now that it's just someone going the same direction as me. This route makes no sense. I'm heading out to the middle of nowhere."

"You need to stop heading to nowhere and come home." There was a brief pause, and then her tone suddenly changed as she said, "Calvin? Calvin, I'm getting a little freaked out now."

"*You're* getting freaked out?"

"Yeah. I don't know where you are and there's someone following you in the dark...and you're really tired."

"What does me being tired have anything to do with anything?" he asked defensively.

"No, nothing. Forget it," she said quickly.

"It's probably just a damn cop waiting to give me the ticket of a lifetime. Like you said."

"But what if it's not? Calvin, you need to head back here...turn around, just don't keep driving further out to nowhere."

"Well if it's *not* a cop I'll beat the shit out of this guy, if he tries anything. I should pull over right now and see what the hell's going on."

"No!" Leah shouted. "Don't pull over...please. I just got really scared, I don't know why. I don't like the sound of this. You're not in the best frame of mind right now and I have a really bad feeling all of a sudden."

"All right, all right. Now *you* calm down," he said

sternly to her. "Everything's under control. Nothing's going happen to me. You think someone is going to beat me up or something?"

"Or something."

"Leah...here, there's a turnoff coming up. I'm going to make a right here. Let's see if he follows me again. If he follows me, I'm stopping. If he doesn't, then he doesn't." Calvin flicked his signal and braked gently this time, making a smooth right onto an unknown dark country road. The truck tires rumbled over some potholes.

He checked his mirror. "All gone," he said over the phone.

She let out a sigh of relief. "Thank god."

"That was weird," he said with a laugh. "I still say the odds are against someone taking the exact same random route I drove, but I guess it's possible. Either that or the cop had enough fun toying with me."

"Or he got another more important call," Leah suggested.

"Could be. I'll be home in a few, once I figure out where I am now."

Leah sat next to Calvin on the couch while he ate the dinner she had saved for him. Some ridiculous reality show about celebrities trading wives was on TV, but neither of them was paying attention to it.

"Something just feels wrong about the whole situation," Calvin said, his brow furrowed, deep in thought.

"Oh, yeah?" Leah said, bringing herself out of her own stupor.

"Since I went up there. It didn't sit right with me

then and it's not sitting well with me now."

"Was there any confusion at all about what caused the fire?" Leah asked in a tone that made it clear she was not in the mood for this conversation.

"No," he answered quickly. "Not from the investigator I talked to and the town's fire investigator."

"Then why would you have any reason to think otherwise, Calvin?"

"I don't know... I have a feeling there was something more. I think the investigator just didn't really know. That's the feeling I got, that he really didn't know what to say caused the fire and how it spread, and he had to come up with something for the insurance company."

"So he just made up the whole thing with the outlet?"

"It was like he wasn't sure he believed it himself but he wanted to make sure that I did."

"Why would a professional investigator do that?" she asked, clearly still very skeptical.

"I could think of a bunch of reasons. It was freezing out, for starters. There wasn't much left to look at, either. The basement had been filled with water and then drained, and then the hoses blasted everything around. I think his job obligated him to come up with some sort of explanation, even though maybe he couldn't for certain say what happened."

"So what do *you* think happened, Calvin?"

He looked at her and shrugged slightly. "I have no idea."

"Well, then I guess you'll just have to take their word for it and let it go. It's not like it should really matter to you, anyway. They're going to give you the money from your policy to buy a new house. Unless you want to rebuild on the lot where you were."

"No. I don't want to live there anymore. The neighbors aren't what they used to be. Ever since Morgan and I broke up. They haven't talked to me much."

"So they'll give you money to buy a new house," Leah said. "That's a pretty nice thing. Think of it as a fresh start."

"It's not quite that simple," Calvin said, hiding some pain.

"I know. I know it's killing you about Hobbes." Leah reached over and rubbed his neck. "And I don't blame you a bit. I don't know how I would deal with that, if I lost my Miko...especially like that."

"You have no idea. He was in my dreams all night trying to get my attention. Barking, pawing, like he's just trying to communicate and break through the barrier separating us."

"You'll get another dog, Calvin," she said, sounding a little more insensitive than she had intended.

"Like you care," he retorted. "You couldn't stand that dog, anyway."

"That's not true."

"Yes, it is."

"I loved Hobbes, too," she argued. "Maybe not as much as you did, but I loved him and would never wish for anything bad to happen to him."

"You wanted to kill him since I met you."

"I didn't want to *kill* him," she said. "He just frustrated me. With pretty much everything he did, like growling at me when I tried to move him off the couch."

"I always let him lay on the couch at my home," Calvin said.

"Okay, how about pissing on my floors when he was here?"

"We never had time to walk him enough," Calvin

said with heavy guilt. "It's my fault."

"See, there you go again, trying to make excuses for him. He was a good dog, Calvin, and I know you miss him a lot, but don't make him into a martyr. He wasn't that great."

"Thanks. That makes me feel a lot better."

"I'm sorry. You can put all this behind you. You can move closer to work, buy a house down in this area. It will be a fresh start. Maybe it will be a new home for both of us. A fresh start for both of us." She scratched his back. "I think this has all worked out perfectly."

Calvin sat in thought for a moment, and then said, "I need to go up there."

"Up where? To the house?"

"Yes."

"What for now?" She moved back a little from him on the couch.

"I need to be up there. To look for something…for some reason why this happened."

"What do you expect to find?" She gave him a skeptical glare. "The fire inspectors have already spent plenty of time there. Do you honestly think you're going to figure something out on your own?"

"I don't know."

"Well, I need you here. *We* need you here. We're your family, and we're your obligation now. It's time to stop thinking of yourself and whatever whim you feel like following."

"I'm not following a whim. This isn't for fun. Look, all I know is that I need to go to the house. I need to see what I can find. I want to see if there is anything left in there. I had a lot of things up there."

"To waste a tank of gas and half of a day?"

"I'm going up as soon as I can. My next day off."

She slapped her leg. "Calvin—w*hat for?*"
"I'm not sure yet."

5

"Calvin! Calvin!" Leah shouted repeatedly, grabbing him and violently shaking him in bed.

Calvin finally snapped to consciousness with a yelp.

"Calm down!" Leah shouted in his face, throwing the weight of her body on top of him, her arms outreached and pinning him on his back. "Calm down, Calvin! Stop!"

Calvin stopped throwing himself around in bed and panted heavily. He was soaked in sweat.

"Calvin! Oh my god..." she cried as she held his head like a mother shelters her child, telling him repeatedly that he was okay.

"I was having a nightmare," Calvin said plainly, lying with his eyes opened widely and staring at the ceiling.

"I figured," Leah said, rolling off of him.

"It was bad...it was about the house again."

"Oh, no, Calvin..."

"I've been having them all night. I can't stop having nightmares about it. It was about Hobbes again, too."

"I'm sorry, Calvin."

"He was trapped upstairs in the house. He was barking down at me. He was barking like crazy and the house was on fire all around me. I was on the ladder, trying to get to him, but the flames kept getting higher, like they were coming after me to burn me alive. The ladder started shaking. I thought I was going to fall into the flames. When I looked down, I saw a guy—I don't know who it was—he was on fire and his face was all burnt, but he was still alive and he was looking up at me on the ladder. His eyes were gone. There were just holes for his eyes. Then he started shaking the ladder again. I was yelling like crazy. Hobbes was barking at me, but I couldn't get to him. He was going to burn alive in front of me. And then I fell. I was kicking around as I fell—I fell so fast—and I knew that I was going to fall into the flames and die."

Leah looked at him in the dark silently. A long moment passed before she spoke. "This needs to stop, Calvin," she said softly. "You can't take it anymore. And *I* can't take it anymore."

"I know. I'm sorry."

"I wish I could tell you what to do, how you could stop having these dreams."

"I just hope they go away soon. I don't think there is anything I can do. It's just like a post-traumatic stress side-effect, I guess."

"You need rest, Calvin. You need to get some rest."

Calvin kept glancing out the front windows at work, as he usually did. The large windows across the front wall gave him a nice glimpse into the outside world, and he was grateful for that. He had worked in enough different places to fully appreciate any sort of window to catch a glimpse of daylight, and he certainly had grown to appreciate the large panes of glass across the front of the building.

Then Billie appeared in view, out in the parking lot, casually walking across the slushy pavement with his outdated leather bomber jacket on. He walked with an exaggerated swagger, trying to look much cooler than he was.

Calvin moved over a little, away from the Apheresis machine he was working at, to watch where he was going. Then he could see Sadie out there, smoking by her car. As he approached her and said something with a gesture, she quickly pulled her phone from her pocket and started talking into it, nodding her head as if pleased to hear from someone.

Billie seemed a little annoyed by this, and pulled out his pack of cigarettes and leaned against the light blue car parked next to hers, allowing her to have her phone conversation, if she was really even talking to anyone, in peace.

He had a lot of nerve, Calvin thought, to lean on someone else's car like he owned it. It was much nicer than what Billie drove, which was a beat-up pickup truck that had been modified with blackout headlights and lowered suspension. That crappy pickup suited him perfectly.

Then Calvin saw him pull a set of keys out of his pocket. He opened the driver side door of the light-blue sedan and fished around for something in the console. Calvin was surprised. Apparently Billie was driving a different car now, and had parked right next to Sadie.

At first, all Calvin could think about was how Billie couldn't afford a new car like that, at least not until he got his ridiculous debt under control. He had been attempting to live large on a very small income. But then Calvin took a closer look at that light-blue sedan he was now sitting in with the door open. There was something very familiar about the shape of the vehicle, its color, and the shape of the taillights. Calvin couldn't be certain. It was impossible to be absolutely sure, but it looked very similar to the car he had seen circling the block at Leah's house.

Calvin's heart accelerated as he stared at the car, which Billie was now exiting and locking up. He tried to calm himself, though. It was a very common car, and there were probably hundreds similar to it on the road in the general area. Calvin's eyes scanned the parking lot. There were even two others just in the parking lot that looked somewhat similar, although not identical. In the dark, they could easily be mistaken for the same vehicle.

Calvin watched Billie reenter the building and slide off his out-of-style leather bomber jacket. He hung the jacket and headed across the donor room.

Calvin casually approached him as he passed and caught his eye, although Billie attempted to avoid eye-contact. "Hey, new wheels?" Calvin said to him, sounding enthused.

"Oh…yeah," Billie replied, barely slowing down to answer. He had a nasty scowl on his face, as though Calvin had no business speaking to him, and certainly had no business asking him personal questions. "That's my new ride."

"That's a pretty nice car," Calvin said, sounding genuinely impressed. "It's not as cool as your low-rider truck, though."

"Nah. No way," Billie said. "But it's my ride now. I blew the engine on my truck drag racing it. So I bought that car off my brother. He just got divorced, so he couldn't afford it anymore."

"Gotcha," Calvin said, nodding, as Billie continued past him with a grunt.

Later that morning, Calvin approached Leah as she was busy reviewing a procedure record.

"Hey, I need to talk to you for a second," he said to her with muffled hostility.

"What is it, Calvin? I'm in the middle of something, here."

"Well, I need to talk to you for just a second. Okay?"

"Oh, boy…" she followed him out of the room into the back hallway. "What's wrong?" she said to him, annoyed.

"Well I'm sorry I pulled you away from your remedial task in there, but I thought we had talked about you and Billie and that shit he pulls with you."

"Uh-huh, we did talk about that several times. And what have I done to offend you now?"

"Leah, he had his hands all over you in there."

"What? When?"

"When he came up behind you at the front desk. He was practically standing on top of you. He was pushed into you. And then he starts giving you a massage."

"My neck was really sore," she said defensively. "I told you this morning that I slept wrong and I could barely move my neck. He saw me rubbing it earlier and knew it was sore. And honestly, it was nice to have someone actually try to make me feel better."

"Oh, please. You think he was trying to make *you* feel better?"

"Calvin, can we not do this today?" She snapped at him. "I'm really tired and I have a lot of work to do and I'm not in the mood for this. And you're really tired too. You haven't been sleeping at all these last few nights. Look at you—your eyes are totally bloodshot. Your hands are shaking. You need to relax and get some rest tonight."

"But you don't understand how him giving you a massage at work is totally inappropriate? Especially when I'm standing right there?"

"Calvin, you have so much going on in your mind, I think you're driving yourself crazy…"

"You don't think that's a dominance game he's playing with me? You don't think he's trying his best to piss me off?"

"I don't know, Calvin," she said slyly with contempt in her voice, "Is that what Sadie was trying to do? Piss me off and show me that she can take you away from me?"

Calvin looked stunned. He didn't say a word.

"Yeah," she went on, irate. "I heard about how she was all over you in the break room."

"She was hugging me because I told her that my house burnt down."

"Well, Billie was just giving me a massage to make my neck hurt less. So I guess we're even. I need to get back to work. You should probably do the same."

Later that day, Calvin pulled Leah aside again. She was obviously still upset with him from their conversation earlier, but he didn't care about that anymore.

"What's wrong now, Calvin?" she said, beside herself, as he grabbed her hand and led her into the break room. He closed the door behind them.

"Leah, I had a very unusual conversation with the investigator a few minutes ago. Remember the one I told you about up at the house?"

"Mr. Rogers sweater?"

"Yeah. Him. He called me today and told me that they want me to send them a whole bunch of stuff. They want my phone records for the last six months, my credit card statements, my utility bills for like the last year. And there was more."

"What do they want that for?"

"I don't know. I really don't like the sound of it, though. I don't like the direction this is taking."

"Me either. I don't know a lot about this sort of thing, but my friend Mary's husband went through this a few years ago when his house burnt down. They didn't ask all those crazy questions and interrogate him. They didn't make him come up with phone records or anything like that."

"Yeah. Phone records," Calvin said. "What else could that mean, besides they think I had something to do with the fire?"

"Maybe they want to check your history just to see who else you were talking to."

"Why?"

"To see if there was anyone else who could have been involved. It may not be about you at all. They may be fishing for clues."

"But they already told me there's nothing more to say about it. They know what happened."

"It sure seems like they don't. Or if they do know, it's not what they're telling you."

"If there was someone else in my phone records I had called, why wouldn't they just ask me if there was anyone else I suspected might have done something like that?"

"Why *would* anyone else do something like that? It doesn't make any sense."

"What's that supposed to mean?"

"I just mean that it wouldn't make sense for anyone else to burn down your house, Calvin."

"Anyone besides me? Is that what you meant?"

"No, that's not what I meant at all…"

"I lost my dog in that fire, not to mention everything I own, so don't even for one second think…"

"That's not what I think, Calvin. God. It's not what I think. It just doesn't look good."

"Great. Thanks."

"Well it seems like you have an awful lot working against you. It would be easy for someone else…anyone else, to draw that conclusion."

"Yeah. Exactly. It's all too easy for people to draw that conclusion without having any idea at all what they're talking about."

"I believe you because I know you so well. I know you could never do something like that, and certainly not harm your dog."

"That's why I didn't want this getting into work. It's nearly impossible to convince people that I had nothing to do with it once they get it into their heads. No matter how many facts you throw at them that debunk their theory, they've already got their minds made up. It's too much to deal with, right now. It's going to cost me my job. There's too much tension here already."

"I'm extremely nervous about this, Calvin. I think you should talk to your lawyer. You need to talk with someone who knows about this sort of thing and try to figure out what's going on, where this is heading. This is really scaring me."

"How do you think I feel? It's scaring the hell out of me too. I'll talk to Alfred."

"Without a lawyer, these people are just going to

screw around with you. You have no idea if they really have the right to ask for these things they've requested, like your phone records. That's your private, personal information that has nothing to do with your house burning down. You don't even know if what they're asking for is legal."

"I'll call him right now. I was going to call him anyway to see how the restaurant lawsuit is going."

"Forget the restaurant lawsuit. This is far more important. I can't have anything happen to you."

"Nothing's going to happen to me."

"We're finally together again, as a family. It's the most wonderful thing that could have happened. And I hate to say it, but we owe it all to your house burning down. If that hadn't happened, we wouldn't have this beautiful second chance..."

"Leah..."

"I just don't want to lose you again. It killed me the first time, and I couldn't go through that again. You are where you belong. We all are now."

"Alfred, I need to talk to you about another personal matter," Calvin said into his phone from his truck. He was freezing and his fingers were numb, but it was the only place at work to get some guaranteed privacy without fear of eavesdroppers. "I haven't brought it up yet because I wanted to focus on the lawsuit and not deal with this right now. But you need to know—there was a fire at my house."

"Oh my god."

"It took everything from me, even my dog."

"The baby and Leah are okay?"

"Yeah, they weren't there at the time," Calvin said. "They were actually out of town. Even if they had been home, they would've been at her house."

"Well, let's just be grateful for that."

"Oh, I am," Calvin said. "I'm counting my blessings right now, even though there aren't very many to count at this point."

"You had insurance, right?"

"Yes. I have insurance."

"Then you should be fine. Except, of course, for your dog. I'm very sorry to hear about that. Truly. But your insurance should take care of everything else and make it right again."

"Well that's the thing," Calvin said. "That's the real reason I wanted to reach out to you today. I may need your help with the house matter."

"What's going on?"

"I'm extremely nervous about the whole situation with the insurance company. I'm getting some pretty strange vibes from the people I've dealt with so far."

"Like what?"

"Well, from the start, when I first met their investigator up at the house, things just didn't seem right. It seemed like he was hiding information. And I kind of got the feeling that he thought I had something to do with it, even though he said repeatedly that he knew I didn't and it was just his job to ask the questions he was asking."

"Listen as soon as you say, 'insurance company', the hair rises on the back of my neck. These people are not your friend. They're not there to take your side or hold your hand through this. They're there to get to the bottom of what happened and look for any reason not to pay you the money they rightfully owe you, as per your contract with them."

"Well that's the thing. They haven't offered a dime for anything yet."

"That's a problem. You should at least be entitled to an advance."

"An advance?"

"That's a portion of money that they are supposed to pay out from your claim to cover your current living expenses as well as providing you a way to replace certain necessities you may have lost, such as clothing."

"They haven't offered anything like that."

"You also didn't know to ask for it, which means they wouldn't want to tell you. That's their game. That may be why you feel like they're keeping information to themselves. The more you know, the more it can cost them. They're not there to protect you. They're there to avoid paying you, even though you paid your premium for all those years. Now it's their turn, and they need to pay up."

"Isn't it illegal for them to do this to people?"

"Insurance companies break the law all the time. They approach these things with the attitude of 'what are you going to do about it?' And the answer to that, for most people, is nothing. Most people in your situation are completely wiped out. They've lost it all. They don't have the money to hire a lawyer and take on an insurance company by themselves. The insurance company is well aware of this, and in fact counts on it. They want you to be as weak and vulnerable as possible. It makes their job that much easier."

"That's pretty twisted," Calvin said.

"It's a pretty twisted world we live in. At least when it comes to money. Speaking of the advance, where are you living right now?"

"With Leah."

"Oh, god...I'm sorry, I know what that situation is

like from all I've heard during my dealings with you thus far. That must be extremely difficult for you."

"It's painful," Calvin said. "I guess it's a chance for us to try to make things work again, whether we like it or not."

"There's nowhere else you can stay for a while?"

"No. If there was, I probably would have tried it."

"We need to fix this for you, Calvin. As soon as possible."

"That would be great. I'd like to get my life back on track."

"So, these people from the insurance company. Who did you actually talk to?"

"I spoke with a bunch of people on the phone. They referred me to a couple different people. I sort of got passed around a lot."

"Typical," Alfred said. "Who was it you were talking to who gave you the bad feelings you spoke of?"

"That was the investigator I met up at the house. He's the only one from the insurance company that I've actually met in person."

"He was an investigator?"

"I thought he was a claims representative at first. That's who they said they'd be sending out to meet me. A claims rep. He only told me later in the interview that he was an investigator."

"That's very unusual, Calvin," Alfred said in dismay.

"Is it?"

"Well, yes. Usually the claims representative is the one to meet you out at the scene and assess the damage. He would be the one to work you up a quote and get the ball rolling for you in the process. It's a long process with many steps. For them to just send an investigator out to meet you, right off the bat is just…strange."

"Should I be concerned about this?"

"Well, I really don't know," Alfred said. "Maybe that's just the way they do business at this particular insurance company. Do you happen to have the fellow's name, or perhaps a card that he left with you?"

Calvin pulled out his wallet. "Yup. Right here. Marshall Hamilton, Special Investigator," he read.

Alfred grunted. "You know what he really was?"

"A special investigator?"

"Well, yes. But he wasn't just a normal inspector or investigator. Apparently your house fire ranked pretty high on their suspicious meter."

"Someone thought that enough to call in a specialist?"

"Yes. Calvin, have you already consulted another attorney about this matter?"

"No. It hadn't even occurred to me."

"Well, it would probably be in your best interest to hire one, whether it's me or someone else."

"But this guy acted like nothing was unusual at all," Calvin said defensively. "He acted like he knew exactly what happened and there was really nothing to even look into."

"Oh, believe me, they're looking into it," Alfred said. "I'm not saying they think that you had anything to do with it, or even that someone else had anything to do with starting the fire. All I'm saying is that they're looking at something for some reason. And they're trying to figure out how they can use that something to avoid paying your claim. That would leave you without your possessions, without your house, and no money in your pocket. You need a lawyer at this point. You're on dangerous ground."

Later that day, Calvin was preparing to begin a procedure on Mrs. Peters. He had programmed the machine, primed the needles, and filled out all the paperwork. He had already gotten her the mandatory three blankets she always needed. She had been donating for thirty years and counting and had the track marks to prove it. Calvin had performed her procedure so many times it was like second nature to him and he could do it with his eyes closed. He enjoyed her company, as always, although it was painfully boring for him internally. There was no challenge left. There was no ambition to succeed, since whatever efforts he made, no matter how great, they would never be rewarded.

He did his best to smile, act enthusiastic, and just be a man and do his job. And he did his job like a sharp-shooter with that needle in his hand.

On the other hand, he also knew to maintain his humility and modesty, as nothing taught humility like sticking needles in people for a living. No matter how great you were, things went wrong. There were always variables like the donor moving his or her arm, or the veins not plumping up the way they normally do because of dehydration, or a tissue plug on the way into the vein blocking blood flow. This killed Calvin. He wanted to be perfect all the time, especially after working there for so many years. He was as good as he would ever get. There was no way for him to get better with a needle. And there was no way to completely eliminate the problems associated with venipuncture. He could never, without doubt, get every vein to work correctly throughout the entire procedure. It was something that could never be fully mastered, and that irritated him to no end.

Calvin had already gotten Mrs. Peter's return needle in, where the fluids would be forcefully shot back into her arm, and was preparing her other arm, the draw arm, when something caught his attention.

There was a cluster of staff up in the glass windows of the office, conspiring about something. Given the monotony of the days there, any such gathering as this brought the hopes of some jolting news about the company or one of the employees, or perhaps even just some juicy gossip. Anything to break up the day.

However, Calvin did not like the look of this gathering up there, particularly because the group kept glancing at him through the glass windows of the office while they talked in a hushed manner.

"Hey," he said to Sadie, catching her as she passed by. "What's going on up there?"

"I don't know. They're all rushing around whispering to each other," she said, obviously alienated by the childish behavior of the staff. "Freaks."

He saw some arguing back and forth between Billie and Sam. Sam shrugged his shoulders and appeared very frustrated.

After a few minutes, the group dissipated. Calvin had not been paying attention to what he was doing.

"Oh, sorry about that," he said to Mrs. Peters.

"Something interesting going on up there?" she said to him with a smile.

"There's always something interesting going on here. Hopefully nothing bad, though."

Calvin's heart was pounding as he stuck the second needle in her skin. A perfect hit, despite his shaky hand.

He felt his mouth get dry. There was something in the air he didn't like.

They knew.

He filled out his paperwork hastily. He kept looking up to the office to see if any more activity was taking place, but everything seemed to have gone back to normal.

His mind wasn't on the procedure at all. He asked Mrs. Peters if she needed anything else before he walked away, and she said no.

He left and hurried to the bathroom. He needed a few minutes alone to get himself under control. He was having a panic attack. He knew what would happen if they found out. And now he had to face them.

He took a deep breath and walked tall back out onto the floor, ready to deal with the attention and questions— the suspicious, insinuating questions, the doubtful glances, and frightened avoidance.

"Calvin, you've really outdone yourself this time," Billie shouted to him as he walked back on the floor.

"What's wrong?" Calvin asked in a daze.

"What's wrong?" Billie held out his arms, infuriated. "This is what's wrong."

Calvin looked at the screen and saw it. He had never actually started the procedure.

"Would you like to explain to Mrs. Peters why she has to be disconnected and sent away for the day?"

"Oh, shit," Calvin said loudly.

"That's an awful waste," Billie explained loudly to Mrs. Peters, shaking his head. "Calvin, here, in his infinite wisdom, just cost us the kit and your donation. What a guy."

"He's doing everything he can to get me fired," Calvin griped to Sam on their way out of work. It was freezing out, even though the sun shined intensely down on the two of them as they walked across the parking lot to their cars.

"He knows they need you here," Sam said. "He's already been trying for a while to do away with you, from what I hear."

"What the hell'd I ever do to him, anyway?"

"You're here," Sam said plainly. "You're in his way."

"None of these women want anything to do with him."

"In his mind, they all do. Especially yours. The way he sees it, if you weren't here, he'd have your girlfriend and every other woman in the office after him. A guy like that can't stand the fact that he's outmatched. All he's accomplished is moving up a rank. That's like becoming the manager at McDonalds. You might think you're a big-ass in your own little grease world, working with a bunch of high school dropouts and acne-faced teens, but in the real world you're still at the bottom of the food chain. And he knows it."

"He's above me on the food chain right now."

"But you've had money," Sam reassured him. "You owned a business flipping houses. Then you owned a restaurant."

"Briefly."

"Doesn't matter. You still did it. No matter what happened with that, even if people want to tear you down because the business fell apart and you're back here, you still did it—on your own. You don't have rich parents giving you money. You started out with nothing, Calvin. And that's pretty amazing, especially in this economy."

"We're all still in the same boat now, though," Calvin said resentfully. "Except he's captain."

"You have a way out."

"Yeah. Someday, maybe."

"Once your lawsuit pulls through for you. You know you'll win that, eventually."

"Eventually. It could be years. I could lose, too, you know."

"You have a bullet-proof case," Sam reassured him.

"There's no such thing in the legal world, from what my lawyer has told me. Even if I win, it may be impossible to ever collect all that money I lost."

"At least you have hope. Now, me, on the other hand..." He shrugged his shoulders. "This is a life sentence for me. And I'm an old man now."

"You can retire soon."

"Not with the price of everything going up. I can't afford to anytime soon. You know, Calvin, when you're young and you move through life, you don't see it. You don't realize your golden age. You always think things will keep getting better as you get older, that you'll make more money the longer you work and you will become successful. There's always that glimmer of hope, too, that somehow things will work out wonderfully for you and all your dreams will come true. Then, one day, you're in my situation, and you realize that your best years have come and gone. You've already experienced the best that your life will ever be, and the sad thing is that you never even realized it while you were living it. You accept that all your hopes and dreams were only that, hopes and dreams. What you're left with is the realization that those few good years, even those few good memories, were your glory days."

Calvin chuckled. "Well I sure as hell hope these aren't my glory days, because I wouldn't want to see what the rest of my life is going to look like."

"Things aren't that bad. They can always get worse, believe me. You have a beautiful, healthy baby. And you have your own health. You're still young and you're not a bad looking guy. You have your whole life ahead of you. Those thoughts, right there, may very well be your glory. Don't waste it."

Calvin walked with Miko across the frozen surface of Grave Lake. He had decided to walk across the lake to the Pizza Shack, which sat on the water's edge on the opposite side of the lake and was one of the few gathering spots around. Leah had taken Pearl to visit a friend of hers for a few hours and Calvin wanted to pick up a pizza to surprise her when she came home.

Calvin loved the openness and solitude of walking out in the middle of the lake with the wind blasting his face and making his nose run. There were dark spots, where the wind had blown the snow cover away, which allowed a peek at the murky, mysterious depths below.

Miko was in his glory, trotting alongside Calvin with his tongue hanging out and what appeared to be a big smile on his face.

Calvin heard the ice crack under his feet. It stunned him for a moment, stopping him in his tracks. Miko galloped ahead, looking back to urge Calvin on. It hadn't been cold enough long enough. Calvin knew that. While the temperatures had been low over the last few weeks, there had been some unseasonably warm days in the mix.

Looking around, Calvin realized that he was directly in the center of the wide lake. He had come a long way, and he had just as far to go. He imagined himself breaking through the thin layer of ice and being swallowed by the water underneath. The ice water would shock his system and soak into his heavy jacket, shoes, and clothes, and drag him down to the graves that lay at the bottom of the lake.

Calvin noticed a vehicle that was stopped in the middle of the bridge that divided the middle and first lakes. It was a blue car with dark tinted windows. There were no other vehicles around, and it seemed strange to Calvin that someone would stop there. He wondered if the driver was looking for a way to warn him of the unsafe ice; but the driver remained inside the car, despite Calvin now staring at it.

Calvin treaded carefully. He lightened his footsteps drastically and crept across the ice the way he always crept across the bedroom floor when trying not to wake Leah. After twenty-feet or so, he turned to his right to see if the car was still on the bridge. It was gone.

He was relieved as he walked up onto the shore in front of the Pizza Shack, but at the same time oddly disappointed to be safe again.

Miko pounced after some seagulls that were raiding some spilled garbage in the snowy parking lot.

"Stay here, boy," Calvin said to Miko as he walked past him onto the wood porch and entered the hot aroma of pizza, beer, and hot wings. The restaurant always looked like it might collapse at any moment and nothing had been updated in over fifty years. All the wood floors were uneven and slanted, which made walking through it to the men's room an adventure after a few beers.

"Calvin Strong," said Annie, the gray-haired owner, from behind the counter as she grabbed his order from the shelf behind you. "One large well-done cheese pizza," she said, handing it to him. "That'll be nine even. You're the only customer we have who orders their pizza well-done."

"It's Leah's thing," Calvin said, getting money out of his wallet.

"You tell Leah I said hello. And you be careful walking across that lake, Calvin. That ice is thin."

"I know. Thanks," Calvin said, shoving his wallet in his pocket as he pushed his way out the door.

Exiting the restaurant, Calvin almost walked right into a man standing outside. Calvin halted and stared into the man's brown eyes, bewildered.

It was Davis. His white hair was a mess. He was unshaven. He looked as though he hadn't slept in days.

"You shouldn't be here," Calvin said, eyes wide.

"I know I shouldn't be here, Calvin," Davis replied with a shaky voice.

"I mean, it's between your lawyer and mine. We shouldn't be talking…"

"Just hear me out. Please."

Miko suddenly appeared at Calvin's side, snarling and showing his teeth.

"*Jesus*," Davis uttered, backing way.

Miko abruptly lunged at Davis and barked, chomping his powerful jaws.

"Miko!" Calvin yelled at him and grabbed him by the fur on the back of his neck.

"Holy shit!" Davis cried in terror. "That's a big freakin' dog, man!" he said with a nervous laugh.

Calvin examined him. Was he there to jump him? Was he going to attack him? Stab him? Shoot him?

Calvin was not a huge man, although good-sized and muscular. He had a certain quality, though, when he found himself in confrontations that would make the opposition back down even if the physical advantage was not in his favor. Calvin intimidated people. There was something about him when you pissed him off, something about his character that warned you that he would not hesitate to knock another man's teeth down his throat if he got in his face. No one picked fights with Calvin—not since he was a kid.

Calvin refused to let his guard down. He knew this was a desperate man in front of him—a desperate man who had obviously been tracking him. A hundred thoughts were going through his mind. On the exterior he was perfectly calm and still, looking the broker, Davis, dead in the eyes. He didn't know what it would take to make him leave, what he came for, and what he wanted.

"I'm broke," Davis blurted out. "I'm financially destroyed."

"I know the feeling," Calvin said with contempt. "Except I have a baby to take care of. Look, I'm sorry you got caught up in the middle of this…there's nothing I can do."

"What do you mean there's nothing you can do? Make it stop. That's what you can do. Please. Make it stop."

"I can't," Calvin said shaking his head. "It's already in the court's hands. There's nothing I can do at this point."

"You have to do something. I'm dying here. I'm in debt up to my ears. My wife just left me. You know what that's like? My wife of seventeen years just up and left me for another man. I don't have anything left, Calvin. Please, I'm begging you. My car broke down and I can't afford to get it fixed." He pointed to the vehicle behind him. "That's my brother's car. I have to drive around my brother's car until I find the money to get mine fixed."

"You ruined my life."

"I didn't ruin shit! It was the idiot who sold you the business. Jake's the one who committed fraud. He's the only one you should be suing. Not me, for Christ sake."

"You set me up," Calvin said with great resentment. He looked Davis dead in the eyes and said what he had wanted to say to him since he had to permanently close the doors to his business. "You knew the business wasn't succeeding."

Davis looked ashamed and hurt at the same time. "Calvin, no…"

"You *knew* it was failing," Calvin said to him resentfully. "You knew Jake altered his sales figures. You knew we were about to have a baby and you went ahead and did this to me anyway."

"I didn't have a choice!" he shouted, throwing out his arms hysterically. "I was losing everything! You think this is what I set out to do? You think this is the sort of thing I got a master's degree in business management to do to people? I needed to close your deal or I was going to lose my job. I had already started it before I ever saw Jake's numbers. I didn't know the numbers were fraudulent until we got further into the deal and he gave me his financials to give to you. That's the first time I knew, Calvin. I swear, that's the first time I knew about this bullshit."

"You could've told me. You could've stopped the deal from happening and allowing me—encouraging me— to sink every penny I had, and then some, into a hopeless business venture."

"It was the *potential* of the business, Calvin…"

"There was no fucking potential!" Calvin erupted with a growling boom in his voice that exploded and echoed around the parking lot. "The business was doomed long before I took it over. I tried everything I could. There was nothing in the world that was going to keep that place open, other than pouring tons of money into it just to keep it afloat. It would never have been profitable."

"Okay, so you're right," Davis said, giving in and softening his tone. "You're right. You're totally, one-hundred percent right. I screwed up. I never imagined how much damage this would do to you. I know what I did was wrong, and if I could take it back I would. What do you want me to do, Calvin? What do you want from me?"

"I want you to get me back all the money I lost."

"I can't do that. I don't have it."

"Then I guess we don't have anything further to discuss," Calvin said coldly, walking towards the shore of Grave Lake. He called Miko to follow him.

"Don't do this!" Davis hollered at him from the parking lot. "Calvin?"

Calvin stomped down and started back across the frozen lake, ignoring him, with Miko trotting beside him.

"Calvin! Don't do this to me!"

Leah was on her way to bed when she reminded Calvin to let the dog in. Part Husky, Miko was perfectly content wandering around outside in the fenced yard even in the coldest of winters.

Calvin opened the door to let Miko in. The frosty air swirled into the kitchen, but there was no dog.

"Miko," Calvin called him, remembering the other night when he wouldn't come to the door because he saw something out in the dark. He waited a moment for him to come trotting up to the door.

Miko didn't come. Calvin didn't bother calling him again. He zipped up his jacket and slipped on a dirty old pair of shoes before venturing out into the yard.

Miko wasn't in the same spot he was a few nights ago when something had him spooked. In fact, Calvin didn't see him at all.

"Miko?" he called him again as he scanned all corners of the fenced-in yard for Leah's dog. He heard only the whistling of the frigid breeze and bare branches clattering against each other.

He was gone.

Calvin went back inside. He left his jacket and shoes on and went back to the bedroom, where Leah was already in bed but still awake.

"Leah," he said to her apprehensively, "Miko isn't in the yard."

"What do you mean he's not in the yard? Where is he?"

"He's not out there. Are you sure the gate was closed?"

"Yes, I'm sure…there's no way he could've gotten out, Calvin. Are you sure he's not just way in back?"

"Yes. I'm sure. I walked the entire yard. I stepped in a ton of dog shit. He's not there."

"That's impossible," Leah argued. "There are no holes in the fence. He can't jump over it. There's no way he got out, unless he learned to fly." Frustrated, she threw the covers off of her and stomped through the house. She put on a jacket, a hat, grabbed a flashlight, and went outside.

Ten minutes later, she was back, now crying. Together they drove around town for almost two hours. They called the local pound, but he hadn't been brought in. Miko had vanished into the night.

Later that evening, while Calvin was preparing the coffee maker for the morning, a flash of light caught his eye from the kitchen window.

He saw car headlights head up the street. They

looked hauntingly familiar and he had a flashback of the other morning. He also remembered what Leah had said, about it just being a neighbor or a delivery guy.

He hated to admit it, but she was probably right. He was losing it.

He shut off the lights and watched from the dark out the kitchen window, waiting. He knew it was ridiculous, but he couldn't stop himself. He was convinced that it was the same car that he saw the other morning, and it would come back. He knew that car, even though he had never gotten a clear glimpse of it in good lighting.

A few minutes passed with him glued to the window. Then he yawned. He was exhausted. His feet hurt terribly. He began to wonder why he was torturing himself.

He snapped himself out of it and pulled himself away from the window. It was an idiotic waste of time and he desperately needed sleep.

The bedroom floor froze the bottoms of his bare feet as he crept across it, trying his best not to make the hardwood floor pop and creak. He gently pulled back the covers and slipped into bed soundlessly next to Leah, who was already snoring. He pulled the comforter up to his chin and shivered for a moment, savoring the delight of going from the cold hard world into a cozy cocoon. He cleared his mind. For the next six hours or so, the world could not bother him. *No one* could bother him, except himself.

6

Calvin awoke suddenly. It was Leah. She was calling him from somewhere distant in the house.

"Calvin! Calvin, come quick!" she hollered to him.

Calvin sprang out of bed in his boxers and ran through the house. He was so dizzy and disoriented that he almost fell over. His heart felt like it was ready to explode.

"What's wrong?" Calvin shouted back at her, finding her in the kitchen.

"Out there! Look!"

Calvin peered out the front kitchen window to find a giant fireball flaming high in the dark night, off to the side of the property. It took a moment to register.

"The dog house," Calvin blurted out. He fumbled like crazy to put some shoes on and ran outside. The blaze was burning wildly and lit up the entire yard. The dog house had been almost entirely consumed already.

Calvin ran to the other side of the house and grabbed the garden hose. Fortunately, due to laziness and total lack of time, neither one of them had ever disconnected the hose and put it in the basement for winter.

He cranked the faucet handle around. Water came

out, much to his relief.

The dog house had pretty much burnt itself out by the time he reached it with the hose, but he proceeded to saturate it anyhow. He realized that it really wasn't near any tree branches or anything else, so it probably wouldn't have caught anything else on fire.

And then it sank in.

"This was no accident," he said to Leah, who was standing out on the porch in her bathrobe. "It didn't spontaneously combust." Calvin had the odd feeling that he was being watched as he extinguished the last of the stubborn glowing embers, allowing the darkness and cold of the night to reclaim the yard.

The dog house still smoked. The burnt smell wafting off of it brought up all-too recent memories for him.

He swiveled around, scanning his surroundings. All was still and quiet. The fire had been intentionally set, he was sure of that, and whoever had set it was still fairly close by, possibly to see him panicked by the fire.

The dog house had burnt quickly—entirely too quickly, and far hotter than it should have, it seemed.

Calvin's eyes kept wandering out the wall of windows on the front of the building, watching every car wiz by out on the main road past the parking lot. He kept noticing small sedans like the one he had seen outside Leah's house.

Every one that went by and caught his eye he examined and tried to picture it in the dark. He was suspicious of white sedans, silver ones, and light-blue ones as well. Seeing how many he saw and how many roused his senses, he began to realize that his memory of the car outside Leah's house was beginning to fail him. The picture he had in his head was becoming blurry, as is often the case with witnesses to crimes or accidents.

"Hey," Billie's voice jolted Calvin from the right. Calvin glanced over at him, startled.

"What the hell are you doing? There are patients waiting." Billie huffed and shook his head. "Retard," he muttered under his breath as he headed back towards his office.

Calvin noticed that everyone was behaving very strangely around him at work. It wasn't the usual wacky, upbeat atmosphere. He could feel the tension in the air surrounding him, and he knew it wasn't paranoia. They were avoiding him, moving far out of his way when he walked around the site. He caught them in his peripheral vision staring at him, glancing his way more than usual. He detected them whispering to each other and then silencing when he approached. The break room hushed when he entered. They all looked at him awkwardly, avoiding eye contact and trying to act like nothing was going on.

It had happened. The truth had infiltrated his previously safe haven of work and spread through it like cancer. It had instantly rotted away every relationship he had spent years forming and had permanently stained his character. It was completely beyond his control and there was no going back now.

But no one said a thing to him. Except Billie.

"Going out for a smoke," Billie announced as he passed by Calvin. "Got any matches?" he asked Calvin with an evil smile.

Calvin glared at him.

"Hey, you did a great job chasing Leah out of here yesterday," Billie said to him. "You sure know how to treat a lady." He leaned closer to Calvin, lowered his voice and said sleazily, "That's why I let her go home a little early yesterday. It gave me time to stop by and make sure her neck and shoulders were feeling better. And I made a few other things on her feel better while I was there."

Calvin stared into his eyes, jaw trembling. His right hand lowered behind him and balled into a fist.

"Oh, do it," Billie taunted him. "Punch me. Punch me right now, I beg you. Please, do it in front of all the staff. Give me the reason I need to get you out of here for good."

Calvin controlled himself. His blood pressure was soaring. His adrenaline was pumping hot blood through his veins and he could feel his savage inner animal coming out. He knew that if he hit Billie at that moment, it would've broken his jaw or his nose, wherever his fist landed. It would've knocked that scumbag halfway across the room. But he couldn't. He needed his job. It was the only thing keeping him alive.

Billie snorted in his face in disgust. "Pussy," he remarked, shaking his head and walking away.

Later in the day, Calvin was lost in his work, fumbling through the repetitive motions of his job in a stupor, when he had a rude awakening.

"Calvin," Billie called him into his office loudly and obnoxiously.

Calvin dropped what he was doing and headed towards the office. He could see Billie through the large window that faced the floor of the donor area. He was looking over paperwork. Calvin wondered what Billie wanted now, or what he was going to say or do to try to provoke him. Calvin paused and took a deep breath before entering the office. He knew nothing good would come of this encounter.

"Oh, hey, here," Billie said, shoving a stack of papers at Calvin. "This is from your fuck-up yesterday. It's a written warning."

"A written warning?" Calvin said in disbelief. "For making a mistake?"

"One too many," Billie said condescendingly.

"I never make mistakes," Calvin said fiercely. "This is the first time I've ever done anything like that."

"Well, not according to my records," Billie said slyly. "You've made as many mistakes as I say you have."

"Look, I don't know what your problem is…"

"So what did you use to start the fire?"

"Excuse me?"

"What sort of accelerant did you use? My uncle is a firefighter in your town, way up there, and he told me all about your little incident."

"It was an electrical fire," Calvin said, realizing he was admitting that there had actually been a fire. He knew the secret was out, but he hadn't expected to be confronted like that.

"Do you expect anyone to believe that? My uncle sure doesn't. And neither do I. Nobody in that little shit town up there believes that it was an accident, not for one second. And you were the only one to have anything to gain from that fire."

"I don't really care what you believe, Billie."

"I have to hand it to you. I can't believe you actually torched your own dog, man."

"I didn't do anything!" Calvin said, spitting, his

face turning bright red. His hands were shaking. He felt the adrenaline taking hold of him again.

Billie howled with a laugh, imitating a dog in pain. He threw his head back and laughed.

"Shut the fuck up," Calvin growled at him.

Billie shot out of his chair and leaned into Calvin, his nose just inches away from Calvin's face. "Or what?" Billie said spitefully with an evil grin, his dark eyes glistening. "Are you going to light me on fire, too?" He howled right in Calvin's face again, obnoxiously. "You and your fucking dog both got what you deserved."

Calvin's blood pressure was so high that parts of him began going numb.

Billie howled again. "I can't believe you killed your own dog, man. You're going straight to hell…"

Calvin's hands were around his neck before Billie finished his sentence. He had him lifted up off the ground, his shoes dangling in mid-air.

"*I'm already there,*" Calvin growled before slamming Billie's head against the office window behind him.

The thud was loud enough that the entire staff stopped what they were doing and turned to look. They all saw Billie up against the glass, pinned, and Calvin holding him there by the neck.

Calvin instantly knew the consequences of what he had done. He had just been defeated. He had let Billie win.

Calvin let him go.

Billie fell to the floor, stunned. He simply stared up at Calvin, shocked, petrified, and speechless, for once.

Calvin walked briskly to the break room and grabbed his bag of food. He didn't make eye-contact with anyone on his way out the door except Sam, who was grinning from ear to ear.

The SUV glided through the snow up Route 7. The snowstorm hadn't really gotten bad until he was almost to the exit. He hadn't remembered hearing anything about snow in the forecast, but then again he rarely listened or cared what the weather would be like. The only time he paid close attention to the weather was back when he drove the sports cars. He was terrified of getting stuck out in a snowstorm in a light-weight rear-wheel drive vehicle.

The sky was very sullen and overcast, an infinite light gray that spewed large, heavy snowflakes everywhere. He hoped that the snowstorm was only affecting the northernmost point of his journey, because it was going to be a long, long ride home if it was snowing all the way.

His phone rang. He pulled it out to see Alfred's name illuminated on its screen.

"Mr. Strong," Alfred greeted him enthusiastically. "How are you doing today?"

"I've been better."

"One of these day's I'll call and you'll say something different, like 'I'm doing great' or 'not bad'."

"Don't hold your breath."

"Are you free Thursday?"

"What day is today?"

"Today is Tuesday. Thursday is the day after tomorrow, which happens to be Wednesday."

"Right. Thursday is my day off. Why?"

"I scheduled a deposition with the insurance company's lawyer to resolve the claim on your house."

"What is that?"

"It's a recorded statement from you about the house and the circumstances surrounding the fire."

"Are you sure that's a good idea?"

"It's the fastest way to get this resolved. I assume you would like to get this resolved as soon as possible, correct?"

"Yes. Of course I would."

"Good, then. Thursday. I'll email you the address once I find out what it is. We're on for five PM Thursday evening."

"Is this going to cost me a lot more money?"

"Yes."

"How much, exactly, are we talking, here?"

"Very difficult to say. But it's going to be a lot."

"Alfred, you know I'm struggling to make ends meet. You're draining the life out of me."

"We're almost through it. And you need this right now, Calvin. This is not an option for you. You need legal representation on this matter. And I need to bill you for my time."

Calvin sighed. He dropped his head. "Send me the bill."

He reached his street and turned the corner, past his burnt-out home. It looked awful, a sad pathetic site in the falling snow. He remembered every day coming home to that house. It had never been perfect, but it was home to him for seven years, and at his young age that felt like a huge portion of his life.

He remembered the dream he had of opening a business from the house. Being on the main drag, it was a perfect location for a small mortgage business. He figured he could live upstairs, or divide the house into two sections, one for living and one for his business. Like almost all of his other dreams, it was a failed attempt and never came to be. He didn't have enough money at the time, and although he had the support from people who wanted to come work for him, he couldn't come up with the funds quickly enough to make it happen. His connections with people eventually dwindled as they moved out of the mortgage industry or moved out of the area. So it became his home.

Calvin pulled the SUV into the unplowed driveway of his ruined home and stepped out into the deep snow.

The familiar bad smell of the nearby paper mill wafted through the air. It wasn't pleasant, but it was the smell that greeted him almost every time he had arrived home. It was very quiet around him. The neighborhood seemed abandoned, lifeless. All sounds seemed distant and muffled, and he could actually hear the sound of snowflakes hitting the snow-covered ground.

Calvin stepped away from his vehicle and scanned all the surrounding homes for signs of life. It was always such a nice neighborhood to be a part of. It was his haven from work and the busy street in front of the house. He could ride his mountain bike to the trails at the other end of the development or take his dog for long walks.

In the past, he could always count on running into the usual dog-walkers. There would be Jenna with her Golden Retriever, who knew his ex-girlfriend because her brother worked with her. There was the older lady, with the Black Lab, who always seemed a little too anxious to talk to him. She often made him a little uncomfortable because he felt like she had her own scheme in her head of what was going on between them on their chance meetings while their dogs sniffed each other's butts and peed. There was the younger athletic-looking woman with the little Yorkshire terrier, who he always looked forward to running into, although he never quite knew what to say to her. He always wondered if she was married and how old she was, or if she lived alone. She always seemed interested, though, which kept Calvin interested in walking his dog past their usual chance meeting spot.

But he hadn't seen any of the dog walkers in quite a while now.

The neighborhood had always been very friendly and welcoming to him when he bought his first home there. The town had a reputation for not being accepting of outsiders, but once you became a part of their community they would do absolutely anything to help you.

He knew that the neighbors diagonally across the street, past the empty plot of land, always migrated to Florida for the winter. They hadn't been around for a while and wouldn't be for another couple of months.

He spotted Jenna walking with her Golden Retriever through the snow, heading back towards her driveway. She was all bundled up in layers with a hat, scarf, and gloves on. She seemed to be in a hurry.

"Hey," Calvin called to her and waved. He trotted towards her through the snow, which was getting deeper by the minute.

Jenna's reaction to first seeing him bothered him. It was as though she had just run into someone at the supermarket when she was in a giant hurry and really did not feel like talking. She looked almost upset that he had spotted her and stopped her. She did finally give a hesitant wave back, but continued heading towards her back door.

"Jenna," Calvin persisted as he jogged towards her.

She finally paused for a moment and turned to face him. "Hello, Calvin," she yelled over to him hesitantly.

"How are you?" Calvin asked with all the cheer he could muster up.

"I'm all right...I'm actually just heading in the house now..."

"I see that," he said, taken back by her cold attitude. "Hey, I just wanted to ask you a few questions about my house, though, about the fire, if you have just a couple minutes..."

"I don't want any part of it," she said abruptly.

"No, I'm not asking you to do anything, I..."

"No thanks," she said abrasively. "I didn't hear anything, I didn't see anything, and I don't have anything to say about it." She turned her back and hurried into her house, slamming the door behind her.

Calvin stood stunned. He felt lost, betrayed, abandoned. He felt as though he had done something horribly wrong.

His eyes passed the windows of all the little houses, and then landed upon the large kitchen windows of the old white farmhouse across the street. The house was built in the 1860's and was three-times the size of most of the homes that were built around it in the 1950's. The kitchen windows faced his house and were the only direct view of his back door and driveway from any of the surrounding houses.

The white curtains in their kitchen window were suddenly drawn shut by someone hiding from view.

Calvin looked away, bothered by this, feeling he had somehow offended someone inside. He had thought the house was empty. The owners of the old home were the first people he had met when he moved into his house. They had approached him and offered any help they could provide.

Now the curtains remained closed. Their kitchen window was quite a distance from where he stood, so he couldn't say for certain, but there seemed to be someone carefully peering out from behind one edge of the curtains.

Although quite bothered by this act, Calvin tried not

to take it personally and convinced himself that whoever it was hadn't seen him and was simply closing the curtains. He had known them the longest of all the neighbors, and figured if there was anyone he could count on at that moment, it was them.

He trudged across the thick powdery snow on the street and up the walkway that led to their large, wooden front porch, which was really on the side of the house.

Clumps of snow clung heavily to the Hemlocks and nearly brought their lanky evergreen branches to the snowy ground around him.

Calvin was startled by a dog barking and charging him.

"Oh—hey, Hercules." He patted Hercules on the back and rubbed his head. "How ya doing, buddy?" He knew his presence had been announced now.

Calvin climbed the porch steps. His heavy boots thudded across the crackling old boards of the porch and left traces of snow.

He opened the storm door and knocked a few times.

He waited.

He swore he heard footsteps inside.

He opened the storm door again and knocked again on the solid wood door.

He thought he heard a voice from inside. He couldn't be sure, it was so faint.

He waited a few more moments, beginning to feel extremely uncomfortable.

No response came.

Calvin stood patiently facing the door for a good minute, much longer than he felt comfortable staying there. They knew he was there and they obviously did not want to talk to him. He was invading their privacy, now, and felt more intrusive with every second he remained. He didn't know where else to turn.

As he walked down the porch steps and started across his neighbor's snow-covered lawn, he heard a car's engine revving strangely. At first he couldn't place the sound, since cars were traveling by on the main road and pulling out from the convenience store. Then he noticed the old maroon sedan of his next-door neighbor, Mrs. Gooding, lodged peculiarly in the snow at the end of her unplowed driveway.

The engine on the old Buick roared again, but the tires only spun as a fountain of snow shot up from its rear.

This wasn't the first time he had helped her out of a snow bank. Her son always said he would plow her driveway when it snowed, but when he did show up, which was rare, it was too late in the day and she had already tried to make a break for it on her own.

"Mrs. Gooding," Calvin yelled as he crossed the street towards her. The street had still not been plowed and his shoes sank a good ten inches down before reaching solid pavement. He walked on the few tire imprints from cars that had recently passed through, even though they had already filled in quite a bit.

"Mrs. Gooding," Calvin yelled again and waved to her.

He saw her stop what she was doing and focus on him for a moment. It was hard to see her through the glare on the windshield, especially with melting snow sliding down it. She finally acknowledged him with a wave, recognizing him through his winter apparel.

Calvin approached her window and she lowered it for him.

"Mrs. Gooding," Calvin greeted her warmly, so glad he had made contact with someone else and knowing that she would never turn her back on him. "How are you?"

"Oh, hi, Calvin," she said merrily. "Well, I'm doing just fine, thank you, except I'm afraid I've done it again."

"I see that," Calvin said, bending over to examine the peculiar situation she had gotten herself into. "Wow, you got her lodged in pretty good this time."

"Yes, I thought old Bessie had it for sure," she said, baffled. "It won't go at all, now."

"There's almost a foot of snow on the road. Where are you heading that's so important?"

"I have a hair appointment. And now I'm afraid I'm running late."

Calvin couldn't help but smile. He shook his head a little. "The roads aren't even plowed. Are you sure your hair place is still open?"

"Well, they better be. I made that appointment last Tuesday, and there's no way it can wait another few days or a week, who knows, until they can fit me in again."

"All right. Here…" Calvin said, stepping back from her door. "Why don't you get out for a minute. I'll grab your shovel and see what I can do." He trudged up her driveway and found a snow shovel and a dirt shovel in her garage. "These should do it."

Calvin bent down behind the car and assessed the situation. Her back tires were completely suspended off the ground by a mound of snow she had rammed. He crouched down to his elbows and knees and began poking at the mound with the pointed dirt shovel.

"I'm so sorry about your house, dear," she said to him sadly.

"Yeah. Me too. Thanks."

"It was such a beautiful old home. And you did such a nice job maintaining it."

"I did a lot of work over there. That's for sure."

"Well you took it a long way from where the

previous owners left it. For so many years that was a rental property and we just had one lousy tenant after the next. They were so unfriendly and did nothing to keep up the place. The owners never did anything either. It was just income for them. It's at the end of our street, so it was so nice that you fixed it up and restored it. It made the entrance to our street so lovely."

"Oh, that's very nice of you," Calvin said kindly. "And look at it now."

"I just hope they tear it down soon. It's so ugly and frightening-looking."

"I'm sure they will. I don't know exactly how soon it will be."

"They've been asking an awful lot of questions around here," she said.

"Who? The police?" Calvin stopped shoveling.

"No. It wasn't the police. It was a couple of men…one in particular I saw going from house to house over the last few days. I'm home all the time and I don't have much to do. I keep my eyes on the neighborhood, especially your property since you haven't been around as much as you used to."

"They asked you questions too, then?"

"Oh, yes. One man was here for quite a while. I had a tough time getting rid of him, to be honest. And I'm always itching for company since I tend to get pretty lonely by myself here."

"What did he ask you?"

"Oh, just about everything."

"About the fire that morning?"

"Everything," she said, shrugging carelessly. "He asked me about you, about the fire, about the house in general, and he asked plenty about me. I don't understand what business that is of his or what right he had to ask me all those questions. I'm just a boring old lady who needs to get out more."

"What was he asking about the house?"

"He was really interested in who I saw coming and going there. I thought it was rather odd that he seemed so curious about who and what I might have seen even a couple weeks before the fire."

Calvin stopped shoveling and sat up to face her. "Who *did* you see coming and going a couple weeks before the fire?"

"Oh, well, you of course, and your girlfriend. That's about it."

"Wait…Mrs. Gooding, you saw my girlfriend at the house? At my house, right over there?"

"Well, yes…I mean, I didn't actually see *her*, but I saw the car. It was the only car near the house that wasn't yours."

"Wait…Mrs. Gooding, my girlfriend hasn't been around here in months…maybe four or five months…what did the car look like?"

"It was just, you know, a little car. A little smaller than mine. I have no idea what type it was. I'm not very good with cars."

Calvin's face went cold. "Mrs. Gooding, what *color* was the car you saw?"

"Let's see, dear…oh, give me a moment…it was dark, it was at nighttime when I saw it, so I couldn't really say for sure. It was light in color, though. Maybe a light blue, or maybe a silver or gray."

"And it was shaped like your car? A sedan?"

"Yes, like mine but a little smaller, maybe. Like, oh, you know, a normal typical car you see a lot of."

"When did you see this car?"

"I saw it just a couple times. I noticed it driving up

our street after dark. And then, I thought it was odd that when it parked, it parked across the street in front of the empty lot over there, not in your driveway."

"Are you sure the person went to my house, then?"

"I caught a glimpse of a figure heading over there after parking across the street."

"What did the figure look like?"

"I couldn't tell, dear. It was too dark. I just saw motion. There were no lights on at all at your house. You should really leave some lights on, or at least your back door light on when you're not home so that you don't trip going up your steps. You could fall and hurt yourself."

"Thanks, but I don't think we have to worry about that anymore."

"Yes, I suppose not," Mrs. Gooding said.

"So the man who came to your door and was asking you all of these questions—you told him about the car that you saw, the person heading toward my house?"

"Yes. I told him everything I could remember, which at my age isn't a whole lot."

"But you definitely told him about that car you spotted, the silver car that wasn't mine?"

"Yes, dear. He seemed especially interested in that. That seemed to get his attention more than anything else I had to tell him. I don't know why. I had to end the conversation around that point, because he just kept asking more questions. The more I answered the more he asked." She shrugged. "I told him I was sorry but I have a carrot cake in the oven, and as much as I've enjoyed talking it is going to burn." She shrugged again. "I do have *some* pressing matters in my life, you know."

"The man, what did he look like?"

"Totally gray hair. Strange-looking with a funny grin. And he had on the worst sweater."

"Sweater?"

"I wouldn't be caught dead in a sweater like that. And I'm eighty-two."

"Right," Calvin said. His eyes wandered to the snow covered street. "Here, I think I've got this cleared pretty well now. Why don't you let me hop in and give her a try?"

"Why, of course, dear. Thank you so much."

"No problem," Calvin said as he squeezed himself between the steering wheel and the seat. He got stuck for a moment with the steering wheel poking his stomach, but managed to cram himself in. He put the old Buick in drive and tapped the gas. It took a couple tries of reversing and gunning it, but he managed to free the Buick from its snowy prison and it pushed forward onto the snow-covered street.

"There you go," he said, leaving the door open for her."

"Oh, I don't know how to thank you," she said, carefully lowering herself into the driver's seat.

"Thank me by not getting yourself stuck again, at least not when there's this much snow. I won't be around to help you anymore, so please be careful."

"You too, dear," she said as she settled into the maroon cloth interior of her old clunker and waved to him.

Calvin waved back and watched her tires spin as she pulled away in slow-motion and plowed her way down the street.

Calvin stood in the middle of the street with a blizzard around him, making him feel as though he was in a gloomy, depressing snow globe. In the middle of that snow globe sat the burnt corpse of his former home. Calvin noticed that all the windows and doors of the first floor and basement had been boarded up with sheets of plywood.

Most of his tools had been lost in the fire, and he didn't have much else with him to pry an opening.

That house knew something he didn't. That investigator knew something he didn't. All that Calvin knew was that he needed to get inside.

Finally, almost against his will, his feet began treading through the snow towards it. There was only one thing to do now.

Calvin slowly but steadily descended the concrete steps down to the basement opening, which was now blocked by a large sheet of plywood. He ran his fingers around the edges and realized it was nailed in almost obsessively. He grabbed a corner of it and tugged. It gave a little, but made Calvin wonder if he would be able to get it off with his bare hands.

After a minute of tugging and yanking, the plywood ripped loose from the door frame, popping one nail at a time, until there was an opening large enough for Calvin to squeeze through.

Calvin entered the gaping black hole and disappeared into the darkness of the basement. He pulled a flashlight from his pocket, which he normally kept in the glove compartment of his SUV.

He twisted on the flashlight and began probing the walls and shelves of the basement with its narrow light beam. There was very little to see down there, considering how much clutter the basement had accumulated through the years.

He wasn't concerned with the basement, as fascinating as it was to take in the damage the fire had caused. His interests were higher in the house.

Calvin aimed the flashlights beam up at the walls of the great blackened ruins, from the basement floor to the sections of the roof over the attic. An intense pillar of daylight beamed down from the broken roof and illuminated portions of the black walls, but very little of the light penetrated the overwhelming darkness of the house's catacombs.

Calvin stood in one spot and swiveled, neck cranked, to peer upwards at the ascending walls around him. It was a long, long way up.

He looked for a path, something to latch onto to assist a climb. He had done a fair amount of indoor rock climbing in his day, and had even tested his skills outdoors on the famous Gunk's, as they were known to locals of Upstate New York. He knew he had tremendous upper body strength and could pull himself up any distance with just his hands alone, but there was no rope here, there was very little solid to latch onto to make his way up there— and that was where he needed to go, to the ledge of the second story's floor that loomed far above him, protruding out into the daylight and falling snow above.

Calvin went to the garage and pulled down his extendable ladder from where it hung by large nails on the wall. He just hoped it would be long enough.

He threaded the ladder down through the gap he had forged between the plywood and the basement entrance. After slamming it's aluminum sides into wood debris around him noisily, he had the ladder extended up into the light above and precariously teetered it back and forth, trying to keep his balance with its unwieldy weight. The ladder's top found a spot to settle close to the ledge, although it wasn't quite there. Calvin tried to maneuver it closer, but that was as good as it was going to get. It just wasn't quite long enough.

He stepped onto the bottom rung, the second and third, and wiggled his body back and forth to test the stability of the ladder. It shook and shifted slightly, to his dismay, but on the uneven mess of charcoal and ash he knew it was as stable as it could be.

His boots slipped and shifted on each rung of the ladder with each cautious step he took towards the light above. His boots were wet with a slimy gray mixture of melted snow and ash.

Calvin was waiting for the strong wind to begin and the ladder to begin shaking, the house shrieking in his face to get out and end his pursuit of whatever lay above.

He ascended hand over trembling hand, up into the black cathedral, past the floor of the first story. He could peer into most of the first floor now. The blacked wood floors were distorted into little hills. The refrigerator was melted into an almost unrecognizable shape. The kitchen was simply gone; there were no cabinets, no sink, nothing. If he hadn't known the house like the back of his hand, he would never have guessed that there used to be a full kitchen along those walls.

He was already at an intimidating height, but it was the second floor he needed to reach.

Snowflakes swirled around him and stung his eyes with a brief cold. He had to be at least sixteen feet off the basement floor now. He kept his eyes focused on the top of the ladder. He was surprised he had made it this far. His need to know was far greater than his extreme fear of heights.

He shook the melted snow off his face as he neared the top of the ladder. His feet and hands moved with the silent stealth of a cat, perfectly balanced and premeditated. He was too high to make a careless mistake now.

His hands reached the last rung on the ladder. It was the end of the line. His mouth was dry and his muscles were twitching.

He reached up and to the right at the charred ledge

of the second floor. The first section he put pressure on crumbled in his hands, sending the pieces of charcoal and ash dust drifting down into the abyss.

He felt around with his bare hands as his feet pushed him upwards on the top rung of the ladder. His right hand grasped around the corner of the bedroom's wall. His left hand entered the outside of bedroom wall on the stairwell side and latched onto the strips of wood that comprised the walls. The plaster had completely burnt away, leaving just blackened wood strips that still seemed to have their strength.

He tried his best not to think about what would happen if either hand slipped. The fall could possibly kill him, and at the very least would leave him maimed for life. At this point, given the choice between the two, he'd rather die than suffer anymore.

He made the sudden realization that he had passed the point of no return on his journey. He had shifted his support almost fully onto the house structure. He needed one last shove to hurl himself up and over the ledge of the bedroom floor. He had no idea if the floor would support his weight, but looking at it from underneath it appeared mostly intact. Burnt, but sturdy.

He froze for a moment, frightened and exhausted. He had gone too far, though, and something inside him would not allow him to turn back now, even if he could.

Calvin counted to three in his head. He took a deep breath. He had to see that bedroom.

With one quick and powerful heave, he launched himself from the ladder.

His fingers scrambled to accommodate the full weight of his body and pull him up and over, but the fingers of his left hand snapped through one of the strips of wood inside the wall. He flailed and struggled for a split second, desperately grabbing for anything to latch onto.

He knew he had kicked it. The aluminum ladder rustled and fell away as he hurled himself up onto the bedroom ledge, in the doorway of the bedroom. The ladder fell through the darkness until it slammed up against the inside of the front of the house with a horrible clanking and clattering.

Calvin clutched the floor of the bedroom on his stomach, his legs still dangling off, suspended a good twenty-four feet up. With a lunge he pulled himself all the way up and rolled into the mess of debris that occupied the bedroom floor.

He breathed heavily, his eyes wide and fixed on the open sky above and the snow it sprinkled on his face. He didn't dare move for a minute, horrified that any movement would send him crashing all the way to the basement. He had no idea how much weight the structure would hold, especially up this high, given how much its supporting beams had been compromised. The exterior walls had collapsed on the outside of the bedroom, which could cause further decline of the structure's integrity.

It became apparent how dangerous his situation was. His ladder was gone. He was trapped up high in his house and had no way to get down, and didn't even dare move a muscle. Fear swept over him as he tried to gain control of his senses. He shouldn't have gone up there alone. It was a terrible idea.

Calvin stayed flat on his back, petrified, for what seemed like an eternity to him.

He had to move. He had to at least try, or he would die there in the cold.

He gently rolled himself onto his side. If the house was supporting his weight already, he figured, it would continue to as long as he was careful. He didn't weigh that much, either, he thought, thank God. He wasn't puny by any means, but he had never been able to gain a pound if he tried.

He began moving around on the floor of the bedroom. There were pieces of slate and timber everywhere from the collapsed roof, as well as the sections of wall that caved in. There was a lot to go through, and from where he was he couldn't see a thing. There was too much debris in the way.

Calvin gently eased himself to his hands and knees. He delicately then lifted himself to a hunched-over standing position. He couldn't believe he was standing.

He tip-toed around the room as though walking through a stream on slippery rocks, finding the right path to take and gently testing and retesting each step before he gingerly took it.

With each step he became more daring and confident. The floor seemed perfectly stable, although he still had his moments of doubt. Nothing had indicated any weakness.

Calvin began clearing rubble from the roof. He sifted through mountains of two-by-fours and pieces of slate, tossing some over the ledge down into the darkness of the basement and other parts of it into whatever clear spots there were in the room.

There was only one thing he was after.

Calvin's heart began pounding as he cleared more debris from the room. He was able to get a clear picture of the floor now, and he was realizing something was not right. He assumed the mountains of debris had been blocking his view of his furniture, his possessions in that room. The more he cleared, however, the more confused he became as to the whereabouts of his things. The furniture his parents had bought him as a housewarming present when he purchased the home—he couldn't locate them. They were not where they had sat for the last seven years.

He came to the startling conclusion that they were not there at all. His bedroom was bare. The only thing that now occupied it was the debris from the attic and roof.

His bed, gone. His two dressers, gone. The lamp—even the lamp was nowhere to be found. And the nightstand—the nightstand which was the one reason he had gone up there, the reason he climbed that ladder and risked his life—the nightstand that held the gold watch his grandfather had given him, that had been in his family for six generations—it was gone too.

There were no remains of these items. There should have been, looking at the rest of the room and the damage it sustained. The damage from the fire wasn't even that bad in this particular section, as he had assumed from ground level. The major damage to this room came from the roof above.

Calvin frantically began kicking debris aside, his adrenaline taking over. There was nothing but bare floor under all of it—empty, bare carpet. The carpet wasn't even entirely burnt.

There was no reason for all his belongings, especially his gold watch, to be completely absent.

Calvin became more panicked and began spinning about the room, knowing his things had to be there. There had to be *some* trace.

Calvin suddenly yelped.

There was a cracking sound and a pain in his leg. His stomach dropped out as he found himself weightless for a moment.

7

"Hey," said a deep, booming voice from above Calvin. He heard the voice, but his head was spinning and he couldn't get a hold of reality. "Hey," the voice repeated, more firmly.

Then Calvin felt a hard nudge on his shin. He jerked awake to find a gun pointed at him.

"Just what do you think you're doing in here, son?" said the voice again from the man behind the gun. He was a large, heavy-set man with a bushy mustache. Calvin saw the gold badge and knew he was a police officer.

Calvin couldn't answer the cop's question at the moment. He just stared at the man, confused, and then his eyes wandered around his new surroundings.

"You can't be in here," said the cop.

Calvin focused back on him. "Where am I?"

"You're not supposed to be in here," he warned again in a harsh tone. "Why are you in here?"

Calvin looked around at his unfamiliar environment. The last thing he could remember was going through his bedroom upstairs. It all seemed like a dream, another nightmare, except he couldn't seem to wake up from this one. He looked around the room at the warped black walls and snow-covered floor. Flurries whipped in through the hole in the wall where the window used to be.

He was in his downstairs bathroom, the bathroom he had taken showers in for the last seven years. He barely recognized it. He lifted his head to see what he was laying on. He was in the partially-melted bathtub.

"This is my house," Calvin said, rubbing the back of his head. It hurt tremendously and brought him a splitting headache. His hair felt wet in back.

"This isn't anyone's house anymore," the cop said to him, lowering his gun but keeping it out. "You can't stay in here, son. I can refer you to the local shelter if you want, but you can't sleep in here."

"No, this used to be my house," Calvin protested. "I own this house—I owned it before it burnt down."

"You own the house?"

"Yes."

"Do you have some form of ID on you?" the cop asked.

"No, not on me. I usually leave my wallet in my truck."

"You own the truck outside in the driveway?"

"Yes, that's mine, unfortunately," Calvin said.

"I already ran the plates on that vehicle. Is the vehicle registered in your name?"

"Yes. Calvin Strong."

"And, Calvin, could I get your date of birth, please?"

"Sure. April twenty-third, nineteen seventy-nine."

The cop removed a piece of paper from his breast pocket and examined it in the dim light. "Well, that's definitely your vehicle. Now, you say you're the owner of this home?"

"Yes."

"How long have you owned it?"

"About seven years or so," Calvin answered.

"Did you recently have any work done on the house?"

Calvin looked confused. "Yeah. Why?"

"What's the most recent thing you had done to the house?"

"I had a new furnace installed just a couple months ago," Calvin said, perplexed.

"There we go," the cop said, satisfied. "Thank you. Now I know for certain who you are. Calvin, I'm Sergeant Patton. I'm the person you first spoke to about your home fire last week."

"Oh, yes. Hi. I thought I recognized your voice."

"I'm very sorry for your loss," Patton said. "But I still can't allow you to be in here."

"But this is my house, though. I own it," Calvin said plainly.

"That is true. But it is officially considered a crime scene, according to the insurance company, so they have full control over the premises and they've communicated that no one who doesn't work for their company should be entering the property."

"A crime scene?" Calvin asked in disbelief.

"Yes sir."

"What crime was committed here?"

"I have no absolutely no idea," Patton said with a shrug. "They have their own way of operating and they don't share details like that with us. It's none of our concern. They just let us know that they've taken control of the property. Technically, they didn't even refer to it as a crime scene. I've been around long enough to know what it means when an insurance company doesn't tear down a structure like this right away, or doesn't even have a plan to, and they tell the police not to allow anyone near the property."

Calvin pulled himself out of the melted bathtub and rubbed his head again.

"You okay?" Patton asked, concerned. "That's looks like quite a gash on the back of your head."

"Yeah. Fine. I've had worse," Calvin looked down at the tub and saw a splatter of blood. It was still dripping into the base of the tub when he moved.

"Well, I'd get that covered. Get some pressure on it. I think I have a cloth and an ice pack out in the car. I'll get that for you when we leave."

"Thank you," Calvin said kindly, wiping the blood from his hand onto his jeans.

"Let's get you out of here. Follow me. Please, just be careful where you step. I almost went right through the floor when I came in here," Patton said as he led Calvin out of the bathroom and through what used to be the kitchen. "So, just what the hell were you doing in here, anyway?"

"Looking for something," Calvin replied, nearly losing his balance on the hilly, warped kitchen floor.

"It must've been something damn important to risk your life climbing up into that second floor like that. This place is ready to fall down. I don't even feel comfortable standing where we are on the first floor, let alone climbing up there. What was it you were looking for?"

"A watch," Calvin answered quickly. "A gold watch my grandfather gave me. But it wasn't there. Nothing was up there. All my things were gone, including the entire nightstand that I kept that watch in."

"Nothing was up there?" Patton asked, bewildered.

"All my furniture disappeared. Even the huge bed I had and the huge dressers."

"This fire was extremely hot, Calvin. I was the first on the scene…I know you were shaken up at the time when I spoke with you over the phone, but if you remember I told you how I couldn't even enter the structure to make sure no one was in there. I'm glad you weren't. But there was no way any of the firemen would even attempt to enter this building, it was so damn hot. Your things most likely incinerated and didn't leave much behind for us to see."

"Yes, I'm sure," Calvin agreed, "but there was no trace of them, not a single hinge or bolt or nail. Just the pieces of roof that came down. There was no sign that my furniture had ever been there. And the watch is gone. The watch is all I even care about."

The two of them exited the home from the back entry on the first floor, where Patton had pried off another piece of plywood to enter earlier. The two of them stopped in front of the patrol car sitting in the driveway. Patton opened the door of the car and searched around for the icepack he had promised Calvin.

"They also had the fire hoses blasting in there for about three hours," Patton pointed out. "Those hoses are incredibly high pressure, and it's very possible that they blew your possessions into different parts of the house or even outside onto the lawn. Then, who knows, if they were out in the open on the lawn. People around here are very grabby. Lot of poor folks who will take anything they can get their hands on, especially a nice gold watch." He found the ice pack and handed it to Calvin.

"That I know all too well," Calvin said with a chuckle, holding the icepack to the back of his head. "I used to put anything I was trying to get rid of out on the curb in front of the house. I'd go in to get a piece of paper to write 'free' on it, and when I'd come back out a minute later the stuff was already gone. But this is different. I was just up there, and I know no one could've accessed the upstairs in the condition it's in. No one could've gotten those big pieces of furniture out. The way the roof was caved in and where it landed, I could tell it hadn't been disturbed since the fire. No one had touched that since the fire had been extinguished. Nothing was removed from the fire, right?"

"No, no," Patton said, shaking his head. "The fire crews didn't attempt to salvage anything. They figured it wasn't worth their while, and it's not something they normally do. They would only actually remove things from the premises if they caused a further danger to the situation, such as a couch that continued to burn and was contributing to the fire spreading and growing. Otherwise, no. We don't want to be responsible for missing things. When the insurance company sends their guys in, they want to see the property untouched. They want to be able to get the best idea they can of what the structure contained before the fire. They want to know where things were exactly. If police or fire crew mess with that it can cause a lot of legal complications. And believe me, that's the last thing we need more of."

"So then where did it all go?" Calvin asked with some irritation in his voice.

Patton shrugged. "I couldn't really say. Like I said, it may have been shot out onto the lawn and then picked off by the locals."

"Some of those pieces of furniture weighed over three-hundred pounds," Calvin added.

"Well, the hoses wouldn't have messed with those too much. Unless they were already burnt into pieces."

"And they couldn't have been burnt that much," Calvin continued. "I was up there and I could see that the fire didn't affect the upstairs too badly. It was mainly just the attic above that burned. The two bedrooms seemed fine. The closet doors were still mostly intact, and the carpet wasn't even that badly burnt. But there is nothing on the carpet now except pieces of attic and roof."

"The insurance company sends someone in to check all these things out," Patton said.

"Oh, I know," Calvin said, rolling his eyes.

"You've spoken to them about this? They explained everything to you?"

"Yes, they've talked to me and there was no mention of any of this so far," Calvin said.

"And you made your list for them as far as what was in the house, your contents?" Patton asked.

"Yes. Right after the fire," Calvin confirmed. "They seemed to want that right away, so I emailed it over that night."

"And have they said anything about that yet?"

"They haven't said anything about anything."

"Calvin..." Patton sighed. "Well, there seems to be a problem there. If your house is empty with no remnants of contents and possessions and you're saying it was full of the furniture on this list..."

"What are you saying?" Calvin interrupted him anxiously.

"It doesn't look good. Now, relax, I'm not saying it's anything bad. There's just more going on than you and

I realize here. It's possible that the insurance company removed things for their own purposes, maybe analysis for chemicals."

"Why would they do that?"

"Sometimes they will check for use of accelerants in the fire," Patton explained. "Something that might have been used to start the fire and spread it intentionally. It would be something that didn't belong in that portion of the house. They wouldn't be too surprised if they found gasoline in, say, the garage or even the basement. But if they found evidence of it splattered across all the walls, even the upstairs, they would certainly have a good reason to believe the fire was intentionally set."

"They already said it wasn't intentionally set, though," Calvin contested.

"That may be true. You know as much as I do about that. Insurance companies like to keep secrets. They don't like to give more information than they have to, especially on a large claim like this. Remember, this is going to cost them a large amount of money and they want to make absolutely sure the claim is valid before they pay out."

"Valid?" Calvin raised his eyebrows. "You're saying they could not *pay* for any of this?"

"If, say, it was arson, or there was some other wrong-doing of any sort. This is what these investigators do for a living. It's just their job. If I were you I'd read over your policy carefully. And if you have any information to give these people about anything unusual surrounding this fire, even going months back, I would offer that information and let them look into it. It could make the difference between getting your claim paid and having it denied."

"Yes, I do have some new information," Calvin said. "I was just talking to my next-door neighbor, Mrs.

Gooding, right before I came over here. She said she saw a car around here that wasn't one of mine. She didn't think anything of it because she thought it was my girlfriend, for some reason, so she didn't pay much attention."

"What type of car?" Patton asked.

"She could only remember that it was a light colored sedan. Maybe silver—and I've had a silver or white small sedan driving by my house a lot—where I'm staying now, I mean, circling the block at five in the morning."

"You don't know anyone who drives a car like that?" Patton asked.

"No, not really. It's tough to tell exactly what the car looks like since it's always in the dark, and that's when she saw it too. In the dark."

"There are an awful lot of silver or light-colored small sedans on the road, is the problem," Patton said pessimistically.

"I know," Calvin agreed. "I'd recognize this one in the dark if I ever saw it again. I can tell it's the same one every time I see it."

"But you never saw this car around your house up here?"

"No, not me personally," Calvin said.

"Did you tell the insurance company this? The investigator?"

"Mrs. Gooding said she already did," Calvin said. "He was asking a ton of questions and she finally had to end the conversation."

"You might want to give them a call and make sure they got that information, and give them Mrs. Gooding's contact information again."

"Yeah, that's probably a good idea."

"Because it could possibly explain the lack of contents of the house." Patton shrugged.

"You think it was stolen before the fire?"

"I wouldn't rule it out," Patton said. "Especially if someone was seen creeping around who didn't belong, right before the fire."

"Could I file a police report for the stolen property?"

Patton shook his head. "No, no, not yet. We don't even know if anything was removed legally, let alone if it was stolen. Calvin, do you have any receipts for any of the items that were in this house?"

"Receipts? No, not really," he said dimly. "What receipts I had were in the house at the time of the fire. That's the only place they could have been. And most of the furniture was gifts. And my watch I inherited from my grandfather. He got it from his father."

"The problem there, Calvin, is that you can't really show that you ever owned these items, let alone that they were stolen. You're going to have a tough time proving that they were in the house at the time of the fire.

"But they *were*," Calvin said, growing agitated.

"Hey, I believe you," Patton said, putting his hands up defensively. "All I'm saying is there are a bunch of problems with this scenario and I think a lot more has to be straightened out before anyone can really make sense of these circumstances."

"That watch was worth probably six-thousand dollars," Calvin said bitterly. "Whoever took it will definitely be trying to sell it soon."

"They *will* try to sell," Patton concurred. "It's a question of when. It depends how desperate they are for money, because if the person has half-a-brain, he'd hang onto it for a while until things settle down."

"What if I checked pawn shops in the area? Antique stores?"

"There's no harm in trying," Patton said. "Do you have a picture of the watch you could bring around with you?"

"I'm sure I could dig one up."

"Well, that's a fishing expedition. But remember, Calvin, assuming you do find it, you're going to need some sort of proof that the watch belonged to you. You can't just walk into a store and have someone arrested because you recognize it. Were there any initials on it, any unmistakable identifying marks?"

"No. No initials...nothing like that," Calvin said, feeling hopeless. "I would just know it if I saw it."

"I'm afraid there's not much we can do to help you. You can let us know if you do identify it and we can look into it. Jewelry is tough, though. It could belong to anyone and there isn't much of a way to tell who the rightful owner is."

"What if the same person is selling all my pieces of furniture as well?" Calvin asked.

"Well, then we'd have a case to make," Patton said. "Was the furniture really expensive?"

"It wasn't cheap. But it wasn't as expensive as the watch."

"Well, you let us know if that happens and we'll be able to help you out," Patton said, shrugging his shoulders as he got back into his patrol car. He rolled down the window as he pulled away and said, "Hey, you just be careful, now, okay?"

8

"Alfred, I'm glad I got a hold of you today," Calvin said into his phone as Pearl emptied a container of blocks all over the living room floor.

"Calvin. You just caught me, actually. I'm between court sessions. How can I be of service?"

"You have a few minutes?"

"For you, absolutely. What's up?"

"I was up at the house yesterday. I went inside."

"Oh, dear," Alfred said morbidly. "You were inside the house again? Alone?"

"Yes. I went up alone. Something was bothering me about it. I wouldn't have been able to rest again until I went up there. I was having nightmares."

"Calvin, Calvin," Alfred scolded him. "You know you're not supposed to be in there, right?"

"Yes. I know. The cop who found me in there told me all about that."

Alfred let out a long sigh. "You didn't get arrested, did you? Are you calling me from jail?"

"No, I'm not calling you from jail. The cop was cool. It's all right."

"Well that's a relief."

"Here's the thing, though. I was able to reach the second floor of the house with a ladder. When I got up there, there was nothing."

"Nothing?"

"None of my things. Just debris. Just roof and wood beams half-burnt and slate tiles. It was bare floor, though, under all that junk. There was no furniture, no bed, no dressers. There was absolutely no sign of any of my possessions."

"That's certainly peculiar."

"I could even see imprints from the furniture on the floor, in the carpet, where it had been."

"Were you able to see it up there, see the upstairs, I mean, the first time you went to look at the house, when you spoke with the investigator?"

"No. The second floor was totally inaccessible. The investigator told me that anyone who went up there would be risking his life, and they had no plans to try to access the second story of the house. It was too unstable and not worth falling through. And that's exactly what happened to me."

"You fell through the floor?"

"I was up there a while. I was clearing debris, trying to make sense of it all. I figured there had to be some trace of something there, some remains. Even a bad fire would leave something. I was searching like crazy when I don't even know what happened. It was so quick. I felt pain and the next thing I knew I was laying in the bathtub downstairs with a cop aiming his gun at my face and blood pouring from the back of my head."

"Jesus, Calvin, what the hell would possess you to go climbing up in that house like that?"

"I knew there was something wrong with this whole thing from the beginning. There was something up there I knew I had to see. And I found it. That something was nothing. There was nothing up there, no evidence at all that I ever even occupied that house."

"Calvin..." There was a long pause from Alfred.

"This is a big problem. I'm still taking this all in. With what you're telling me I honestly, at this point, have no idea what to make of it. These insurance guys are going to give you a really hard time about this, you know. It doesn't look good at all."

"I know it doesn't look good. Even the cop was telling me that."

"Now, you submitted that list, that inventory of personal belongings that were in the house at the time of the fire, right? You gave that to the insurance company already?"

"Yes. I faxed it to them as soon as I completed it. They seemed to want it right away."

"Calvin, you sent them a list of shit that wasn't in the house."

"But it *was* in the house. They wanted a list of what was in the house at the time of the fire, so that's what I gave them."

"I understand, I totally get that, and I believe you, but from their perspective the house was bare at the time of the fire. They haven't told you about this contradiction yet, probably because they're waiting to see what you say and do. They're not telling you anything they don't have to. They're waiting for you to say something wrong, do something wrong, or for someone else to come forward with some additional information that could shed some light on what happened."

"I don't understand where the stuff went. It must have been the fire company, or the police."

"Is it possible it was stolen before the fire?"

"Anything is possible. But it seems ridiculous. I can't imagine how someone would manage to get all those things out without drawing some sort of attention."

"Have you talked to your neighbors yet?"

"They don't want to talk to me."

"You tried approaching them?"

"They refused to answer the door. One of them practically ran away from me. They said they don't want anything to do with this, that they 'didn't see nuthin' and have nothing to say."

"Hmm." Alfred paused. "That's not good."

"It was that damn investigator. I don't know what he did to my neighbors up there, but he sure freaked them out."

"Who knows," Alfred said. "I could take a good guess, though. He probably asked a whole bunch of highly insinuating questions which made you seem like you were somehow responsible for the fire. He was fishing for clues, firing out some random questions and comments regarding you and your behavior. How often you were up there, who you were with, what sort of temperament you have. He's probably also asking what cars were there most often. And certainly he's asking about the night before the fire, which you were up there. Did you interact with anyone that night?"

"No. I haven't interacted with anyone for a while. I kept to myself. Nobody had been very friendly to me in quite a while. My trip up there yesterday was the first time I had even been able to talk to anyone."

"So you were able to make some contact?"

"I talked to my next door neighbor on the side street, Mrs. Gooding. She was stuck in the snow and I shoveled her out."

"What did she have to say?"

"She said she saw a car there. She thought it was my girlfriend's, so she didn't really think anything of it. She noticed it a few times, though. Always late at night. She's awake practically all the time, due to the medication she's on."

"Did she get a plate number on the car?"

"Unfortunately, no. She wasn't even real sure on the description of the vehicle. It was a silver sedan, one that fit the description of the one that I've seen circling the block at my girlfriend's house. But Leah has me convinced that it was just my imagination. At this point, I wouldn't doubt it. I'm starting to lose it."

"But there could be a connection there. Did she see anything else related to the car, any sightings of people near the house?"

"She saw a figure leaving the vehicle, which was parked across the street from my house, and heading towards my back door."

"She saw the figure go in the back door?"

"No. She wasn't even positive that the person was heading to the door—just in that general direction. She didn't pay attention because for some reason she thought it was Leah's car. I don't know why, she's old…"

"And she didn't see what the person looked like?"

"No. Not at all. Just a figure heading towards the house."

"And that was the only information you managed to pick up while you were up there?"

"That was it."

"Here's what I want you to do, Calvin. You need to go back up there. You need to ask around town. Ask everyone you know. Ask anyone you see walking down the street. It's a small town, right?"

"Yes. Very small."

"And word travels fast. Even if someone you ask hadn't seen anything, they may very well know someone who did. It's amazing how these things sometimes come out. Especially in a little town like that where everyone knows everyone else's business."

"It's right in the village, too, on the main line."

"Exactly. There are eyes everywhere. Somebody somewhere saw *something* that is essential information to you. I know you're a very busy guy right now and you've had a lot of bad luck lately, but this is vital to you. This takes priority. Finding something out will most likely make the difference between your claim being paid or denied. I hate to say this, Calvin, but it could also make the difference of freedom and spending the next five to ten years in prison."

"Please don't say that," Calvin said, horrified.

"I don't even want to think about it. I'm sure you don't either. But as your lawyer, I have to, and I have to tell you that *you* have to think about it as well."

"I know."

"There's one more thing you should do. You should have an independent analysis done of the fire. It's going to cost some money, but this is something you should really look into. I wouldn't be doing my job if I didn't tell you that this is crucial. The insurance company is being very vague in its investigation and we need to decipher what exactly they're trying to do so we don't get blindsided."

"How do I go about getting the testing done?"

"I know a guy who does this for a living," Alfred said. "He's an expert on fire investigation. He's a master at what he does, and he's well worth the price."

"The price? How much is this going to cost me?"

"I know money is tight right now, Calvin. You need to do this, though. It will probably run you about a thousand dollars. Shouldn't be too much more than that."

"A thousand...I don't know how I'm going to come up with it. I'll have to find a way."

"I'll email you the fire investigator's contact info. I

strongly suggest that you contact him today. Tell him I told you to call him and that you need him to do this as soon as possible.

"I'll call as soon as I get it."

"Good. This is no game, Calvin. This is your life we're talking about, here."

"Leah, I need to talk to you about something."

She sighed and dropped her head down. "That's never a good opening."

"It's nothing that bad."

"Nothing good ever comes out of a conversation that starts like that," she said. "What's the matter?"

"I talked to Alfred."

"And?"

"And he thinks it's a really good idea for me to get testing done on the house."

"Testing for what?"

"For signs of arson."

"Wasn't that part of the investigation? Isn't it their job to do all that stuff?"

"They supposedly did testing," Calvin said. "I don't know if they really did, if they're lying and just saying they did because they didn't feel like spending the time and money, or if there is some other reason why they would be hiding something from me."

"They're not hiding something from you. It's a major insurance company. They're nationwide. They're not going to do something illegal over your crappy old house. They have much larger claims out there. You're small potatoes to them, Calvin. No offense, but your claim just isn't that big of a deal that they're going to do something unethical or illegal."

"Well something's up," Calvin said. "I'm telling you, something's going on with this."

"That's all in your head, Calvin. There's nothing up with it, other than people trying to do their jobs and get on with their lives. I wish you would do just that. Do your job and get on with your life."

"I don't have much of a life left to get on with," Calvin blurted out.

"What's that supposed to mean?"

"Nothing. I'm just living the dream."

"You think this is perfect for me? Yeah, I want us to be together, but this is turning into a nightmare, Calvin. You've changed. You're becoming someone else, who I'm not even sure I want to be around anymore."

"I'm not becoming someone else," Calvin said. "I'm the same person I've always been, and you've just never really known me. You've only seen me as this person you created in your head who you feel like I should look like, act like, and talk like. I can't ever be right for you. Everything I say and do will never live up to these childish expectations you have of me."

"They're not childish expectations, but I do have certain expectations of you. You're the father of my child and whether you chose to be that or not, it's who you are now and you need to step it up and stop living in a fantasy world. You're house is gone, Calvin. It's gone and nothing is going to bring it back the way it was. Your dog is gone too. Get over it. Seriously, get over it."

"Sometimes I swear to god I couldn't possibly have ended up with someone worse, not even if I tried."

"I feel the same way, believe me," she said, appalled.

"Well I'm glad that's mutual."

"Let's just not fight in front of the baby. She doesn't need to hear that."

"Of course she doesn't," Calvin said. "I never want to be yelling or swearing in front of her. Never."

"Agreed."

"While you're pissed off at me, I may as well finish what I was saying about the house. Alfred wants me to do a second test on it. He knows a guy who's an expert on fires and arson. He'll be able to tell me faster than anyone else what really happened there. He's going to check out the sight for himself and do detailed analysis. He's even going to take samples from all different parts of the house, especially near where the fire seemed to originate, and test for signs of any accelerant used. He's looking for anything that may indicate that the fire was not an accident."

"And how much is this wonderful, elaborate service going to cost?"

"About a grand."

"A thousand dollars! Calvin, you don't have a thousand dollars to your name!"

"I will. I get paid in two days. I'll give him a check. The paycheck will clear by the time he cashes it."

"That money's for me!" she shouted in his face. "Remember, for the bills? You're supposed to be paying me to live here. Remember that arrangement? You're not staying here for free."

"Look, I'll give you the money for the bills as soon as I can," Calvin said. "It's just going to have to wait until the next pay period."

"Why can't your idiotic investigation project wait until the next paycheck?"

"Because the longer we wait, the greater the chance of the results being skewed. Someone could tamper with something…a storm could come and knock it all down. Rain could affect the chemical analysis."

"The chemical analysis, Calvin?"

"Yes. The residue left behind…"

"I'm sorry, and I hate to say it like this, but I'm trying to live in the real world here. And in the real world, my mortgage is going to be late."

"Well, I'm sorry," Calvin said without shame. "You don't have any padding in your bank account?"

"No! I don't! When you moved back out I was left with all the bills, remember? It wiped me out. Did you think I had someone else paying them in your absence? And now I have a child to take care of, on top of that. It's not like I'm getting child support, or anything."

"Look, I'm sorry, but I'll get you my share of the money as soon as I can."

"That's great, Calvin. Way to step up."

"This is important. I wouldn't be doing it if it wasn't absolutely necessary. We need to know what really happened. If it's nothing, then it's nothing. But if something really happened up there that shouldn't have, I need to know about it so that I can get the proper legal representation and take the right steps."

"Okay. I think it's pretty clear what your priorities are."

"My priority is my daughter. I want to make sure that she is safe and taken care of. In order to do that, I need to make sure that I'll be around to take care of her."

"What's that supposed to mean?"

"Nothing. Forget it. You'll get your money soon. I'm sorry for the inconvenience."

9

Calvin pulled into work early the next morning. He sat in his truck a few moments longer than usual, taking comfort in the fact that he was actually a few minutes early, instead of his usual skidding into the parking lot on two wheels and running into work.

He glanced in the rearview mirror and sighed. His eyes were bloodshot. He hadn't gotten a decent night's sleep since the fire, and he could feel his mind faltering.

He was dreading going inside. He had been nothing but a ball of stress since the incident with Billie the day before. It was bothering him, deep down, knowing that he may have just cost himself a job by losing it like that. He had failed himself, and failed his daughter. The one thing that he had to do was stay calm. He was good at his job. He was great at it, and they would never touch him unless something extreme like this happened. His ability to think rationally and reasonably had been slipping lately, further day by day, and he just wasn't able to hold on to his temper any longer.

He just hoped that all would be okay and everything would be forgotten as he climbed out of the SUV and headed towards those glass double doors to start his long and tiring day. The bitter cold nipped the fingers of his right hand, which was exposed to hold the plastic bag full of his food for the day.

He had just walked through the second set of glass doors when he found himself face-to-face with the regional manager, Jerry White.

Jerry stood directly in Calvin's path, calmly waiting for him with his arms crossed. He was tall, lanky, bald and awkward-looking in his expensive business attire.

Calvin had stopped in mid-step, distressed.

"Calvin," Jerry greeted him cheerlessly. "Follow me. We'd like to have a word with you."

Calvin's heart dropped. "Sure," he said grudgingly, knowing he had no say in the matter.

Jerry led him to one of the conference rooms off to the side of the main hallway, where he was surprised to find the human resources supervisor, Dan, sitting and waiting for him as well. Dan was a heavy-set, overstressed walking heart attack whose tie flopped over his round gut as he sat.

"Calvin," Dan greeted him, "Take a seat."

Calvin rolled out a chair from the conference table and sat. Jerry sat opposite him, next to Dan.

"Now, Calvin, I think you know why we're all gathered here today."

"Of course. To discuss my raise," Calvin said.

Both men chuckled a little, unexpectedly.

"Ah, well, no, not exactly," Jerry said, still smiling. "We're here to talk to you about what happened yesterday."

"Yesterday?" Calvin said, seeming confused.

"Yes. You do remember what happened yesterday, with Billie, don't you?"

"I have a one-year-old. I don't remember what I did five minutes ago."

"Well, yes, Calvin, but what we're referring to is the physical altercation that you had with your site supervisor, Billie, yesterday."

"Oh," Calvin said. "That."

"Yes, that," Jerry said, adjusting his glasses. "He told us that you grabbed him and slammed his head into the wall? Is that accurate?"

"Yes," Calvin answered plainly. "That is accurate."

"And why…" Jerry couldn't find the right words. "In what way, in what sense, would you deem it appropriate to lay your hands on any other employee, let alone your site supervisor?"

"He was being a dick," Calvin said.

"That's your excuse for physically assaulting him on company property?"

"Physically assaulting him seems a rather excessive allegation."

"But you did…"

"Someone had to put him in his place," Calvin said, abruptly raising his voice. "Day after day I put up with him torturing me and the other staff. Day after day I watch him touch every single female working at this site—or, I take that back, every *attractive* female working at this site, including the mother of my child. No one else was going to do anything about it. You two sure as hell weren't going to do anything about it. And I had taken enough of the harassment and the abuse from that little prick. Someone had to do it. I'm just sorry it had to be me."

All three of them were silent for a moment.

Then Dan finally cleared his throat and said, "Well, all right...Calvin, I understand you had some issues with this particular employee. He had mentioned a number of times before that you had used harsh language with him in front of the patients..."

"Bullshit!" Calvin shouted furiously. "I never lost my temper with that asshole. Never. I put up with it day after day after day and I always kept my cool until yesterday. I couldn't take it anymore."

Dan looked troubled. "I believe your demeanor at the moment is a pretty fair indicator of your behavior as far as Billie is concerned. You're shouting at us, Calvin."

"That's because this isn't fair."

"Calvin, you've made it extremely difficult to even consider your side of the story. Your behavior just doesn't support it. We cannot, I mean absolutely *cannot* have employees acting like this in what should be a strictly professional environment. We can't allow any staff member to go shoving another person, cracking their head into a wall. It's a major liability for us. We'll be lucky if we don't get sued."

"I didn't have a choice," Calvin protested. "He pushed me too far."

"You've left *us* with no choice, Calvin," Dan said. "I think it's in our best interest to shake hands and part ways with you at this point."

"No," Calvin said softly, taken back, even though he had expected it. "I've worked here forever. I'm the best at what I do. You need me."

"No, we don't"

"I can get every staff in here to back me up in sexual harassment charges," Calvin said. "I can take you to court and you'll be responsible as well, since you knew about it and chose to ignore it. Just try it. My lawyer would love a class-action lawsuit."

"Well, that may be the case, I don't know," Dan said indifferently. "But we still can't keep you on. I'm sorry."

"Listen, I have a baby at home I'm trying to support, here. I need this job." It disgusted Calvin to grovel so pathetically, but he didn't care. He had responsibilities. "I'll find another job soon and switch, but please just let me stay on until I do."

"I'm afraid it's a no, Calvin," Dan said, rising from his chair.

Jerry stood as well and they headed out of the room, leaving Calvin sitting alone in silence at the large conference table.

Calvin sat in a daze as he drove up the Northway on his way to the house again. The thought of seeing that burnt-out structure again was making him feel sick to his stomach. He couldn't get the images out of his head from the last time he was there, and he had enough of the nightmares that haunted him throughout his days as well as his nights. He wanted the demons to leave him alone.

But Alfred had told him to go up there, and he was right. He needed more information. Someone had to have seen something, he kept telling himself.

It wasn't time yet to wash his hands of this whole situation. He had a feeling it would be a while before this was over completely. He also had a feeling that he wouldn't be seeing a dime from this anytime soon. His financial situation was becoming dyer and it was now affecting his home life and his relationship. More importantly, it was affecting the quality of the time he spent with his child. She would only be this age once, and he didn't want to miss these times because of his financial woes and the drama in his relationship. He needed to keep a level head and focus on her.

He had called the independent fire investigator and hired him, upon Alfred's strong recommendation. He needed all the help he could get right now. The investigator, Charles, had been very pleasant to deal with on the phone, although he didn't seem overly interested in helping Calvin out, despite the thousand-dollar fee. He agreed to take on the case, though. He was going to make it up there the next day, Thursday. Charles explained that he rarely responded to a case on such short notice, but Calvin had stressed how time-sensitive this issue was and that he was having problems with the investigator from the insurance company. As soon as Calvin brought up the insurance company, Charles took an interest in the case. He was obviously highly knowledgeable and seemed to crave an opportunity to prove another investigator wrong, especially from such a large and prestigious insurance firm.

Calvin was on Route 7, approaching the flashing yellow light that signaled his house would be the next street on the right.

He held his breath, waiting for those sad remains to come into view again. He prepared himself. He needed to control his emotions and look at this from a strictly rational perspective.

All that went out the window when the house came into view. The first thing he saw was flashing lights and yellow and black striped barricades and cones. There was large construction machinery surrounding the familiar horrid remains of the house, and a flurry of activity from construction workers around it. They wore bright orange vests and hard-hats and hustled around to ready their front-end loader, bulldozer, and the small crane that had pulled into the back yard.

Calvin quickly swung the SUV onto the side street and screeched to a stop next to the activity.

"Hey! What are you doing!" he shouted as he ran out of his vehicle.

No one could hear him over the noise. One worker turned and noticed him, but made a face of indifference and continued walking towards the house.

"Hey!" Calvin shouted as he jumped out of the SUV. He ran towards the man in the crane that had already started ripping into the side of the house.

The crane stopped in mid-scoop of the outer wall. The worker controlling it threw the gears into neutral and shut the beast off. He climbed down from the seat to meet Calvin.

"Hey, what are you doing?" Calvin asked him abruptly.

"We're here to take her down," the worker said, motioning towards the burnt house.

"Wait a second!" Calvin yelled. "Nobody's tearing this house down."

"We were hired to do it yesterday. So here we are."

"You can't tear this house down yet. I'm the owner of the house, and I'm telling you that I don't want it torn down yet."

"You're the owner of this property?"

"Yes."

"Well, we got the order from the insurance company," the worker said, taking off his hardhat. "Prestige Insurance Company."

"That's the company that insured this property. They shouldn't have told you to tear it down yet, and definitely not without my permission."

"We already have all our equipment here. As you can see, we've started the demolition."

"I see that. But you weren't supposed to. There's still testing to be done on this house. You have to leave it intact, exactly the way it was after the fire. You can't just come in and start tearing it apart before the investigation is complete."

"We were told the investigation was complete."

"By who?'

"By..." he checked a pink piece of paper that he pulled from his breast pocket. "By Mr. Marshall Hamilton."

"Well it's not complete. He had no right to tell you that. This is my house, burnt or not, and I still have more investigating of my own do to here before it gets torn down. Once you guys take it down, all evidence regarding this fire is gone. We're not done with that yet."

"That's fine. We can stop work for the day, here, but someone's going to have to reimburse me and my crew for bringing all these machines out here and for all these guys' time."

"Bill the insurance company. It's their mistake, so that's their problem. I don't have any money. This wasn't supposed to happen yet, and certainly not without my permission."

"I'll talk to them. You're right; it's not your fault. If you're the owner, we can't legally tear this structure down without your consent. I was under the impression that this insurance guy had already gotten your signed consent. You may want to have a word with him about this. I'm sure going to."

The worker snorted, pissed off, and turned to his men. "Come on, guys," he shouted to them. "We're outta here for the day. I've got the owner right here and he says we're not supposed to take this place down yet."

      Calvin looked around the neighborhood as he stood in the salt-covered street next to the snow bank lining the edge of his property. All the houses seemed abandoned. As was before, there was no sign of life anywhere. Maybe Calvin was being paranoid, but it almost seemed like the second he pulled up in his truck everyone ran into their houses and closed their blinds.

      He saw some smoke coming from Mrs. Gooding's chimney next door. Her car was out in the driveway. It was unusual for her to leave the car out, especially in such cold weather.

      Calvin didn't know where else to turn. She seemed to be the only person so far who had seen anything at all strange around the time of his house fire, even though her memory was cloudy and vague. Perhaps if he probed further, she could remember something else. At the very least, maybe she could point him in the direction of someone who had seen something.

      He entered her glass-enclosed porch and knocked on the side door of the house.

      There was no answer.

      A plow thundered its way up the street, spreading more salt on the already dry roads. They must be expecting a major snowstorm, Calvin thought.

      He knocked again on the solid wood door. He chuckled at the goofy snowman she had hanging high on the door. It wore earmuffs and boots that had faces of snowmen on them.

      There was still no answer from within and, as far as he could tell, no movement. He leaned his head against the door and listened. He could hear what sounded like voices.

It was commercials. She had the TV on.

Calvin had never known her to watch TV at all, especially during the day. She listened to classical music and sewed. She often said how much she hated TV and that the only reason she even had cable was for her grandchildren when they came to visit.

Calvin twisted the door knob a little. It was unlocked. He pushed it open a crack and yelled inside, "Mrs. Gooding?"

All was quiet inside, besides the TV.

"Mrs. Gooding? Are you in there? It's me, Calvin, from next door."

Still no reply.

Calvin was starting to worry. He had watched out for her since he bought his house seven years earlier, and he had bailed her out of trouble enough times to know when something was wrong.

He swung open the door and entered the kitchen. His boots squeaked across the old linoleum floor. He could see the TV on in the other room. It was some daytime game show.

He saw Mrs. Gooding's silver hair puffed up from the back of the old Victorian arm chair which faced the TV. He couldn't see the rest of her.

"Mrs. Gooding?" Calvin asked, desperately hoping that she had fallen asleep in front of the TV.

As he approached the side of the chair slowly, cautiously, afraid of what he would find, he could see that she was slumped down in the chair, hanging in an unnatural manner with the chair holding her up and in place.

She was motionless. Her face came into view. She was very pale, almost white, outlined with dark patches. Her chest did not move up and down.

Calvin reached out and felt her left wrist. It was ice

cold.

He stepped back and stared at her for a moment, still in shock. He had only seen a dead body at a funeral, after it had been dressed up and had make-up applied, restored to a happier, plastic-looking version of the person when they were alive. She looked horribly sickly, pale, and her skin looked lifeless and stiff.

He pulled out his phone and called 911.

After a few minutes with two local police officers, a third officer, who looked awfully familiar, entered.

"You again," Officer Patton said when he saw Calvin standing in the kitchen. "You haven't been inside that house again, have you?"

"No. No, I just came up here to see what I could find out. They were about to tear down my house."

"Well, the sooner the better. It's an eyesore. And it's really dangerous, being so close to the street and to the other houses."

"It wasn't my idea to tear it down. I had to stop them. The insurance investigator I'm working with told them to go ahead with it."

"Well, I guess they were done with their investigation and wanted to let the town get back to normal."

"But I wasn't done with mine."

"I see."

"I'm having more testing done. I'm paying for it myself, to try to find out what really happened. I don't believe this guy's story for a minute. Something just isn't right."

"I understand you found Mrs. Gooding's body?"

"Yeah. She wouldn't answer the door, so I went

inside to check on her. It wasn't locked."

"Why were you at her door?"

"I had talked to her when I was up here yesterday, when I went inside the house…"

"Yes, I remember. You told me about your conversation with her."

"I wanted to talk to her again about what she saw. She saw *something*. I wanted to see if I could get any more information out of her, anything to help me figure out what might've happened to my house or who could've been involved."

"You told me…she saw a car, right? An unusual car circling the block and parked near your home?"

"Yes."

"And you were saying you think that same car kept driving by where you are living now, in…in, ah…"

"Grave Lake."

"Yes, right. Have you had any more incidents with that vehicle?"

"I'm not sure."

"You're not sure?"

"I thought I was being followed one night…but I can't be sure about that. Our doghouse was set on fire, though, three nights ago."

"Someone lit your dog house on fire?"

"It burned like crazy. There was something put on it, some sort of accelerant. It wasn't just the wood burning. It was incinerated within a few minutes."

"Might've just been some kids," Patton suggested carefully, seeming to be trying his best to take Calvin seriously.

"I didn't get that feeling. But it's possible."

"Did you see anyone around? Hear anything when that happened?"

"No. I was busy putting out the fire. I had the feeling I was being watched, but I didn't see or hear anyone."

"It's very hard to say if there's any sort of connection between your house up here and what has been going on where you're staying on Grave Lake. I wouldn't rule it out, though. I'm going to get in touch with the Grave Lake police department, just in case. Especially since we have a death involved now."

"You don't think there was a connection with my house fire to her dying, do you?"

"No. I don't. But it is an interesting coincidence that she was the only person who seemed to have any information regarding sightings of strangers around your house before the fire, and now she's dead."

"Will they do an autopsy?"

"Looks like natural causes. I don't know if they will. It's up to the family, really."

"I was just talking to her two days ago," Calvin said mournfully. "I shoveled her car out of the snow bank."

"She was old, Calvin. She had been living here alone since I started patrolling this town, and that was over twenty years ago. I've seen lots of old people pass on my watch. I'm going to keep an eye on things for you personally. I highly doubt there is a correlation, but I believe there is reason to at least check it out."

10

It was 5pm Thursday afternoon, the time that Alfred had set up the deposition with the insurance company's attorney. Calvin found the downtown high-rise with his GPS, but quickly realized there was no place to park at all. He ended up on the second story of a packed parking garage two blocks away. He hadn't worn his black dress shoes often and they were less comfortable than he had realized on the long walk, irritating the heel spur on his left foot.

Calvin entered the high rise and took the elevator to the fifth floor. He approached the glass doors with the firm's title, Trident, written across them and tried to open it. It was locked. There was no doorbell. Looking into the office hallway he could see there was no receptionist, either. They must be watching him on camera, he figured. Soon they would notice him and let him in.

Calvin paced for a few minutes anxiously. Nothing was happening. He kept checking the time on his phone. It was past five now, the time they were supposed to all meet. He peered into the office again. There was no one around for him to flag down.

He decided to hit the men's room while he waited. The restroom was overwhelmingly fancy, with classical music playing and mahogany columns around the stalls. There was nothing like hearing the polished notes of Mozart's String Quintets punctuated by random flatulence and urinals flushing.

He admired the way he looked in his suit while he washed his hands at the granite countertop. He looked like a model or a movie star all dressed, quite the contrary to his actual situation. He heard someone enter the restroom behind him and turned his head to say, "Good evening."

"Good evening to you, sir," the man responded in an all-too familiar voice.

Calvin turned around. He would recognize that sweater anywhere. It was Marshall Hamilton.

"How's little Pearl doing?" he asked in a creepy voice that sent chills through Calvin.

"She's good," Calvin replied hesitantly.

"Wonderful," he said with a giant fake smile and headed into one of the stalls.

As soon as Calvin was outside the bathroom he whipped out his cell phone and called his lawyer.

"Alfred," Calvin said.

"Hey, Calvin, what's up?"

"I didn't know that guy I told you about was going to be here."

"Which guy?"

"The investigator. The one with the sweater."

"Oh, yes. Mr. Rogers."

"Yeah. Well he's here. And he's actually wearing the same goddamn sweater."

"No way."

"Yeah. I just didn't think he would be a part of this.

I really don't like the guy."

"What can I say? They can do what they want, and obviously this guy feels he has a reason to be there. The investigation is apparently ongoing, so he may very well be trying to sniff something out."

"Of me?"

"Out of the entire situation."

"I thought this was over," Calvin complained. "I thought they were going to pay my mortgage and give me the money they owe me for a new house."

"Not until they're ready, I'm afraid. And something tells me they're not ready."

"You don't understand...I can't stay where I am for much longer. It's not a good situation, and it's getting worse quickly."

"I know, I'm sorry, but let's just deal with this right now. Please just get here as soon as you can."

"I'm here," Calvin stated.

There was a pause before Alfred asked, "Where?"

"I'm waiting outside the door. I can't get in."

"Outside the door of the building?"

"No, outside the door of the law firm," Calvin said.

"I'm standing outside the door of the law firm right now too," Alfred said, bewildered. "I don't see you."

"I don't see you either."

"I'm looking right at the door with Trident printed on it."

"So am I."

"Well there's no one else here besides me."

"Are we in different dimensions or something?" Calvin asked, starting to feel like he was really losing it. "Did I die on the way over here?"

"There's a receptionist right behind the big glass doors. They aren't locked, Calvin."

"There's no receptionist," Calvin argued. "I can't see anyone inside. It just looks like a hallway."

"Wait a second..." Alfred said. "What floor are you on?"

"Five."

"Okay. I'm on six. That must be a second entrance for them. The firm is two stories."

"Jesus...someone told me it was on the fifth floor. All right, be right up."

The elevator doors opened and Calvin saw Alfred standing there.

"Hey, that's more like it," Alfred said with a laugh.

Alfred stood about the same height as Calvin. He was a few years younger than Calvin, and much heavier. The black suit jacket he wore was ridiculously small on him, exposing the sleeves of his white button-down shirt and allowing his gut to pop out from the middle.

"Suits aren't supposed to go in the dryer, you know," Calvin said.

"Yes...yes," Alfred said, looking down at himself. "I believe I may have gained a few pounds."

They quickly met with the other opposing attorney, Charles Rosen, who had very pale skin and bags under his very pink lower eyelids. He had a rather cold demeanor when meeting them, as if they were just another customer bothering him on a busy day.

They all settled into a conference room, including Marshall Hamilton, who sat next to Mr. Rosen.

"You look absolutely great, today, Calvin," Marshall said to him with an exaggerated grin.

"Thanks." Calvin could sense that the investigator knew he made him uncomfortable. He could also sense that it didn't offend him or even bother him much.

Mr. Rosen, "We already have a lot of information that you gave to Mr. Hamilton, so we won't need to go over that again, thankfully. That will save us sometime today and hopefully we'll be out of here at a reasonable hour."

"That would be nice," Alfred said.

"Now, Calvin, I'm going to ask you some more questions about your house," Mr. Rosen continued. "You owned it for seven years?"

"Yes."

"Did you purchase the home with anyone else?"

"No. I'm the only one on the deed and the mortgage."

"You were working at the time, I take it?"

"Yes."

"What sort of work were you doing?"

"I worked for a mortgage company as a loan officer."

"So you made the appropriate income to cover the mortgage?"

"Yes. It was a stated income mortgage, though, since I worked in sales. With the stated income you didn't have to show that you made enough to actually cover the mortgage, just that you had a job. They don't do those types of loans anymore."

"And with good reason. Were you ever late on your mortgage, before this whole situation with the business going under?"

"No. It was definitely a struggle some months, but I always managed to pay it on time...or at least within the fifteen-day grace period."

"And that is reflected in your credit report. How many vehicles do you own at the moment?"

"Just the one. My SUV."

"You had more than one up until recently, correct?"

"Yes, that's correct. I had a Porsche and a commuter car that I drove back and forth to work."

"Neighbors saw you coming and going?"

"Yes, pretty much every day."

"Your SUV, the only vehicle you drive right now, where did you park that when you were at your house?"

"I always parked in the garage."

"Why?"

"Because I had one. I spent enough years without one to appreciate having it. It blows my mind how people with garages still park outside in the driveway."

"Have you talked to your neighbors since the fire?"

"I talked to my next door neighbor, Mrs. Gooding."

"Did you talk to anyone else while you were up there?"

"No. No one else seemed too interested in talking to me."

"How close were you with your neighbors?"

"I used to be very close with most of them."

"You used to be? Why aren't you close to them now?"

"They all took a bit of a step back from me when my last girlfriend and I broke up. It was a really nasty breakup and I forced her out of the house. It was my house and she wouldn't leave."

"She wouldn't leave?"

"She wasn't paying rent, or contributing to bills, I should say, and she didn't have another place to go. I was okay with her staying there for a while, but she was making my life miserable. She would pick fights with me about anything when I was just trying to mind my own business. Then she started seeing this other guy, some loser, while she was still staying at my house. She would talk to him on the phone in front of me and he'd pick her up outside my house. The cops were called to our house a few times because the fighting got so out of hand. They finally said it would be better if she just found another place to stay."

"She left?"

"She did, but not without ruining my name in town. A lot of people hated me for the way I forced her out of my home, even though she didn't leave me with much of a choice."

"Do you think that she may have had something to do with the fire?"

"No," Calvin said, taken back by the thought of it. "She doesn't have the time or energy to shave her legs, let alone that. And she had another boyfriend instantly anyway, so I don't think she even cared."

"Do you think the boyfriend had something to do with it—some jealousy issues, maybe?"

"I doubt it. No, I don't think so."

"How long ago was the breakup?"

"About two years ago."

"And how long have you been with your current girlfriend?"

"About a year-and-a-half. I started seeing her just a few months after the other relationship ended."

"And now you have a baby together?"

"Yes. She's seven months old."

"How would you describe your relationship with your current girlfriend?"

"Not good."

"Not good? You maintain separate residences?"

"We were."

"You live together now?"

"Yes, for the moment. Until this all gets resolved and I can move on with my life."

"Is there any chance you will continue to live with your girlfriend?"

"Maybe. I doubt it, but maybe."

"Was the pregnancy planned?"

Calvin sighed, getting extremely uncomfortable. "No."

"Did your girlfriend want to have a baby at this point in her life?"

"Yes. She did."

"She was excited about being pregnant?"

"Yes."

"And you were willing to do whatever was necessary to provide for the baby and take care of her?"

"Yes. Of course."

"Interesting... Tell me a little about your business ventures...you bought a business about a year ago?"

"Yes. A restaurant franchise."

"What happened there?"

"The guy who sold it to me committed fraud. The restaurant was hemorrhaging money. I couldn't keep it afloat any longer and had to shut it down."

"How long did you manage to keep it open for?"

"Two months. We have a lawsuit going now against the seller and the broker agency that brokered the deal."

"How did you come up with the money to buy the business?"

"I had been flipping houses before that, and then trading stocks for a while."

"Flipping houses...why did you stop doing that?"

"The market turned. Real estate wasn't selling well, so I switched over to the stock market. Same problem with the stock market about a year later, though."

"Did you do a lot of the work on the houses yourself?"

"I did almost everything myself. Everything except entire-house plumbing jobs and furnaces. And roofs. I'm afraid of heights."

"You hired contractors for those other things?"

"Yes."

"This isn't your background—fixing houses. How did you learn to do all of this?"

"I just taught myself as I went. With each house I picked up more skills."

"You found this to be profitable?"

"Yes. Very profitable, since I paid cash for the houses and did almost all the work myself."

"You paid cash for them?"

"Yes.

"That's a good amount of cash. How did you come up with the cash to pay for your first flip-house?"

"It was a combination of a few things. I had refinanced my mortgage on my main house and took some cash out of it with the new loan. I saved a good amount of money since I had help from my girlfriend at the time with the bills. And I had a minor lawsuit I was part of, a class-action suit for unpaid overtime from a mortgage company that I had worked for."

"So you paid cash for the house, fixed it up, and then listed it for sale?"

"I listed it myself. I figured out a way to get on the Multiple Listing Service for dirt cheap. I sold that first house in three weeks."

"And how much of a profit did you make?"

"About thirty-six thousand dollars."

"And you put that into your next project?"

"Yes."

"How much did you make on the next house you bought and sold?"

"About the same."

Mr. Rosen sifted through the pile of papers in front of him and pulled one out. "We have this list you wrote of contents that were supposedly in the house."

"They *were* in the house."

"Yes...we've had a chance to review this list. I've sat down and spoken with Mr. Hamilton for quite a while about it. It's an interesting list." He looked up at Calvin. "You made this list yourself?"

"Yes. Of course."

"And all these items were in the house at the time of the fire?"

"Yes."

"How do you know that for sure?"

"I was there the night before. Everything was there."

"Every single item on this list was in the house when you left the night before?"

"Yes...well it's impossible to be sure about every single item. I didn't take stock of everything every time I left the house."

"But to the best of your knowledge, the items on the list were there?"

"Yes."

"And you left the house at what time, again?"

"About nine."

"And the fire occurred around five-thirty the next morning. Do you think it's possible that someone broke in and stole all the possessions in the house during that brief time period?"

"I don't know. I suppose it's possible...I don't know."

"Because that seems highly unlikely, that someone could move all those items out without anyone, including your neighbors, seeing anything."

"Yes, that does seem unlikely."

"Did anyone, the police or the fire department, say anything to you about removing pieces of furniture from the home for any reason?"

"No. There were some remnants of things out on the lawn. They said they didn't remove anything intentionally."

"Well, Mr. Hamilton was able to gain access to the entire house after the fire. He was even able to access the second floor, which was much more stable and intact than he at first thought. After doing a thorough search of the house, including the entire upstairs bedrooms and closets, it is his determination that there are no visible remains of the items that you describe in detail on this contents list you gave us. How do you explain that?"

"I don't know."

"In fact, it's Mr. Hamilton's professional opinion that those items were never in the house at all. They simply were not there at the time of the fire. Where did all those things go?"

"I have no idea. They were there when I left."

"Did you sell those items before the fire?"

"No."

"Do you have any gambling debts?"

"No. I don't gamble."

"Do you owe anyone money for anything at all?"

"Just my mortgage. I don't have much debt."

"You have balances on credit cards, I see from your credit report."

"That was only since the business went under. I had racked them up while I was struggling to stay open. There isn't much, though. Only about four-thousand total."

"Did you have a plan to pay that off?"

"Yes. I was making substantial payments out of my

paychecks…up until this happened. Now that plan has been derailed."

"Have you ever had any dealings with drugs?"

"With drugs?"

"Drug deals gone bad?"

"No. No drug deals at all, actually, bad or good. I don't do any sort of drugs. I don't have the time or money."

"But you used to have the time and money."

"Yes, but that's still something I've never been into."

"Do you take any medication for any sort of mental condition?"

"No."

"Have you ever suffered from any mental illness?"

"No. Never."

"Calvin, did you burn your house down?"

"No." Anger took to his face. "No," he said, more forcefully.

"Because, forgive me for saying so, but it certainly appears that you did, to all of us."

"Objection," Alfred rang in.

"Withdrawn," Mr. Rosen answered. "So you owned a business that failed right before the fire occurred?"

"Several months before, not *right* before."

"You lost a business that you had sunk every penny you had into, several months before the fire?"

"Not every penny."

"Answer the question," the Mr. Rosen directed, raising his voice. "You lost nearly all the money you had invested in this business that failed, which was nearly all the money you had to your name?"

"Yes," Calvin answered quietly. "That's correct."

"Your mortgage was in default, was it not?"

"Yes, but I have explained that before to Mr.

Hamilton......"

"But it was in default, correct?"

"Well, yes, but..."

"So your mortgage was not being paid according to the contract signed when you took on the mortgage?" he shook his head obnoxiously, belittling Calvin.

"No, it wasn't being paid..."

"And you weren't currently living there at the time of the fire?"

"No, that's not true. I *was* living there, just not all the time. I work in Albany, so I was commuting back and forth, and with the baby sometimes I ended up staying at my girlfriend's house since it was closer to work..."

"Your 'girlfriend' who you have the baby with?"

"Yes."

"And where, Calvin, are you residing at the present time?"

"I'm staying with my girlfriend for the time being, but..."

"So you were staying there before, and you're staying there now as well?"

"Well, no, I was staying there only occasionally when I had to work early the next morning...it didn't make sense for me to drive all the way back to my house just to sleep, then drive all the way back down to Albany in the morning. Her house is so much closer than mine to work."

"So this has worked out well for you, now, living with your girlfriend?"

"Well, no, not really..."

"But you have a baby together and now you're nice and close to work."

"It's not permanent...she was nice enough to let me stay there for a little while."

"Being her boyfriend."

"No, being the father of her child."

"So, it wouldn't be entirely outlandish to draw the conclusion that the two of you had planned on living together full-time?"

"What? No."

"It certainly appears to us that it made sense. Why were you maintaining separate residences?"

"Because we don't get along. We've never gotten along, but now we have a baby together."

"But even when things have gotten difficult financially for you, after all these hardships, you still maintained your own house—a three-bedroom house, approximately three-thousand square feet—for just you and your dog?"

"Yes. I didn't want to pay for a whole house for just me to live in alone, but it was what I had at the time and I wasn't in any position to switch residences."

"Had you considered selling the house?"

"Yes, but I hadn't gotten there yet. I've had too much going on to mess around with that, and I didn't really know where else to go once I had sold it. I didn't know what to do."

"Well, Calvin, the answer to you 'not knowing what to do' seems all too apparent to us at this juncture. I mean, put yourself in our shoes. Or, for that matter, anyone else's shoes. The facts we've gathered do not paint a pretty picture of you. It doesn't look good at all. Did you consider yourself to be in a desperate situation?"

"Look—no, I wasn't desperate, I wasn't even that overly concerned with the whole thing, and I didn't have anything to do with that house burning down. I don't know what you guys are trying to get at…"

"If you didn't do it, who did?"

"I haven't done anything wrong! I'm here on my

own free will. I'm not on trial and I haven't committed any crime. I paid my damn insurance premium for the last seven years to you people and now that something's actually happened where I need your help, you're treating me like a criminal. I'm your customer, your paying customer. What's the point of having insurance if you're going to do this to people when they have something tragic occur in their lives? My goddamn life has been ruined. This has taken nearly everything from me, and I've had about enough of this." Calvin shoved himself back from the table and stood, ready to walk out.

"Calvin, you understand by leaving this deposition you are failing to cooperate with this investigation," Mr. Rosen warned. "Failing to cooperate will likely lead to your claim being denied in its entirety. And I *will* personally make sure that your claim is denied in its entirety, including the entire replacement value of the house, the demolition, your mortgage payoff, and the contents of the house. Do you understand that?"

Calvin stood at the table for what seemed like an eternity. His heart was pounding. He could feel the heat in his face and knew it was getting red.

Calvin finally slowly sat back down. "Yes. I understand that," he said sullenly.

"Okay, then. Good," said Mr. Rosen, taking a deep breath as he shuffled through the papers in front of him.

"My dog was killed in this fire," Calvin added, his voice more calm now. "I didn't do this. I could never have done that to him."

"No evidence was found of your dog being in the house at the time of the fire," Mr. Rosen stated plainly.

"What?"

"We're not saying the dog wasn't there. All we know is that we did not specifically find a body of the dog in the remains. Only the collar. There was a lot of debris, though, and it does not surprise me that we could not decipher the corpse in all the ash. Tell me, Calvin, you claim you were staying at the house…"

"I *was* staying at the house…"

"Please stop interrupting me," Mr. Rosen shouted. "You need to stop interrupting me when I am speaking. So you *were* staying at the house. Did you eat when you were at the house?"

"What?"

"Did you eat when you were at the house?"

"Did I eat?"

"Yes."

"Of course I ate."

"Can you tell me why the refrigerator was practically bare inside?

"I don't keep a lot of food. I lived alone, so I usually just ate out, or grabbed something on the way home from work."

The lawyer paused for a moment. He had the expression of someone who had just lost a game of chess, but was doing his best not to let it show on his face. Mr. Rosen regrouped himself, and then continued methodically, "So you were late on your mortgage. You just had a business that failed miserably, leaving you flat broke. You have a baby to take care of and a 'girlfriend' who has her own house, which you're now living in with her. You gave us a list of items in the house which simply were not there. The house was bare. And now you're having your own independent testing done on the house by someone you hired? Is there anything else you would like to add, along with the results of that test? Perhaps a signed statement of confession?"

Calvin glared at him.

"I believe that will be all for today," the Mr. Rosen said, gathering his papers and shoving them into his briefcase. "We'll be in touch with our 'decision' on your coverage."

Mr. Rosen said to Marshall, on his way past him, "Nice to see you again, Mr. Hamilton. Until next time."

"Always a pleasure," Marshall said to him as Mr. Rosen walked out of the room without acknowledging Calvin or Alfred.

Marshall rose from his seat. There were no papers for him to gather. He shoved his hands into his pockets and said, with his usual fake smile, "See, Calvin? I told you we'd be keeping an eye on you."

"Calvin, hang on a second," Alfred said to him as they left the building together, motioning for him to come closer.

"Yeah?"

"I need to talk to you about this for a minute," Alfred said in a somewhat hushed tone, being mindful of the people passing by.

"That went well, Alfred. Don't you think?" Calvin said sarcastically.

"Yes...yes, indeed," Alfred said, clearly troubled. "That didn't go well at all, Calvin. That was not what I expected."

"What am I supposed to do now?"

"I don't know, Calvin."

"What do you mean, you don't know? You're the lawyer, here."

"I *am* a lawyer. I'm a *good* lawyer, Calvin. But this is beyond my abilities. It is beyond my experience."

"What are you trying to say?"

"I'm trying to say that I'm not going to be able to represent you in this matter any longer."

"What? You're dropping my case?"

"I don't have much of a choice."

"Is this about the money? I'll get you the money that I owe you..."

"It's not about the money. Although I will have to charge you for today. Keep that in mind. I expect payment for services rendered. And your tab has added up to about four-thousand dollars now, on this case and your franchise lawsuit. I don't mean to sound like a debt collector, but you do still owe me all that money."

"I'll get you your money," Calvin said, frustrated and a little disgusted with him. "And I'll get you the money for whatever else you do for me on this insurance case. Just don't drop the case. *Please*."

"It's not the money, Calvin. I don't feel that I can appropriately represent you on this matter. I don't feel competent. It's for your own good, really. I'm sorry."

"I can't believe this. You're bailing on me."

"I'm sorry, Calvin. I have failed you as an attorney. You need to get someone with much more experience than I have, or, I hate to say this, you are in some pretty deep shit."

11

"Hey, it's me," Calvin said into the phone while driving down a country road in the dark.

"Hi," Leah answered. "Where are you?"

"On my way home. About another ten minutes.

"Honey, it's daddy," Leah said to Pearl in the background. "You're on speaker. Say goodnight to her."

"Hi, sweety. Hi, baby. Daddy loves you. I miss you."

"She's reaching for the phone and smiling," Leah said with a giggle.

"That's my little daddy's girl. I'm surprised she's not asleep yet. It's late."

"Yeah. What's up with that? How did it go?"

"Oh, you don't want to know," Calvin said with a sigh.

"Not good?"

"No. Not good at all. I feel sick to my stomach."

"What happened?"

"They think I did it, Leah. They think I burnt my own house down and I'm committing insurance fraud."

"What? They actually said that to you?"

"Yup."

"I thought this meeting tonight was supposed to settle all this," she complained.

"That's what I thought, too."

"I thought this was the end...you said this was the fastest way to settle this. Your lawyer told you that."

"They don't want to settle it," Calvin said. "They want to not pay me anything."

"But that's ridiculous. You have insurance. This is *why* you have insurance."

"I feel like I'm going to throw up. This is like a living nightmare."

"What did your lawyer..." Leah's sentence was cut off by a sharp clicking sound.

"Are you still there?" Calvin asked.

No reply came.

"Leah? Are you still there? Did I lose you?" Calvin checked the display on his phone. The call had been disconnected.

He became aware of the headlights behind him. He had no idea how long a car had been behind him on this road and he wondered how he hadn't noticed it earlier. The headlights were strangely familiar, although it was nearly impossible to recognize any headlights behind him in the dark. He thought back to the other day with the headlights that wouldn't leave his rearview no matter how many turns he made.

He checked his phone for signal. He had four out of five bars, which was unusual for these back roads. He thumbed down to Leah's number and tried her back again.

Her phone rang several times without answer.

Calvin eyed the headlights behind him. They were keeping a considerable distance from his bumper, a little further than most drivers deem necessary. There was something odd about the way they followed him around every turn, something peculiar about how the distance was always constant, as though the driver was trying to avoid suspicion.

Calvin shook it off. Even *he* felt he was being paranoid now. It made him wonder if it really was him all along. How much of what was going on was in his head? He had been so stressed with everything. His life was falling apart. Maybe this was his version of a mental breakdown.

Leah's phone went to voicemail. He dialed it again. It didn't seem like she was ready to end the conversation. She had hung up on him many times in their two-year relationship, but usually it was fairly obvious why she hung up and he always felt it coming. If her phone disconnected she would instantly call him back, usually at least two or three times, playing phone tag as they tried to redial each other at the same time.

Her phone rang until it went to voicemail.

Calvin flicked on his blinker and gently slowed to make a left onto a shortcut he sometimes took. A few seconds after accelerating down that road, he noticed the headlights behind him reappear in the darkness.

He refused to let himself be paranoid about the car behind him this time. It was just someone driving home from work. The odds *were* against someone driving the exact same way as him, sure, but it had happened before.

He did have the right, though, to take a different path home tonight, he decided. *That* wasn't being paranoid. It was being *adventurous*, trying to mix things up in his boring daily routine. There was nothing weird about that.

He braked quickly to take a sharp right that caught his eye. He knew it would get him where he wanted to go, even if it did take a minute longer. The scenic route.

The headlights followed a moment later.

Calvin struggled to remain calm. He could feel his blood pressure rising. The SUV rumbled over some jagged pavement, vibrating his white knuckles on the steering wheel.

Calvin had always accelerated in Math in school, and he was mentally calculating what the odds were of some random driver taking exactly the same route as him at the exact same time of night. Then throw in the fact that the car behind him was one of only two vehicles he had seen in the last ten minutes.

Calvin's foot hit the brake and he shot up another snaking desolate road. This time he would know for certain. This road didn't lead in the same direction. It led right back to where they he had just come from. It made no sense for him to drive it, and it would make even less sense for the person behind to follow.

All was black behind him. He realized how heavy his heart was pounding and how agitated he had become.

Then he saw a few tree trunks light up as he rounded a turn. The headlights smoothly glided up behind him again, keeping their respectable distance but on him like glue.

"*Come on,*" Calvin yelled to himself in frustration, slamming his palms on the steering wheel. He didn't know what to do. He couldn't lead this person back to his home, to his baby, if they didn't already know where he was living. He couldn't keep driving around in circles forever. It was getting late and he was running low on gas. He wanted nothing more than to get home and get something to eat. He was starving and his blood sugar was dropping. He thought about leading the car back to the city area to lose him, but that would take him another ten minutes just to get there, and then there was no guarantee he would lose whomever was following him.

His fear and stress were turning into adrenaline-fueled anger. He had had enough of this game and he wasn't going to play anymore.

The road was pitch-black without even a road sign in sight. There was no moon visible and there was absolutely no one around.

He didn't care. He jerked the SUV off the road onto the gravel shoulder. The tires skipped a little and the traction control buzzed as he slid.

If this guy wanted to play with him out here in the middle of nowhere on one of the worst days of his life, with no witnesses in sight, then Calvin would be more than happy to lay his ass out. It was the wrong day to mess with him.

The headlights stayed their constant distance behind and slowed to a stop in the road. They lingered maybe a hundred feet back, waiting for him to continue.

Calvin remained on the shoulder and threw on his right turn signal.

The car behind waited.

"*What the hell*," Calvin growled to himself, letting his temper go wild. "*What the hell are you doing! Go!*"

The headlights refused to budge.

Calvin lowered his window and waved his arm out frantically for the car to pass around him and continue on its way.

Silence.

Calvin stuck his head out the window and screamed out the window, much louder than he expected, "Let's go! Go around!"

The headlights sat perfectly still.

And then Calvin lost it.

He whipped his door open so violently that it

sprung back and nearly closed again. He went to lunge out of the truck and got snagged on the seatbelt, which he furiously fumbled with until he unlatched it.

"*Hey*!" Calvin shouted as he tore out of the truck. "What the fuck are you doing!"

No answer came.

Calvin stormed just a few steps quickly towards the car and shouted, "Come on!" He flailed his arms out furiously.

He could hear the car idling as he stood illuminated in its headlights. He knew the driver could see him clearly, and surely could see the ferociousness on his face.

But still no answer came.

The car sat perfectly still, waiting for Calvin to either approach it or to continue on his way so it could follow.

Calvin let his arms fall to his side. His expression faded from anger to concern. This was not at all the reaction he had expected. He expected to exchange words, maybe even have a fist fight. He would have loved a fist fight at that moment. But this was far, far more daunting.

He had no idea who was in that car. He had no idea how many people were in that car. He certainly had absolutely no clue why he was being followed.

What he did know was that the driver was not going to leave the vehicle. The driver was forcing him to approach, blinded by its headlights while whoever was in the car watched his every move as he walked up. What if the person had a gun and was waiting to blow his brains out when he came near?

The 'old' Calvin almost certainly would have blown his fuse and rushed right up to that car in the dark. He would have put his fist right through that driver's window. Things had changed now, and it was the thought of his adorable little girl calling him 'dada' that made him stop in his tracks and let his anger go.

It did more than calm him, though. It made him *afraid*.

With all his anger now dissipated, Calvin stepped backward to his truck and swung himself up into the seat, all the while keeping those headlights in the corner of his eye. He closed his door, put the truck in drive, and pulled off of the gravel shoulder onto the road.

After a moment, the headlights followed again behind him.

"Oh, shit..." he muttered to himself. "Oh shit, oh shit, oh shit..."

Calvin was trembling now. His foot stomped down the gas pedal to the floor.

The truck's engine roared and hurled him forwards down the curving road at an alarming pace.

The car behind kept pace with him, but no longer kept its distance. Those headlights were riding up Calvin's tail, so close he almost couldn't see the lights, just the top of the windshield and the roof of the car.

The truck's tires screeched around the bends in the road, frantically trying to hang on and keep the large vehicle upright. This was not the Porsche he used to drive. He knew the SUV had its limitations and was not meant for aggressive driving like this, but he had lost control of his senses and could only think of evading his pursuer.

The SUV sloppily slid around a sharp curve in the road. Calvin could feel the steering wheel losing effect on the tires, but kept his foot glued to the floor.

There was a sudden jolt from behind.

Calvin yelped. He had been hit. He caught a flicker of the headlights behind him swerving for a moment, and then coming back under control.

The truck's tail slid out. Calvin cranked the wheel to try to keep it straight, but its unwieldy weight had shifted too far.

He found himself on his right two wheels, flying off the road. There was a quick flash in his headlights of brush and trees.

He slammed to a stop with a brain-pounding thud. His body had been jerked forward like a rag doll against the safety belt.

All went quiet.

Calvin lifted his head and looked around, surprising himself by how little he was fazed physically by what just happened. He immediately checked his arms, legs, and fingers for problems. He felt all over himself for the warm wetness of blood. He seemed fine.

The force of the impact had thrown a hammer from the trunk up into the dashboard. His seatbelt had restrained him perfectly. He couldn't believe that it didn't hurt at all where it had absorbed all the shock of the impact.

He looked in his mirror, then out every window of the truck. The car following him was nowhere to be seen.

His own headlights still illuminated the brush in front of him, but there was no sound from his engine. He turned the key in the ignition. It cranked and the headlights dimmed, but the engine didn't fire up.

He unlatched his seatbelt and stepped out of the truck with his phone. Crickets and other unknown bugs chirped and hummed all around him, but there was no sign of anyone around.

He opened the back door on the driver's side, reached under the seat and pulled out a crowbar. He swiveled around, paranoid, as he pulled his phone from his pocket and dialed Leah.

There was still no answer on her end. The second

two attempts also failed to be answered. He called 911.

"Yes, someone just ran me off the road and I crashed into a tree," he said to the overly calm operator. "Yes, I'm okay, I think. But my car's not. I'll need a tow truck, or something. No, I have no idea where I am."

"Sadie," Calvin said into his phone from the tow station's waiting room. "Hey, I'm sorry to call you so late…it's an emergency."

"Calvin—what's up?"

"I need a lift. I wrecked my car."

"Oh my god…are you okay?"

"I'm fine. I just can't get a hold of Leah. I've been trying for two hours now and she won't answer her damn phone."

"That's not like her."

"No, it's not. I normally can't get her to stop calling me. Even if she's pissed at me, she'll call me to tell me how pissed she is. I'm sorry to bother you, but I didn't know who else to call. No one else I know lives out this way."

"No problem…just give me a few minutes to get myself together and I'll be there as soon as I can…actually, I'll just throw on a coat and head there in my pajamas. Where are you?"

"I'm at Karnie's Garage," Calvin said. "Do you know it?"

"Oh, yeah. Pass by it every day. I know exactly where you are. I'll be there in a few. You're sure you're okay?"

"I'm okay. Thanks."

As Sadie's car pulled up under the lights of the

towing station, Calvin couldn't help but notice that it resembled the car he had seen circling the block at Leah's house. It didn't exactly match, but then again it looked a lot different in the light than in the dark.

He shook off that thought. It did look like the car that had been circling the block, but it also looked like hundreds of other cars out on the road of similar shape and size. He needed to calm his imagination. He was becoming irrational and directing his fear and stress onto those closest to him.

He knew she had gotten the car just a few months ago. She was so happy just to have something that started every time without her having to get under the hood.

"Hey, Sadie," he said as he sat down next to her and closed his door. "Thank you so much...you have no idea."

"Hey, no problem," she said warmly. "So what happened?"

"Someone ran me off the road," Calvin said with fear in his voice. "I think someone's trying to kill me. For real."

"Did you talk to the police?"

"Yeah, I filled out a police report while I was getting towed. There wasn't much for them to go on, though. I didn't get a license plate or even really saw what the car looked like. It's pretty much hopeless."

"No one saw anything?"

"I was in the middle of nowhere. There was no one else for miles around. Just me and this psycho that chased me and ran me off the road. He actually hit the back of my truck."

"Well there should be something there then," she said. "On the back of your truck—a scuffmark or dent..."

"Nothing," Calvin said hopelessly. "There are scuffmarks and dents, but you can't even tell what was from what. I looked at it myself and couldn't tell which one the car made tonight. It didn't do much damage, apparently. Just enough to push my back-end out and make me fishtail off the road."

"How fast were you going?"

"I don't know," Calvin said. "Fast. Fast enough that I couldn't keep the truck on the road. I was being chased."

"You have no idea who could've done it?"

"None. After I explained the incident to the cops and gave the best description I could, the one was like, 'Ah, could you be any vaguer?' They don't have a clue where to start, and they're probably not going to start. It was a set of headlights in the dark on a back country road with no witnesses. If they even had a description of the vehicle, they would have *something* to go on."

"So you have no idea who the other driver could've been?" she asked him.

"No. Not really."

"Did you do something to piss him off, like pass him or cut him off or something?"

"No," he said, shaking his head. "Nothing like that."

"I've heard stories about people totally flipping out and chasing down drivers because they had their high beams on and didn't shut them off when they passed…crazy fucks."

"No, nothing like that. I was being followed."

"Followed?"

"For a while," he said. "It wasn't the first time, either. Just the first time something happened."

"Why? Who would be following you?"

"I'm not sure," he said. "Look, there's a lot more going on in my life than you realize right now, a lot more than anyone at work realizes. I just try to keep my personal life personal, even about something like this. I try to keep it out of work, you know, so that I can just go there and work…well, not anymore."

"Calvin, someone followed you and basically tried to kill you. You're obviously in danger. Is there anyone in your life who would be doing this to you? Or even anyone who you had a chance encounter with, that didn't go so well?"

Calvin chuckled and held his forehead in his palm. "Yeah, lately I seem to make enemies pretty quickly. I don't think any of them would ever take things to this extreme, though."

"Like who? What enemies have you made recently?"

"Oh, like the guy who sold me the business. Jake Caruso. He's one. I've told you about the lawsuit, right?"

"Yeah."

"Well, he's in a heap of trouble. I've got him on fraud. The best case scenario for him is that I win the lawsuit and basically take every penny he has to his name, including his house."

"Well, I could imagine he's pretty upset with you at this point."

"Yeah, well, he had it coming. He committed a crime and now he's going to pay for it, even if it messes up his life. He messed up mine, that's for sure. Right when Leah and I were having our baby."

"Do you think it was him following you?"

"No. I thought about it, but I seriously doubt it. He's not the type. He has a wife, kids, and dog that keep him plenty busy. His job he's working now has him running seven days a week. I can't imagine him finding the time to mess with me and follow me places. It wasn't his car, anyway. I could tell that much by the headlights. It wasn't his wife's or his kids' car either. I know that for sure. He would never take it to this level, either, no matter what I did to him. This was something scary…something very psychotic. It felt evil to me…it's hard to explain."

"How do you mean?" Sadie asked.

"Both times the car followed me it seemed very premeditated, thought-out. The way the car drove and followed me, and then sat there motionless and soundless when I stopped and got out of my truck. There was no emotion—that's it. There was no anger, no temper flaring. It was as though this person was very calmly and rationally carrying out a plan. Not what I would expect from someone furious enough with me to do something like this."

"Is there anyone else you can think of?"

"The broker on the deal, too. Because of my lawsuit against their broker agency, the broker who handled the sale of the business, this guy Davis, got fired. He was caught falsifying my signature on a document. He's the reason that the broker agency will most likely be found responsible. If it wasn't for that forged signature, I wouldn't have a thing on them. And he's been calling me obsessively."

"Davis?"

"Yeah. And then he even followed me out to the lake—to the Pizza Shack, to try to talk to me."

"Jesus, Calvin…Sounds like you've pissed off a lot of people lately."

"I can't seem to *not* piss people off lately. But I'm not one to lie down and take that sort of thing. I get back on my feet and fight. And the thing is, even if something happened to me, that lawsuit will still go on. The seller of the business is still guilty of criminal charges, even if I'm out of the picture. It just doesn't really make sense to me why they would do that. It's not worth it to any of them just for revenge." Calvin took a deep breath and sighed. He lowered his head and rubbed his temples. "I'm just really worried about Leah."

"Have you talked to her since you called me?"

"No. I can't get her on her phone," Calvin said, panicked. "She won't pick up; it just rings and goes to voicemail. It's killing me. She's home alone there with my baby and I almost just got killed. What if someone is at the house with her?"

"I'll get you there soon. Don't worry."

"What if while someone was following me, someone else was at the house with them? What if the person following me was trying to keep me away from the house?"

"Calvin, I get it, but you need to calm down. You don't know that anything is going on at home. You haven't talked to her."

"What am I supposed to do now? What if someone is waiting for me now every time I leave the house, waiting to finish the job? They meant to kill me, I'm pretty sure of that. I think they'll come back for me."

"Do a lot of people know where Leah's house is?" Sadie asked.

"No. Not too many. She's not listed online or anything."

"Who knows that you stay there?"

"Just close friends, I guess," Calvin said. "There's no way for anyone else to know I'm there. Unless they follow me home."

"Have you been followed more than just today and the other day?"

"Not that I've noticed."

"Is it possible someone followed you all the way home to Leah's house without you realizing it?"

"Yeah, I guess it's possible. I'm usually pretty

observant when I'm driving. But yeah, someone could have followed me for most of the trip without me noticing if they hung back a ways and I was busy on my phone or playing with the radio."

The wheels rumbled onto the gravel as Sadie pulled into the driveway in front of the cottage. All appeared quiet. A few lights were on inside, making the little house glow eerily like a pumpkin in the dark.

"I don't see anything unusual," Sadie said.

They both got out of her car and quickly made their way down the stone path to the front door.

The door swung open right as they reached it, startling Calvin and making Sadie jump back a step.

Leah stood in the doorway, glaring at him.

"Leah," Calvin said with great relief. "Leah, I was so worried."

"Where the hell have you been?" she snapped at him.

"You don't even want to know."

She looked past him to Sadie and, in a rather accusing tone, said, "Hello, Sadie."

"Hi," Sadie answered timidly.

"Where's the baby?" Calvin asked.

"She's asleep. Would you mind keeping it down? She's been really cranky and I finally got her to sleep. I'll be pretty annoyed if she wakes up again. So where were you this whole time?"

"My car went off the road. Somebody hit me."

"Are you okay?" Leah asked, sounding rather insensitive. She was obviously still very much bothered by Sadie's presence.

"Yeah. I'm fine, just shaken up," he answered.

"Where's your car?"

"It's in the shop now. It wasn't drivable the way it

was. That's why Sadie drove me home. She was the only person I could get a hold of who lived out this way…"

"She was the *only* person you could reach?" Leah asked accusingly. "How many people did you try calling?"

"Well, just her," Calvin said timidly. "But she's the only one who lives out this way. You know that."

"Why didn't you call *me*?"

"I tried," he said defensively. "You weren't answering. I was scared to death. I tried you like twenty times and you wouldn't answer, and meanwhile someone was out there running me off the road. I had no idea what was going on here, if someone was here trying to hurt you or the baby."

"Why would someone be here?" Leah asked. "What does that have to do with the accident?"

"It has to do with it because it wasn't an accident," Calvin said. "That was no accident."

"You think someone intentionally ran you off the road and wrecked your car?"

"I know for a fact that someone hit the back of my car to try to knock me off the road."

"Oh, okay," Leah said, obviously not buying his story yet. "And was Sadie in your car with you when this happened?"

"What? No. Why would you even say that?"

"Oh, I don't know, you just mysteriously show up with her at my door and give me some wild story about someone intentionally hitting your truck and making you crash."

"Someone tried to kill me," Calvin said with both fear and anger in his voice, offended by the way she was reacting.

"Where did that happen?"

"Out in the middle of nowhere. Down some back

road near Wynantskill. I don't know for sure."

"What were you doing all the way out there?"

"Trying to lose whoever was following me."

"The person who ran you off the road and tried to kill you?"

"Yes."

"Excuse me," Leah said to Calvin and looked past him to Sadie. "Sadie, if you don't mind, I think it would be best if Calvin came inside and settled down a bit. Apparently he's had some excitement tonight and I think we need to figure some things out together."

"No, I understand," Sadie said, stepping back from the doorway. "You just take care, Calvin. Be safe."

Calvin nodded to her and she headed up the stone path to her car.

"I just don't understand you sometimes," Leah said to Calvin. "I try and I try, and I'm so patient and understanding with you…"

"You're not patient at all with me, and you're the least understanding person I've ever been with. You have no idea what I've been through tonight."

"You know, I don't even care, Calvin. I've just had enough of this. I'm getting sick of hearing what people at work are constantly saying about you and Sadie, and hearing them tell me what you said about me…"

"I don't say anything about you at work…"

"Bullshit! People tell me things."

"Who?"

"People there I trust. They tell me things about you, and how you always spend so much time with Sadie and the way you look at her. How you 'admire' her so much. How about 'admiring' me for a change? I'm the mother of your child. We have a baby together, Calvin. And I've had it with this ridiculousness."

"This isn't fun and games here, Leah. And this isn't about Sadie. There's something going on and you're not listening to me."

"You're delusional, Calvin, you're so delusional if you think this is all really happening to you. Why can't you see how much I love you? Why can't you embrace how hard I try to please you?"

"You're not even hearing what I'm saying."

"Things have been stressful since the baby came along. Well, since we found out about the baby. But I've never changed the way I felt about you. I know I'm difficult to be around sometimes and my temper is pretty bad and my body doesn't look the way it used to. But that's your fault! You did this too, so don't blame me for the way things are between us."

"This isn't about us right now."

"It never is."

"This really isn't about us. There's something wrong and someone is really trying to hurt me—and maybe you, too."

"What would someone possibly have to gain by hurting you, Calvin?"

"I don't know."

"You're not worth someone going to jail over, Calvin," she said in a snotty, insulting tone. "You don't *have* anything. You have *nothing*…"

"I know!" he shouted in her face. "I don't need you to tell me what a loser I am right now. I'm just trying to figure out why someone did this to me, and you're making things a hundred times worse, so just stop!"

The sound of a crying baby silenced them both.

"Great," Leah commented, throwing her arms up. "You had to go and yell and wake the baby up."

"You were yelling a lot louder than I was."

"No, I wasn't," she argued. "It's always someone else's fault, isn't it? And now I'm going to be up all night with her, because you're a paranoid schizophrenic who can't control his temper."

"I can't deal with you right now," Calvin said, closing his eyes and holding his head. "Just…please, just get away from me."

"I *am*," she announced loudly. "I'm getting my daughter."

A minute later, the baby's crying quieted as Leah soothed her in the living room.

"She wants to be rocked," Calvin said to her, his voice calmed down. "Here, let me," he reached out to take the baby from her.

Leah reluctantly gave the baby to Calvin, refusing to look at him.

Calvin took Pearl in his arms and rocked her. He held her tightly and closely as he spun around the room. She closed her eyes and yawned.

"I'm sorry," Leah said with tears in her eyes. "I've just been really depressed lately."

"Misery loves company."

"And I feel like shit about myself. I hate pretty much everything about myself, and I hate what I've done with my life at this point. Except her, of course. There are just so many pretty girls out there. I see them flirting with you, and they're always looking at you and trying to get your attention. And here I am, stuck here with a baby and a gut I can't get rid of, while you look better than you ever have…it isn't fair."

"Leah…"

"I get really scared about losing you. I need you to be a part of my life, and most importantly a part of hers. What would happen if you weren't around? I don't know what I'd do. I couldn't imagine living without you." She gave him a kiss on the cheek. "I would do anything to make things work between us."

12

"Leah, I found it!" Calvin yelled to her in the kitchen. "I got it!"

"What did you find?"

"My watch!"

"What watch?"

"My grandfather's watch. The one that was in the house fire…here it is! Come look."

Leah walked over casually, trying not to roll her eyes or appear bored. The baby squirmed in her arms. She had been extremely cranky that evening and her mood had obviously taken its toll on Leah.

"All right, I'm coming," she said as she bent over to look over Calvin's shoulder. "Is this what you've been doing all day?"

"That's it. That's my watch."

"How do you know?"

"Because that's it! Look at it!"

"It does look a lot like the one you had," she said encouragingly and shrugged her shoulders. "I never really looked too much at the watch you lost, so I can't say for sure. It does look like it, though."

"That's because it *is* it."

"All right, okay, relax."

"This is kind of a big deal," he said, a little annoyed by her lack of enthusiasm. "This is the watch that was supposedly lost in the fire, never to be seen again—just like the rest of my furniture and all my other expensive things. And here it is."

"I just don't know how you can say for sure that that is your watch, Calvin."

"It's identical. It has to be it."

"Well I don't think yours was the only one in existence. There are a lot of those floating around out there."

"And what are the odds that this one would happen to turn up for sale online right after I lost it in a house fire?"

"You don't know how long it was for sale," she said.

"No...I don't, but the odds of it being for sale in this same area...it can't be a coincidence. It just can't."

"Stranger things have happened. But yeah, I guess I see your point. The watch had to have gone somewhere..."

"Along with the rest of the furniture."

"Yes, well, a lot of the other things are explainable," Leah said. "It was a hot fire, the whole place got trashed and everything got blown around."

"That nightstand that it was in weighed a good hundred pounds," Calvin contended. "There's no way a hose blast could blow it out of the room upstairs."

"But if it did, or somehow it came out and landed on the lawn, then the watch would be fair game for anyone walking by, including the firemen and police. What would they care, since they'd figure it's already considered lost."

"There's no way it came out. It's impossible."

"So someone went in there after the fire, probably during the night, and somehow got up to the second story and took the watch out."

"And all the furniture, half-burnt?" Calvin asked.

"It's possible."

"It's far more likely that the watch and furniture were removed before the fire, since there was absolutely no sign that they had been in there. There were no door hinges, no pieces of dresser or bed, no remains of mattresses, there was nothing but bare carpet under all the debris from the roof."

"So, even if that is your watch, so what?" Leah said uninterestedly. "So someone stole your watch at some point. You're covered by your insurance policy for all that stuff, so just let them know it was in there."

"Leah...that's the problem. I didn't tell you about this yet because I didn't want to freak you out. The fact that things were missing from the house after the fire, or before the fire, is a major problem with the insurance company."

"They told you this already?"

"Yes. They did," Calvin said somberly. "They said that it will probably result in the claim being denied, and possibly worse."

"What's possibly worse?"

"I don't know for sure. It doesn't look good though, for me. It's easy for them to look at it as insurance fraud, plain and simple, and Alfred said they'll often try to make a connection to the fire itself."

"Do you mean arson?" she asked with fear in her eyes.

"Yes."

"But Calvin, you didn't do anything wrong, right?"

"Of course I didn't," he declared. "Of course I didn't. I'm worried, though about how this is looking."

"It doesn't paint a very good picture for you."

"No."

"Can't Alfred help you with this?"

"Alfred dropped my case."

"What? When?"

"After the deposition."

"What are you supposed to do, then?" she asked.

"For starters, figure out who has my watch and why they have it. Alfred said I had better find *something* to explain what's going on here. This watch online is the best thing that I could have found. If there's any reason why I can tell it's not my watch in person, then I'll give up on that and just hope that someone else saw something happening that night."

"Wait...when you see it in person?" she asked incredulously. "You're actually going to meet up with this person who you think stole your watch?"

"Yes."

"What if it's someone you know?"

"Then I'll know," he said plainly.

"This just seems crazy, Calvin..."

"I figure that even if it's just some random person who came across it, at least it's some proof that I didn't just make up the contents of the house."

"And you think the person is just going to give the watch back to you, assuming it is actually yours, without any proof at all on your part?"

"I'll take care of it."

"What does that mean?"

"It means I'll take care of it," he repeated. "If that is actually my watch, then I'll get it back one way or another."

"Calvin, I don't like the sound of this at all," she warned him.

"You're making way too much of it."

"It sounds dangerous to me."

"Well I don't have much of a choice at this point, now do I?"

She sighed and shook her head. "I don't like this, Calvin," she said in a lowered voice as she headed into the bedroom.

Calvin drove Leah's car towards a location he had not been before. He took her car after she was home with Pearl. He told her he needed to get out. As usual, it was an argument, since she had worked all day and didn't appreciate being left alone with the baby as soon as she got home. He had been cooped up in that tiny house too long, though, and his insecurities and paranoia were eating him alive. Despite offending Leah, he knew it was best that he get out of the house for a while. And something in the back of his mind had been bothering him.

Calvin let his GPS guide him towards the address of the man who sold him the failed business, Jake Caruso. Calvin found his address on the court paperwork from his lawsuit against Jake. Calvin didn't know exactly why he was heading there or what purpose it would serve. He just knew that he had to see who this man really was and how he lived—and how much money could be extracted from him in the lawsuit.

When Calvin finally turned onto the suburban street that the GPS told him was his destination, he was surprised to see Jake Caruso right outside of his house, spreading salt on his driveway. Calvin kept his speed constant. He was in Leah's car, so he knew that Jake wouldn't recognize it.

The sight of Jake's lovely house made Calvin's blood boil. It wasn't a mansion, by any means, but it was a very upscale home, a picture of suburban perfection. Calvin knew it was his money that was funding that pretty house. His anger grew as he thought about how he and Leah couldn't afford the special formula that Pearl needed, all because of this man.

Jake picked up a shovel on the ground next to him and began chipping away at a spot of ice. The garage door was open. Calvin could clearly see the vehicles inside. On the right was a fairly new minivan. On the left side was a white sedan. Calvin did a double-take at the sedan on the left side. It didn't look exactly like the one he had seen so many times in the dark, but he could only see the back end and most of it was hidden in the garage. The taillights were sleeker and wider. It appeared to be a newer car than the one that had been following him.

Jake looked up from what he was doing, noticing the car passing his driveway. He nonchalantly waved, only half-looking at the car, perhaps assuming it was a neighbor at first but then realizing he didn't recognize it. He went back to working on his driveway.

Calvin wondered what was going through his mind as he chipped away at his driveway in the freezing cold. Was he terrified about the impending lawsuit and the inevitable decision that a court would make? Did he just not care? Maybe he thought he had a way to weasel out of it.

Calvin thought about stopping the car and getting

out. He thought about walking right up to that asshole and landing a haymaker into his jaw.

He calmed himself. It would all be settled in court. If he took any action on his own against Jake, it would only compromise his case.

Calvin wondered, though, if that was indeed Jake outside Leah's house at night. While Jake kept up the façade of living the perfect life, the suburban dream, Calvin knew his life was about to be destroyed. Jake must have known it, too. The more he thought about it, Calvin realized that the white car in the garage was very similar to the one stalking him. In fact, he was becoming quite certain, as he drove home, that it was the same car.

13

Calvin rode in Sadie's car with her, listening to Neil Young singing "Rockin' in the Free World". She dangled her cigarette out the cracked window on her side as she sang along. Smoking cigarettes was definitely not a quality that Calvin found attractive in a girl, but as much as he hated to admit it, it did give her a certain level of coolness and confidence. Even the way her silver bracelet dangled around her thin, feminine wrist while ashing her cigarette attracted him. Every square inch of her seemed almost too good to be real—or at least far too good for him.

"So where exactly are we meeting this guy, again?" Calvin asked, letting his eyes shamefully roam her cleavage when he was fairly sure that she wouldn't notice him staring. Her skin was so milky and impossibly soft in appearance; it was a torturous tease.

"The village plaza," she replied, taking a drag on her cigarette and leaning towards her window to blow the smoke out. "I know pretty much where it is. It's very public."

"Well it's a lot of money he expects to get and he has a watch that's very valuable. I don't blame him." Calvin smelled traces of her perfume, or possibly her deodorant, mixed with the cigarette smoke that had blown into the car.

"He sounded like a bit of a weirdo when I talked to him," Sadie said, seeming a little bothered.

"What was his voice like?"

"Deep. Really deep, like he was using some sort of voice altering device, like you hear on TV when a person wants to remain anonymous."

"You didn't recognize the voice at all?"

"No. It didn't even sound similar to anyone I know. And he was insistent on meeting at night."

"At night? Did he give a reason why?"

"No. He finally said he'd do it during the day, but I could tell he really didn't want to. I wasn't about to encounter this guy in the dark."

"I can't wait to see this guy."

"You're not going to, like, run out and deck him, are you?"

"Not unless it's someone I know. If I recognize this guy then his ass is mine."

"Do you think it was one of your neighbors?"

"Could be."

"Or one of the cops, maybe. Or even one of the

firefighters."

"It's possible. No matter what, though, I want to make sure that it really is my watch. Otherwise, I have nothing. I want to be sure of it first."

"Yeah. You don't want to go assaulting innocent people for no reason, crazy man," she said with a smile.

"You have no idea how crazy I feel lately."

"What you've been through is enough to make anyone a little nuts. You're fine. I think you're keeping a very level head through all of this."

"That's only because of my daughter. If it wasn't for her being in my life, I'd probably be in jail right now."

"Or an asylum," she laughed. "You really love your little girl, don't you?"

"More than life itself."

She was silent for a moment with a small smile on her face. "So what did you tell Leah you were doing today?"

"Oh, she knows I'm going to meet the guy about the watch."

"She knows you're with me?"

"No. God, no."

"Calvin," she jokingly scolded him.

"I don't mean to be dishonest with her…it's the last thing I want to do. I don't mean any disrespect by it, honestly. She's just not very understanding."

"She definitely wouldn't be very understanding of you hanging out alone with me."

"No. She'd freak. She just doesn't get it. I needed your help. She wasn't about to help me with any of this. Even if she was, whoever has my watch might recognize her or her car. I needed someone unknown to help me— someone who looked serious."

"That's me. Unknown and serious."

"I really appreciate you doing this with me. It's a big deal."

"No problem. I think this will be kind of fun, actually. So this should be pretty safe, though, right?"

"We should be fine. We'll be in a very public place. And there's no way he would know you or your car."

"And what about you? Are you going to go up to meet him with me?"

"I'll hang back in the car for a minute. I want to see who this guy is. If I recognize him right off the bat, then I'll handle it however I feel like handling it. If I don't recognize him, then I'll want to get out of the car and take a close look at the watch. I'll want to make sure it's really mine."

"So, here we are," Sadie announced. "The gorgeous village plaza. Home to the village dollar store, village auto parts, and village supermarket."

"Where did he say to meet, exactly?"

"In front of the supermarket."

"Good. Plenty of traffic, lots of people. Glass windows on the front of the supermarket, so lots of people will see if anything happens."

Sadie pulled them into a parking spot after circling twice, looking for the best vantage point of the supermarket. She parked and turned the car off. She left the radio on. They sat facing the supermarket two spots back from the front row with a perfect view of everyone who came and went near the store.

"Did he say what sort of car he'll be driving?"

"No. We didn't get into that. He said he'll be standing up there with a black overcoat on."

"Nothing yet, then."

"Nope."

They waited in silence for a few moments, listening

to the radio. It was Tom Petty singing 'American Girl'.

"I love this song," she said in a daze and sang a few bars.

"Wow, you actually have a decent voice."

"Really? No, I'm just messing around. I can't carry a tune at all. Eric says I destroy songs."

"Sounds pretty good to me," Calvin said, honestly impressed. "You know, with your looks and your voice, you could really make it somewhere. Have you ever thought about that?"

Sadie laughed a little and blushed. "Thanks," she said, looking out her window. "But I tried. It seems pretty stupid now, but yeah, I thought I was something special. The truth is, I just wasn't good enough. There are girls out there who are prettier than me and can sing so much better," she said, her voice beginning to quiver. She nodded her head, clearly deeply bothered by the memory. "One guy I auditioned for said that the only thing I would ever do in show business would be porn."

"You didn't do it, did you?"

"Calvin," she said with a laugh, shaking her head. "Of course not. I just accepted reality for what it was. I'm getting older. My looks are fading and they'll continue to. And I have a job I can't stand that I'm not all that great at." Sadie took a final drag on her cigarette and flicked the butt out the window. "Sorry," she apologized with a forced smile at Calvin.

"Oh. Don't be," Calvin said awkwardly. He was shocked by this sudden outpouring of truth from Sadie. She had always been so guarded when it came to her emotions and weaknesses. Calvin sensed she was very upset and changed the subject. "What time do you have?"

"Two-fifty-eight."

"He's not early."

"Let's just hope he shows. This is the only hope I have right now." There was a long, empty pause. Calvin's mind was racing about the man they were supposed to be meeting. His heart started pumping hard, ready for fight-mode, and he knew he needed to calm himself down and remain rational. He decided to change the subject with Sadie to anything that would distract him. "How is Eric doing, anyway?"

"Oh, you know." She shrugged. "He's the same as usual."

"I haven't seen him around much."

"No, he's been really busy with everything. He's always busy."

"I remember when you first started working there he was in almost every day, it seemed."

"Yeah."

"Bringing you flowers or lunch. Or even driving all that way just to bring you a banana."

"Yeah, well things have definitely changed a lot since then."

"Things are okay, right?"

"They're all right. Not great. We've been having some problems."

"Really? I never would've guessed."

"We're only human. And we've had a rough time lately."

"I always pictured you as the perfect couple, honestly. It actually made me mad sometimes…maybe not mad, but just a little depressed. Seeing everything going so well for you while my life went down the drain."

"Appearances can be deceiving."

"Well, when you see a couple like you two, always happy and perfect in every way…I guess it just makes a lot of people jealous. It makes them realize how imperfect their lives and their relationships are. So what the hell happened?"

"We've been drifting apart for a long time. It seems like every day for the last year or so we became further and further separated from each other, emotionally. I don't know what to do about it."

"Have you considered counseling, maybe?"

"There's nothing to counsel. We just don't feel much for each other. We're just together now. Just living together and eating together. Actually, we don't even do a whole lot of that. His schedule is so erratic and busy; we hardly ever see each other. That's a huge part of it. We don't spend any time together anymore. Maybe that's the way he wants it."

"I doubt that."

"It's true. Sometimes I don't even want to be around myself so much."

"Join the club. I'm my own worst enemy."

"There's something else I haven't told you. No one at work knows, just because I don't think it's any of their business."

"I won't tell anyone. You've kept my secret about the crash and the fire. I promise I won't tell anyone."

"His mother died about two months ago."

"Oh my god…she couldn't have been that old, right?"

"Fifty-four. Totally unexpected. It was Christmas morning when she died. Heart failure. Nothing in particular brought it on, and there's nothing that could have been done to save her. She just woke up, wasn't feeling well, and then dropped dead a few minutes later on the kitchen floor while baking some pastries for breakfast."

"I had no idea…"

"It really messed him up. He hasn't been the same

since that happened. I mean, we were already pretty distant by that point, but that was just what put him over the edge, I guess. He totally withdrew from me and everyone else in his life. He was totally cold to me. I tried to be there for him, but he said that I could never understand. And I couldn't understand. I couldn't understand why he was being so mean to me. It was like he was taking it out on me, what happened. But because she wasn't my mother, he was mad at me for sympathizing and trying to help him through it. Somehow, he took it as a personal insult to the relationship he had with her."

"You were just trying to help. What do you say in a situation like that?"

"There isn't much you can say or do that will help. And things just got worse from there. We're still together, we're still a couple. But at this point, I don't really see any future with him. I'm sure he feels the same way about me, but he just won't say it."

"Have you tried talking to him about where things are heading?"

"I try all the time. He doesn't want to discuss it, but he won't just end our relationship, either. He doesn't know what he wants right now. He's hurting. In a way, he still needs me more than ever, even though he acts like he doesn't want anything to do with me."

"At least you two are going through this without kids."

"I'm so glad we chose to wait on having kids. That's the only thing that could make this worse, if we had a baby being dragged through this awful drama."

"I would never have guessed in a million years that you were going through all that. I always see you as this overwhelmingly perfect person who can do nothing wrong. I always saw you as blessed in every way. It always intimidated me."

"You were intimidated by me? Is that why it took you so long to start talking to me at work?"

"I always saw you as being so far above everyone else, on a pedestal. It's kind of funny now, and embarrassing, but I didn't understand why someone like you would be at all interested in talking to someone like me."

"That is ridiculous."

"I know. I guess I always felt like crap when you talked to me, or when I was around you."

"What? That's bizarre. Why would you feel like crap?"

"Because being around you and Eric was like a constant slap in the face of how screwed up my life is. There you were, looking like Miss America and saying and doing everything perfectly, and there was Eric, looking like an underwear model or something."

She laughed.

"You two gave off this vibe of being perfect. I don't think you meant to, it's just the way I perceived it. It kind of rubbed in my face all the things I always wanted but wasn't going to get."

"What is it exactly that you want?"

"I'm not even sure at this point. I don't think there's any one path that makes sense for me. Do you know what I mean? It's like there is no right thing to do, not without other major consequences."

"Well, Calvin, you'll get your money from the insurance company one way or another, sooner or later, and you'll be able to buy a nice house somewhere else, maybe in a better location, and you'll just have to start a new life there."

"Alone."

"That's up to you. You need to figure out your relationship. This was a chance for the two of you to make it work. It wasn't a sign from God; it was just another random incident in your life that could allow you to take a different path. I think you know what you need to do, though."

"Yeah. I just don't want to think about it. There are so many negative things that are going to come with getting my own place again. This time, it would be for good."

They sat in silence for a moment, listening to the radio and staring at the supermarket in front of them. Calvin's eyes wandered down and traced the sleek curves of her legs in her tight jeans. He marveled out how she could be so slender but still have such a luscious figure with feminine shaping in all the right places.

"Would you like to know what I thought of you until recently?" Sadie asked out of nowhere.

"What?"

"I thought you were a player."

"A player? That's about the furthest thing from who I am."

"You're so different than what I thought you were."

"Different how?" Calvin was intrigued.

"Just different. You seemed like just another jackass guy who was going to make cheesy passes at me and think that you had some claim on me."

"Like Billie?"

"Exactly like Billie. But you're so different. I never would have guessed by looking at you or first meeting you that you're so...down to earth and honest. I guess that's why I was so interested in you. I don't mean in a sexual way..."

"Gotcha."

"I mean I would just watch you sometimes. I wouldn't even be paying attention to my own work; I would be so busy watching you do your job. There's this focus you have, this intent on getting things perfect. It's fascinating to watch. You move in the same patterns, almost robotically, but beautifully, like an artist at work."

"I'm usually just thinking about sex or beer."

"Well it's captivating to watch you think about sex and beer. I don't know what it is. I've just never been so interested in watching someone. I don't really care about other people that much, what they're doing. I live in my own little world and try not to get into other peoples' business."

"I didn't think anyone really cared what I did at work."

"That was one of the reasons Eric and I were having problems, too."

"What do you mean?"

"He started getting a little annoyed that I talked about you so much at home. He'd say he didn't want to hear about what happened on my job that day. I talked about work a lot because I felt like it was the only thing I had to talk about with him. Anything else would just somehow turn into a fight or send him on an emotional rampage for the rest of the day, or just plain alienate him. But every time I brought your name up that especially bothered him."

"Why? I've known him for a long time."

"He's mentioned that it makes him a little uncomfortable, the fact that we work together. The same schedule and all. He also came into work one time to bring me Japanese food and we were sitting together on lunch. I never even knew he had been there until someone mentioned something later about the food and how nice it was for him to bring it. I guess it may have fueled some paranoia he was having about the two of us."

"The two of us? I never would have guessed that...I've never sensed any insecurity from him, or any jealousy."

"His head hasn't been in the right place lately."

"I don't know when that was, but I can't think of any reason why it looked like we were doing something wrong at lunch."

"We weren't. Of course we weren't. He just already had suspicions, and whatever he saw, maybe we were laughing together about something, made him feel like we were having a better time than he and I have, or have had in a long time.

"I'm very sorry...but I have to say, I'm actually kind of flattered at the same time, that I could actually pose a threat to your perfect relationship."

"You and everything else, it seems. We're just falling apart. I started looking for apartments about a month ago. Then I have to worry about bills. I didn't give money a second thought before, when things were good with us. The money I made at my job was just the icing on the cake. We didn't need it. It was vacation money, spending money. I think that's part of the reason I've stuck it out as long as I have. I'm worried about how things will be for me."

"You'll be fine. You're strong and independent. I'm sure you'll be better off without him, anyway, even if things are a little tight financially for a while. Hey, is this our guy?" Calvin said, noticing a man in a black overcoat stepping onto the sidewalk in front of the supermarket.

"Holy shit," Sadie exclaimed in shock.

"Oh my god..." Calvin was stunned as the monstrosity of a human being approached the sidewalk limping with his enormous, heavy head tilted to one side.

He was hunched over, as though his spine was curved in all different directions and it was a struggle for him to stand up straight. He had long stubble covering his droopy face. He wore aviator sunglasses that looked like spectacles on his giant grizzly face. A long black trench coat swayed around him like a cape, large enough for a normal-sized man to make a tent out of.

"So much for jumping him," Calvin said. "That guy could pick me up and throw me through that brick wall."

"Do you recognize him?" Sadie asked.

"No, " Calvin answered without thinking about it. "Not at all. I have no idea who the hell that is…or *what* the hell that is. I've never seen him before in my life."

"What is that, a birthmark on the side of his face?"

"Looks like a big scar."

"He looks like a freak to me," Sadie said, sounding intimidated. "I can't believe how tall he is. Is he wearing stilts or something? You're sure you want to go through with this?"

"As long as you're game."

"I'm game. As far as I'm concerned, I'm just a girl trying to buy a piece of jewelry. Nothing illegal or wrong about that."

The giant man kept looking around impatiently. He appeared very awkward, nervous, like he wasn't used to being seen out in public and just wanted to get out of there. He moved aside clumsily to let a mom and her three kids pass by, after they almost walked right into him. The three kids craned their necks to stare at the giant man in horror and awe, one of them tripping on the sidewalk. The mother stared as well for a moment in disbelief, before cautiously herding her kids together and ushering them along into the store.

"Bombs away," Sadie said, getting out of the car.

She walked straight for the giant man without hesitance, strutting like a business woman in heels on a mission. She didn't look back.

"Wait up," Calvin called after her, getting out of the car. He caught up and together they walked towards the man in the overcoat, who had now realized they were approaching. It was perfect, since he hadn't seen which car they had come from. There were at least a hundred other cars in the busy parking lot.

The giant man caught them in his sight through his dark sunglasses.

Calvin raised a hand at him, as if hailing a cab, to let him know who they were. The man waved back to acknowledge them and reached into the inside pocket of his overcoat. He pulled out a folded plastic bag with a watch inside.

"Hello," Sadie said, walking up to him with a warm smile.

"Hello," the man said to her in a voice so deep and booming that both Calvin and Sadie could feel the sound waves pass through them.

Up close, it became apparent just how big this giant was. Calvin, who was above average in height, was at eye level with the man's belt buckle. The man was slouched over strangely, too, making him appear shorter than he actually was. Based on Calvin's own height, he estimated the height of the man to be about ten feet.

"You must be Tom?" Sadie said to the man.

"That's me," Tom replied in his deep voice.

"I'm Tricia," Sadie said. "And this is my boyfriend, Scott," she said, putting her arm around Calvin's back.

"So why are you interested in this watch, again?" Tom asked them. His words were difficult to understand, being so low in tone.

"We're collectors. More of investors, I should say. We seek out jewelry like this, old pieces that have great potential to increase in value over time. I probably shouldn't tell you that, though, right? You're not going to want to part with it now."

"I'm afraid I need the money now for an operation," Tom said. "I would never part with it otherwise."

"How did you come to be the owner of this magnificent piece, if you don't mind me asking?"

"It was handed down through my family, three generations. And now I'm the jerk who's going to go and sell it off. What can I say? I don't really have a choice. I'm sure my grandfather would've wanted me to just get rid of it if he knew how much pain I have in my back. I never use the thing, anyway. I would never wear something like this, so it just sits in a drawer. What's the point of that?"

"Well that's where we're happy to come in. With the price of gold on the rise every day, we figure we can't go wrong with this."

"That's absolutely true," Tom said. "And good for you. This is quite a deal you're getting."

"So I assume the price we discussed over the phone is still valid?"

"Of course."

"Would you consider accepting any less for it?"

"Well, given the investment opportunity here...I guess I could knock a couple hundred off, but I really wouldn't go any lower than that."

The giant's eyes were blocked by the dark sunglasses, making it impossible for Calvin to see where he was looking, but he seemed to be highly focused on Calvin. He couldn't be sure, but given the way his head was turned slightly towards him, the man appeared to be examining him very carefully, even while talking to Sadie and appearing to give her his full attention.

"So how long has it actually been in your possession?" Calvin asked.

"Oh, I'd say about ten years now. Since my dad passed away."

"They don't make them like this anymore," Calvin said, running his thumb around the face of the watch.

"No, they certainly don't," Tom agreed.

"Hey, babe?" Sadie said to Calvin.

"Yeah?"

"Did you remember the cash?"

"What? I thought you had it."

"No. I left it on the table and told you to grab it on your way out."

"I didn't hear that. I just heard that you had it."

"Great,"

"Well, what are we supposed to do now?"

"Is there any way we could meet you another time, same place?"

"Uh, yeah. I suppose. I'd stay and wait for you to run home now, but I have an appointment to get to."

The giant was visibly starting to get a little nervous. He slid the watch back into the plastic bag and slipped it back into his inside pocket.

"We're so sorry about this," Sadie said sweetly.

"No big deal. We'll try again another day. You have my cell number now, miss. Just give me a call."

"Okay. Bye now."

They turned and started walking back to Sadie's car together, holding hands. She squeezed his hand tightly twice.

"Oh, hey," Calvin yelled, turning around to face the man, who was now heading back to his own vehicle. "Hey, Tom?"

The man stopped and turned. "Yes?"

"I remembered something I wanted to ask you about the watch."

"Yes?"

"The tiny letters on the bottom of the face of the watch. I just noticed them when I held the watch—the letters RM—what is the significance of those letters?"

He paused a moment, as if uncertain what Calvin was asking.

"The letters on the back of the watch," Calvin repeated, "underneath the face. Are those someone's initials?"

"Oh, yes. RM. Those were my grandfather's initials."

"Oh, okay," Calvin said with an indifferent nod. "Just wondering. Thanks again."

"See you soon," the giant man said.

"Yes, you will," Calvin said, walking away with Sadie.

As they headed for Sadie's car Calvin looked over his shoulder to make sure that the giant was not following them or watching where they were going. He appeared to have absolutely no interest in them. Calvin watched until he got into a large, beat-up old pickup truck.

"We need to follow him out of the lot," Calvin said to Sadie as they both sat into her car. "At least long enough for me to write down his license plate."

"Which car?"

"An old rusty pickup truck, three rows that way."

"You think that was your watch?" Sadie asked as she whipped out of the parking space and threw the little car in drive.

"I *know* that was my watch."

"You're certain of it?"

"Yes."

"You knew when you held it?"

"I was pretty sure when I held it. I knew for certain when he told me what the initials on it were for."

"Yeah," Sadie agreed. "He hesitated. It seemed like he really didn't know what the initials were there for."

"There *were* no initials on it. Just like there were no initials on my watch. That's why the cop said I would have such a hard time identifying it to get it back and press charges."

"There he is."

The pickup's brake lights flashed at the pedestrian crosswalk in front of the supermarket. The pickup tilted heavily to the left side under the incredible weight of the giant. Calvin wondered how he was able to fit into the truck's cab. The truck reeked of exhaust and puffed out some blue smoke as it accelerated. It either had holes in its muffler or had no muffler at all, since its heavy old engine cylinders beat loudly like helicopter blades.

"Follow him right out of here, if you can. I have a piece of paper and a pen..." Calvin jotted the plate number down. "There, got it."

"You're good?"

"Got it."

"Because I don't think I'll be able to follow him through this turn. This road is really busy and it will be a minute before I can pull out after him."

"Don't worry about it. I've got what I need."

Later that afternoon, Calvin was attempting to feed pieces of potato and carrots to Pearl, who kept swatting them off her tray with a devious smile. She shook her bottle of milk upside-down until it splattered her tray, and then finger-painted with the milk she had spilled. Calvin dropped his head into his hands and sighed.

It had been a long, unusual day for him. Pearl hadn't napped at Mrs. Cotter's house, their neighbor who watched her when they needed a sitter. She was in rare form since he picked her up and he was too exhausted to deal with it.

Then something caught his eye out the front kitchen window. There was a car turning the corner. Calvin's heart thumped. It was a light-blue sedan slowly rounding the corner, past the hedges. The sight of the vehicle, through the hedges, bared an uncanny resemblance to the car he had seen so many times at night stalking their street.

The car stopped at the edge of the driveway. The hair on Calvin's neck stood up. He went into fight mode. This was really happening, right now in broad daylight.

The passenger side door popped open. Leah stepped out, carrying her purse and a water bottle.

Calvin's mind raced. He couldn't believe his eyes. He stared intensely to see who the driver was as the sedan turned around on the street. With the late afternoon sun's glare, it was tough, but he was able to get a clear view for a moment. It was Billie. He was driving the new car that Calvin had seen him with at work.

"What the hell's going on!" Calvin opened the door and shouted at Leah before she made it to the front porch.

"What?"

"Why are you driving with Billie? Why did he come here?"

"He gave me a ride home. I didn't have a car."

"I thought you were going to call me when you were ready."

"I told you I'd either call you or find a ride with someone else."

"I didn't think you meant *him*!"

"What's your problem, anyway? I thought I was doing you a favor by not making you drive all the way to get me with the baby."

"My problem is you being alone with that scumbag—in his car! That's the car that's been driving around here, Leah, at night!"

"What? Are you crazy? He's never even been out here before. He had no idea where he was going without me directing him."

"Bullshit!"

"Listen...You want to know the real reason why I didn't call you? Because I needed a break from you, Calvin. I didn't want to ride in the car with you and get into a fight in front of the baby."

"So you'd rather be alone with that asshole?"

"He's not an asshole to *me*. It was nice to be around a man who isn't acting crazy all the time and flying off the handle."

Calvin grabbed her keys off the table. "I hope you're in for the night. I need to leave now."

Calvin stood in the dark outside of his burnt home. He didn't know why he went there. He had to get away from his situation with Leah in that tiny house. He always felt like there was no escape and the pressure built up until there was an explosion.

Calvin remembered what Officer Patton had said

about going into the property as he pulled at the plywood covering over the basement door. He didn't care. It was his house and his nightmare. If he wanted to go inside and look around, investigate, or just hang out in there and do whatever the hell he wanted to do, it was his goddamn business, not the police department's. He loudly and forcefully ripped the plywood from the basement entrance.

As he wandered through the dark chasms of his home, he felt an odd sense of familiarity. The walls were charred and all was misshapen and distorted, but the structure still managed to retain all the memories, both good and bad. Every corner of the home, every radiator, every door knob, every window, spurred at least one memory of someone or some event. In much the way a person visits the grave of a deceased loved one, this had become his sanctuary.

He didn't think he would find anything. He didn't know where else to go, and somehow he felt like he would find answers there—answers to more than just what happened to his house. He wanted answers to where his life had gone so horribly wrong.

"*Hey, killer,*" a voice suddenly said from somewhere in the room.

Calvin jumped and gasped as he spun around. His fists went up. Shocked, he looked for the source of the voice.

"Nice place you've got here," the voice said again.

Calvin spotted the figure in the dark. He recognized the voice now. It was the Davis. He was inside the house.

Davis stepped into the light a little more, closer to Calvin. "Beautiful work," he said with his arms out, admiring the charred structure around him. "Did you do this?"

"I didn't do anything," Calvin said, still in shock.

"Sure you didn't. Neither did I," Davis said, stumbling over some debris. His words were slurred. It became clear that he was heavily intoxicated.

"Did you follow me here?" Calvin asked apprehensively.

"No rest for the wicked, Calvin. No rest for you. No rest for me. We're both losing our minds."

"You've been tracking me? Is that your car that's been driving around my girlfriend's house?"

"My car is sitting in the impound lot, thanks to you. I'm a total bust. My life, as I knew it…is no more," he slurred as he took a bow.

"You just stay the hell away from us," Calvin said as forcefully as he could, trying not to let his voice tremble.

"I don't know what else to do," the broker said slyly. "I don't know how else to get through to you. I did my best to talk to you man to man about this. I never wanted anything bad to happen to you, Calvin. All I wanted was to make a sale. I sold my soul for a goddamn sale. And now I may as well send myself straight to hell."

Calvin saw him pull something shiny from the pocket of his overcoat. Davis raised his arms. Calvin heard the unmistakable sound of a gun cocking.

"What does it feel like to know you're about to die, Calvin?" Davis said with the long steel barrel aimed directly at his face.

Calvin's arms instinctively went up. He was defenseless.

"I want to know…" Davis struggled on, "because I don't feel anything anymore. I don't even feel the alcohol…or the blow anymore. I used to get excited about things…I used to feel right…and I can't get back there."

Davis suddenly turned the gun on himself. He gulped its long barrel into his mouth, practically shoving it down his throat. Calvin could see the whites of his eyes widen in the dark as he smiled with his finger on the trigger.

Calvin's arms remained up in the air. His mouth dropped open.

The trigger clicked. Silence.

Davis cackled loudly as he pulled the gun from his throat. He stared at Calvin with bulging eyes as he ran his tongue up its barrel.

Calvin pulled his phone out of his pocket, ready to call the police, when a piece of burnt wood came flying at him. He flinched and ducked to avoid being hit.

Davis cackled as he disappeared out the basement doorway, up the steps, and back into the night. He was gone.

14

"Alfred, I need a favor from you," Calvin said into his phone. He sat on the living room carpet with Pearl, who was playing with a piece of paper beside him.

"Mr. Strong, how can I be of service to you today?"

"I need a huge favor from you. I wouldn't be asking you for this if it wasn't extremely important."

"How huge of a favor?"

"I need you to run a license plate for me. You said you have connections, right?"

"I do…it depends, I guess. What information are you looking for?"

"I have the plate number. I need to find out who the car belongs to and where he lives. If possible, I also need a background check and criminal record."

"Whoa, slow down, Calvin. That isn't information that can just be handed out, even if I am able to actually get it."

"I know, but this is an emergency and I know you can get me that information if you really want to. I'll pay you for it."

"Now, Calvin. Bribery is a crime. And I would be more than willing to commit that crime if you had any money."

"I'll come up with money for you."

Alfred snorted, amused. "You still owe me thousands. I'm not worried about that right now. Whose plates are we running and why is it so important?"

"It's about the house. You said to find something, anything that can help my case. Well, I did. I found the person who has my watch."

"This is the watch you lost in the house fire?"

"Yes. I went out to meet this guy with a friend, pretending to be interested in buying it off him. When he left, I was able to take down his license plate number."

"Calvin...how can you be certain that this is your watch?"

"I know it is."

"Well, I don't mean any disrespect by this, but everything about this just seems...well, crazy."

"This guy somehow ended up with my watch. He might have all my other things, too. He knows something. He has to. How could he have possibly ended up with that watch?"

"Or, it could be just a guy selling his watch. I know you're certain it's yours, but in a court of law you're going to have a very tough time proving that...in fact, I'd have to say it's impossible to prove, unless you have some form of evidence. Even a picture—do you have a picture of the watch?"

"Everything was lost in the fire."

"Right. Of course. So we have absolutely no proof

that this is actually your watch, or that it was stolen in the first place."

"Look, I just want to know who this guy is and what connection he has to me."

"It seems like there is no connection, Calvin. I mean, even if I get you this information, what are you going to do with it?"

"I'm going to get my watch back and find a way to prove that he took it, along with all my other things."

"This all sounds extremely reckless to me, to be honest. I think you're opening up a whole new world of trouble. If you feel like going and taking matters into your own hands and doing something crazy, chances are you're going to end up in jail."

"That's where I'm headed anyway. Isn't it, Alfred?"

Alfred sighed. There was a long pause.

"Isn't it? Isn't that what's going to happen to me?"

"It's possible."

"It's a lot more than possible. I'm not an idiot. I can see the writing on the wall. I can see where this whole thing is going, this goddamn investigation. Even my girlfriend thinks I did it."

"She thinks you did it? Really?"

"She hasn't said that, but I can tell. And you know what? I don't blame her a bit. It makes perfect sense that I did it. Why wouldn't I? I've got nothing else to lose and it looked like I had everything to gain."

"Calvin, you didn't do this."

"You even think I did."

"No, Calvin. I don't. I believe every word you've said."

"Then why did you drop my case?"

"Because I don't think I am capable of defending you. I'm a good lawyer, Calvin. But I know my limitations.

I don't have enough experience to help you with a matter this serious. This is life and death for you. I don't want the responsibility of guiding the outcome of this matter."

"You're saying it looks that bad?"

"I'm saying I don't know of anything I can do to help you."

"Alfred, I need that information. You have to get it for me. I'm not going to sit by and let this happen. I have a little girl at home who needs me. I don't want to spend the next ten years away from her. If anything happens to me, please forward whatever information you have to Officer Patton with the police department in White Falls. Please, have your friend run the plates. Tell me what I need to know. Do it for my little girl. Do it for Pearl."

There was a long pause and an awkward sigh from Alfred. "You should have never brought that baby into my office," he said. "She's the only reason I haven't been able to say no to you so far."

15

"I really appreciate you doing this with me," Calvin said to Sadie as she drove him through the suburban streets, dangling her cigarette out the cracked window in between drags.

"I like trouble," she said with devilish sweetness. "Might be fun. I didn't have anything else going on tonight, anyway."

"Take a right here," Calvin directed her.

"You really know your way around here, don't you?"

"It's not my first time out here," Calvin said. "I've been coming out here the past few nights. I take Leah's car, after she goes to bed. I finally got my truck back again yesterday."

"That's good. It must be strange driving, it, though. After what happened, I mean."

"It is. It's tough to drive it without thinking about the crash. It's still great to have my truck back, though. I don't feel stuck at home. Oh…and take a left here. It will be your next right."

"What street was it, again?"

"Chestnut."

"So you think you're really going to go through with this tonight?"

"We'll see. I don't know yet. I have to see what the situation is, who is around at the time. I'm not just going to break into someone's house without being careful."

"You're not afraid of much at this point, are you?"

"No. I'm not."

"Well just take your time and feel it out. Don't let your adrenaline carry you away."

"I won't. I need to keep my head."

"What if there's an alarm system?"

"Then I'm not going in. I'm no professional burglar, that's for sure."

"My brother knows how to disarm them. Any of them."

"Well, maybe we'll give him a call if there is one. I doubt it, though. Not in the neighborhood we're heading to."

"Seems pretty laid-back out here."

"Extremely. Half these people don't lock their doors at all, let alone have a security system."

"Here it is…Chestnut," Sadie said as she turned the corner.

"Quiet neighborhood".

"The houses are bigger than I expected. And older."

"Number 9. There it is," Calvin said, pointing to the ugly old house.

Sadie slowed a little, but didn't stop. "I'm not going to pull up right now. I'll circle the block and come back around. I don't want it to be obvious that we're pulling up near his house."

"Good idea," Calvin agreed. "This seems like the type of neighborhood where everyone is always peaking out their windows."

Sadie approached the house again after turning around the block and stopped about a hundred feet from it this time.

"Calvin, looks like someone's still in there," Sadie said, noticing the movement across the window in the well-lit room. The curtains were pulled closed before they could make out the figure inside.

"Great," Calvin said. "Tonight's his night to stay home."

"We may have to try back another night, that's all," Sadie said with surprising disappointment. She was clearly enjoying this.

"Yeah. I think this is a no-go for tonight," Calvin said.

"We can wait for a little while, if you want."

"What? No, I don't want to hold you up any more."

"You're not holding me up from anything," Sadie said in a mischievous tone, her dark side showing through again.

"I don't think he's going to leave this late at night. It's already nine-fifteen."

"I'm willing to stick it out for a little bit longer if you are."

"Yeah. Yeah, I don't really mind waiting. The baby's already asleep, so I'm not missing any time with her."

"And you're probably not *missing* time with Leah, right?"

"I wouldn't mind a break. If I don't see her tonight, it's just one less fight we'll have."

"That bad, huh?"

"She's all right. I care a lot about her, and I do miss spending time with her. She tries. It's just been difficult lately. It's tough to find a reason to stay together, other than the baby."

"Do you think you would be with her if you guys didn't have the baby?"

"I don't think so," Calvin said, sounding heavily burdened. "But maybe things will work out in the long run because of it. It would definitely be a lot easier that way."

"A lot easier than dealing with a messy breakup and having Pearl grow up in a broken home."

"Yeah. It's a lot of pressure on us. People don't understand it until they have kids. I never understood why anyone would stay in a bad relationship just for their children's sake. I totally understand now why so many people do it. It's not about their own interests, that's why. It's not about the child support payments, either, although that's usually a factor to some degree. It's because they can't stand the thought of doing that to their kids, being responsible for their child growing up with parents who aren't together. It's tough enough that my parents aren't around anymore. I couldn't imagine growing without them."

"My parents divorced when I was ten. It messed me up for a while, but I moved on and accepted it. Better to just end it while the baby's still a baby, too young to realize what's going on. That way she'll never know the two of you together and she won't have to deal with the change."

"She'll still have to deal with the other people in our lives."

"Ah, the new replacement boyfriend."

"I can't stand the thought of some other man stepping in and trying to take my place as her father. Doing things with her and taking care of her while I get visitation rights every-other weekend and pay child support."

"And that's the best-case scenario."

"That's the horrifying part. It scares the life out of me to think what could happen, what sort of freaks and weirdo's she could subject my child to if she starts seeing other men."

"And you have no control over who she's going to bring home and who she's going to decide to trust."

"I don't even want to think about it."

"But what about you, Calvin?"

"What about me?"

"What about you being happy and living your life?"

"Forget about me. That ship has sailed. I screwed up my life pretty good this time, and now I have to live with it."

"You're not interested in dating other girls?"

"Of course I am, but there's no room in my life for that right now."

"How long are you going to keep trying at this relationship?"

"As long as it takes. I have a lot of reasons now to overlook all the problems we had before. They seem pretty insignificant compared to what I could face with the baby if we broke up. I'd rather be tolerant and try to tough it out."

"You shouldn't have to tough out love, Calvin."

"No, you shouldn't."

"And where does she think you are right now?"

"I told her I was working late and then going out for a beer with Mike."

"You've been hanging out with him a lot lately."

"Have I?"

"I think it's funny that you hang out with an old guy like that."

"I like Mike. He listens to all my shit. And, to be perfectly honest, I don't have a whole lot of friends lately."

"You seem like a pretty popular guy to me, at least around work—and what I've seen of you outside of work."

"Not really. Not at all, actually. I don't have much time for friends these days. I've been too busy trying to fix my life and make it go somewhere."

"Sometimes I feel like I don't have a lot of close girlfriends. I think it's because I clash with them. Guys are just so much easier to get along with."

"So what does Eric think about you hanging around all your guy-friends?'

"He doesn't care."

"So he doesn't care at all that you're out with me tonight?"

"No. He does care."

Calvin looked over at her. Her face was still, staring ahead at the lights inside the house.

"Is it a problem with him?" Calvin said, more seriously.

"It's a problem with him and me," she replied without much emotion, nodding her head.

"Well, maybe we should call it a night, then."

"Why?"

"Look, I don't want to be the problem, or even part of the problem between you two. I've known Eric for a while, and he's a good guy. After what you told me before, about what he's going through right now and how he's acting all paranoid, I don't think it's a good idea to fuel his paranoia, especially since us being here is totally unnecessary right now. This guy isn't going anywhere for the night…"

"You don't know that," Sadie said firmly.

"No, I don't know that for sure…"

"Then stay with me. Please."

"Sadie…"

"Just stay for a little while," she said softly and sweetly as she leaned across the armrest.

Calvin suddenly found himself pressing his lips against hers. They were impossibly soft and supple. The smell of her perfume rose up from her chest and teased his senses. It felt so strange, so wonderful yet so awkward to be kissing another woman. It had been so long since he had so much as touched a woman other than Leah.

She swung her leg over him and straddled him in the passenger seat, kissing him voraciously and cupping his face with her palms.

Her body was so different from Leah's, so sleek and slender. She was softer than he thought she would be, given how firm and toned her body always appeared. Her body— the body he had spent so many hours staring at during work, the curves he watched sway back and forth as she walked across the lab, her delicate thin figure with fullness in all the right places. Since they had started working together he hadn't missed a day of fantasizing about her, especially during his times of difficulty with Leah. She was so dark, mysterious, and seductive; it always made him certain that she was wildly sexual. Watching that body move in the tight clothes she wore, how jealous he always was of Eric and their perfect little life together.

It felt absolutely glorious, having her on top of him, not only physically, but mentally as well, and her wanting him so badly was making him crazy. But it all felt so wrong, and maybe that was part of why it felt so good. It was lined with guilt and fear. No matter how many times he had fantasized about this beautiful girl, this was making him sick.

"Stop," he said abruptly as he pushed her face away

from his.

"What? Why?" she said, gasping for air, a perplexed expression on her face.

"We need to stop this."

She leaned in and kissed him again.

"Sadie…come on, I'm serious. This isn't right. At all."

Sadie closed her gaping mouth and moved her face back from his a little. He could see in her eyes that she was hurt.

"Any other time, any other situation, and oh my god…you are so incredible, but this is so wrong on so many levels. I never thought I would say this to any girl as hot as you in my life—but I can't do this. It's making me feel sick to my stomach."

"I'm sorry I have that effect on you."

"You know it's not you. My head's in a rough place right now. I'm scared of losing my little girl. I'm scared of upsetting my relationship with Leah. I can't do this to her, as much as she pisses me off and drives me nuts. I need to try to make things work with her. If she found out about this she would break it off with me and then I would lose my baby…"

"You don't have to explain, Calvin."

"I do, though…"

"No, you don't. My head's in a bad place right now, too. I'm sorry. I shouldn't have done that."

"Don't be sorry. Any other time, any other situation…you don't know how much this is killing me right now."

"You have no idea how bad it's killing me."

"I never knew you even looked at me like…that."

"I've always liked you, Calvin. Since the day I met you."

"Could've fooled me."

"I did. Watching you work, the way you interact with everyone and the way you focus so intensely on what you're doing. And the way I saw how good you are with your baby. You have very good character, Calvin. That's why I believe you. I wouldn't doubt you for a second."

"Thank you. Maybe we should…"

"Oh, yeah, right…" she fumbled to un-straddle him and flipped herself back into the driver's seat. "My relationship is over," she said bluntly. "I've been in a weird place lately, just like you. I'm sorry."

They sat in silence for a minute, staring distantly at the house with the lights still on.

"Hey—look at that," Calvin said, noticing a portion of the driveway illuminate.

A pair of headlights appeared from the garage, heading down the driveway. The loud, rusty old pickup rumbled its way onto the street and headed away from them.

"That's him," Calvin said.

"Wow. I totally lost focus on what we were here for. Please be careful, Calvin. Call me if you need help. I have my phone right here if you need me."

"I will," he said, stepping out of the car.

"Be careful," she said with a sweet smile, looking up at him with those pretty big brown eyes. God, she was gorgeous. He couldn't believe someone like that was actually interested in him. He walked on the grass, not the sidewalk, to avoid making unnecessary noise. He knew without doubt that it was Tom's old pickup that they saw departing, but he had no way of knowing if there was anyone else was in the house. He thought about going right up to the front porch and ringing the doorbell, but decided it was too well-lit and would give him away to the neighbors or anyone driving by, should they happen to see him.

He crept along the side of the house on a jagged slate pathway and was able to peek into the large bay-windows. He could see inside, plain as day, since there were so many lights on within and no curtains were drawn. He peered into a living room with sparse furniture, mostly old-looking, like antiques. There were no signs of life inside. There was no movement, no voices, and the television wasn't on. He came around the side of the house to the back door, which he decided would be his point of entry.

The surroundings were reassuring. He felt safe creeping next to the house, given the distance of the neighbors and the privacy that the hedges and trees offered. His biggest fear at that moment was that a dog would bark or a door would suddenly open, alerting someone to his presence.

The only sound was his boots struggling to tread on the icy slate pathway, which had eroded and shifted with time and become irregular. Being the dead of winter, all the neighbors' windows were closed.

He checked the door knob to the back entry. It was locked. There was no deadbolt on it, though. Calvin pulled his wallet from his pocket and slipped out his blood donation card. He didn't want to risk scraping up his credit card or license.

He inserted the card between the weather stripping of the frame and the door where the latch ran from the knob. It was an art form he had perfected as a teenager, always forgetting his key to his parents house and, in his later years, his own house. It was usually a reliable method for opening locked doors, although it often took a few tries to catch the latch. You have to get just the right angle and push the card through the slot.

Calvin jiggled the card in for a third time, trying a different approach, when the door suddenly popped open, swinging inward.

The stench of rot and decay flooded his nose with a wave of heat from inside. The back hall was eerily dim and vacant. He gently closed the back door behind him. Calvin's boots squeaked on the old hardwood floors as he crept his way down the hallway, leaving footprints of mud and water all the way. He looked down at his feet. He would have to wipe that up later, since it was pretty obvious someone had been walking in there.

"Hello?" he called out to the empty hallway. His voice echoed on the hardwood floor and empty walls. He had to make sure there was no one else in the house as he walked through. At the point where he was at he could still talk his way out of being in their back hallway. Perhaps he could create a story that there was a car accident and he was just trying to get someone's attention inside the house, or he thought he heard a scream and wanted to investigate.

There was no response.

The smell of the house bothered him, nearly making him gag. It smelled like death.

Satisfied that the house was empty, Calvin treaded more confidently on the wood floors. His boots clunked through the hallway and into what appeared to be the living room.

The living room was surprisingly devoid of furniture and belongings. There was very little on the walls, just a few small paintings hung by string, crooked. The furniture was mostly comprised of small, ugly antiques, inappropriate for such a large room. He noticed that none of the furniture matched. It was all random pieces, sloppily thrown together with total disregard to style, era, and color.

The floor was covered by a hideous green carpet, matted flat and worn, which looked old enough to match the age of the radio he had just noticed.

Classical music was playing from the antique radio that had been left on. A soft orange glow came from its outdated and oversized display panel. Calvin had only seen radios like that in movies set in the thirties or forties.

There were a few drawers in an end table. Calvin pulled them open, but found nothing.

His eyes scanned the room for something, anything unusual besides a horrible example of interior decorating. There wasn't much he could see out of the ordinary. It looked like a very sad, lonely existence. There was a certain taste and knowledge of antiques and objects of a past era, but there seemed to be no ambition to keep anything clean. Dust covered everything and in some corners accumulated dust bunnies nearly the size of real rabbits.

The entire room was dimly lit and eerily void of signs of life. Yet, at the same time, he had a very unusual feeling of walking into a trap, as though someone had been expecting him.

Calvin's head whipped around as some headlights caught his attention outside. His heart jumped. They turned into the driveway across the street. He needed to keep moving. There was nothing more for him to see in the living room.

He regained his focus and darted from the living room into the kitchen, which was partially illuminated by the living room lights.

The first thing that caught his attention was a giant pile of papers on the kitchen table. It was covered, every square inch of table, making it clear that no one sat and ate here.

Calvin peered over them, struggling to see them in the dim light. He picked up a few opened letters and brought them closer to the living room for examination. Each one was addressed to Thomas Grissom.

He slid his fingers inside one and pulled out the front page of the letter. It was a collection notice for a medical bill for $1,734. Calvin slid the bill back in and slid out the next one. It was also a medical collection notice, this one for $2030.43. He opened a few more and found the same thing, medical bill after medical bill, and then a bill for a personal loan that was six months past due. Then there was a utility bill notice that wasn't yet opened. Calvin recognized the envelope, since he had been through many rough times in his life. He had seen this typical exterior of the bills before, and it was a sure sign of a shutoff notice.

Calvin set all the bills back on the table, trying the best he could to arrange them in the order that he found them. He didn't think it would be too noticeable, considering the condition of the table and the house surrounding it.

On the kitchen counter, amidst a mess of dirty dishes and glasses, he noticed a large collection of medication bottles. He picked up a few and read them, but had no idea what the medication was or what it was used for. He had never seen so many different bottles of pills, all colors and shapes. It appeared as though the user had given up trying to put them all away.

Calvin pulled open a few drawers, not expecting to find much. There was only dirty silverware and some random dishes, most of which did not match. All the cups and glasses were from different sets as well.

There was grease and grime all over handles to the drawers and all over the appliances. It was disgusting, even to Calvin, who had never kept an overly-clean home. The house definitely had the vibe of a college fraternity house or a bachelor pad, minus the partying.

He could feel the tension. Simply breathing the rotten, stale air was making him want to vomit. It had to be a sad, lonely existence for the homeowner.

Calvin checked the bathroom, which was disgusting and smelled of old urine. The floor was slightly wet, either from urine on the floor or a leaky toilet. He could barely see his own reflection in the mirror; it was so smudged and blotched with grease and soap scum.

There was only one drawer. It screeched open when he yanked it. It held an ancient hair brush, its bristles covered in mildew, and an old pair of coke-bottle eye glasses without a case.

The smell of mildew and mold mixed with urine was making Calvin sick to his stomach. He couldn't understand how someone could live there, and it really made him wonder what sort of monster—or monsters—he was dealing with.

The dining room held practically nothing besides the big fancy table in the middle of it. Strangely, there were only two chairs placed at it, which obviously did not go with the table. The table was a dark cherry color, antique and fancy-looking, and the two chairs were light-oak and country style.

There was a smaller table in one of the corners with something resting on it. Calvin could barely make out what it was in the dim light, but on closer inspection, he realized it was a gun. It was a large, old handgun, a vicious-looking, cold-blooded killer with a long barrel. A few bullets lay around it randomly. He didn't dare touch it.

Calvin backed out of the room. He was starting to become unnerved. He decided he'd better check in with Sadie. He pulled out his phone and dialed her as he crept up the old wooden stairs to the second floor.

"Hey," she said anxiously. "Everything okay in there?"

"Yeah. I guess," Calvin replied, surprised by how shaky his voice sounded.

"Find anything?"

"Just a bunch of weird stuff. Lots of past due bills. Majorly past due. Not much furniture. Lots of things missing, like incomplete sets. And there are a lot of antiques just laying around, not really placed anywhere in particular. And there's a gun in here."

"What sort of gun?"

"A colt 45. Just sitting in the dining room with bullets right by it."

"What the hell for?"

"I don't know. Who leaves a gun like that out in the open, in the dining room? Why would you do that?"

"Calvin, maybe it's time you get out of there," Sadie said, trying not to sound worried.

"I'm already upstairs. This place is really giving me the creeps. It's like something out of a horror movie. I feel like someone's going to pop out of a closet with a chainsaw any second."

"Calvin, I'm really not liking the feel of this anymore. I mean I didn't like it to begin with, but now I'm getting nervous."

"There's nothing going on out there, right?"

"No. Nothing."

"You can see perfectly, though, right? If someone came home?"

"Yeah. I'm right here. I should be able to see if anyone comes near the house."

"Then I should be all right. I'm almost done, anyway. I need to check these last couple rooms. The bedrooms upstairs."

"Calvin, maybe you should just bail," she said, sounding more desperate.

"I have to keep going. I've come this far, I'm not bailing now. I've already broken the law. I'm at least going to find my watch and find out anything else I can."

"Please just get the watch and get out of there."

"I will. Just call me if you see something happen out there."

"Of course."

Calvin slipped his phone back into his pocket as he entered a room to his right, the closest to where the stairs brought him. It was filled with clutter from floor to ceiling. Chairs were turned upside down and stacked on chairs of different types and styles. He saw a sewing machine in the mix, an elaborate stereo system, a huge flat-screen television, and various small tables turned on their sides in the mountain of random furniture.

Calvin wondered why someone would have something like a flat screen television and keep it unused in a room upstairs, while the living room was so bare and void of possessions.

Physically unable to enter the room, he could only peer in from the doorway. If something of his was hidden in there it would be extremely difficult to locate.

Calvin headed towards the other bedroom. He kept pondering what he would say if someone else suddenly appeared in the house. It made him extremely nervous, being trapped upstairs, since there was absolutely no excuse he could think of for being there.

The other bedroom was not completely bare like most of the other rooms. The bed was large and wooden, larger than the one he had lost in the fire. There were a couple night stands, but they were also very different than the one he had lost.

It was very dark in this bedroom and he was tempted to flick on one of the lamps. He knew, however, that it was the worst thing he could do. A different light on in the house would be visible from outside to anyone who happened to be looking, despite the shades being drawn. It would be a dead-giveaway that someone was skulking around inside.

Calvin went straight to the first nightstand. He pulled the small blue flashlight from his pocket and twisted it on. Its beam was much brighter than he wanted it to be, but there was no way to control it. The only way he could dim its beam was to keep it very low and cover part of it with his index finger.

The drawer of the first nightstand held a load of pennies, some wrappers to candy or gum, and a couple paperclips.

He went to the second nightstand, and found it held only a book of matches, a bunch of receipts, and some random manuals for a toaster and a lawnmower.

Calvin knelt down on the flattened, filthy carpet and peered under the king-size bed. The smell from the carpet stung his nostrils, probably thirty years of dirt, pet dander, and mold smashed into the carpet fibers. The flashlight's beam probed the carpet underneath, finding only dark dust bunnies and a few boxes. The boxes proved to be either empty or filled with a few random things, such as a paperback novel and a small space heater.

Calvin was getting frustrated. He knew it had to be here, unless this guy had already sold it in the few days since they met him. He had to find it.

He tore open the closet door and was hit with a waft of must and mothballs. He shined the flashlight in. These people were lazy, he thought. Careless, lazy, and disorganized.

The flashlight's beam caught something familiar. He took a closer look. It was the giant overcoat that the giant man had worn when they met him. Calvin reached his hand inside the jacket, behind the buttons, where he had seen Tom repeatedly remove and replace the watch.

Calvin couldn't believe it. His hand latched onto something in plastic. He pulled it out excitedly. It was his watch, still in the same plastic bag that the man had shown it to them in.

Calvin's heart surged. He had found it. All the money in the world couldn't replace it, and he had taken huge chances and gotten it back in his family again.

He had found what he had come for. Now it was time to get out. He knew he had to leave, but it was the inner daredevil in him and his insatiable curiosity that made him linger. He couldn't leave just yet. He wanted more. He wanted to push the envelope. He was alone in the house of the person or people who stole his most beloved belongings and he wanted to know more. He wanted to know how and why. He wanted to know what happened to the rest of his things.

He had time. All was quiet from Sadie, so he knew that no one was on their way into the house. The street outside seemed perfectly quiet and dark as well.

There was a haunting feeling telling him to leave, that he needed to get out right now. It made his adrenaline surge, and it *did* frighten him. The reality of his situation was setting in, now that he had found what he had come for. Instead of scaring him away, however, it made him angrier. He had the upper hand now, for the first time in a long time. He had won something back and he wanted to keep going.

He knew his furniture had to be in the other room,

piled high with all the other items he had seen. What was all of that stuff, anyway? Why would they leave all of that in one room while the house was so scarcely furnished? Were all those items stolen?

He had to know. He had to find something to file a police report. If he could get some sort of identification off of one of the items, maybe the serial number off the large flat screen TV, maybe the police would be able to identify it as stolen. The furniture held little hope for identification, since very few pieces of furniture have serial numbers. Electronics, however, are easily traceable.

Calvin walked across the hallway to the other bedroom and opened the squeaky door again. He was again confronted with the giant pile of precariously stacked furniture and electronics, which created an obstacle course of chair legs and table tops in the way of the television he could see sticking up from the middle.

He shined his flashlight on the back of the television and could spot the location of the serial number from where he stood, four feet away at the edge of the mountain. He plotted a way to weave through the chairs and tables, getting closer to it every moment while being extremely cautious not to upset the pile. One wrong move could trigger an avalanche, and he knew there was no way he could restack everything exactly the way it had been, making his presence here very obvious when the inhabitants returned home.

He could now read the serial number with the flashlight shined directly on it. He slid the pad from his pocket and searched for a pen. He found it and quickly scribbled down the number on the paper, taking care to write legibly enough that at least he could read it, if no one else. It would be useless if he couldn't decipher his own numbers and letters. It was very difficult writing in this awkward position, his body extended well beyond his feet.

There was suddenly a low boom sound that came from either downstairs or outside the house.

Calvin froze in place. He didn't breath. He listened for any other sounds. None came.

He slowly backed his body out of the entanglement and shoved the paper and pen back in his pocket.

He spun in place, silently, peering out in the hallway and trying to catch a glimpse of something out one of the windows.

There was nothing. No further sounds, no lights.

Calvin's heart pounded. He tried to calm and reassured himself that it was just a random noise from the house or one of the neighbors doing something, perhaps closing a garage door. It was possible, too, that in his investigations he had shifted something which fell.

He remembered Sadie outside. It soothed him to know that she was keeping an eye out for him. He thought he'd better check his phone anyway, just to make sure that somehow it hadn't shut off on him or been silenced.

He slid his hand into his left pants pocket. His heart skipped a beat.

His phone wasn't in his pocket.

He frantically patted his other pockets, including his jacket pockets, thinking he had accidentally put it in one of the others.

The phone was missing.

He froze in place again. He listened. There was nothing. All was silent. He was still okay. He knew he needed to get out. He was really spooked now and needed to leave. But he needed to find his phone first. He couldn't leave that behind. It was proof that he was in there, that he had broken into their home and gone through their things— and now stolen an expensive antique watch from them.

He darted back into the master bedroom, where he had found the watch. The flashlight quickly probed the room, darting around the floor and by the nightstands. He didn't see it anywhere. It couldn't have gone that far. It was impossible.

A horn honk outside snapped Calvin back to reality. He had lost all focus and forgotten where he was or what he was doing. The reality of the situation came rushing back to him all at once, surging his adrenaline. He spun in circles in a panic, unsure of what he was even looking for. His phone, he remembered. He had to find the phone.

The horn honked outside again, distant but audible.

A thud came from downstairs, followed by a scraping sound.

A door had opened.

Calvin stared at the light from the stairwell, frozen in place, and listened to the thumping of two sets of shoes walking into the house on the hardwood floor.

Calvin went into panic mode. His eyes darted around the bedroom. If he had been downstairs there was always the other door to try to sneak out of, or at worst *run* out of. He had no place to turn. There was only the one stairway leading back downstairs.

He heard voices underneath him, two men talking back and forth, but he couldn't understand what they were saying. He didn't dare move. He knew that the old creaky floors would surely give him away in a second if he so much as took one step.

He heard the voices move into what sounded like the living room.

Calvin heard one of the men walking across the hardwood floors. He took the opportunity to move himself. He tiptoed across the bedroom floor towards the window. Based on his memory of the exterior of the house, that window should be over the lower roof of the garage.

The movement downstairs ceased once again and Calvin froze in mid-step on the old moldy carpet.

"Need to get to the pharmacy again tomorrow," the booming voice of Tom said, now understandable.

"You're almost out of this one, too," said the other, normal voice.

Calvin heard a plastic bottle being thrown across the room, hitting the floor and bouncing. He heard one of the men groan deeply. He knew at least one of them was in the kitchen.

"Want any of this?" the other voice said.

"Yeah," Tom grumbled.

Cabinets squeaked open and banged shut in the kitchen.

One of the men swore to himself.

There was a minute of silence. Then there was a long groan of relief. "That's so much better," Tom said.

"Yeah? Well enjoy it, because you're cut off until I actually get some money again."

"You have the money for tomorrow?" Tom asked in a stupor.

"Yeah," the other voice said. "We're good for now."

"How much longer is this gonna be?"

"A lot fucking longer now, thanks to you."

"I can't take it anymore. Just fucking kill me," Tom mumbled. "Just fucking kill me," he groaned in a stupor. "Why is this taking so long? When are you going to have the money?"

"This should've been done by now!" the other man's voice exploded. "You're asking *me* when I'm going to have the money? I'll have the money when you actually do what you're supposed to do! This is getting out of hand.

I'm losing control over this. This has never happened before, but it's getting away from me and we need to stop this shit. I've never had a problem with this until you got involved. This is all your goddamn fault. And now you need to fix it.

"Yes," Tom answered with horrifying submission.

"This is out of control," the voice said, becoming enraged. "Where the fuck is he?"

"I don't know."

"What the fuck is he doing?"

"I don't know," Tom cried.

"And why can't you do anything right?"

"I don't know, I don't know…"

"What the hell is wrong with you? You're going to lay there and cry like a baby, you fucking freak? You're going to cry about it now? This is my ass on the line here and I've got a big baby crying at me!"

Calvin was rocked by a loud thud that shook the entire house.

"Fucking freak!" the voice screamed.

Tom could be heard growling and sobbing.

Another loud pounding noise came from downstairs.

"You know what's going to happen if you don't have me?" the voice snapped at Tom. "You're going to die. You'll last a week. They're not going to take care of you like I do. They're going to let you rot and throw you to the dogs in there and they're going tear you apart and eat the pieces. I am the only thing keeping you alive. I am your master. Understand? I'm the only thing keeping you sane. I should throw you back into the hole in the ground I found you in."

"Yes," Tom said obediently. "You are the only thing keeping me normal."

"You're goddamn straight I am. And you're still about the furthest thing from normal I've ever seen."

"I'll do it. Just please stop, I hurt so bad. I should've done it when I had the chance…"

"Oh?" the voice got quiet. "Is that what you think? Do you think you should have done it when you had the chance? Do you think you should've done the one simple task you were supposed to do when you had the chance?"

"I want to die," Tom groveled.

"You'll fucking die when I choose to fucking kill you!" the voice screamed at him. "Here…you want to die?"

"No…"

"You want to die right now?"

"No, don't point that at me!"

"I thought you wanted to die. Didn't you just say that?"

"No…please…"

"You want me to pull this fucking trigger right now?"

"Please…"

"I should ram this barrel right down your throat, you worthless piece of shit!"

"Oh, god, no…"

"There is no god, sweetheart. There is only me. We're both in hell and I'm the devil. And you want to know what the devil says? The devil says it's time to blow your fucking brains all over that wall behind you."

Calvin was startled by a sudden crashing sound. There was a struggle. He heard feet stomping on the floor, grunting and groaning, and then glass shattering with a boom that rattled every window in the house.

One of the men let out a howl. There was a series of groans and moans like they were both being tortured as he heard them slam into walls and knock everything in their path to the floor.

"What the fuck is that?" the voice fired, suddenly silencing the chaos. All motion ceased.

A chill went up Calvin's spine. The hair stood up on the back of his neck.

"What's all this water and mud?"

"You didn't come in that way?" Tom asked in a daze.

"No. I didn't," the voice snapped at him. "And neither did you. Remember?"

Calvin heard both pairs of shoes stomping around the hallway below.

"What the hell's this shit?"

"Those are boot prints."

"The door's still locked."

"Those are fresh boot prints. Our feet are totally dry. I didn't go out back for a cigarette. I just went outside the garage. I wasn't in snow."

"Those are fresh footprints."

Calvin's heart pounded.

"What the fuck...what the fuck!"

Suddenly both pairs of boots thundered through the house over the hardwoods, vibrating the tables upstairs and rattling an old clock on the dresser.

Calvin heard doors fly open and hit the walls in their frenzied search. He knew it wouldn't be long before they shot upstairs, since it was the only other place someone could be hiding.

Calvin abandoned his tip-toeing and sprang for the window. He unlocked it with a flick of his finger and shoved it up furiously. He threw up the old window screen and knocked it off its tracks.

A blast of cold winter air hit his face. He looked out and was grateful to see the garage roof right below. It was steep and covered in snow, but it was still the greatest relief he had experienced in years.

He flung himself up and out the little window with remarkable agility, surprising himself by how quickly his adrenaline made him move. He had a soft muffled landing on the few inches of snow on the roof.

Through the open window, inside he could hear the men crashing up the stairs. He quickly pulled the window closed in a hopeless attempt to cover his tracks. He climbed a few feet up to the peak of the garage roof, where he was able to gain better footing, and haphazardly sprinted across its peak to the outer edge of the garage. It was too high. He ran a few steps down the roof towards the backyard and slipped onto his back. He slid the rest of the way down and right off the roof, landing in a snow-covered evergreen tree that cracked under his weight.

Calvin lay still for a moment, uncertain if he had just broken his back. The wind had been knocked out of him and he couldn't yet sit up.

Then he heard the men yelling. It sounded like they had opened the window where he had escaped, and now certainly saw the imprints he had just made in the snow on their roof. They wouldn't follow him. They were going to go back downstairs and out the door.

Calvin struggled to his feet, freeing himself from the entanglement of crushed evergreen branches, and darted for the driveway. He saw Sadie's car up the street, right where he had left her.

Her car started up and shot up the road towards him as he rushed out of the driveway into the street. She slammed on her brakes and he flung himself into the little car.

"Go! Go!" he hollered at her in a craze.

She stomped the gas pedal to the floor and the little

car rocketed up the quiet suburban street, screeching around the corner and weaving an untraceable path to distance them from the house.

"Are you okay?" Sadie shouted at him with tears in her eyes.

"I don't know. I think so," he shouted back, out of breath. "Those people are crazy!"

"What the hell happened? I was calling you like mad!"

"I lost my phone in there."

"You lost your phone? You mean it's still in there?"

"It must be. I have no idea where it went."

"Oh, no…Calvin…this is bad…"

"Only if they find it."

"It's your phone. With all your contact information. They'll know you were in there."

"I know. They won't call the cops. I can tell you that much."

"Why not?"

"They've got a ton of stuff in there I'm pretty sure is stolen. One whole room is filled with random TV's and furniture. I took down a serial number off a big TV that was stacked in a bedroom with a bunch of other stuff. We'll see what the cops have to say about that."

"Did they see you in there?"

"Almost. I made it out just in time. It was the giant guy with my watch. It was him and some other guy. I couldn't tell who it was. And they're both totally insane. I mean psychotic."

Sadie glanced over at him, her face blank and her eyes wide. Her idea of a fun adventure had taken a severely twisted and disturbing turn.

"Did anyone see you outside?" Calvin asked urgently.

"No," Sadie said. "A few cars went by, but nobody seemed suspicious. Nobody seemed to care."

"Good. They didn't see me inside. They didn't see you outside. Let's just pray they don't find the phone. Those people scare the shit out of me."

16

Calvin snapped awake to a pounding on the front door. He shot out off the couch where he had finally passed out from exhaustion the night before.

He struggled to gain his bearings, shocked to find it was light out and that he had slept as long as he had.

The knock came again at the door.

Calvin grabbed the baseball bat where he had left it leaning against the fireplace and headed to the front of the small house. He peaked through the curtains as if he expected at any moment for the door to fly open and knock him down.

It was Alfred.

Calvin opened the door.

"Mr. Strong," Alfred said, seemingly relieved. "I'm glad I found you in. I thought something might have happened to you."

"No. Not yet," Calvin said, surprising himself by

how cryptic that sounded.

"I was worried. I've been trying to reach you all morning. We need to talk. Do you have a moment?"

"Yes, of course. Come in," Calvin said.

"Expecting company?" Alfred said, noticing the baseball bat in Calvin's right hand.

"Yes. I think I am."

"What's going on? Who do you think is coming here?"

"The men who stole my watch."

"Dare I ask, why do you think they would be paying you a visit?"

"Because I was in their house last night."

"Oh…Calvin."

"I didn't know what else to do. I had to find something out."

"You've committed a pretty serious crime here, you realize."

"I don't care."

"And did you find the watch that you believe to be yours in their residence?"

"Yeah. I've got it right here."

"Calvin…that may very well be your watch, but I'm afraid there isn't much we can do about it. What would we tell the police, exactly? That you broke into someone's house and stole a highly valuable antique watch?"

"I know, I know. I got a serial number off a TV that I found in there, too."

"A TV in their living room, like most people have?"

"No, no. It was with a bunch of other random, mismatched items stacked in a bedroom. It wasn't being used, for some reason. From the looks of it all I think it was stolen stuff."

"Did you see anything else from your house in

there?"

"No. I didn't see any of my furniture."

"Just the watch…so you got a serial number off this TV, you were saying?"

"Yeah. It's right here. Can you contact your cop friend and find out if it was reported stolen?"

"I could, possibly…the problem is how you discovered this item in their house. That's going to be very difficult to explain. And unless there's some other wrongdoing on their behalf, I really don't know how the police could possibly even obtain a search warrant to go into the house."

"And the watch?"

"The watch will land you in jail, Calvin. If I were you I would keep that little secret to yourself, because to anyone else it would appear as though you're the only one committing any crimes here."

"There was a gun on the table…I heard them talking…"

"Again, while you were trespassing after breaking and entering and stealing from their home. Look, I'm sorry, Calvin, but I don't know what I can do for you on that matter."

"Just have your friend run that serial number for me. Please"

"I'm running out of favors from him. Cops don't like to give out random information when they don't even know who is obtaining that information or why they want to know."

"Please, just try."

"I'll try. If I catch him on a slow day he might do it for fun, but I can't promise anything."

"It would mean a lot to me. Thank you."

"The real reason I tracked you down and drove all

the out here to the middle of nowhere was because I have an important message for you."

"About what?"

"About your fire investigation. The guy I told you about, who you hired, has been trying to get in touch with you. It sounded really urgent, and I've never known him to get excited about anything—and I mean anything."

"What's the message?"

"All I can tell you is that you need to get in touch with him as soon as possible. He sounded frantic. I don't know what's going on, but he was freaked out enough to call me and have me track you down for him."

"He couldn't tell you anything?"

"You're the one paying him, so no, he couldn't tell me a thing. I'm sorry."

"Alfred, if anything happens to me...if I suddenly disappear or turn up dead or anything, just get whatever information you find to the White Falls Police Department. Give it to Officer Patton. Please."

"Will do, Calvin. You can count on me. I have to go now. I'll try this serial number, and you please just get in touch with this guy."

"I will. Thank you, Alfred."

"And Calvin, that Louisville Slugger might be great for knocking a ball out of the park, but if you want to knock someone's head out of the park you should buy a twelve-gage."

Calvin found the small office of Stan, private fire investigator, in the back corner of an office complex. He pulled into the parking lot and hopped out of his truck.

"Mr. Strong," he said in a snotty tone, before Calvin

could even greet him.

"Yes, hello, Stan…"

"You're not an easy man to get a hold of."

"Normally I am. I lost my phone…"

"I've been calling you for about the last twenty-four hours. I left probably seven messages for you."

"You left messages on my phone?" Calvin's expression changed to terror.

"Well, yes," Stan said with an attitude. "Where else would you expect me to leave messages? I don't have your address, or I would have driven out there myself. I had to call that lawyer of yours to get in touch with you. I don't have time for this sort of thing, and quite frankly, neither do you."

"What do you mean?"

"I saw where they started the demolition prematurely, but it really didn't affect any of the testing that I had to do. That part of the house was completely irrelevant to my investigation. It had nothing to do with the fire. I spent a great deal of time in your prior home, Mr. Strong. Almost two full days. I never do that in a case like this, Calvin, because there normally isn't a need to, and my fee does not cover that sort of intense analysis and labor. And by the way, your check bounced."

"It bounced?"

"Yes. It bounced. And I don't mean literally, because it didn't literally bounce, it fell to pieces on the floor after I tore it up. But never mind that, I don't even care. This was an unusual case for me and I took a personal interest. We'll settle up on money later, if you're able to. I'm much more interested in what happened to your house than I am in a fee."

"What happened to the house?"

"If you'll let me explain. Your house, Calvin,

essentially ate itself. It ate itself from the inside out. The fire originated from within the walls themselves. And not just from one point. The walls must have combusted simultaneously from within. Your report says, what, that it was an electrical fire?"

"Yes. An outlet that wasn't wired right and had exposed..."

"Bullshit," he spat in Calvin's face. "That was no wire. That was no outlet. This was not an electrical fire. This was something very different, a whole breed of its own. Most people would never know the difference. Most inspectors and investigators would never see the difference either. It's only because I've seen it before. Not often, not a lot. But a few times in the region."

"Where did you see it before?"

"There was a house in Jackson. Burned to the ground. An elderly couple died in that fire, along with their three cats. It was brushed off as accidental, a cigarette left burning. The whole family swore that they both had given up smoking decades earlier and couldn't believe that a lit cigarette had caused the fire, even though an old pack of cigarettes was found in the debris, half-burnt. It seemed like one of them had maybe decided to have one for old-time's sake, light up and choke a little more since death was impending anyway, and then left it lit somewhere without realizing. It's almost believable, but I know that's not what really happened. I know it because I spent way too long in the remains of that house, even all night with a flashlight, because I couldn't shake the feeling that something wasn't right about the fire. It was the family, too, who kept me going. They knew their parents and grandparents, and they didn't believe the story for a second. It took a great deal of analysis and a ton of samples from all over the interiors of the walls and framework of the house, but eventually I realized that the fire had been of a highly unusual nature. I got the data back from the lab a few days later on the samples I had taken. It was a chemical they couldn't clearly identify, or at least the residue left by a chemical they couldn't identify. It was everywhere. It somehow had been spread through the walls themselves, dousing the interior of every wall in the lower portion of the house. The residue traces were weak, almost undetectable, but they were there. They were there in every sample I took. I can only imagine what that must have looked like. The house must have caught fire from all angles at once and then within seconds burned upwards through the roof, collapsing the entire structure into the basement and killing the old couple inside. They never had a chance. There were smoke detectors in every room. The old couple never had time to respond to them because they were probably melted before they ever went off. There was no escape, either, with a ferocious blaze like that. There was no way out."

"So what happened with all the information you got from the tests?"

"Nothing."

"What do you mean?"

"They didn't do anything. I was extremely excited about what I had learned about the fire and was shouting at the insurance company to take a look. They didn't seem to care, though. They said that the traces I had found in the walls were simply a result of the old insulation burning, a common chemical reaction to extreme heat. They called this normal. They ruled it a simple case of accidental fire due to a lit cigarette and then they dropped it. They ignored all the tests I had run and the results. It was disregarded as nonsense and tossed aside. This was no accident, Calvin. You were targeted. I don't know by who or why, but you were definitely targeted and this was very intentional. Someone went through a great deal of difficulty to burn your house down and make it seem like an accident."

17

Calvin sat in a daze at the kitchen table, feeding spoonfuls of peach baby food to Pearl in her highchair. He stared at her, expressionless, as she gobbled down the spoonfuls he offered and made 'mmmm' sounds.

"Are you okay today, babe?" Leah asked him from the bathroom as she brushed her hair. "You seem awfully distant. And spacey."

"I'm always spacey," Calvin replied. "Isn't that what you always say?"

"More so than usual," she said. "Something you want to talk about?"

"No. Just a lot on my mind, that's all."

"Well, all right. I just worry about you. Things have been good between us, you know. And I just want things to keep going so well."

"You think things have been good between us?" Calvin asked with distant indifference.

"Yes. I do." she replied with conviction. "I think

things are going great and I'm excited about spending more time together. I think about the future a lot."

"Leah...I'm not even on that page right now."

"Well, we're living together. If we're not staying together as a couple and you don't see a future between us, why are you still here? And don't even say you have nowhere else to go. I know you could find a place easily enough."

"I could find a place if I wanted to. I don't want to leave, I've told you a hundred times. I want things to work between us, but I'm just trying to take it one day at a time right now. I try not to think too much about the future. I just think about now."

"So I'm 'Miss Right Now'?"

"You're the mother of my child and I love you," Calvin stated without emotion. "Is that what you want to hear?"

"It's a start."

"There's a lot going on right now that has me stressed. Really stressed."

"That's why we need to maybe get away for a bit. Take a vacation," Leah said in a chipper tone.

"I don't need a vacation right now..."

"You're stressed. You're brain is on overload. You're not thinking clearly. I don't mean to say it like that, but you're not. I know you don't see it, but I do."

"I'm not losing it. Okay?"

"It's okay. I understand," Leah soothed him. "I've talked to a lot of people about what's happening to you and I want you to know that I understand and it's okay and I'll stand by you no matter what."

"Damnit, Leah, I'm not losing my mind!" Calvin yelled at her. "Why are you telling people that?"

"I'm sorry. I'm sorry. I didn't mean to put it like

that. Bad choice of words."

"No matter what words you use, I'm not losing my mind. I know what's going on and I've never been more rational or more aware of reality. And unfortunately, my reality sucks."

"Things will get better."

Calvin snorted. Then the expression on his face became very serious. "You know what?" he said, putting Pearl's spoon down and turning to face Leah. "Maybe a vacation is just what we need right now. The three of us. That's not such a bad idea at all. How about we pile in the car tonight and just take off somewhere for a week or two?"

"What? Calvin, I can't," she said, laughing a little. "That sounds great, but I can't just not show up to work and call in for a week or two. I have to give at least a couple weeks notice before taking any vacation time, especially that much."

"Forget work."

"Yeah. Easy for you to say. You don't have 'work' anymore."

"They'll find someone to fill in for you."

"Calvin, no," she said with a laugh.

Calvin was dead serious, though, now. "Then call in."

"Call in?"

"Yeah. Call in and say there's a medical emergency. Say you need to have surgery or something that's going to keep you out for a couple weeks."

"Calvin, why would I do that?"

"What if it were an emergency? What if I'm the emergency, and our need for a vacation together is the emergency?"

"An emergency vacation. Hmm…I like the sound of

that."

"Then let's do it," Calvin said firmly.

"Oh, really? Well you go right ahead and book it. Where on Earth will we go? Paris? China? Aruba?"

"Wherever you want."

"And we'll fly on your private jet?"

"I don't care how we get there or where we go. As long as we're away from here."

"You're really determined to get us all some rest and relaxation, aren't you? I like this change in you. Normally it seems like I can't get you to leave the house."

"Yes. I definitely think it's time to leave the house." Calvin's eyes were glazed-over, now fixed on his baby in the high chair.

"Hang on," she said as she went to grab her vibrating cell phone off the kitchen table. "This must be our travel agent calling right now to book it."

She looked at the illuminated screen of the phone before answering it. "Calvin?" she said to him. "Why is your phone calling me?"

Calvin's face went pale. He had no response for her. He stared into her eyes with pure fear.

"Why is your number calling me? You're right here. Why would your phone be calling me?"

She answered it. "Hello?" she said with great uncertainty. Her forehead scrunched as she stared at Calvin, mystified. "Yes, he's right here," she said with hesitation in her voice. "It's some guy calling for you."

He stared at her as she handed the phone towards him.

"Well? Are you going to take it?"

Calvin took the phone in his hand as though it was a deadly weapon. "Yeah, this is Calvin," he said in a dull tone, trying to hide the fear that was eating away at his nerves.

The voice on the other end was low and growling and slowly said, *"This is the boogey man, Calvin. I've been watching you. I've been waiting. And now I'm coming for you and your girlfriend and your baby. I'll make sure that you're the last of the three, so you can watch me rip the other two apart."*

Calvin dropped the phone to the table. He fumbled to pick it up and press the button to end the call.

"What the hell was that?" she asked him in dismay.

"Nothing. Nothing."

"Well who was calling me from your phone? Where is your phone? Who was that?"

"I lost my phone."

"You didn't tell me that."

"I didn't know it until just now."

"Who was that calling from it then?"

"Just some punk. Nobody. Just somebody who found it and thought it would be funny to call up people on my contacts list and prank me."

"How did the guy know that you'd be sitting right next to me?"

Calvin looked at her.

"How would anyone know that? That you'd be right here with me and I could hand the phone to you when he asked for you?"

Calvin shrugged. "He must have just taken a chance. I don't know...I don't know, Leah."

"Why are you so shaken up by it? What did he say?"

"Nothing," Calvin snapped. "I don't want to repeat it. It was just some damn kid. Some stupid shit-stain in the world with nothing better to do than call me up and piss me off."

"Calm down, it's no big deal."

"I am calm!"

"Is that why you're yelling at me?"

"I'm just a little stressed right now. That's all."

"So you're going to have to get a new phone then?"

"I guess so."

"The person isn't giving it back to you, I take it?"

"No, Leah. He's not."

"You look like you've seen a ghost."

"I feel a little sick. I'm tired. I don't feel good. Maybe I just need to take a walk or something. I need a little space. I don't know."

"Okay. All right." She went quiet for a moment and rinsed dishes in the sink. "I'm going to run out to the store. There's a bunch of things we need, so I'll be a little bit. You just take it easy and relax. Just forget about it, okay? You'll get a new phone. It's no big deal, babe."

"No. It's not a big deal," he said, forcing a brief smile for show. "Pick me up some Pop-tarts."

"Blueberry unfrosted? You got it."

"They don't make them store-brand. They only make the frosted ones store-brand."

"Yes, dear. I know." She gave him a kiss on the cheek. "I'll be home a little later. Love you."

He watched her walk across the kitchen. "Love you too."

Calvin stood at the front door and watched her get into her car. As soon as she backed out of the driveway and headed up the street, he sprang into action.

"I'm sorry, sweetie," he said to Pearl. "You're going to have to stay put for a bit. Daddy's got a lot to do right now. I'm sorry."

Pearl watched him rush around the room with those big adorable eyes. She held out her arms toward him and said, "Dada."

"Daddy's never going to let anything bad happen to you, sweetie. No matter what."

"I'm home," Leah said, pushing through the door with bags of groceries.

"Oh, hey there," Calvin said, rushing through the living room to greet her.

"Where were you, just now?"

"Oh, just putting some laundry away."

"You look all sweaty."

"I guess I stayed active while you were gone."

"Well that's good, I guess…"

"Let me help you with the groceries, there…"

"Thanks. There's more in the car."

"I'll get them," Calvin insisted.

"Okay. Twist my arm. I'll start putting them away then. Hi," she said cheerily to Pearl. "Mommy missed you!"

Pearl smiled widely and kicked her feet in the highchair.

"You haven't had her in the highchair the whole time, have you?" she asked Calvin accusingly.

"What? No. We just decided to have some more lunch," he said as he closed the front door quickly behind him.

He hurried out to the trunk of her car to grab the rest of her groceries. He took six bags of food, normally enough for two trips. His adrenaline was pumping and he didn't feel the weight or the bag handles cutting into his fingers. He just didn't want her to come back out near the cars.

"Here we go. This is everything," he announced,

plopping the bags on the counter.

"Thanks. I got you a bunch of food in there, too. Cold-cuts, milk, ice cream, and, of course, cookies for you."

"Thanks," Calvin said, rushing to help her put things away.

"So, hey," Calvin started, taking a deep breath, "I know you just got back from the store and you probably don't feel like going out. But how do you feel about running to the Home Warehouse with me?"

"Really? For what?"

"Well, some trim, for starters. I want to finish the baby's room that I never got to."

"Really? That would sure be nice. It's only been a year and a half since you started your trim project that should have taken an hour."

"Yeah, I don't know what I've been doing with all my free time lately," he said sarcastically. "I've been bored out of my mind."

"I know things have been hectic."

"Hectic is not the word."

"I appreciate the offer, and it's really nice to see you taking initiative like this, but you're a strong guy, Calvin. You don't need me to help you carry a few pieces of trim to your truck."

"Oh, I know. It's not just the trim. I need some other things too. I thought I would pick up some bags of concrete to patch the basement floor."

"Really? Wow. That would be great if you do that."

"So you'll go?"

"Oh, I don't know," she said uncertainly. "You can still lift those by yourself, easily. You don't need a little girl like me to help you with that."

"Of course I don't. I want to spend time with you,"

Calvin said sincerely, knowing how to play off her emotions.

"Aww," she said, smiling at him. Her cheeks blushed. "That's very nice to hear. I just got home, though…I don't know, I don't really feel like going out again. I'm kind of in for the night."

"Oh, come on. It will be a quick trip. We'll pick some things up and be on our way. It will be a nice ride. We'll stop and grab you a coffee on the way."

"Oh, all right. Since you put it that way. You know I can't resist coffee at this time of day. I'm dragging. Just give me a few minutes to get ready and get Pearl ready and we'll go."

"I'll take care of her. Just get yourself ready."

Together they drove.

"This is so nice," she said to him. "Spending time together. The two of us are never off on the same day anymore. Well you're off all the time now, sort of."

"Yeah."

"I can't wait for the spring to come. We'll plant a garden this year. We'll grow fresh tomatoes and cucumbers. Maybe some cherry tomatoes and squash."

"Sure. Sounds good."

"Are you feeling all right?"

"Yeah. I'm fine."

"You don't seem fine."

"I'm perfectly fine. Just driving. Why?"

"You're quiet. And extremely focused."

"I'm just tired. Lot on my mind."

"Anything you want to talk about?"

He remained silent for a moment. "No," he said

hesitantly. He knew he had to tell her, but he couldn't find the right moment. He knew it wasn't going to go over well and she would never understand.

"Huh," Leah said, looking confused. "This is a different way to go to the Home Warehouse."

"Yeah. Scenic route."

"If you say so…"

Pearl started crying in the back.

"I thought she was asleep already," Calvin said, surprised.

"Me too. She didn't make a peep so far."

"Leah, there's something I need to talk to you about."

"Oh, okay…" Leah said, distracted and annoyed. "Well, now she's crying back there…"

"I know, but just forget about the baby for the moment."

"She's crying her head off, Calvin."

"I know, but she's fine. She's in her seat and there's nothing wrong with her. I really need to talk to you for a minute."

"Now you want to talk, all of a sudden? Now that we can't?"

Pearl's crying intensified.

"Are you sure she ate while I was gone, Calvin?"

"She ate…she might be hungry still."

"She's crying like she's starving and hasn't eaten in five hours."

"She'll be okay for a few minutes," Calvin said, growing frustrated. " We'll stop somewhere on the way."

"Calvin, I'm not going to let her just cry her head off back there. She never cries in the car. She usually just passes right out. This isn't normal. She's either starving or something is seriously wrong. Either way, I need to tend to her." She unlatched her seatbelt and started to crawl in between the driver and passenger seat.

"Leah..."

"Shhh...it's all right, it's all right," she calmed Pearl as she climbed into the back seat.

"Leah..." Calvin struggled to get her attention.

"Mommy's going to get you some food, since somebody's trying to starve you to death," Leah said facetiously. "Poor starving baby."

"Leah, we need to talk..."

"Calvin?" she asked suddenly and stopped going through the bag to find a bottle. "What is all this in the back of the truck?"

"I was trying to talk to you about that."

"What is all this? Why is your truck totally packed up? Why are there suitcases in here and all these bags of...clothes and food? Her portable crib is in here too...why is this in the car, Calvin? Why is it in here?"

"We're going out of town for a little while."

"What? Are you kidding me?"

"No."

"You're being totally serious right now?"

Pearl began screaming.

"Yeah, I'm serious," Calvin shouted over the baby's crying. "I tried to tell you. You make it so difficult to talk about anything serious..."

"What?"

"You won't listen to me. This is serious. I've been trying to tell you and you just won't listen to me."

"Calvin, where are we going?"

"We're heading to a friend's house. For a few weeks."

"A few weeks, Calvin? When I said we needed a vacation, this is not what I had in mind. I can't do this right now. Are you crazy?"

"No, I'm not crazy," he replied defensively.

"I can't do this," she hollered at him. "You know that. I have to go to work tomorrow, Calvin. To my job. I can't just leave town for a few weeks on the spur of the moment. I appreciate you being spontaneous and all, but this is not the time or the way to do it! Why would you do this? Why did you pack up all our things in the car and trick me into going on a drive with you to the hardware store?"

"Because we're in danger, Leah."

"What? What sort of danger?"

"I'm in trouble. Listen to me, and listen carefully. There are people who are trying to hurt me. They may want to hurt you and the baby, too. We need to leave town for a while."

"Okay, Calvin, this is just crazy…"

"You need to trust me on this one. Just trust me this one time."

"No. No, no, no. Is this all about the house burning down again? Is that what this is all about? You're still driving yourself crazy about the house burning down and your dog dying?"

"There's more to it than you realize, Leah."

"Oh, please…"

"You have no idea what's going on. We need to leave the area and make sure we're all safe."

"No, Calvin! This has gone way too far now!"

"People have threatened my life. And yours. And our child's."

"Calvin, what are you talking about? Is this just like the car that was circling the block? The car that turned out to be the paper delivery guy making his rounds?"

"You don't know that for sure. That car keeps

turning up…"

"Oh, following you again? Chasing you? Because you think you're so interesting that someone wants to follow you and watch everything you do?"

"Someone *was* following me. Someone *was* chasing me. Someone ran me off the road and tried to kill me."

"Oh, right. Where are the marks on your truck, Calvin? Why aren't there any marks from another car on the back of your truck where he supposedly hit you to run you off the road?"

"There *are* marks," he said firmly.

"No, there aren't!"

"There were already a lot of marks on the back. That's why you can't tell which ones are from the car hitting me."

"No one else seems to think you were hit from behind," she said doubtfully. "And all I know is that you show up with Sadie in her car while I was sitting there at home waiting for you, worried sick, and there isn't really any damage to the back of your truck."

"You don't get it. You're not listening. I found my watch. I found it online and I went to meet the guy who had it. He tried to sell it to me. It *was* my watch, Leah. I have it right here," he pulled it from his pocket in the plastic bag. "*This* is my watch."

"Your watch was lost in the fire, Calvin. If that is your watch, then how did you get it back?"

"I tracked down the guy who stole it from me. I had Alfred run his plates and we found his house. We waited until he wasn't home and I went inside."

"Who's we? Calvin? Who's we?"

"Me and Sadie."

"Oh my god. That's great, Calvin. That's just awesome."

"I went inside their house and I found the watch in there. And here it is. This is my watch."

"So you went with Sadie to break into some guy's house and then stole his antique watch out of his house?"

"I didn't *steal* it—this is *my* watch. He stole it first."

"Are you even listening to yourself right now? Do you hear what's coming out of your mouth?"

"There was other stolen stuff in there. It wasn't just the watch I found."

"Was your other stuff in their house?"

"No, I didn't see that. But I know the other things they had were stolen."

"And how do you know that?"

"They had piles of crap stacked up in rooms upstairs—all kinds of things that seemed out of place. And there wasn't much in the rest of the house, just empty rooms. If you had all this nice furniture and nice TV's, wouldn't you be using them instead of…"

"Did it occur to you that they had just moved in? Or were getting ready to move out? Or maybe they're just lazy slobs who keep clutter around?"

"You don't understand," Calvin yelled defensively. "You weren't there."

"No. And I wouldn't have been there. I don't break into people's homes on wild assumptions with other men I work with…"

"You wouldn't help me! You never believe me! Those guys had something to do with the fire. I'd bet my life on it."

"Sounds like you already did."

"I heard them talking," Calvin struggled to explain. "Through the floor."

"You were in the house while they were home?"

"They came home while I was in the house. And

they were talking about me. They were talking about what they had done and what they needed to do to me. And I lost my phone inside the house. It slipped out of my pocket. And then they called. When you answered the phone—that was them calling me from my phone. They must have found it and found your number in it."

"So maybe it was just a random guy who found your phone in his house and was really pissed off that you broke in and stole his valuable watch. Did that occur to you?"

"They've been watching, Leah," Calvin said anxiously. "That's how they knew I'd be standing right next to you when he called. It all makes sense..." his voice trailed off. "It all makes sense."

"Listen, I know you're going through rough times right now, and I truly love you," Leah said as calmly as she could, her voice trembling fiercely. "You're the father of my child and I'm doing everything I can to ignore the way you've been acting lately. You're not well, though, Calvin. Someone needs to say it to you. There's something wrong with you."

"I'm fine! I'm not insane! This is really happening to me!"

"Nothing is happening to you, Calvin. It's all in your head. All of it. You're sick, Calvin. And I'm starting to really worry about you."

"Oh, please, don't do me any favors. You don't need to worry about me."

"No. I mean I worry about you being around me. I worry about you being around the baby. This is getting out of control. Absolutely out of control."

Calvin glanced at her with fire in his eyes. "Don't you *ever* say anything like that to me..."

"That you're unsafe around your child? If you told

anyone in the world what you've told me, they would think you're crazy, too. There's not a person out there who would go along with this ridiculous paranoia and these crazy delusions you've been having. I don't know how to handle it. I don't know what's wrong with you or how to fix it. I'm afraid to even talk to anyone about it. They'd tell me to get away from you. And stay away."

"Yeah, well Sadie believes me. She hasn't doubted me for a second."

"That's it! I want you out! I want you out of my house and out of my life! For good! You're totally crazy Calvin, completely fucking crazy! And you know what I think? I think it was *you*!"

"You think *what* was me?"

"It was *you*, Calvin! You burnt your house down!"

"What?"

"Everyone else thinks the same thing!"

"Don't say that!"

"It was *you*, Calvin!"

"No!"

"And you don't even realize you did it! You're head is so fucked up!"

"I didn't kill my dog! I didn't do anything…"

"You're so out of your mind right now…Please, just take us home! I don't care what you did. Please don't do this with the baby in the car!"

"You're not taking my baby away from me, if that's what you're thinking…"

"I'll take her wherever I want! We'll move back to California, across the country, if that means we're both safe from you! Just take us home now!"

Calvin focused in the rear view intensely. The SUV ran over the edge of the road. The whole car jerked and rocked as he yanked the wheel, fighting to keep it on pavement and avoid a tree.

"What the hell are you doing!" she shouted in his ear.

"That's the car! Behind me!"

"What?" She glanced in the rearview. "Are you fucking kidding me!"

"That's the goddamn car that's been following me home from work and circling our goddamn block every night! That's it!"

"That looks like a million other cars on the road, Calvin. That's just a normal car being driven by some normal person on their way home from work. Normal, Calvin! Not like you. Normal!"

"I *am* normal! I'm not crazy, I know that's the car…I'd recognize it anywhere." He frantically shook his head. His knuckles whitened on the steering wheel. "I'm gonna run this fucker right into a tree…"

"Calvin! The baby's in here!"

"I'm gonna smash the shit out of this guy! They ruined my life!" He shook himself violently on the steering wheel. "They took everything from me!"

"What the fuck is wrong with you!"

"I'm gonna kill him!"

"You're crazy, Calvin! You're crazy! You're fucking crazy! Stop it! *You're fucking crazy!*"

18

"Calvin," a female voice echoed in Calvin's brain.
Everything else was quiet.

"Calvin," the voice came again, agitating Calvin, pulling him back. He had no idea where he had been, but he knew for certain he was not ready to come back.

"Calvin," the voice persisted. "Why are you doing that?"

Calvin struggled to open his eyes. They cracked slightly and shut instantly. It was bright and they would not stay open.

"Calvin, why are you doing that?" the voice insisted, becoming more desperate. "You need to tell me why you're gasping like that. Why do you keep gasping and jerking like that? You need to wake up."

His eyes opened slightly again. Everything was blurred, but he could see enough to make out human forms around him. He knew he had the answer. He understood what they wanted now, because the problem was becoming apparent to him as well. He wasn't sure he could talk. His voice cracked and he was surprised sound came out at all. "I can't breathe," he muttered.

Calvin saw the blurry people rush around for a moment, then felt an unpleasant intrusion in his throat. He was out again.

19

"He's waking up again," a voice hollered in the background.

Calvin became aware of buzzing and humming noises for the first time, although he had the feeling they had been there for quite a while. He whipped his head to one side, jolted by the unfamiliarity of his surroundings. His eyes kept trying to close, but he forced them open. He was in a bed in a room with a heavy blanket over him. He went to shift in the bed and encountered great difficulty. He was uncomfortable and he felt this position was making it hard to breathe. The room was a blur around him. He tried to focus, but everything kept spinning. It seemed so familiar now, but he couldn't figure out where he was or why.

"Yes, he's waking up again," the same woman's voice repeated anxiously.

Calvin could hear a conversation taking place outside the doorway between a man and a woman. Their voices were lowered in an attempt not to be overheard. Then a man entered the doorway with a very serious expression on his face.

"Mr. Strong," the man said to him. "How are you

doing now?"

Calvin grumbled and tried to turn in bed again. He wanted to talk, but words were not coming out.

"I'm sorry about the restraints," the man said. "But we couldn't have you acting up again. The last time you woke up, you woke up swinging. It took nearly half the floor to get you under control. We're not playing that game again. You're quite a strong fellow, as your name implies. Much stronger than you look. But you seem much more under control now. I'm sorry, I should introduce myself. I'm Doctor Fletcher. I've been overseeing your care since you arrived. Are you able to speak to me?"

Calvin made a few attempts and was finally able to ask, in a hoarse voice, "Where am I?"

"You're in Empire Hospital, in Albany, on the fourth floor."

"The hospital?"

"Yes, Mr. Strong. You are in a hospital."

"Why?"

"You were in a very serious accident, I'm afraid."

"What happened?"

"Well, there's been a lot of curiosity about exactly what happened. Do you remember anything about the accident you had yesterday?"

"Yesterday?"

"Yes, you've been out for just over twenty-four hours. You've been with us the whole time. We've been keeping a close watch on you and we've been waiting for you to wake up. You were involved in a very serious car accident, Calvin. You suffered a head trauma and broken ribs. Your injuries seem well under control, and of course it's the head trauma that we're mostly concerned with. You've been under very close observation. Do you remember anything at all about the accident when it happened? Or why it happened?"

"No…" Calvin looked him in the eyes, perplexed. "I don't remember anything about an accident."

"You were driving your car with your wife and your baby in the back…"

"Pearl…" Calvin spat out.

"Yes, your wife and baby were in the car with you at the time of the accident."

"My baby…oh, god, the baby…"

"Your baby is perfectly fine, Mr. Calvin," he said soothingly, as though telling a child that there are no monsters under the bed. "We have her in our pediatric ward and she is under observation. She didn't have any obvious injuries from the crash and we've done several ultrasounds to make sure that there were no internal injuries. That car seat saved her life. She seems perfectly fine, and exceptionally happy and hungry," he said with a reassuring smile.

"Leah…she is okay, too?"

"Mr. Strong…" he shifted his posture and leaned closer to the bed. His face became more serious. "Your wife is under our care as well."

"She's not my wife…but she's okay, right?"

"We're keeping a very close eye on her, Mr. Strong. She sustained quite a few more injuries than you or the baby did in the crash. She wasn't wearing a seatbelt at the time of the accident and was thrown into the windshield. She's suffering from a major head trauma. She has what we call a subdural hematoma and we may have to perform surgery to relieve the pressure on her brain. She's still not conscious. We haven't had any luck yet with getting her to respond. We're hopeful, though."

"I need to see her…I need to see my baby."

"I'm afraid you'll have to stay put for the moment."

"No, you don't understand...I need to see her, I need to see that she's okay."

"You will see your baby soon. We can't let you see her right now. You're in no condition. We need to keep you in that bed right now, restrained, for your own safety and the safety of others in this hospital."

"No...No! Let me up! I don't need to be tied down! Please let me see her."

"Nurse!" the doctor yelled out into the hallway. "We're going to give you a sedative," he said calmly to Calvin. "Would that be okay with you?"

"No! I don't need a sedative! I need to get out of this bed! I need to see Pearl and Leah!"

The doctor hurried out of the room and a nurse walked in. She quickly pressed a button on the left of Calvin's bed.

Calvin's legs suddenly felt like they were wrapped tightly in cloth, as though there were inflatable pants on him that were overfilling with air. He felt warm and heavy. He was out.

20

Pale daylight filled the room. Calvin could see through the smudged window that it was flurrying outside. The snowflakes went practically sideways, caught in the updraft along the high walls of the hospital.

"Mr. Strong," a woman's voice said as she walked into his room.

Calvin raised his head slightly. He could see a middle-aged nurse with her hair up in a bun entering his room.

"Nice to see you awake again," she announced cheerfully. "You seem much more rested than before. And much calmer. How are you feeling today?"

"Like I got run over," Calvin grumbled.

"Your body went through a lot. It's going to take some time to fully recover. Fortunately, you've retained all your motor skills and your verbal abilities. That was quite a nasty head injury you got. You're very lucky that you haven't sustained any brain damage."

"Lucky is not the word I would use. I'm anything but lucky lately."

"You will be back to normal in no time," she said, pulling an empty bag from his IV pole. "We've been waiting for you to wake up today because there's someone here to see you."

Calvin perked up, finally making eye-contact with her. "Who?"

"He's a police officer with the town of White falls. He traveled all the way down here to have a talk with you. I guess you've met him before. He said you have. But I needed to make sure that you're okay for a visit. Do you feel up for it right now, Calvin?"

"Yes. That's fine."

"Good. I'll have him join you in just a moment. I think he just stepped away to grab a cup of coffee."

"Sure."

A minute later, Calvin was surprised to see Officer Patton appear in his doorway.

"Mr. Strong," he said in that familiar deep, hearty voice.

"Yes. Hello, Officer Patton."

"That's great—you remember who I am. They said you might not. Are you feeling all right today?"

"I'm in a lot of pain," Calvin said. "Other than that, great."

"I just want to make sure you know who you are and where you are. I have a lot of questions for you, and I want to make certain you are in the right frame of mind to be answering them."

"Sure. Yeah, I'm all here." Calvin shrugged carelessly. "I'm a little groggy from this medication, whatever they're giving me. It's making me a little loopy. I feel drunk. But I can answer whatever questions you have."

"Good." Patton settled into the hospital chair next to the bed and leaned forward towards Calvin. He clasped his hands together on his lap. "Now, Calvin...what do you remember about the accident?"

"I didn't remember much until that doctor was in here. He brought it up and it suddenly came back to me."

"You remember driving into the tree?"

"No. I don't remember anything about a tree. I remember about a week ago when I was run off the road into a tree and it messed up my truck..."

"Do you remember the events that led up to *this* crash?"

"Somewhat. Yes. Yes, I do."

"Can you tell me...what was going on at the time of the accident? Or, rather, I should say, what was going on in the car the few minutes before the accident occurred?"

"We were in a fight," Calvin stated.

"By *we*, I assume you mean you and your wife?"

"She's not my wife."

"I'm sorry. You're....?"

"Girlfriend. Sort of."

"Your girlfriend, sort of, and you were having a fight in the car?"

"Yes."

"An intense fight?"

"Yes. Fairly intense."

"What was the fight about?"

"It was about everything that had been going on lately," Calvin said slowly, slurring his speech. "She didn't believe me. She didn't believe anything I said and she thought it was all made up in my mind."

"She thought *what* was all in your mind?"

"That someone was trying to kill me."

"Why would someone be trying to kill you?"

"Because I had pushed too far. I had found out more than I should have, even though I don't understand it."

"This all has to do with your house burning down?"

"Yes. Ever since then, someone has been watching me. Then trying to kill me, or at least scare me into thinking they were trying to kill me."

"What would someone have to gain by killing you, Calvin?"

"I don't know," Calvin said blankly. "Like I said, I felt like I had learned too much, I was on their trail. I think they're worried that I really have something on them."

"Calvin, who is *they*?"

"They, the men. The two men who live together. The giant man who tried to sell me the watch he stole from me, Tom. I forgot his last name. I have it written down."

"You mentioned the watch that was stolen from you. I remember you told me about that when we met up north. Is *this* that watch, Calvin?" he said, pulling the watch in the plastic bag from his pocket.

"Yes." Calvin's eyes lit up. "That's my grandfather's watch he gave me."

"How did you get this watch back, Calvin?"

"I...I'd rather not say right now."

"How did it get from Tom's hands into yours again?"

"I can't get into that right now."

"His name is Tom Grissom. He contacted the local police to report this watch as stolen from his home three nights ago. Are you sure this is your watch?"

"Yes. Positive."

"He filed a police report with the locals. He is claiming that you broke into his home and went through his belongings, then found and stole this watch that I'm holding right here in my hand."

"That's *my* watch," Calvin insisted.

"I believe you, Calvin. But it's not just me you have to convince. I want to believe you and I do, but to anyone else, this is all a little difficult to swallow."

"That *is* my watch. And there's all kinds of other stolen stuff in that house too. They have stacks of stolen property piled up in their upstairs rooms."

"So, you were in the house?"

"Yeah...No...I'm not answering that right now. I have a serial number, though, that might be of interest to you. I wrote it down. It's in my wallet."

"All right." Patton sighed and shifted in his chair. "I'll do a search on this serial number and I'll see if anything turns up. No harm in trying."

"There was another man in the house. It wasn't just the giant man."

"There's another man living there?"

"I think he lives there. I'm not sure.

"We'll look into that," Patton said, taking a moment to jot something down on his notepad. "Now, back to the moments before the crash. You were in a heated argument with your girlfriend?"

"Yes."

"Were you aware that she had dialed 911 on her phone during that fight?"

"What?" Calvin glared at him. "No. I wasn't."

"She never said anything," Patton continued. "She just dialed it. The emergency dispatcher picked up, but she never answered. The line was kept open, though. She never hung up. We have a large portion of the fight leading up to the crash on tape. I've listened to it myself, several times, and it brought up more questions than it answered. Where was your girlfriend at the time of the accident?"

"She had gone in back to try to feed the baby...she

never fed her, though."

"Why not?"

"She saw the things in my trunk."

"Yes. I wanted to ask you about that. That was brought to my attention by the local police department. They said your truck was packed with quite a few belongings, as though you were planning to stay away from home for a while."

"Yes. That's true."

"Where were you heading, exactly?"

"Anywhere but home."

"Why?"

"I was afraid for my child's safety, and that of Leah and myself."

"So she was in back with the baby?"

"She was sort of between the two front seats, leaning forward while we were fighting."

"So that's why she didn't have her seatbelt on? Because she was feeding the baby?"

"Yes."

"Calvin, you mention on the tape, right before the crash, that someone was behind you, following you in a car?"

"Yes. There was someone behind me. It was the car that I had been seeing around since the fire. It was the car that ran me off the road the first time. I'd recognize it anywhere."

"You seem pretty convinced of that in the recording."

"I know it was the same car."

"And you think this car rammed the back of your truck, ran you off the road into the tree?"

"I don't know. I assume so. I don't remember exactly what happened. I just remember the fight and seeing the car behind us."

"Calvin, there *was* a witness to the crash. A man who lives very nearby was plowing a driveway. He didn't actually see the crash happen, but was there just moments after it occurred. He said that there didn't seem to be another car involved."

"No…there was another car…"

"He said it was just your truck and that he didn't see any other vehicles. There was, however, a man who stopped to try to help. He's the one who actually ended up calling 911 to report the accident."

"That was him…the man who stopped…it had to have been. Who was it? What was his name?"

"I can't release that to you, unfortunately. But it appears to be just a random driver who came upon the scene. There doesn't seem to be anything suspicious about any of it. In fact, we're having a tough time understanding why your truck ended up in the tree."

"I'm a good driver…I had my baby in the car…"

"Were your eyes on the road while you were fighting with your girlfriend?"

"Yes…except when I was looking at the car behind me coming up fast. I was watching the road."

"Because it really looked to the police at the scene as though you had simply driven off the road, maybe lost control of the vehicle, and slammed it into the tree. But you're saying there was another car involved, that there was another car right behind you?"

"Yes, there was…there was another car."

"Your girlfriend supports that part on tape. We can hear that she saw the car as well, although she does not find it suspicious at all. The two of you continued to fight about that."

"She didn't believe me. She never believed me

about any of it."

"Any of what?"

"That I was being followed. That someone ran me off the road. She thought I was just out cheating on her or something. I tried to warn her. I tried to keep her safe."

"And that's why you were trying to leave town with her?"

"I had to get us out of there. Especially the baby."

"Even if it meant taking her away against her will?"

"She didn't know what was happening. She thought it was all in my head. Her ignorance was a danger to us all, especially to our child who never had a say in the matter."

"I want to believe you, Calvin. I'm here to try to help you. I'm not trying to get you in trouble."

"Then let me see my daughter."

"That I can't do."

"I don't understand. Why is it so hard to just let me go see her? Everyone is telling me that she's just fine, she's perfectly okay, but they won't let me go see her. And I want to see my girlfriend."

"Calvin...your girlfriend...Leah is in very rough shape, from what I've been told. I haven't seen her myself...but you need to be prepared for the worst. They have her in the ICU right now and they're keeping a close eye on her. I have to be honest with you... No one I've talked to is overly optimistic about her recovery. She still hasn't woken up or even responded to the doctors yet. There's still hope, though. I don't want to get you down. You just need to know what you're facing. I don't want to tell you that everything is going to be fine. You're just lucky as hell that you had the baby strapped in well in the car seat. It saved her life."

"I need to see her. Why can't I just go to wherever they have her and see her? I want to hold her and know that she's all right."

"You can't."

"What do you mean I can't?"

"I can't allow you to do that. It's not up to me. The doctors have given their orders."

"What do you mean I can't? I'm fine. I'm fine. I can walk, I can get out of bed and walk there. If they want they can wheel me there right in this bed, I don't care…"

"They have given strict orders that you are not allowed to leave this room, Calvin."

"Why can't I leave? Why can't I just go down the hall? I'm not going to hurt myself anymore than I already have."

"They're worried about your safety. They're worried about your behavior and what the police have learned about you."

"I don't understand…"

"Calvin…do you know where you are?"

"I…I don't know. I'm in the hospital. I'm in Empire Hospital."

"Calvin, I'm not the one who should be explaining all this to you. They really should have told you more…"

"What's going on?"

"I'd rather it be this way, though. I'd rather be here to explain it to you, even though this isn't my job or even my place."

"Explain what?"

"Calvin, you *are* in the hospital. That is true. You were taken to the emergency room after your accident. Then, after your behavior when you first woke up…the way you were acting, combined with the police report that had been filed…and then the local police got involved and had the 911 tape and reviewed it, it was decided that you should be moved to a more…secure room in the hospital."

"What the hell does that mean?"

"It means that you have a lot of people keeping watch over you, and they're all here to help you get well again, or at least until we sort some of this out and figure out what's really going on."

"What the hell do you mean?" Calvin hollered, shaking his head.

"Calvin, this is very temporary. You have to understand where the doctors are coming from. It was determined that it would be best to keep you in a section of the hospital that would allow a more thorough—and secure—evaluation of your mental health, as well as your physical health."

"What are you saying? They put me in the nut ward?"

Patton sighed and looked at the floor.

"They threw me in the psych ward of the hospital?" Calvin erupted. "Are you kidding me?"

"Calvin, the best thing you can do is stay calm and relax. Just rest and get better," Patton said slowly. "Then they'll let you out of here."

"I want to get out of here now. I'm fine. None of this even hurts."

"You can't leave just yet, Calvin."

"The hell I can't!"

"There's a guard at the end of the hallway. The doors are always locked. You can't just walk out. Only hospital staff are allowed through the doors. Like I said, just stay put and stay focused on being calm, and that's your best ticket out of here."

"I'm not crazy!" Calvin yelled, throwing himself against the restraints on his bed.

"I know you're not. I can tell you're not just by talking to you. You're scared. You've been shaken up.

You're angry. You're on edge. I know something happened to you, Calvin. I don't know exactly what it was, but hopefully we'll find out. In the meantime, you're safe here. You're in good hands. And hopefully we can get all of this…straightened out."

21

Pacing the hallway with his IV pole trailing along side of him, Calvin did laps back and forth over the glossy blue and gray floor tiles. The light pale blue of the walls mixed with the florescent lighting in the most unpleasant way. The air tasted sour with loneliness and distress.

Calvin watched the workings of his prison. He only glanced when someone came or left, never looking for more than a split-second, so as not to be noticed.

It's like when you put a gerbil in a cage. The first thing it does is investigate every corner of its cell, searching for any potential exits. Once it realizes that all exits are blocked, it proceeds to look for weaknesses within its prison, something that could perhaps be chewed wide enough to squeeze through. The gerbil will spend its entire stay in that cage trying to get out.

The same happened to people in a psych unit. It's

human nature, to try to find freedom, to protest being confined against one's will, even if nothing better awaits outside the prison walls. Most of the people in there wouldn't know what to do if they were suddenly released. They might even beg to come back in.

Calvin did not socialize with most of the other patients. He did observe them closely, however. He spent his time trying to figure out what sort of problem brought them to this sad, lonely state. There were some young patients and some old ones. None of them talked much, besides 'Mickey', who would latch onto whoever was near and never shut up. She walked and talked in slow-motion, only wore Mickey Mouse attire, and never stopped smiling like something wonderful was happening in front of her.

Calvin heard piano music coming from the common area. The common room was a large, open space with a television, an old upright piano, and tables and chairs for eating.

Whoever was playing was clearly an accomplished pianist, although some of the notes were curiously missed. Calvin approached the room, drawn in by the haunting melody. He stopped in the wide doorway and watched.

There was a fairly tall, lanky man sitting on the bench playing. He was probably in his early thirties and had his hair spiked up and colored green like a rock star. Both of his wrists were entirely bandaged, from his forearms to the base of his fingers.

"Looking for a way out, bud?" the man said while continuing to play, his back to Calvin.

Calvin paused a moment, uncertain if the man was talking to him or not. He looked around and concluded that he was the only other person in the area. "A way out of what?" Calvin asked, intrigued.

"A way out of here," the man said, continuing to

play. "You're looking for a way out."

"How did you know that?"

"I've seen you walking up and down the hallway pretending you're not noticing everything that's going on."

"Then, yes," Calvin said. "I am looking for a way out."

"There's no point," the man said, still continuing to struggle through his difficult piece of music. "They'll just find you and stick you right back in here. Trust me. And then it's worse."

"How is it worse?"

"Then they keep you in here longer. They keep you on closer watch, too. Suddenly you're a flight risk. They don't want to risk you getting out again and, who the hell knows, hurting someone else or something because they couldn't keep you in like they're supposed to. Then they get sued and all that shit."

"You've gotten out before?"

The man laughed. "This is my fourth ride on the crazy train. The name's Mike, by the way."

"I'm Calvin."

"Yes, I've gotten out before. They brought me right back once they found me. It wasn't tough, because I was lying in a pool of my own blood."

"What happened to you?"

Mike stopped playing the piano. He lowered his bandaged hands to his sides and said, "I tried to kill myself again."

Calvin didn't know how to respond to that. "Why did you do that?" he asked, feeling rather insensitive after he said it.

"Because it didn't work the previous three times."

"What made you want to do it in the first place?"

"I'm tired of living. I've had a rough life, an

upbringing from hell, and I can't take any more pain. I'm messed up, man. Once you're messed up enough, you just can't fix it. Especially if you're young when it happens. I was just a kid. I just wanted to play with toy trucks and trains. I didn't ask for any of this. I never asked someone to turn me into what I am." He was quiet for a moment, slumped in his chair. He turned around on the piano bench to finally face Calvin.

Calvin was surprised to find that his pupils were jet black. He had scars all over his face.

"I'm back in here, now, once again, because of this girl I was seeing a couple months ago," Mike said, lost in his own world. "And she was, like, the most beautiful thing I've ever had in my life. She was absolute perfection. And it was the greatest feeling I've ever experienced...ever. I would've done anything for her, to hold onto her and keep her mine forever. And I tried, but I couldn't. It was going well until I started weirding her out...maybe because I was trying so hard. And then she ended it. She told me she didn't want anything to do with me. That was the last time I ended up in here. Then I got out. I wanted to see her, to at least try to talk to her about what we had. So I escaped from here and went to her house. Needless to say, that didn't go so well. She was pretty freaked out and called the cops. Go figure. While they were on the way, I kept trying to just talk to her. She told me to get lost, go home or she was going to have her new boyfriend come over and beat the shit out of me. I told her that if we couldn't be together then I didn't want to live anymore. She said that's fine, do what you gotta do. So I went into her backyard, where there's this big garden. I found a glass ornament and broke it on a rock. Then I used the broken pieces of glass to slice both of my wrists. I cut them as hard and deep as I could. I wanted to make sure the arteries were severed. It was supposed to be the last time. I wasn't supposed to be here again. And here I am."

"It's a shame," Calvin said. "Most people wish they could play the piano like you."

"I play like shit now. I cut so deep that I damaged the tendons in my wrists. But somehow I still managed to screw it up and live. Can't even kill myself right."

"So they found you and put you back in here?"

"Yeah. After an extensive visit in the ER and a couple of surgeries. Those doctors spent forever working on my wrists, trying to repair the damage I did. What a waste."

"Why was it a waste?"

"I'll be dead by Thursday. They have to let me out by Wednesday. They can only hold you against your will in here for three days. Good to know."

It was either late at night or very early in the morning. Calvin couldn't tell anymore. He stopped looking at the clock hours ago. He couldn't sleep. He wasn't hungry. He didn't know quite what he was feeling, but he knew it was unpleasant and he wanted it to end. He sat on his bed, his head hanging low. The medication was kicking his ass. He was sluggish and felt heavy, tired all the time.

An unfamiliar alarm suddenly shouted at him from within his room and made him jump up from the bed. Panicked, he looked over to the small table beside his bed.

The phone in his room lit up as it rang.

He stared at it. The phone hadn't rang since he'd been in there. It continued to ring loudly, piercingly, and it was making his nerves stand on end. He looked at it as though he had never seen a phone before and didn't know what to do with it.

He slowly walked over to it, staring at it the entire time. He had a strange feeling that it would never stop ringing until he answered it.

"Hello?" he said in slurred speech.

"*Calvin,*" a frightening voice said on the other end.

"Yes. Hello?"

"*Calvin. We've been looking for you.*"

Calvin looked around frantically.

"Who is this?"

"*You know who it is.*"

"Why are you doing this to me?"

"*Because you're still alive.*"

"What did I do to you!"

"*You wouldn't let it go.*"

"Wouldn't let *what* go?"

"*You were supposed to be in that house.*"

"What house?"

"*Your house.*"

"What the hell did I do to you!" Calvin held his forehead and squeezed.

"*You can't get us out of your head, Calvin,*" the voice taunted him.

"I didn't do anything to you! I didn't do anything wrong!"

"*It's a nice night for a fire, Calvin. And you know what I'm in the mood for barbecuing? I'll give you a clue. I'm watching her right now through the kitchen window drinking a bottle.*"

"Fuck you! My baby's not even there, you sick fuck! She's not even there!"

"*Oh. Then it must be someone else's baby in your house being held by that old hag.*"

"I don't know what you're on…my baby's with me in the hospital. She's perfectly safe here."

"Are you sure about that, Calvin?"

"Yes."

"Are you sure you're sure?"

"Yes."

"Would you bet your little baby's head on it?"

"I know she's here! Leave me the hell alone!"

"We're never going to leave you alone, Calvin. We're in your head now. Once we're in your head, you'll never get us out. You'll never get us out. You'll never get us out. You'll never get us out. You'll never get us out. You'll never get us out. You'll never get us…"

Calvin screamed into the phone and slammed it down on the receiver. He stared at it as he cautiously backed away from it. He felt two tears dripping down his cheeks. He was trembling. He clutched his temples with his palms and squeezed as hard as he could, groaning as if being tortured.

"What did I do, what did I do…" he said to himself as he walked in circles in his room. "What did I do, what did I do to you, Leah…Oh my god, what did I do to you, Leah? You were right, you were right…"

"Calvin," a voice said from the doorway firmly, jolting him, he spun around so quickly and violently that the nurse at the door gasped and flinched. "Oh—you scared me," she said, looking very afraid of him. Her tone became overly cautious. "Are you okay in here?"

"Yes," he answered quickly.

"They wanted me to check on you. Some of the staff said that they heard a commotion coming from your room."

"Yeah. I'm okay."

"Did something happen in here?"

"No. Nothing happened. I'm calm. I'm fine now and I'm calm."

"Okay…all right…Calvin, you look like you've just seen a ghost."

"I must have fallen asleep. I guess I had a nightmare, or something. I'm a little freaked out, that's all. I scared myself."

"It may be a reaction to the drugs we're giving you. We need to know about these things, too, given the hit you took to your head. We need to know about any strange impulses or mood changes."

"Is my baby still in the hospital?"

"What? Well, yes, Calvin, as far as I know…"

"I need to know," he cut her off. "I have to know where she is."

"She's in the pediatric unit. The doctor told you that. You've asked us *several* times already, too. I know you want to see her, and I can only imagine how difficult this must be for you to be kept from her like this. I have two children of my own and I couldn't imagine…"

"Is she there?"

"Is she…in the pediatric unit?"

"Yes. I need to know if she is still in there. Please. I just had a really bad dream and I'm very scared. I have a very bad feeling, and it would really help me right now to know that she's in the hospital here and that she's safe and sound."

"Okay. I'll see what I can…"

"Please."

"I'll see what I can do. I'll make a call for you. I assure you, Calvin, she's still here. So just relax in the meantime."

Calvin watched her illuminate in the florescent light of the hallway before she disappeared around the corner.

He knew she had to be there. Leah was unconscious in a hospital bed in the other end of the hospital. The baby was there. She had to be.

And he knew what that meant.

It was him. It was all him. He had lit his house on fire. He had killed his dog. He had driven their car into a tree with the baby and his girlfriend in the car. He had almost killed all three of them.

He felt dangerous. There was something very wrong with him and he didn't understand it, but there was no other way around it. Leah was right the whole time. None of it was happening to him. It was all a creation of his. He must have suffered some sort of total mental breakdown when he lost the business and his life fell into ruins. He must have blown a gasket and truly lost his mind without ever realizing it. He was dangerous. He was in the right place, now. He just hoped that there was something that could be done to fix whatever was wrong with him.

And then it occurred to him.

He needed to end this. He couldn't accept the horrible things that he must have done and the people he had hurt. He nearly killed his girlfriend, the mother of his child, and put his own child's life in danger.

He wanted to die. He looked around the room. He needed some way to escape the pain.

Was it possible? The voice on the phone wasn't real. Maybe the whole conversation wasn't even real. Did the phone even ring? No one else seemed to hear it. Did he really answer it? Did that conversation really take place, or was that just his deluded mind playing tricks on him?

"Calvin," the nurses voice came from the doorway again. "I have some great news for you." She walked in with a smile on her face. "I was totally unaware of this, and I apologize, but your baby was actually discharged from the hospital."

"Discharged?" Calvin practically shouted at her. "To who?"

"I guess one of your neighbors was able to take her. She was listed as an emergency contact for the baby and she was happy to do it. She's even staying at your house with the baby so that she has everything she needs right there and she can sleep in her own crib in her own house."

"I was never asked about this...I never said anyone could send her home with anyone else."

"They had to release her. I thought it would be great news to you that nothing was wrong with her. They ran all their tests and she seemed perfectly fine. We can't just keep her in the hospital forever if nothing is wrong with her. They tried calling anyone else, your girlfriend's parents...and I guess there were no family members listed for you. They weren't able to get a hold of anyone besides this neighbor who was willing to help out for a little while. We're still trying to get a hold of Leah's parents or some other relative, but until then, she's perfectly safe."

"No, she isn't! I didn't okay this! She is not perfectly safe!"

"Calvin, you need to just relax and take it easy..."

"You don't understand!"

"I know you miss her and you're worried about her, especially after what happened."

"You have no idea! I need to get to her. I need to go get her and be with her."

"Not just yet, Calvin. In time. All in time. Right now we need to keep you here for at least a little longer and make sure you're all healed."

"I'm healed! I'm fine! Let me go now!"

"Mr. Strong, I need you to calm down now. This isn't helping matters, and it won't help you get out of here any sooner. You need to relax. Your baby's just fine."

Calvin fell silent. His head dropped. He breathed heavily and he felt his head spinning.

"Maybe I should call the doctor for you…"

"No," Calvin snapped. "I'm fine. I'm calm. I'm fine. I just need to rest and relax. I need to get my mind off things."

"That would be a good idea. Are you sure you're okay now?"

"Yes. Thank you. I feel much better and I'm calm now. Sorry about that. I'm very calm."

"Don't be sorry. We'll all be just up the hall, at the station, if you need anything or you start feeling anxious again." She turned away with a smile and headed up the hall, her heels clip-clopping all the way down.

Calvin paced the hallways, making loops up and down the long blue halls. Every time he passed a nurse he nodded to her and gave a fake smile. They were everywhere. He noticed the security guard in his usual spot by the door. There must be another way out. There had to be for fire code, but this appeared to be the only exit and it was heavily guarded with another set of doors just past it.

The guard was a large man, very heavy with plenty of muscle. He wasn't athletic by any means, but he was solid and well-built. Calvin knew that the guard could stop him. He wouldn't be able to get past him if he charged the door.

He had seen how they open the door with the red button hidden behind the counter of the nurses' station. There were nurses seated behind it, and several more wandering around making their rounds and eating dinner, or lunch, or whatever they considered this meal on the graveyard shift.

The piano music from Mike echoed eerily through the empty halls, ringing through the florescent lit halls with ghostly tones. Every few lines Calvin could hear him miss a key, but he kept playing. He was getting better.

Calvin approached him. His body swayed as he played the ghostly melody, putting forth much more effort to play accurately than it would normally take him if he had full use of his hands and fingers.

Calvin walked into the common room and stopped behind Mike.

"I need to go now," Calvin announced to Mike's back as he played.

Mike continued playing and missed a note. His eyes were closed. He sighed as he missed another note, but struggled onward.

"My baby is in danger," Calvin said, feeling as though he was talking to himself. "I'm not crazy. I'm not crazy, Mike. There's a man watching my house and he says he's going to kill her."

Mike kept playing. His body jerked with each note.

"I have to get out of here. I have to go now."

Mike continued to play. His eyes stayed closed. His bandaged hands trudged onward with the notes, as though he hadn't heard a word Calvin had said.

"I need to go now," Calvin said, his voice shaking. "I need to get out of here right now."

Mike just kept playing.

Calvin heard the doors to the ward open. Food trays clanked as the food cart rumbled and squeaked out in the hallway. Voices chattered back and forth from the front desk.

The piano playing suddenly stopped.

Mike grabbed his hair with his bandaged hands and began tearing at it. He erupted with the most horrid-sounding, animalistic scream Calvin had ever heard.

Calvin jumped backward away from him.

The nurses came crashing into the room.

"What's going on here!" one of them shouted, stopping short of mike, who sat in front of the piano shrieking into his bandaged hands. He then stood up from the piano bench and began thrashing himself around the room violently, screaming the entire time at the nurses, who were attempting to keep him under control but didn't dare touch him.

The large security guard came thundering towards them all a moment later, hustling his unwieldy body mass down the hallway as fast as it would go. He shoved Calvin out of his way, nearly throwing him to the tile floor. He ran up and instantly grabbed Mike in a giant bear hung, but he could barely hang onto him with all the thrashing. There was yelling and screaming along with Mike's shrieking as the entire ward turned to chaos.

Calvin backed out of the entryway to the common room. He glanced down at the nurses' station near the end of the hall. There was still a food cart halfway through the doors. The security guard was gone. There were no nurses at the station, as they had all abandoned it to help with the situation.

Calvin didn't give it a second thought. Before he realized he was moving, his unlaced shoes slapped the smooth tile floor as he sprinted down the blue hallway towards the open security door.

He flew out the door and into the next corridor. There was no one around. He spun in circles for a moment, looking for an exit. He knew he was on the fourth floor. He needed an elevator. But an elevator would be too slow and he could get caught in it. He found the stairwell and bolted through the door. His feet barely touched the stairs as he flew down them, jumping half the distance and only picked up a few steps here and there. He was descending rapidly, but not rapid enough for him. When he had gone down as low as he could, he blew through the door and flew out into a parking garage.

"Hey!" an unknown man's voice shouted after him. "Hey! You! Stop!"

The voice faded behind Calvin as he weaved his way through the maze of parked cars with incredible agility, like a deer escaping through a wooded area.

"Hey! Get back here!" the voice insisted somewhere behind him.

Calvin didn't look back. He didn't know where he was going, and at the moment he didn't care. As long as he was out. He was free.

He heard commotion behind him, but it didn't worry him. It only made his adrenaline pump harder, and that made him run even faster. He was by no means in the athletic shape he used to be, but he knew for damn sure that there was no way those overweight and out-of-shape security guards were going to catch him.

He became aware, however, that he did need a plan. He needed to lose them. They could catch up to him in cars. They could find him if he didn't weave himself into the landscape well enough.

He shot through a thin patch of woods on what must have been a man-made trail. He emerged from the other side into a rundown neighborhood. He had no idea where he was. He knew that they wouldn't either, and, at the moment, that's all that mattered.

The sidewalk he ran down was littered with dirt and garbage under a layer of snow. Some of the structures were boarded up with plywood.

He had no idea where he had ended up, but he was clearly in a rough section of town. There were no cars driving past at all. There were no signs of life around. And he was freezing.

Calvin kept running until he began coughing up phlegm. He couldn't breathe any longer. He was out of shape, out of breath, and the bitter cold air was biting at his lungs, which had already sustained damage from the crash.

His feet slipped on the sidewalk and he fell down hard. He hit with a smack, cracking the back of his head on the concrete.

He lay for a moment, watching the snowflakes swirl down in the light from the streetlamp. Illuminated briefly by the lamp, they danced like a thousand fireflies on a warm summer's night.

Everything was hushed around him.

He realized he couldn't feel his arms or his feet anymore. He was freezing, colder than he had ever been.

The bitter cold stung him like a thousand bees all over his body. He needed warmth. He needed a jacket or gloves or a hat, anything to keep some body heat in. He could feel it slowing him down mentally.

He didn't want to run anymore. He didn't want to move. He wanted to sleep, right there on the sidewalk with the flurries falling down around him like feathers. It didn't even feel cold now. It felt like nothing.

Calvin closed his eyes. He felt himself drifting off. And then he remembered his child. He remembered her laughing and smiling at him, the way she smiled widely in the morning when he went in to get her out of bed and she held her arms wide open for him to pick her up. She needed him.

Calvin's heart surged. He rocked his body around in

the snow, shaking off the pain. He groaned as he climbed to his feet once again, reaching back behind his head to feel the blood, already freezing in his hair and cracking with his touch.

He began walking, limping. Then he began running, hobbling. He didn't know what he was looking for. He needed someone, anyone. He needed a phone—a pay phone. Did they still make those? Everyone has cell phones nowadays and he thought he remembered hearing that they were doing away with payphones all together in most cities. But this was a poor area. There must be one somewhere.

He saw a car cruising down the street through the slush, an old Cadillac that looked weighed down in the back. He was desperate. He stepped out into the mess of snow and slush on the street and waved his arms over his head.

The Cadillac swerved towards him, but did not slow down. It came so close as it passed that it nearly threw Calvin back as it covered him with a giant splash of brown slush and ice water.

Calvin cried in agony. He was drenched from head to foot. His shoes were soaked. His hair was saturated. It felt as though he had been stabbed with a thousand needles over every portion of his body. He screamed.

Someone inside the car yelled something loudly at him as it rolled away into the night.

Calvin staggered in pain. He clutched himself tightly with his arms wrapped around his upper body, pushing himself to keep going. He had to make it home. He didn't care what it took, even if he had to walk all the way to the lake soaked head to foot in the freezing cold. He was slowing down, though. He could feel it again. He was losing his will. His body was not responding to what his mind was telling him to do.

And then he saw it. It was a payphone on the street corner. It was probably one of the worst sections of town in the entire city, but he had found a payphone and it was the most beautiful thing he had ever seen.

He just needed money now. He had no change, no currency of any type at all on him. They had taken all that away from him in the hospital.

He tried to flag down a passing Lexus, despite his fears of getting covered in freezing slush again. The driver honked at him furiously and swerved far away from him, all the way into the oncoming lane.

The other cars he tried did the same, refusing to acknowledge him or moving greatly out of their way to avoid driving anywhere near him.

"Excuse me," he said to a woman at the stop light who had her window down to hold out a cigarette. She looked nervous and fumbled to find the button to roll her window up. "I just need a quarter for the pay phone," Calvin pleaded. "Can I please just borrow a quarter from you...Hey!" She was already gone. She peeled out and ran the red light.

Calvin stumbled along the sidewalk, weaving back and forth. It was hopeless. He was too cold and too tired. He was giving up hope. He couldn't go any further.

He saw a bum crouched into a corner between a stairwell and the side of an apartment building. He was bundled up with several brown and gray coats on, a wool hat down almost over his eyes, and another round hat resting on top of it. He rocked a little, and moved his cheeks as if chewing something, but for the most part remained still. He looked beaten, battered by the streets. He had been stripped of anything that could possibly be taken from him.

"Hey, brother man," the old bum said to Calvin,

noticing him as he approached. There were heavy bags under the bum's eyes, which were nearly swollen shut. Calvin wondered if he could see at all or if he had only heard him approaching.

"Wha you doin' out in dis kind a weather without a jacket on, man?"

"I need to get home. It's an emergency."

"You don't belong here," the bum said.

"I'm just trying to get a quarter so I can use the pay phone over there so I can get home," Calvin said, struggling to breathe.

"Dat's all you need, man? You need a quarter?"

"I just need to make a phone call. That's all."

The bum reached into his jacket and pulled out a jar of coins with a very shaky hand. He held it up towards Calvin.

"You take what you need, son. Go on, now. Take it."

Calvin reached in and pulled out a shiny quarter. "Thank you," Calvin said gratefully, clutching the quarter. "You have no idea how much this means to me right now."

"You need it more than I do, son."

22

Calvin spotted Sadie's little silver car pulling up along the curb a hundred feet away from him. He could see her looking around for him.

He struggled to get himself to his feet. He had been sitting since he called her. He couldn't walk any further, and he was losing the strength to even stand. His legs were totally numb. He couldn't feel the skin on his arms anymore. His fingers were frozen. He just hoped he wouldn't get frostbite. He had heard all these stories about people having fingers amputated from frostbite.

He stumbled backwards. He waved a hand up in the cold air at Sadie.

Then the car suddenly whipped around and the headlights raced towards him. She had seen him. He felt so relieved he could have cried, if the tears wouldn't have instantly turned to icicles.

"Calvin!" she shouted to him as she flew out of her car. "Are you okay?"

"Frozen," was all he could reply.

"Let's get you in the car…" she grabbed his right arm and helped him to his feet. "Oh my god! You're skin is like ice! Calvin!"

Calvin shuddered and shook the cold off. He felt the warmth from the car before he was even close to it. He felt the heat radiating off the engine. He slipped into the passenger seat and held himself, shaking.

"Oh my god, Calvin…what are you doing? Why are you all the way out here?"

Calvin just trembled uncontrollably.

"Let me find you something…" Sadie said urgently, looking around the car.

"We need to go," Calvin muttered.

"I have a blanket in the trunk…hold on just a second, it's right here," she said as she disappeared around the back of the car. She hurried back and threw a blanket over him. She wrapped it around him and tucked him into the car seat tightly like a cocoon. "Why aren't you wearing a jacket?" she asked, cupping his cheeks with her palms. You're freezing cold, Calvin. You're entire face is frozen," she said, horrified as she pressed her body against the blanket and held him.

"I'm so cold," he said, shuddering.

"We'll get you warmed up in a minute," she said, flicking the thermostat in the dashboard and cranking the fan all the way up.

"We need to go. It's an emergency," he said.

"We'll go, we'll go…just tell me where you need to go."

"I need to get home as soon as I can."

Sadie carefully shut his door and ran around the car to get in on her side. "This is a rough patch of town you ended up in," she said, surprised, as they sped up the street.

"It's bad."

"It's the worst neighborhood in the entire city," she said. "I'm afraid to even ask how you wound up here in just a T-shirt and jeans."

"They think I did it," he said to her.

"They think you did what?"

"Everything."

"You mean with the house?" she asked, confused.

"Everything. They think it was all me."

"Who are *they*?"

"The people at the hospital…all the doctors and nurses, and even Leah."

"They all think you did *what*?"

"They think I burnt down the house. They think I crashed my own car with the baby and my girlfriend in it. They think it was all me. And I was starting to think it was me, too."

"Calvin, it wasn't you."

"They put me in a crazy ward in the hospital, Sadie. They thought that I was a danger to my child and so they wouldn't even let me see her to make sure that she was okay. They wouldn't let me see Leah, either."

"You're not crazy, Calvin," Sadie reassured him.

"I'm glad you think so. You're about the only person in the world who thinks that right now."

"I knew two minutes after meeting you what you were like. You might be a little eccentric at times, definitely a little different, but you're not crazy or scary or anything like that. You just have a different way of looking at things, and honestly, I think you're probably one of the sanest people I've ever met. You're not capable of doing anything bad, Calvin. You're a sweetheart. I remember when you saved a baby bird from being crushed by a bay door, even though it meant holding up an entire team of workers and making them all late. Maybe that is crazy, to be so worried about something so little and unimportant. But if you're crazy, then we should all be so lucky to be crazy like you."

"Thank you for just believing me," he said.

"I wouldn't doubt you for a second. I don't understand how anyone else who knows you could."

"Then believe me, these guys are bad, Sadie. They're real bad. They're psychotic, like totally out of their minds, and they want to kill me. That's why I was trying to leave town when we had the accident. It *wasn't* an accident. It was them behind me and I know they pushed us off the road. I didn't just drive off. Even though I don't remember exactly what happened, I remember seeing the car behind me and I know that they did it. They called me in the hospital threatening me and my child's life. And she's home, now. They sent my baby home with a neighbor."

"Why the hell did they do that?"

"They said they couldn't contact anyone else and Leah had listed her as her emergency contact."

"Not her parents or anyone else? A friend?"

"No. Her parents are too far away and they're never home. Her friends are never around and they're not local either. I guess she really trusts this lady and she's known her for a while. She's part of the reason that Leah bought the house when she did. This lady told her about it and ended up getting her a good deal on it. They're real close."

"How is Leah doing?"

"Not good. She's not good. And my baby's at home with someone I don't even know. And there's somebody threatening her life."

"Should I call the cops or something?"

"No. No, I can't call the cops now," Calvin said with great frustration. "Don't you see? It looks like it was all me. They'll come and get me and throw me back in that nut ward. They'll lock me up again and leave my baby totally unprotected. They'll also press criminal charges on me for breaking into the house and stealing the watch. They'll get me on everything, including burning the house down, and I'll end up in jail, since I'm not really crazy. They'll figure out pretty quickly that I'm perfectly sane and I don't have much of a way to defend myself against all the charges that I'll face."

"What are you going to do, then?"

Calvin was silent.

"What are you going to do when we get to the house?" Sadie asked again.

"I don't know. All I know is that I need to be with her. I need to be there for my child."

"But you can't take her anywhere. You don't have a car, do you?"

"My truck was totaled in the accident, from what I heard."

"So how are you going to get around, then? Where are you going to go?"

"I don't know," Calvin said. "I don't know what to do."

"Calvin, I'll drive you guys wherever you need to go. I'll help you any way I can."

"That's nice of you, but no. I can't accept your help."

"Why not?"

"I don't want you involved in this any more than you are. I don't want to endanger your life too. You don't have anything to do with it, and I want it to stay that way."

"I don't care if you endanger me, Calvin. You need help. Who else is going to help you?"

Calvin shrugged his shoulders. "I'll figure it out."

"Let me help you," she insisted more quietly.

"Sadie..."

"Let me help you. I'll drive you far away from here, wherever you want to go. I'll call in sick to work and we'll just leave."

"No, Sadie...these people want me dead. I can't drag you into that. I can't. Then you'll get caught in the crossfire."

"I don't care," she said defiantly. "You need help. Your baby needs help. And I'm going to help you."

Calvin had nothing more to say.

"I'm going to help you," she repeated more quietly.

They pulled into the driveway loudly, gravel crunching under the tires, even though she had tried to pull in quietly. The headlights illuminated the ugly front fascia of the house for a moment before Sadie shut them off. The house appeared calm. There were no lights coming from within.

Calvin nearly shrieked as the bitter cold from outside hit his already red skin and shot knives through his nerves. He swore loudly, surprising himself.

"We'll have you inside in a minute."

"I'm soaking wet...I can't get warm."

They headed down the stone path to the house, Sadie holding onto his arm.

He hated a woman holding him up, supporting him, but it felt good at the same time to have someone so concerned and so willing to take care of him. He needed some comfort right now, a warm heart.

"Calvin, you're whole body is shaking."

"I know...I can't stop."

"I'm going to come in with you. I want to make

sure you're okay."

Calvin nodded as he shook.

"Should we knock? Or just walk in?"

"Knock," Calvin said.

"Right. I suppose we don't want to scare the hell out of this lady and have her keel over."

Sadie knocked on the door fairly loudly.

They waited a few moments. There was no answer, and there didn't seem to be movement from within.

Calvin knocked on the door, a little louder. "Ms. Cotter?" he yelled at the door.

A light flicked on from far within the house. He could see a bit of movement through the thin curtains that covered the window of the front door. Footsteps approached on the wood planks of the kitchen floor.

The curtains moved a little and parted slightly, allowing Ms. Cotter to peak out from the dim light within. The porch light was on, but Calvin knew it was still difficult to make out faces in the dark outside.

"Mrs. Cotter, it's me. It's Calvin. I live here now."

A moment later, he heard the deadbolt unlatch and the door creaked open.

"Calvin?" She said as she opened the door. Her eyes were very squinty, straining to take in the sight of him and Sadie. "I thought you were still in the hospital, dear," she said.

"I'm out now."

"Are you okay?"

"Yes. I'm fine. We're fine."

"Oh my goodness...I heard about what happened, with the accident, and...oh my goodness, I couldn't believe that happened, right up the road here. I felt so horrible...I didn't expect to see you anytime soon. They asked me to take care of Pearl for you until one of you was released from the hospital. Being a nurse for thirty years, I hardly minded. I was so worried about you, though. I'm so glad to see that you're okay and safe and sound."

"We're just glad the baby's okay. Do you mind if we come in?" Calvin said, ready to lose it, trying to keep his calm in the extreme cold.

"Oh, of course, of course...forgive me...I just woke up. I was sound asleep."

"Sorry to barge in on you so late," Calvin said. "I wanted to get home to the baby as soon as possible. I didn't want to spend one extra minute away from her."

"Oh, I understand," Mrs. Cotter said, looking Calvin up and down. "What happened to you? Why are you all covered up?"

"Oh, nothing," Calvin said casually. "No big deal. I just fell in the snow in the parking lot. I got pretty wet. I had to take my jacket off, since it was soaked."

"Oh...well okay, then. And who is this?" she said, glancing at Sadie.

"This is my cousin, Sadie," Calvin said to her, thinking quickly.

"Oh," Mrs. Cotter said, examining Sadie. "Hello. Nice to meet you."

"Nice to meet you too," Sadie answered with a smile.

"She was my ride home from the hospital,"

"Oh, of course. Your car. I heard it was totaled...I'm so sorry."

"It's just a car. I'll get another."

Mrs. Cotter glanced at the clock on the oven. "Well, I suppose I should get myself back home then for the rest of the night."

"We really appreciate you doing this for us," Calvin said.

"Oh, my pleasure. I'll just gather up my things...I'm a little groggy still..."

"Sure, thank you, Mrs. Cotter."

"You're welcome, dear."

Mrs. Cotter walked back and forth through the living room several times, looking all over for anything she might have brought over to the house with her. Finally satisfied that she had everything together and bundled into the plastic shopping bags she carried, she said, "She had her last bottle at around eight this evening. She has just been a perfect little angel. Such a delight to be around. What a precious child."

"Thank you. Take care now," Calvin said as he gently closed the door behind her. Once the door was closed, he exhaled and clutched his forehead in his freezing palms.

"Thank god. I didn't think she would ever leave. We need to get you warm," Sadie said, quickly snapping into action. She shot into the living room and instantly found the thermostat, which she slid all the way up. The furnace responded immediately from below in the basement, the burner firing up and the fan humming. The house vibrated a little as the noisy system forced warm air through the ducts.

Calvin groaned. "I feel dizzy. I need to sit." He nearly collapsed into one of the kitchen chairs around the table. He still clutched himself tightly, with the blanket around him, struggling to retain any warmth he had.

"Hold still," she said, approaching him from behind. "Let's get this blanket off for the moment. You need to get that shirt off. You're soaked and that's making it impossible to get warm. Here..." she said, slipping a hand under the shirt down by his navel. "Lift up your arms," she said as she helped him slide the shirt over his head. She threw it on the kitchen floor. "Good God...she exclaimed, "You're red as a lobster." She reached around him and rubbed his shoulders and biceps. "I'm trying to increase circulation. Your skin is like ice."

Calvin couldn't help but notice that her massaging seemed to be as much for her benefit as for his. Her warm fingertips made their way around across his abdomen and up around his biceps. He certainly didn't mind, and wasn't about to object. It was probably the only thing in the world that could make him feel good at a time like this. Her touch was so soft and sensual, as much agony as he was in, it still made him feel incredible, that such a beautiful woman with so much power over so many poor men's hearts would take an interest in him. It was almost enough to make him forget everything else.

But there was an unpleasant feeling coming over him. He was starting to warm up, but there was a very sick feeling in his stomach. He noticed his hands were trembling.

"I don't feel right," he said to Sadie.

"Let's get you in a warm shirt," she said. "I found this sweatshirt in back. Here," she said, helping him slide it on.

"It's not just the cold," he said to her with worry in his voice. "I feel sick. I'm not even cold anymore and I'm shaking. I feel perfectly warm and I can't stop shaking like this."

"It's probably from the medication. The morphine or whatever pain killers they were giving you. They're wearing off now. You're going through withdrawal. Let's get you onto the couch."

"We should get out of here," Calvin protested.

"We will. I think it's best that we stay here for the rest of the night. It's already so late. The baby's sound asleep and you're in no shape to travel anywhere else. You need to rest and stay warm here."

"No…the police will come looking for me."

"If they do, I'll answer the door and tell them that I'm the neighbor watching the baby."

"But what if the freaks come for us? They know where we are, they're always watching."

"Shh…" she calmed him. "We'll leave first thing in the morning. You need rest now. We'll be okay tonight. It's only a few hours until daybreak. Then we'll be safe."

Sadie clicked off the lights, much to his surprise. She climbed onto the couch with Calvin and gently wrapped her soft curves around his quivering body.

"Body heat will help keep you warm," she whispered in his ear.

Calvin felt her hands slide up and down his back, caressing him gently, now in more of a motherly manner than a sensual one. His body ached. The tremors and muscle spasms were starting to make his muscles sore. He had been shivering for hours now.

Sadie wrapped herself even more tightly around him, weaving her legs with his.

They both fell asleep instantly, weaved together, listening to each other's breaths and absorbing each other's precious body heat.

23

Calvin awoke to the baby crying. He rolled around, confused by what was trapping him, keeping him from getting up.

"You okay?" Sadie asked in a daze.

"Yeah. I'm okay," Calvin told her. "The baby's up, that's all."

Calvin went in and found her standing in her crib waiting for him with a great big smile on her face. She held her arms out to greet him and almost fell backwards, having let go of the crib's rail.

"Here, sweetheart. Daddy's here, sweetie. It's okay." He embraced her and held her tightly, that precious little bundle of pajamas curled up in his arms and snuggled into his chest.

He took her to the kitchen to get her a bottle. He had become a pro at preparing a bottle while holding a screaming baby in the other arm. He was glad she wasn't screaming this time, though. She actually seemed very much at peace.

"Here, sweetheart," he said, handing her the bottle as he settled into a kitchen chair with her cradled in his arms. He pet the top of her head with his fingers, amazed by how tiny her little head was and how soft her hair was. She drank serenely with her eyes closed.

Calvin caught a flicker of light outside the kitchen window. He watched a vehicle round the corner and glide by, partially visible through the leafless brush at the edge of the property. It reminded him of the car that he had seen circling the block right after the fire. It chilled him.

His eyes stayed with the vehicle. It slowed and glided to a stop behind Sadie's car. Calvin could see it was a police cruiser. He stood up with the baby and backed away from the window.

The police cruiser's door popped open and the light came on inside. An officer got out and walked towards Sadie's car, probing it with a flashlight. Then the flashlight's beam illuminated the path to the house.

Calvin could hear the radio from inside the patrol car sounding. He couldn't make out what was being said over it, just a lot of static.

Calvin stood in the dark in the middle of the kitchen. He knew that they couldn't enter the home without a warrant. He could hear Sadie snoring on the couch. He would have to wake her up. She could pretend to be the neighbor watching the baby, and hopefully the police officer wouldn't have too much information and would buy that.

The officer moved his flashlight around the exterior of the house. Calvin jumped out of the way with the baby as the flashlight's beam probed inside, illuminating the kitchen cabinets and the opposite wall. Then the beam left. Calvin moved forward towards the window.

The police cruiser's radio sounded again in the background, the only noise on a silent night at two in the morning.

All was quiet. He couldn't see the cop's flashlight anymore or hear his footsteps. Calvin tiptoed through the kitchen and into the living room. He crept from window to window, trying to figure out where the cop had gone and what he was looking for. He wasn't on the side of the house, so Calvin snuck into the back bedroom and cautiously peered out the large windows, pressing his face against the glass to look in either direction as far as he could. There was nothing but snow and darkness and trees.

A door thumped shut out front. He moved back through the house to the kitchen and quickly peeked out. The cruiser was gone.

Calvin breathed a sigh of relief. His hands were still shaking with the baby in them. She had fallen asleep with the bottle in her mouth. He took a deep breath. He had never felt so exhausted and he knew the drugs were having an effect on him. He wasn't sure if it was the morphine wearing off or painkillers they had given him. He had no idea what else they had doped him up with to get him under control in the hospital. The room was spinning. He was shaking as though entering hypothermia, even though he was perfectly warm. The world was functioning in slow motion around him. He had to put the baby back into her crib.

He passed by Sadie on his way to Pearl's bedroom. She was still sound-asleep.

His eyelids felt heavy and kept sliding closed as he walked into Pearl's room. He held her closely in his arms and admired her for a moment. Such a beautiful, pure thing. Such innocence, he thought. It made his whole life seem worthwhile to know that he brought her into this world.

"Goodnight," he whispered and kissed her on the forehead. "Daddy will be here when you wake up. Don't worry. Sleep well, little angel. Sleep well."

He gently laid her down in her crib and pulled her Winnie the Pooh blanket over her, up around her chin. Her little arms snuggled the blanket closer and she sighed, and then she was out.

Calvin's head was spinning. He felt as though he might be violently ill at any moment. His mind and his heart wouldn't stop racing. He wasn't tired. He wasn't hungry. He wasn't cold. He just felt terrible, jittery, anxious, and had a horrible feeling of dread that plagued him. He was scared about the police. They would be back. He didn't understand why they didn't even knock on the door. They'd be looking for him. And so would the men trying to kill him.

Calvin shuddered alone in an arm chair. He didn't want to wake Sadie. His nerves were taking over his body and he hardly felt like cuddling. He wasn't cold anymore. He wanted to be left alone right now, to deal with the horrible anxiety that was eating him alive. He had never felt so scared, so vulnerable. He knew it was partially the drugs. At least he wanted to believe that.

He found himself sifting through the bedroom closet, keeping as quiet as he could. He hoped he was being quiet, since his senses seemed pretty off at the moment. Then he found what he was looking for. He pulled the baseball bat out of a corner of the closet, where it had leaned against the two walls, covered by clothes.

He slid his hand under the bed and searched around until his fingertips came upon the large, sheathed army knife.

And then he sat. He sat in the recliner like a statue, eyes fixed on the door, bat in hand, knife at his side. He trembled and convulsed in the dark. The baby was sound asleep. Sadie was sound asleep. He was alone with his thoughts, his fears. And the dark. It would be morning soon. They would leave this house and never come back again. He didn't know where they would end up, but he would make sure that no one could find out where he was. He didn't care where they had to go or how far. There was nothing more important than the safety of his daughter, and he couldn't do anything to put her in harm's way. He felt he had put her in enough danger already.

And so he sat, shaking, eyes wide open. His brain was fried. His body was exhausted. He rocked on his own in the recliner, which was not a rocker. He was the last line of defense. He had to stay awake, at least until daybreak. He had to.

He had to stay awake.

He had to stay awake.

He had to stay awake.

The furnace kicked on and filled the house with humming and whooshing noises. With everything else so quiet, it sounded like a freight train in the night. It almost seemed deafening.

A strange odor washed over Calvin's senses. He had the sensation of free-falling. His head struggled to clear itself and regain some sense of reality. He had no idea where he was or what he was doing there. He was in a dark room that seemed totally unfamiliar to him. His rationality struggled to get a hold of something, to get some sort of bearings on what was going on. He had no idea where his mind had been or for how long, or if this was even reality or a dream that he was suddenly thrust into.

There was movement around him. He tried to turn his head, but couldn't. He wanted to move, but couldn't move his arms or his legs. Each sound he heard around him froze him solid in place.

Something wasn't right.

In fact, he had the overwhelming feeling that something was very, very wrong around him. Goosebumps covered his body. The hair on the back of his neck stood straight up and he felt electrified. And there was that strange, toxic odor in the air that flooded his lungs.

There were footsteps. The old wood floor creaked and popped with the slow, cautious steps.

The footsteps were moving from behind his chair to behind the couch, making their way through the living room.

Calvin held his breath.

A tall, dark figure came into his line of vision, like a blacked out cartoon character in the night. It stealthily slinked its way around the couch to the floor directly in front of where Calvin sat.

Calvin's head spun. He struggled to maintain focus on the figure, which had something in both of its hands.

"*Calvin,*" a voice whispered his name.

Calvin struggled to gain his bearings.

"*Oh, Calvin,*" the voice called him, a little louder, taunting him.

Calvin sat petrified with fear, trying to wake up.

"*We got out of your head, Calvin,*" the voice said.

Calvin wiggled his fingers. The army knife was no longer in his grasp.

"*And we came to get you.*"

Calvin looked out of the corner of his eye for the baseball bat he had leaned against the chair. He didn't see it. It was possible that it had fallen to the floor.

"*Are you afraid, Calvin?*"

Calvin knew that voice.

"*Are you afraid of the truth?*"

Calvin heard a click and was startled by a large, bright flame that suddenly appeared in the figure's outstretched hand.

The figure moved closer to Calvin with the flame, then leaned its head in closer, lower, towards Calvin, until the figure's face was fully illuminated in its dancing orange glow.

Calvin got the feeling of being on a rollercoaster in its first big drop. He knew instantly who it was, even with his features distorted by the lighter's flame in the dark room.

It was Marshall Hamilton.

Calvin was flooded with adrenaline. He still hadn't moved. His body wouldn't respond. He had only experienced this sort of paralysis in a dream before.

But he wouldn't wake up. He was already awake, he knew for sure now, and this was really happening right in front of him.

Marshall had a red jug of something in the hand he held the lighter with. In the other hand, he held a clear bottle of vodka.

"*Boo*," said Marshall, as if frightening a child.

Sadie was motionless on the couch. She hadn't stirred. Calvin had no idea if she was alive or not. He could now see clearly that the knife was gone from his lap. He could see the end of the baseball bat, though, sticking out from under the side of the chair. He must have dropped it when he fell asleep.

"*It's the boogey man, Calvin,*" Marshall said with a frozen smile. "*The boogey man's coming to get you. And your little baby, too.*"

Marshall laughed as he jerked the bottle of alcohol and splashed Sadie with it. She still did not move.

Then he splashed Calvin with it as well.

Calvin gasped as the fluid hit him. The fumes were overwhelming.

The lighter stayed lit in Marshall's hand, just inches from the spray of alcohol.

"What are you doing!" Calvin cried out in horror. He was in such shock and so confused that the words barely came out.

"*Just some house cleaning.*"

"What did I do to you?" Calvin yelled. "What did I do to you!"

"*You didn't do anything,*" Marshall said with a sick smile.

Calvin's eyes widened in horror.

"*You were just the right guy, Calvin. The right guy in the right house in the right situation. All the stars were aligned. Until you went and fucked it all up for us. But I'll forgive you for that. I'm going to clean up all that mess right now. You'll see your dog again soon. Promise. One for the road, eh, Calvin?*"

Marshall lifted the bottle of alcohol and threw back his head. He chugged it.

Calvin reached a hand down to the side of his recliner. His fingers instantly located the bat.

Marshall held the bottle high to his lips, downing the last drops, with the lighter still lit in his opposite hand.

Calvin wasn't aware of leaving the chair or swinging the bat. He only felt it smash the bottle of vodka Marshall was drinking. The bat smashed it from its bottom right into Marshall's face, hammering the majority of the shards of glass straight into his mouth and jamming it down his throat.

Marshall's other hand flew up in defense, the lighter still lit, as he screamed.

The alcohol ignited on his face.

A plume of fire exploded from deep within his esophagus as he howled in horror. The room lit up brighter than daytime as the flames engulfed his head and the rest of his body.

Sadie woke up screaming and jumped off the couch.

"Look out!" Calvin shouted at her as the flaming figure walked towards them, flailing and shooting fire out of its mouth like a dragon.

The container in Marshall's hand caught fire as well and bounced onto the couch where Sadie had been laying. It spilled its contents as if pouring out liquid fire and instantly set the couch ablaze.

The smoke detectors all went off at the same time.

The flaming figure came at Calvin.

Calvin swung the bat furiously and made contact with Marshall's fiery head. The blow nearly knocked Marshall across the room. He struggled on the floor, convulsing and squealing like a piglet as the flames ate him alive.

The entire living room had become an inferno.

"The baby!" he shouted at Sadie, busting into the baby's room. He heard Pearl crying.

The heat was overwhelming. It almost knocked Calvin down. The air was so hot that he almost couldn't take another breath. He grabbed Pearl up from her crib and bundled her in her blanket. He crouched low and ran out of the room with her.

"Calvin!" Sadie shouted his name from the living room.

As he ran out of the baby's room, Calvin slammed into what felt like a wall. He suddenly found himself airborne, flying backwards a good eight feet. He collided harshly with the back wall of the baby's room and dropped to the floor. Stunned, he felt Pearl, who was now screaming. He hoped he had protected her from the impact.

The fire's light was almost entirely blocked in the doorway to the living room. It was Tom Grissom looming in the doorway. He had thrown Calvin across the room like a ragdoll.

There was a loud smack. Tom's giant head jolted and he staggered back out of the doorway and hit his head on the ceiling.

Sadie screamed as she was thrown backwards across the living room.

Tom suddenly stopped and turned to the flaming figure on the floor. He let out a low, bellowing howl as he threw his giant hands up over his face. "*Dad,*" he cried at the flaming, now motionless figure in a blaze on the floor. "*No! Dad!*" He thundered his way across the burning living room. He shoved the flaming couch out of his way with a flick of his wrist and knelt before Marshall's fiery corpse.

Calvin watched in horror as Tom picked up Marshalls body and cradled it like a baby. Marshall's flames lit Tom's giant cloak on fire as he tried to carry the body through the house towards the door.

Tom screamed as the flames ate into his bare hands and his facial hair caught fire. He threw his head back in agony as he tried to fit through the doorway to the kitchen with Marshall's in his arms.

The fire was quickly spreading to the other rooms now. Calvin could barely breathe. Pearl was squirming and gasping in his arms.

But Tom was blocking the front door.

Calvin saw Sadie fly by and furiously crack Tom in the head with the bat again.

Tom let out a low, bellowing shriek as he toppled to the floor with a thud like a tree falling. The whole house shook. Marshall's lifeless, flaming body rolled out of

Tom's arms onto the living room floor.

Tom lay motionless as his giant deformed body was consumed by the flames.

Calvin covered the baby's head with the blanket and wrapped the rest of her tightly. He jumped through the burning doorway to the kitchen. He fumbled with the door handle. It was locked. The deadbolt was still locked as well. He frantically unlocked the door and ran outside into the freezing night air with the baby.

"Oh my god!" Sadie shouted into the night as she ran behind him, choking on smoke. "Oh my god!" she shouted again, her voice crackling.

"Are you okay?" Calvin yelled at her.

"I don't know...I don't know...oh my god..."

The baby was crying like crazy. He unwrapped her face from the blanket. She seemed fine, just upset. Tears were pouring down her face as she wailed. Calvin held her tightly, holding her face away from the unbelievable heat of the fire.

They were forty feet away and the heat from the fire was unbearable.

"We need to get further back!" he hollered at Sadie. "This is dangerous!"

Sadie broke down and started crying. She dropped to her knees and buried her face into her palms. She sobbed uncontrollably.

Calvin put his hand on her shoulder. He held Pearl tightly and kissed her, telling her it would be all right, as he stood in the snow and watched their home burn to the ground.

24

Calvin stood with Sadie in front of the smoldering remains of Leah's home, which was unrecognizable. About half of the house had collapsed into the basement. The house had burnt wildly while the firefighters struggled to reach water by drilling holes through the deep layer of ice on Grave Lake. Hydrants had not been required by code for homes within hose-length of the lake. It took over two hours to completely extinguish the flames, at least to the point where it was safe to venture inside the smoking rubble.

Calvin had left the baby with the neighbor next door who had been watching her. She was perfectly fine and in desperate need of a nap. The police had insisted that she go to the hospital and get checked over just in case, but Calvin figured he would do that later in the day if he felt a reason to. She had been through enough, and all she wanted now was a nice long nap in a peaceful place where she was safe.

Calvin knew she was fine the second they were out of the house. Once things had calmed down she was back to her normal self, watching the fire trucks in the early morning darkness and oohing and aahing as she pointed at them. She was smiling at the firemen and warming their hearts with such a beautiful display of joy during such an awful event.

He and Sadie stood facing the remains of the house, up in the parking area, leaning against Sadie's car, each with a blanket wrapped around them that the neighbor had offered. It was a frosty morning, around thirty-seven degrees. Not as cold as it had been, but still chilly by anyone's standards.

The scene had turned into somewhat of a social event for the firefighters, who now lingered around talking over doughnuts and coffee.

Calvin and Sadie had been there the whole time since the fire occurred. There were lots of questions being asked. They had given the same story ten times now and the local police were very interested in what actually occurred.

Calvin noticed a police officer walking through the crowd of firefighters. They pointed him in the direction of Calvin and Sadie, where they leaned against the hood of her car.

Calvin recognized the mustache. It was Officer Patton.

"Are you two all right?" He said, walking up to them.

"We're okay now," Calvin said calmly.

He shook his head. "Never seen anything like this. So, they already filled me in. They called me as soon as the call came in from the local police. They have me on speed dial for you now. They told me you're all okay. Is that true?"

"Yes, thank god."

"The baby? She's okay?"

"She's fine. She's just taking a nap at the neighbor's."

"This could've been a lot worse, Calvin. I can't even imagine what you two have been through. I just wish there was more I could have done, faster. I found out a lot. I took you seriously in the hospital, when you told me that crazy story. I really didn't think you had lost your mind. I got right on everything you told me. I looked into this guy, this Marshall Hamilton. He was the one who witnessed your car crash and called 911. I couldn't tell you his name at the time, but I'm glad I pulled all his records. This guy was a real psychopath, Calvin. I mean, this guy was seriously disturbed. I was able to look into his medical history and everything. He's been in and out of mental homes since about the age of nine. He was put in the psych ward the first time for torturing animals, cats and squirrels. He grew up with foster parents. He was abandoned at birth, left for dead. Someone left him there like they knew there was something wrong with him when he was just a baby. From everything else I've discovered, this guy was pure evil. With a major fetish for fire. Just recently he was suspected in three cases of arson, but none of them stuck."

"What the hell was he doing investigating fires, then?"

"Sometimes these big companies don't look into medical history as much as they should. Either that or he faked his identity with them. He was an expert on fire. He was very passionate about fires, how they started and spread and grew. He spent many hundreds of hours online researching information on fires that had taken place, whether they were arson or accidental."

"Where did you find all this out?"

"The records from the investigations on him."

"Then why wasn't he fired from the insurance company? Why would they keep someone like that around?"

"They never knew about it. He was never convicted of anything. The police never had enough on him to make any charges stick, so technically he didn't do anything, as far as the legal system was concerned. And unless he went into work bragging about his crimes to his boss, no one would ever know he'd even been accused of anything. He just went about his usual business of investigating fires."

"Why me?" Calvin asked angrily.

The cop sighed and stayed silent for a moment.

"Out of all the people out there, why me?"

"We may never know exactly why. I can tell you this much, though. From everything I've learned about your case so far, it sounds to me like you were the perfect target for this guy. Your business failed recently, you have no money, and your credit was destroyed. You were desperate financially. You were weak. You were in need. You couldn't afford your house anymore. You just had a baby you had to take care of. There were a lot of factors, Calvin, that painted a very bad picture for you, as far as arson goes."

"He knew that it would look like I did it."

"And it worked. You even ended up in a mental ward facing charges of arson, fraud, theft, and breaking and entering."

"But all for what? So they could steal my furniture? My watch?"

"We searched the house early this morning, before coming here, once we had the information from you about the address and the crime that had been committed. I want you to know, I was with the party that entered the home. It was empty. Of people, I mean. There was no one inside. We did find a lot of interesting items, though, which we're currently looking into."

"To see if they're stolen, like I told you?"

"Yes. I'm not sure we'll turn up anything, but I have a pretty strong feeling."

"What about my other things? My furniture?"

"We didn't find any of your items inside the house. We found them out back in the shed."

"What?"

"We found every single item that you described to us, locked in the storage shed towards the back of the property, behind the house."

"But why did they do this, then? Why didn't they just steal my stuff? Why torch the place and go through all this trouble? Why even bother burning the house down? I don't get it."

"No, the stuff they took out of your home was just the icing on the cake for them. That wasn't the only thing this guy was after. It was about denying your claim."

Calvin looked at him, perplexed.

"They set you up to deny your claim. They made it look like you had submitted a fraudulent contents claim, saying things were inside the house at the time of the fire that weren't there. The insurance company was right in that respect. They weren't there at the time of the fire."

"I saw that for myself when I went into the upstairs of the house."

"Your things were long-gone by the time they set the house on fire."

"But why? What's in it for them if the insurance company denies my claim and accuses me of fraud?"

"These people, and by these people I mean people like Marshall Hamilton, receive enormous bonuses by revealing cases of fraud or discovering any other reason why the insurance company should not pay out the claim."

"Like arson."

"Like arson. Like your contents claim that looked fraudulent. These are the exact reasons why these investigators are involved, to evaluate the remains and your story and provide information substantial enough for your claim to be denied. And for that, they receive huge amounts of money, since the insurance company now doesn't have to pay out hundreds of thousands of dollars."

"He stole my stuff and torched my house."

"So he would have gotten an enormous bonus for his work from the insurance company, in addition to whatever he happened to make selling your possessions, which in your case would have been a decent amount of money. Especially with that watch. And these guys were desperate, Calvin. I mean desperate. They've been at this a while and they've done a great job covering their tracks, pulling it off flawlessly, but they really screwed up on you. They got sloppy. Posting your watch for sale so quickly, that was crazy. Well, this guy was crazy, so there you go. They were bound to get caught sooner or later. I'm just sorry that it was you. I'm sorry you got involved in this insanity."

"You have no idea."

"You're not the first one, Calvin. But at least for this guy, you'll be the last. They've been doing this for a while now. We don't know exactly how long, but given the results from the independent investigator you hired, we've been able to determine that this guy has struck at least two other times. We verified that in those cases, no money was ever paid out on the claims. And it could've been worse, Calvin, believe it or not, from what we've learned. In at least one of these incidents, murder was involved. He seems to have intentionally ignited the house while the residents were asleep upstairs. An elderly couple who had never had a chance. The house went up within seconds, the way this guy lined the walls with whatever accelerant he was using. It's something the guys at the lab still haven't figured out yet. But he injected it right into the walls themselves. Must've drilled holes or something. But once it was in there, just a minor fire in the right part of the house would turn it into an instant inferno. The whole house would be a giant fireball within seconds."

"He told me that I was supposed to be inside." "He told me that I was supposed to have been in that fire."

"It wouldn't surprise me. Calvin, do you have any family close to you?"

"No. I don't have any family left at all. I lost my parents in an accident about ten years ago. My brother committed suicide."

"So there was no one else who would pursue a claim?"

"No...I guess not. There wasn't. That's why I was supposed to be in the fire."

The cop nodded. "You learned too much. They needed you out of the picture. They were scared, Calvin. They were scared of what you were learning. You had unknowingly uncovered their whole plot, the same plot they had been pulling off flawlessly for who knows how long. That's why they came after you. That's why they tormented you and followed you and ran you off the road. We found the car you described to me when I spoke with you up at your house. It's parked around the corner on the side of the street. A silver Chevy sedan. It was the same style car that was driven by Marshall Hamilton when he called 911 at the scene of your car crash. It was a company car that belonged to Prestige Insurance Company. They apparently always send these investigators out into the field with company cars, rather than their own. They want to protect their identity."

"The car was circling the block, here, every day," Calvin said. "They had been watching me since the fire."

Patton nodded. "Most likely. They wanted to keep an eye on you. Learn your schedule. Learn where you were really staying and who else was there. They were probably watching you to see what you were up to, to see what you were learning. If you were going about your normal life or if you were trying to figure out what had really happened. You were too close on their trail."

"If I had known all that, I would've just let the whole thing go. It wasn't worth it...the house, the watch, the insurance money, whatever, it wasn't worth it. All I want is safety for my child. All I can ask for now is that we'll be safe."

"You should be safe now, Calvin."

"They found him, right?"

"They found who?"

"The investigator, Marshall Hamilton. They found his remains in the house, right?"

"They just started going through the ashes a little while ago. The house is a mess, so it will take a little time to find anything in there, since the whole structure collapsed in on itself."

Calvin and Sadie exchanged nervous glances.

"Let me go check with the team on this one. Hold on one sec." Patton walked down towards the ruined house and got the attention of one of the men in an orange jacket. Together they disappeared around the side of the structure. They were gone for a few minutes before reemerging.

Patton walked back up to the two of them, looking sick to his stomach. His skin was pale. "We found a body," he said to Calvin, sounding ill.

"You saw him?"

"I saw the body, yes. Towards the back of the house."

"The living room," Calvin said. He was in the living room when he caught on fire and hit the floor."

"The body is burnt to a crisp," Patton said. "He's got pieces of glass shoved in his mouth, like he ate a bottle."

"That's him. That's Marshall Hamilton," Calvin said. "I hit the bottle with a baseball bat and broke it in his mouth."

"What was he doing with the bottle in his mouth?"

"Drinking it. After dousing us both with alcohol."

"Jesus..." Patton rubbed his forehead, trying to maintain his composure as he wrapped his mind around what had happened.

"What about the other body—the giant man, Tom?"

"The other body?" Patton's forehead crinkled.

"The giant guy who attacked us in the house."

"Oh—I didn't realize there was another person in the house attacking you. Tom—the big guy who tried to sell you the watch—you're saying he was in the fire?"

"I hit him twice with a baseball bat," Sadie said. "He fell to the floor and we ran out of the house."

"No...they haven't found any other body in there," Patton said slowly, appearing confused. "I'll check with them again, but Dan over there only mentioned the one, the man who started the fire. They didn't find any other bodies. Especially not a giant corpse."

"No," Calvin protested. "There should be another body in there. An enormous man's body. Near the doorway to the kitchen, the doorway between the kitchen and the living room."

"You're sure he was actually in the house when it burned?"

"He was out cold on the floor," Sadie said. "He dropped. I hit him hard, really hard. I hit him so hard that I felt the blood spray from his face."

The cop stared at both of them. He cautiously said, "There's only the one body in there. I'll check again, like I said, but Dan would have mentioned that to me. He would've told me if they found a second body…"

"There's another body in there," Calvin insisted. "There's got to be."

Patton could see the fear in their eyes. "I understand you two have been through a lot," he said calmly. "Believe me, though, you've got nothing to worry about. If this other guy did somehow make it out of the fire, he doesn't pose much of a threat anymore. We know where he lives and we'll have every cop in the area on the lookout for him. He'll be running, and he won't get very far. He won't be sticking around here, though. I can tell you that much. And he's hurt, from what you told me. We'll check all the local hospitals to see if anyone checked in with burn wounds and head wounds. He won't be difficult to find. We may even find him in the woods nearby, dead, or face-down in the lake. It sounds like he was in pretty rough shape after you got through with him."

Calvin shared a look of concern with Sadie.

"I do just have one more question for you," Patton said. "The team mentioned to me that all the doors were still locked on the house. All the deadbolts were bolted, and you had to unlock the front door to get out. Were any windows open? Or was there any other way into the house after you got here last night?"

"No," Calvin answered firmly. "The doors were locked and dead bolted. I triple-checked. All the windows were closed and locked, too."

"That's the conclusion that the crew, over there, has come to as well."

"Then how did they get in while we were sleeping?" Calvin asked anxiously. "How did they get into the house?"

"Now, we'll never know this for certain..." Patton said carefully. "But there doesn't seem to be any other explanation or any other way it could've happened... It appears that they were already inside the house before you got home."

Calvin's stomach bottomed out. He and Sadie fell silent pondering the unspeakable evil that had been lurking somewhere in the house, possibly just feet from them, while they thought they were alone—and safe.

Calvin's expression must have spoken volumes to Patton, who said, "Relax," as he started stepping away from the two of them. "You'll both be just fine. We'll find the giant man. Don't give it a second thought. You just love every moment you have with that beautiful little girl of yours." He turned around to look Calvin in the eyes. "I'll be praying for her mother."

25

Calvin was working on strapping Pearl into the car seat when Sadie approached him. Most of the commotion at the scene of the fire had died down, and it was time for the two of them to move on as well.

"It was pretty nice of Mrs. Cotting to loan you her car," Sadie said, patting Calvin on the shoulder as he buckled pearl up.

"It was incredibly nice. And the car seat, too. Good thing she has grandchildren."

Pearl grinned widely at Sadie, who couldn't help but smile back.

"So, where are you going to go now?" Sadie asked him.

"I'm not sure."

"Where are you going to live?"

"I don't know," Calvin replied, not bothered or worried at all by this.

"But you have the baby. You need a warm place to stay, Calvin, to take care of her."

"I'll figure something out," he said optimistically. "I always do."

"Stay with me," she said, as though she had been waiting for the proper moment to pop the question but it hadn't come.

Calvin stopped buckling Pearl in. He looked Sadie in the eyes. "No, Sadie. I can't."

"You can stay with me for just a little while, until you figure out where you're going. There's plenty of room in my apartment. I can help take care of the baby."

"I need to be there for Leah."

"I'm not talking about getting married, here. I'm just talking about you crashing on my couch for a while. Only as long as it takes for you to get back on your feet."

"I know you're trying to help, and we appreciate it. You've done so much for us already."

"Then let me help you with this."

"I don't want to risk losing the only family I have, even if it isn't ideal. It's all I have right now. I created it, I'm responsible for it, and I'm going to stand by it and try to make it work. I already almost lost them once. I'm terrified of losing either one of them."

"I'm not trying to take advantage of you. I mean, I'm not trying to take advantage of the situation, with her in the hospital, or anything like that."

"I know."

"I'm just following my heart. I know how rough this must be for you right now. And I understand why you can't take me up on the offer. I get it."

"Sadie…another place, another time, another situation…"

"I know, I know. Another life."

"Another life. Yes. You're everything I dreamed I would want in a wife when I was growing up. If I had described my ideal woman right down to every finite detail, if I could have anything I wanted, it would be you."

Tears began to make her eyes glossy.

"And it's almost like we were aligned to be together…but somewhere along the way things went wrong. Life took a wrong turn, or maybe a right turn. I think this is where I was supposed to end up, with my baby and Leah. If we hadn't gotten together, then Pearl wouldn't exist. And she's everything to me. She's the light of my world, and the only thing making me happy these days. And, honestly, the only thing keeping me going."

"Just remember that I'm here for you, any time you need me."

"I will."

She leaned in quickly and threw her arms around him. They hugged tightly for what seemed like minutes before parting ways.

Calvin stood with Pearl on the leveled lot where his house used to stand. The driveway and concrete front porch were the only signs left of the house that had stood majestically for ninety-seven years.

He held Pearl tightly and pulled her knitted baby-blue hat down over her ears. It was cold out. It was getting late in the day and the sun was starting to set, tinting the sky a pretty violet color. Together they stood before the crude wooden cross that Calvin had driven into the ground. He felt that the cross was rather insufficient, but it was all he could do at the time. Calvin had inscribed it, as well.

It read, simply,

Hobbes

My best friend

Ashes to ashes, dust to dust

Calvin pulled Hobbes' collar from his jacket pocket. He reached down and placed it on the base of the cross. It was the last time he would ever set foot on that property.

In the hospital room, Calvin read a book to Pearl, who cuddled in his lap right next to Leah while she slept peacefully. She kept them company with the steady beep of the heart monitor next to her bed.

Calvin didn't care that he was ruined financially, unemployed, and homeless. All that mattered was that they were still together.

No one could take this moment away from them. They loved each other. The future wasn't so important. The past didn't matter. At least Pearl could see her mother for a little longer.

Pearl cooed and pointed at a picture of a puppy in her book with her chubby little fingers. "Dog," she said proudly and smiled up at Calvin.

Calvin smiled back at her and kissed her on the

head.

Calvin didn't notice when Leah's eyes fluttered and opened for a moment. He had no idea that she saw baby Pearl on his lap and the two of them reading the book about the lost little puppy. Her pretty lips formed a very faint smile before her eyes gently closed again.

Calvin continued to read until he and Pearl both fell sound asleep, perfectly content in the hospital chair next to Leah, a beautiful angel.

Cory Toth, author of *No Man's Land*, has been writing fictional novels since the age of fifteen. While naturally gravitating toward Suspense and Mystery genres, through the years he has also written Science Fiction and Horror. Toth was born and raised in Upstate New York and draws inspiration for his novels from local towns and landscapes.

Made in the USA
Lexington, KY
18 December 2013